Maggie's War

Shirley Mann is a Derbyshire-based journalist who spent most of her career at the BBC. She then made short films for organisations such as the Heritage Lottery Fund. Her first novel, *Lily's War*, was inspired by Shirley's mother, who was a WAAF, and her father, who was in the Eighth Army. *Maggie's War* is the fifth book in the collection.

Also by Shirley Mann

Lily's War
Bobby's War
Hannah's War
Bridget's War

Maggie's War

Shirley Mann

ZAFFRE

First published in the UK in 2025 by
ZAFFRE
An imprint of Bonnier Books UK
5th Floor, HYLO, 105 Bunhill Row,
London, EC1Y 8LZ

This is a work of fiction. Names, places, events and
incidents are either the products of the author's
imagination or used fictitiously. Any resemblance to
actual persons, living or dead, or actual
events is purely coincidental.

A CIP catalogue record for this book is
available from the British Library.

ISBN: 978-1-80418-875-0

Also available as an ebook and an audiobook

1 3 5 7 9 10 8 6 4 2

Typeset by IDSUK (Data Connection) Ltd
Printed and bound in Great Britain by Clays Ltd, Elcograf S.p.A.

MIX
Paper | Supporting
responsible forestry
FSC® C018072
FSC
www.fsc.org

The authorised representative in the EEA is Bonnier Books
UK (Ireland) Limited.
Registered office address: Floor 3, Block 3, Miesian Plaza,
Dublin 2, D02 Y754, Ireland
compliance@bonnierbooks.ie
www.bonnierbooks.co.uk

For our wonderful granddaughters, Skye and Evie.
May you be as inspired by these amazing
women as I have been

Chapter 1

The Grand Union Canal, November 1942

Maggie tilted her chin towards the sunlight slowly disappearing over the horizon as the seventy-foot narrowboat sank down in the canal lock. The brick walls echoed with the sound of her rendition of 'Chattanooga Choo Choo' and she had a moment of satisfaction, thinking that her school music teacher, Mrs Hanley, would finally have been impressed by her tone-deaf pupil.

'Maggie!'

The scream pierced her moment of calm.

'Maggie, for God's sake, the cill!'

Twisting around the long wooden tiller to look behind her, Maggie gasped. The boat had been thrown backwards with the force of the water gushing out from the open gates at the front and was in danger of being caught on the narrow cill behind her. After days of locks taking the boat up-canal, this was the first one that operated in the other direction and she had completely forgotten about the risk of getting caught on the revealed ledge.

She was about to yell to Gloria to close the paddles but was relieved to see her already turning the metal windlass against the force of the water to wind them back down.

The younger girl's experienced hands worked efficiently and fast but at the same time, Gloria was shaking her head, not sure whether her speed would be enough to stem the gushing flow.

Maggie turned the other way to see their third crew member, Elizabeth, rapidly opening the top gate paddles to let more water back into the lock and hopefully take the propellor out of danger. Quickly assessing how long she'd got, Maggie watched the water in the lock rise at a painfully slow rate then saw Gloria step back, thrust her thumbs up and cross her fingers dramatically.

Maggie pushed the lever into gear and prayed.

It would be pure luck whether the other two had halted the emptying of the lock in time and there was a chilling moment when the boat seemed to hang in the air but then there was a loud clunk as the huge vessel dropped forwards into the safety of the water.

Gloria jumped from the top of the lock onto the roof of the boat, landing with a gentle thud, her slight weight barely registering.

She took one look at Maggie's pale face and ran to the stern to grab the tiller off her.

'You go below,' she ordered, 'I'll get us out of here.'

Maggie stumbled past her down the three steps leading to the tiny cabin and sank down on her bunk, her hands under her thighs, to rock forwards and backwards.

She gave a little whimper.

* * *

Tea that night was a subdued affair. Maggie hadn't spoken a word since the drama at Marsworth Locks and certainly hadn't been any use on their way to the village of Startop where the girls were mooring for the night. Gloria had cycled off along the grass towpath to find fish and chips, but Maggie was only playing with her meal. She slumped down and raised a fork with a soggy chip on it halfway to her mouth, then left it dangling there to look at both her fellow boaters with a stricken expression.

'I'm so sorry, I'm so sorry.'

'It could have happened to any of us,' Gloria told her gently.

'No, it couldn't,' Elizabeth retorted, putting her knife and fork on the chipped plate balanced on her knee, 'it's one of the first lessons we learned. You know that, Maggie.' She glared with the superiority of someone who had more life experience than the girl nodding in abject misery in front of her. 'Getting stuck on a cill is so dangerous, to us and the boat. There's nothing that can be done with a heavy boat that's tipped on its end. I mean it's twelve tons before it's loaded. That's how people drown, never mind what would have happened to the load. All that steel would have sunk us within seconds. What were you thinking?'

Maggie had been preparing answers to this question all afternoon, but she knew none of them would satisfy the censorious Elizabeth.

She shrugged her shoulders and said feebly: 'I'd forgotten that we were going *down* the canal. All the locks we'd done before were going up.'

Gloria got to her feet; at only five foot tall, she was the only one who could stand up fully under the slightly domed roof near the entrance.

'You can talk,' she snapped at Elizabeth, 'you were the one who let the snubber go and we nearly lost the butty boat.'

Elizabeth glared at her. Older than the other girls by several years, she hated being criticised and she felt protective of the *Florence*, an engineless boat of a similar size that all boaters pulled behind them to increase their load capacity. She'd made the girls' butty into her own little domain, but, on the first day out, had forgotten to tie one end of the connecting 'snubber' rope.

Maggie quietly moved her still full plate to one side.

'It was completely my fault and I'm sorry. I will never, ever do it again.'

'None of us will,' Gloria agreed, reaching out her hand to place it on Maggie's arm.

* * *

The three girls weren't totally new to the world of the 'cut' – the miles and miles of canal waterways that threaded around the country – but this was their first solo trip after six weeks of training and they were a long way from possessing the natural experience of the boatmen, their spindly children scampering up and down lock gate ladders as if they were squirrels in a tree. At least five times a day, Maggie wondered how on earth a photo in the newspaper of a ridiculously healthy girl with a boat hook had persuaded her this job would be the escape she craved. She'd applied on the spur of the moment and while the training may have prepared her technically for the challenges ahead, she'd totally underestimated the toll the physicality of the job would take on her slim frame or how living cheek by jowl with two strangers would test her patience, fortitude and sense of humour. When the three trainees met for the first time just a few days earlier at Hayes, they'd eyed each other up warily, and now, Maggie was beginning to think that sharing a tiny world with someone who wore pearls and a twinset under her mackintosh and another who knew more about the canals than she ever would was perhaps not such a good idea after all.

Sadly, Maggie Carpenter was all too aware of why she'd rushed to join the Inland Waterways instead of accepting her first teaching job after college. That night, she wearily tucked the blanket around her in her little bunk while a warm tear trickled onto her cheek. Gloria was snoring contentedly at her feet and Elizabeth had retired to her own bed on *Florence*, giving a final stern glance in Maggie's direction as she firmly closed the wooden hatch doors behind her.

Maggie moaned and pulled her feather pillow around her. She was glad of the one luxury she had allowed herself when, at the age of twenty, she'd abandoned her comfortable life in Manchester to deliver goods for the Inland Waterways between London and Birmingham. The call had gone out in the newspapers for women to take over the arduous work to allow more men to join up. Her stunned grandparents had argued against her plans to give up the offer of a job as a teacher at Manchester High School for Girls to become what they disparagingly called a 'water gypsy'. They had no idea of the real reason their beloved granddaughter needed to flee the familiar streets of south Manchester, and she was too ashamed to tell them. She simply welcomed the spartan existence as a suitable punishment for someone who deserved to suffer and, at that moment, the comfort of a decent pillow was the only thing between her and abject misery.

* * *

The first thing Maggie heard the next morning was Gloria's whistling and the welcome sound of the kettle bubbling on the little iron stove.

'Come on, lazybones, sun's nearly up,' Gloria said, ruffling the bedclothes.

Maggie normally loved these early winter mornings when the weak sun edged above the eastern ridges, mist hovered above the water and the ducks emerged from the reeds looking for scraps of bread, but this morning she buried her head in her pillow. 'I don't want to get up, I don't want to face Elizabeth.'

'Oh, don't be such a scaredy-cat. Come on, out of that bed.' And with that, Gloria grabbed the blanket covering Maggie and tugged.

Gloria's mischievous green eyes and friendly smile had immediately put Maggie at ease whereas Elizabeth's superior tones and haughty air somehow made her feel like a naughty pupil before the headmistress.

At that moment, Elizabeth pushed back the doors and stood, projecting a looming shadow against the light behind her.

Immediately, the cold November air hit Maggie and she shivered.

'Aren't you up yet?' Elizabeth demanded, squeezing down the steps into the limited space. 'Come on, let's get moving or the Spencers will get to the locks before us. I've already heard them filling up with water.'

With that, Maggie jumped out of bed and grabbed her coat to pull it on over her pyjamas. She ran her fingers through her wavy, golden hair and reached down for her socks. There was huge competition to get to the locks first in the morning and already the girls had been jockeying for position with the well-known boating family, the Spencers. Like their new female rivals, they too were delivering essential goods like coal, steel, bricks and concrete between the South and the Midlands but, while the girls were inexperienced, the Spencers were experts at the job and especially at outmanoeuvring any challengers. This morning, it looked like the Spencers were once again going to beat them.

With her head bowed, Maggie mumbled: 'I'm so sorry about yesterday, Elizabeth. I really am.'

Elizabeth looked down her nose. 'No point worrying about it now. We need to get moving. I've got to get to Tyseley on time, the boys are on an exeat.'

Gloria nodded, in awe of this housewife who juggled work on the canals with being a mother of two while her husband was in the Mediterranean with the Royal Navy.

She didn't want to say she had no idea what an exeat was but suspected it was something to do with the strange world of boarding schools.

Maggie leaned over and scooped some tea out of the caddy on the thin wooden shelf. She added it to the boiling water and stirred before pouring into the waiting mugs.

'Tea, both of you?'

She held out a cup to Elizabeth like an olive branch but there was no responding smile.

'Well,' Elizabeth said haughtily, patting her immaculate pin curls into place, 'I don't know how you can get it so wrong, after all there are two of you, I have to manage *Florence* on my own.'

'Even so,' Gloria started, 'you nearly los—'

Maggie gave Gloria a nudge and butted in: 'Anyway, let's get on. I've learned my lesson, I'll never do it again.'

'Just make sure you don't and let's see if we can get through today without any more disasters,' Elizabeth said, standing up and hitting her head on the roof as she went to stalk out of the boat. 'I can hear the Spencers' engine turning over. It's so cold, I don't think it's starting so let's see if we can get ours running, then we can sneak in front.'

It was only when she was out of sight that she reached up to rub her head.

Maggie and Gloria sprang into action, each to their practised stations to either check and start up the engine or to gather in the iron mooring pegs.

As they worked in harmony on the early winter morning, their fingers hardly noticing the cold, they glanced up to glare at the green and black decorated boat, *Buffalo*, that was now edging its way past them, dogging their progress up the Grand

Union Canal. Mr Spencer, standing casually on the tiny deck space on the back of the boat, puffed on his pipe and barely acknowledged the girls but Gloria spotted Mrs Spencer's head popping out of the cabin with a satisfied smile on her lips, content that, once again this morning, the girls would have to fill the locks back up once her family had passed through.

Gloria whispered to Maggie: 'Don't worry, we've got an easy morning, there aren't many locks between here and Linslade. We should be able to catch them up.'

There was always a frenetic ten minutes while the girls got the *Nancy May* and *Florence* ready to leave their mooring, but once they were underway a feeling of calm normally descended on them all. This morning, though, Maggie felt on edge and kept looking back at Elizabeth who was on the butty, too far away to communicate by anything except hand signals while Gloria was at the helm of the Lister-engined *Nancy May*, manoeuvring the 'ram's head' or tiller behind her. Maggie shook her head when Gloria asked whether she wanted to steer, needing more than her morning tea to get her confidence back, and went below to tidy up the cabin where the two beds had been abandoned so quickly just half an hour before.

The cabin, or 'house' as Gloria called it, was less than seven foot wide and ten foot long and on her first exploration of the boat, Maggie had gasped at the ingenuity of cupboards that dropped down to turn into beds or tables, the shelves that were packed with everything from cutlery to potatoes and the hooks that held gleaming copper pans. Every tiny bit of space was utilised and all the little knick-knacks the girls had thought they needed in the beginning had now been whittled down to absolute essentials. The hub of the tiny cabin was a stove that not only provided their only heat but was also used for cooking and boiling the kettle. Each bit of wood was painted and grained to look like expensive mahogany or oak and in a rebellion against the austerity of canal-dwellers' belongings, had previously been adorned with romanticised pictures of castles surrounded by everlasting roses. This boat had seen more experienced handlers than them, Maggie acknowledged. The girls didn't have the brasses and crocheted lace curtains that had been handed down from generation to generation by the traditional boat dwellers but the Grand Union Canal Company had added a small shelf for books for the trainees and with a few cushions that Maggie had brought from home, a colourful rug on the floor and the stove lit, the cabin provided a cosy haven once the mooring stakes were hammered into the towpath.

Maggie rolled up the beds, washed the pots in the cracked pot bowl, eking out as little water as possible from the jug, and put the kettle on again prompted by a hopeful shout from Gloria above the hatch. She had a moment's guilty satisfaction that Elizabeth was alone on the butty boat behind with a flask of tepid tea made an hour earlier and breathed in the warming steam from the bubbling kettle.

There had been so many locks on this bottom part of the Grand Union that their progress had been painfully slow and Maggie had hardly had a minute to appreciate her surroundings but now, carrying two hot drinks and a welcome biscuit for each of them, she emerged onto the tiny deck, called the counter, and, holding on to her own chipped cup, looked around her.

They were leaving the hills of the Chilterns behind them and there was open grassland on both banks. The morning mist had cleared to reveal a grebe bobbing along next to them, its spiky haircut reminding Maggie of one of her brothers first thing in the morning. She spotted some coots hiding in the rushes, while in the distance, a pigeon cooed. At the bow of the boat, a gentle triangle of water parted to let the heavy vessel power its way through. She thought how the waterways were sometimes like a hectic highway or, like this morning, more of a country lane with just the gentle put-put of the engines or the huffing of a horse as it pulled its waterborne load along the towpath. A nod or an occasional greeting were the only sounds of human occupation and, while the boaters looked part of the scenery, the female inhabitants of *Nancy May* and *Florence* stood out like aliens. Lulled by it all, Maggie breathed in deeply, relishing the gentle lapping of the water beneath the hull and the complete separation that the waterways created away from the chaos she had left behind. Unlike for so many of her friends who had joined the services, there were no rules on this waterway, no officious superiors to answer to, a few days off at the end of every trip and, best of all, at moments like this the war and the mess she had made of her own life seemed a million miles away. Listening to the rippling of the water, Maggie tried to push all those disturbing thoughts and the drama of the day before to the back of her mind, but even so, when she held out her hand, there was a slight tremor to it.

She had never imagined that what seemed like a slow, peaceful journey to an onlooker could harbour so many potential disasters and she was making far too many mistakes. It had been drummed into them all during training that the cut was a dangerous place where a bridge could take your head off, a hand could get jammed in the metal as the paddle spindle unwound or a leg could get caught between a lock wall and the boat. Maggie had already lost two precious windlasses, dropping them into the water as she jumped ashore to open a lock, her head was covered in bruises from forgetting to duck on her way out of the cabin and now she had nearly sunk the boat by getting it caught on the rear cill. The initial confidence she'd had when she'd been under the guidance of the keen eye of Kit, the trainer, had been completely eradicated once she joined the other two on their own boat and she was finding that with each mistake, she was becoming more and more nervous, which, in itself, led to more errors. Many other girls had given up – sometimes after just one day – so she took some comfort in having passed both her training and the written test, but that didn't stop her feeling increasingly clumsy and inept. In the meantime, the three girls had a demanding delivery sheet and an impossible timeframe to get from London to Birmingham at less than four miles per hour.

For the first time, she wondered whether she should give up the idea of a life on the cut and go home.

Chapter 2

'You OK?' Gloria asked, glancing at the pale face next to her while deftly moving around the tiller to negotiate the bend in front.

'Yes, fine,' Maggie answered, defensively cupping her hands around her tea. 'Well,' she went on, noting Gloria's sceptical look, 'Sort of. Still a bit shaken. There's so much to learn on the boats and I came from standing in front of a classroom of fourteen-year-olds to this. It all comes so naturally to you, Gloria.'

'Well, it may do,' Gloria said in an uncharacteristically sharp voice, 'but don't think for one minute that this is going to be my life for evermore. I'm only helping out while the war's on. I'm getting off these canals, you mark my words. Anyway, if you're a teacher, you'll know bags more than I do,' Gloria said, not daring to take her eyes off the water in front of them, aware that a moment's inattention would cause the boat to veer into the reeds at the side of the canal.

Maggie looked with respect at Gloria. She was so young but in her seventeen years had acquired so much knowledge that all Maggie's training to become a teacher seemed a waste of time. Gloria may want to deny her roots, but she still knew how the canal system worked, how the water was fed from reservoirs like the ones at Tring near Marsworth, how to fix an engine and most important of all, how to cook a tasty meal on the tiny stove. In comparison, Maggie's ability to reel off every king and queen through history seemed somehow irrelevant.

'But,' Gloria was saying, 'I did grow up around boats and my mam and dad had their own so I often helped out with loading and unloading. Mind you, they weren't boaters,' she added proudly, 'we've got a house and my dad came home every night. And of course, we went to school,' she ended with pride. Gloria went on to explain how the rivalries on the waterways divided the groups very firmly into different factions and how each one guarded its specialities jealously. The traditional boat families who lived and worked the canals travelled up and down the cut with a knowledge gained from years of passing through the same locks, mooring up at the same favourite spots and being aware of where the water and fuel supplies were.

'They know every bend, every shallow spot and all the best pubs,' Gloria told her, 'but their little 'uns don't often get to school. I mean, there's only a few places for them to learn on the cut and the boaters never stop for long. So, most of them don't read and write,' she finished.

'You certainly look the part, no matter what you say,' Maggie told her, taking in the dungarees that Gloria wore with the ease of the men on the cut.

'Well, I don't want to.' Gloria's response was like that of a petulant child. 'I really want to do something different. I just don't know what yet, but you just wait, Maggie, I'm going to escape these canals. I really don't want to be here, Mags, but the trouble was, I knew I had to do something and apart from the Land Army, I couldn't join anything else until I was eighteen – which is in a couple of days I'll have you know.' She cheered up at the thought.

Maggie glanced round to see a swan following in their slipstream and the weak winter sunlight glistening on the water reflecting its late morning rays through the trees. The hoar frosts gave the trees an air of mystery in the mornings and in the evenings, as the sun dipped below the horizon, a pink glow often reminded her of an Impressionist painting.

Glancing around the picture postcard scene, she asked, 'But how can you not love this? It's so beautiful.'

Gloria glared determinedly straight ahead, refusing to appreciate the surrounding countryside.

She'd never admit it, but she did see it; she just didn't want to, any more than she'd wanted to accept that the interview panel at the Women's Training Scheme had been speaking a language she'd immediately understood.

She changed the subject. 'What I've never worked out, though, is how toffs like you and Elizabeth thought it would be a life for you.'

'I'm not a toff, just a girl longing for adventure,' Maggie replied casually. 'I don't know about Elizabeth. I mean they put adverts in all the posh magazines, so perhaps they thought rich girls like her would be so used to tough boarding schools, they'd cope, and, in any case, they'd be too proud to admit it if they couldn't.'

'Hmm,' Gloria said dismissively, 'let's see how many of them are still here when this dreadful war finishes.'

Maggie gave a wry smile; no matter how much this girl pretended she didn't belong on the cut, she was as much a part of the canal network as families like the Spencers.

'Anyway,' Maggie went on, 'I don't think we could have done it without you. Whether you like it or not, this is all second nature to you. The only boat I'd ever been on was a rowing boat in Heaton Park. All this,' she said with an expansive wave of her hand, 'is like another planet to me.'

'What really made you join up, Mags?' Gloria asked, hoping to turn the attention away from herself. 'After all, as a teacher you'd have been in a reserved occupation.'

Maggie mumbled something about 'needing to do her bit' but the reality was, she simply had to get out of Manchester.

* * *

The following day was one of those consistently wet ones, the type that allows drip after drip of freezing rain to penetrate the neck of a sou'wester, gradually seeping down the girls' threadbare jumpers and leaving them feeling laden and miserable. The idyllic winter scene of the day before became a distant memory.

Gloria had insisted Elizabeth needed to take her turn on the tiller of the *Nancy May* and Maggie had moved back to steer the butty. Unlike Elizabeth, she hated that job, as without an engine, there was no control, and it simply meant she had to mirror the snaking around corners that the *Nancy May* did in front of her. To her, it was the most boring task in the world and left far too much time for thinking. Brushing the drips of rain from the end of her nose with her sleeve, she tried to make herself concentrate on the stern of the boat ahead, but Gloria's question had unearthed memories that had led to a night of tossing and turning and very little sleep.

'Damn, damn, damn,' she said, brushing a tear from her eye. She had avoided being on her own since she joined the Grand Union Canal Company at Bull's Bridge in Hayes, determined to fill her mind with the complex world of the canals, but was woefully aware her strategy wasn't really working.

'The engine's grinding,' Gloria called back through cupped hands to Maggie, making her look up with a start. Signalling towards the towpath, Gloria left little time for the butty to slow down and Maggie narrowly avoided shunting into them from behind and almost rammed into the bank. She cursed the fact these boats had no brakes and only just managed to stop in time by using the reeds on the edge. With *Florence* finally safely secured, she approached the *Nancy May* where Gloria pointed down meaningfully at the propeller. Maggie felt a nervous qualm while wrapping her arms around herself protectively, knowing what was coming next. The engine had seemed all right after the lock fiasco but to make sure, one of them would have to get down into the freezing water to check for damage. She sighed; that would have to be her.

With resignation, Maggie went below to take off as many layers of clothing as she could bear and came back out in her underwear, shivering in the winter chill with her arms around herself as Elizabeth stood to one side, her grey eyes glinting and a satisfied expression suggesting it was a just punishment after yesterday's inattention. Maggie waited for the engine to stop before moving gingerly to where Gloria reached out her arms to help lower her into the water.

'It's shallow here, you should be all right,' Gloria told her.

Maggie gulped as she submerged herself in the freezing cold muddy waters. She didn't dare think what was floating around her, knowing that 'bucket and chuck it' was the age-old adage of every single craft on the canals.

She felt the muddy bottom of the canal and winced at the sensation of years of detritus squelching through her toes. She had never done this before, but the procedure was explained to every trainee and it was a manoeuvre she had had nightmares about, not knowing which was worse: the thought that a pike might decide to take a chunk out of her foot or that the waste from those metal buckets that everyone on the canal crouched over was floating around her legs.

Her teeth started to chatter with the cold but then she heard Elizabeth's voice.

'Get a move on, we're already behind.'

Reaching down gingerly with one hand, Maggie felt around the 'screw'. She said a quick prayer that her momentary lapse in concentration hadn't damaged the propeller permanently and felt her way around its blades, biting her lip in concentration.

'Are the blades OK?' Gloria shouted from above her.

'Yes, I think so, but there's a pile of weed attached to them. Pass me a knife and I'll loosen it.'

Maggie started to loosen the weeds and sighed in relief as the blades started to shift slightly. She'd dreaded telling Elizabeth they would lose two days getting a new propeller or admitting to Gloria that they would have to pay for it.

Once trained, the girls only received wages of £3 a week, leaving them to rely on supplementary payment when they delivered their goods so, at this stage of their first solo trip, Gloria, and strangely, Elizabeth too, had already complained they were struggling for funds.

Maggie took the knife from Gloria and started to work slowly and methodically to clear the prop of the slimy weeds but straining too hard, the knife slipped and sliced into the palm of her hand, making her yelp with pain.

'Hurry up and get out of there,' Elizabeth shouted from the towpath.

'Done it!' Maggie finally shouted triumphantly, feeling the prop move more freely, and handed the knife back to Gloria. 'Now, for God's sake, help me up.'

As she emerged, shivering, onto the small wooden stern, Elizabeth immediately doused her in precious, clean water.

Maggie was so relieved that she hadn't damaged the propeller, she only gave a small gasp as the bucket of freezing water was thrown over her.

'Just in case,' said Elizabeth. 'That water's full of things that could cause an infection.' She peered carefully at Maggie's hand. 'You need Germolene on that immediately.' Elizabeth always seemed to know about the dire diseases that lurked in the murky waters of the cut.

'Right, inside and get warm and for crying out loud, can we get on, now? I'll take over *Florence*,' her imperious voice boomed and she marched back to the butty, leaving no opportunity for argument.

It was warm in the cabin and Maggie wrapped the old towel around herself firmly. She would have given anything to curl up on the little bunk, but they were only at Slapton and there was a long way to go so she huffed out a sigh and got dressed quickly before going back onto the wooden counter at the back to hear some unexpected, good news.

'We've got a nice stretch without locks,' Gloria said, 'so why don't you put the kettle on, I'm sure you could do with a warm drink. There's some cocoa on the shelf, let's treat ourselves, but don't tell Elizabeth.' She gave a conspiratorial grin.

While waiting for the kettle to boil, Maggie opened the post they'd picked up at Leighton Buzzard. There was a letter from her grandmother. She fingered the envelope with affection, feeling a sudden wave of homesickness.

Dearest Margaret,

We do hope you're well and keeping warm. It must be so cold on those boats. I'm knitting you some socks that should be with you by the end of the week. The house seems horribly empty, even your grandfather said so and you know how much he likes peace and quiet to read his paper. Although, there isn't much good news to read in the press at the moment, is there? Africa looks to be on a knife-edge. I do feel sorry for those boys out there. Mrs Tomkin's in a terrible state. Her Percy is 'Missing in Action' somewhere in the Mediterranean so I'm terribly thankful you three are still on English soil. The vicar said prayers for Percy at Sunday Service – I hope God is listening. His nephew's coming this week; he's an army chaplain and had a terrible time at Dunkirk apparently. He's been given some leave to come and help Reverend Moore. You know our poor vicar had a bit of a heart problem a few weeks ago. I think he's on the mend but to be honest, I suspect he's struggling to cope with his stricken flock at the moment! We all seem to need his gentle words more than ever.

I'm so glad our two are ground crew and not flying. I am getting more letters from them both, which is lovely, particularly Patrick; Billy's not such a good correspondent. I do wish they'd both stayed on at school a little longer, their writing would be better. It's so hard to read sometimes, especially Billy's, but at least they write so I'm grateful for that. Billy seems to be enjoying Scotland – or rather the Scottish lassies he's working his way through up there! Patrick seems fine in Lincolnshire although – more from what they didn't say, rather than what they did – I gather there's a lot of action going at both stations. I think they're working on Lancasters. We often hear those huge Merlin engines thundering over our house and it's a lot more reassuring than hearing those dreadful German bombers.

I can't imagine you're meeting any nice young men on those canals but maybe you could find a serviceman to write to? I do feel for those young men, so far from home, and I'm sure they'd love to receive some post. You and the boys are all we have, and we feel a huge responsibility to see you all settled. After all, we're not getting any younger!

Anyway, I must go, the queues at the butcher's are ridiculous and I need to spend up to two hours standing in the cold to get even a bit of liver.

Your grandfather sends his love and I send mine too.
Granny

Reading her grandmother's words again, Maggie felt a familiar wave of misery waft over her and a huge amount of shame. Of course, her grandmother wanted her to find a 'nice young man'. She had no idea of the guilty secret Maggie clutched to her heart.

Chapter 3

Maggie heard Gloria calling from above.

'Lock ahead.'

Jumping to her feet, Maggie wiped her eyes and grabbed an extra scarf to ward off the fog that had suddenly enveloped the canal and ran up onto the stern.

'Gracious, you can hardly see the towpath,' she commented to Gloria who was craning her neck to look down the canal for any oncoming boats.

'I know, it's come in like a pea-souper,' Gloria said, narrowing her eyes in concentration 'but we can't allow it to slow us down. It'll clear by lunchtime,' she added with the confidence of someone whose family's livelihood was dominated by the weather.

The girls were entering the Ouzel valley where the canal seemed more like a river than the familiar straight industrial highway. As they approached the area near Bletchley, they were surprised to see little groups of service people huddling together to light up cigarettes.

'There must be some sort of camp around here,' Gloria said. 'Maybe we should moor up and get some supplies; we're almost out of tea. It's cleared a bit, but Elizabeth must be frozen back there and we've gained some ground without as many locks to deal with.'

As if in answer, a call came from behind them, and they turned to see Elizabeth cupping her hands and blowing on them. Maggie gave a thumbs-up sign and while Gloria went below, she tied up.

'You stationed locally?' she called to one little group huddled under a bridge.

'Yep, nearby,' one girl said vaguely.

'There's a lot of you,' Maggie went on, scanning the groups that were dotted all the way along the canal, their bikes strewn by the side of the towpath.

'Oh, it's just the best place to get some fresh air and a ciggie,' another one said.

Elizabeth looked curiously at the little group. She knew they were near Bletchley Park where two of her friends worked, claiming they did boring admin work, but as they were both very bright girls, she suspected there was more going on there than anyone knew. As always, she said nothing. Elizabeth had made a career out of silence; it was a habit learned at the nursery tea table with her strict Norland nanny and parents who believed children should be seen but not heard. Her hair, bullied into place with kirby grips and a tortoiseshell slide certainly never showed any sign of rebellion, and her pearls were around her neck before she put her Aran sweater on. She had perfected her superior expression that suggested a knowledge of everything and a sharing of nothing.

'Not much fresh air today, well, not that you can see,' Maggie said with a chuckle, looping the mooring rope through a metal hoop and jumping back on board with the end of it.

'You girls working the canals?' one serviceman asked, puzzled.

'Yes, we are.'

'Didn't know women were allowed to do that.'

'They need us,' Gloria said, poking her head out of the hatch.

The man looked appraisingly along the tarpaulin covering the steel.

'Well, fancy that. You must be stronger than you look.' He smiled at Gloria's small frame.

A scornful glance made him regret his remark and he took a second look at the pretty girl with auburn hair in front of him before saying hurriedly: 'You're not hanging around to go the pub tonight, are you?'

Gloria examined him up and down and then gave a disappointed shrug.

'Sorry, no, gotta get on. We're behind and need to get to Stoke Bruerne .'

At this, he came nearer to the boat to say in a quieter voice, 'So when are you next passing this way?'

He was in his early twenties and had nice brown hair that fell over a freckled forehead.

Gloria tilted her head from side to side, assessing the young man's possibilities. He was totally different from most of the men she had dated and she hurriedly adjusted her Cockney lilt to try to emulate Maggie who spoke nicely but without the la-di-da tones of Elizabeth.

'Hm, well, maybe in a few weeks, we might be back.'

He got out a pencil and a piece of paper and quickly scrawled a telephone number on it.

'My name's William, Will for short. This is my landlady. Leave a message with a time and place and I'll take you for that drink,' he said, smiling.

'I might, I might not,' she replied teasingly, and turned back to the boat, tossing her head.

Ribald laughter emanated from the towpath and the young man relit his cigarette with a flourish while looking back casually at the attractive young girl on the boat.

'Ah, the *Nancy May*,' one of his friends said, looking at the name on the boat, 'she may or she may not. You'll just have to wait and see, Will.'

* * *

It was almost dark on the following evening when the girls approached Stoke Bruerne. They'd passed through the village and locks here when they were each training, but this was the first time they'd had the chance to appreciate what a hub of activity it was.

'Chuck us that rope over,' a gruff voice said, and Maggie looked up to see a man with a lined, tanned face and a wooden pipe protruding from his lips. She couldn't decide whether his face was dirty or tanned with years in the fresh air, but she recognised the boaters' uniform – an obligatory pair of brown corduroy trousers and old jacket with a red neckerchief.

As soon as the line had been passed back to the two girls on the back deck, he moved forward to take Elizabeth's rope.

'Oh, thank you so much,' she said in an accent that hadn't been heard before around this boat fraternity. The man looked up through his bushy eyebrows and raised them into an arch like the bridge beyond.

'Uh-huh,' he said enigmatically – a myriad of unsaid comments going around in his head.

'Would you happen to know if there are any washrooms here?' Elizabeth went on, oblivious.

'Nope, not that girls like you can use, that's for sure. I suppose the pub might let you use the scullery,' he said, pointing to the Boat Inn.

Elizabeth's delighted expression made him forget his years and he drew his shoulders back like the young man he had once been.

Elizabeth walked briskly towards the *Nancy May*, clasping her hands together excitedly.

'We might be able to get a wash here.'

Within a few minutes, with a flannel between them and a tiny bit of soap, the three girls went tentatively into the Boat Inn. The small bar area was crammed with canal people who all stopped talking the moment the three women appeared in the doorway. The atmosphere was thick and smoky and the banjo and melodeon players in the corner all put down their instruments to curiously assess the new arrivals.

'What yer want?' a rough woman's voice said from behind the bar. Maggie and Elizabeth pushed Gloria forward, hoping her slight Cockney twang might be more recognisable than their carefully pronounced vowels.

'Um, we wondered if we could use your scullery to get a wash,' Gloria said, suddenly embarrassed at all the eyes that were trained on her.

'You off the boats?'

'Yeah, we are,' Gloria said with a pleading expression. 'We've heard how friendly you are at Stoke Bruerne and hoped we might be able to get us a wash here.'

At this, the woman seemed to soften.

'Friendly? Aye, that we are. S'pose you're some of them new trainees working the cut, are yer?'

Maggie nodded. There were murmurs around the room, some were disapproving and some were supportive. Elizabeth's erstwhile helper was nudging the two men next to him with a knowing nod towards the women.

'See, told yers,' he pronounced, 'wimmen on the boats on their own, who'd 'ave thought it.'

While the landlady lifted up a hinged timber section of counter and the girls followed her to the back kitchen, a fierce division in opinions on their presence erupted.

'Thank you ever so much,' Elizabeth said, reaching out her hand to shake the other woman's with a warm smile. Maggie raised her eyebrows in surprise at this new, friendly side to Elizabeth. Instead of grasping the outstretched hand, the barmaid took hold of it and turned it over and back again, examining it closely.

'Ye'll need some warm water and petroleum jelly for those blisters,' she said and turned towards a shelf near the door where she picked up a small jar. 'Here, try this.'

The woman stood back and gave the three girls in front of her a thorough assessment while they scrubbed.

'Oh dear, you ain't used to this life, are yer?' she asked Maggie and Elizabeth. '*You* look as if you'll do all right,' she said to Gloria, 'but I give you two a week.'

'We've already done six weeks training and we're nearly a week into on our first solo trip,' Maggie said proudly.

The woman shook her head in pretend wonder, making the grey bun on the top of her head wobble.

'Well, well, fancy that. OK, well, I'm Betsy Miller. Mess with me and you'll be in trouble. Keep on my good side and you'll . . . Well, let's just say, you'll be all right.'

While the girls washed gratefully in the tin bowl that was on the side, they introduced themselves and, feeling the kindness of an older woman, told her a little of the disasters they had experienced since they left London.

Charmed by their honesty, by the time the girls had finished washing and were wiping their hands on an old towel, Betsy had decided to take them under her wing. Their innocent admissions as to how hard they were finding canal life appealed to the grandmother in her and she told them to sit at the wooden table in the corner while she found them some stew.

Chapter 4

Stoke Bruerne proved to be a haven for boat dwellers and as the girls waved a friendly goodbye to Betsy the following morning, they'd each taken a mental note of the wide variety of useful skills that could be found there. There were rope makers, brick makers, millers and, most importantly, men who could fix engines, leaking pipes or a faulty fire. They'd also managed to replenish supplies from the kiosk on the side of the lock and Elizabeth, in particular, was looking forward to the coffee she'd managed to buy.

'I'm so glad they've stopped rationing it,' she said, reverently hugging the jar of coffee under her arm. 'I was fed up of that Camp stuff. It tastes nothing like coffee.' Gloria winced. She'd tried coffee once and sworn never to touch it again. 'I heard there's a nurse here,' Elizabeth went on. 'Might be useful, I suppose.'

Elizabeth looked almost with longing towards the brick house across from the Boat Inn, remembering how she used to dress up as a nurse to 'treat' all the horses in the family stables. She'd loved pretending she could cure them.

'It never ceases to amaze me the complete world that's been created to keep these canals going,' Maggie was saying. 'I bet some people never venture more than half a mile from them in their whole lives.'

Near the lock, there was the lock-keeper's cottage and a little building advertising 'leggers', the men who would lie on planks and 'walk' their way through tunnels for horse-drawn boats; there were signs offering rope making and repairs and in addition to the little kiosk selling supplies, there was a miller, a brick maker and a coal merchant. Maggie gazed in fascination.

They made their way the short distance to the dark, foreboding entrance to Blisworth Tunnel, passing the stables, farrier and blacksmith's building. At nearly two miles long, it was a part of the journey they were all dreading. Unable to see the other end, their safe passage relied on any oncoming boat illuminating its lamp to warn of its approach. Gloria slowly entered the pitch-black of the tunnel, immediately feeling the chill and the drips of water from the ceiling.

'This tunnel's been in operation since 1805,' Gloria said unhelpfully while Maggie adjusted her eyes to peer nervously at the old bricks that lined it, wondering at the perfect dome that loomed above them. The silence was only punctuated by the chug, chug of their engine and there was a gentle lapping as the hull made its way through the inky waters. It was incredibly hard to hold their course in the pitch-black and only the week before some trainees had crashed their butty, so Elizabeth concentrated on the rear of *Nancy May* to keep it in sight.

Going into a dark tunnel was a little like going into a dark cinema that was hazy with cigarette smoke but in this case, it was the fires from all the boats that choked the air. Gloria had been the obvious choice to steer, given her experience, especially once Maggie admitted to feeling disorientated and terrified of banging the sides on the walls.

There were intermittent little waterfalls dripping relentlessly from above and Gloria complained about how they always seemed to find the space between her sou'wester and oilskins.

The girls were about a quarter of the way in when they heard a horn sound from the other end.

'Damnation,' Gloria said.

She cupped her hands around her mouth and yelled: 'You'll have to go back. We've got a butty. And,' she muttered to herself, 'today's my birthday and if you want to mess with an eighteen-year-old then good luck to you.'

The reply was another impatient toot on the horn.

'What are we going to do?' Elizabeth shouted forward, her voice echoing in the chasm.

Gloria set her mouth stubbornly and turned the wheel to accelerate.

'They'll have to move,' was her uncompromising reply.

As the boats approached each other, Maggie went to the front and shouted loudly again, 'We've got a butty, you'll have to go back.'

'You's better breathe in then,' came a gruff voice out of the dark.

Maggie shouted to Gloria, 'He's not budging.'

'Do you think we'll make it?' Elizabeth yelled to Gloria, positioning her pole to fend off any encroaching hull. As the two boats got nearer to each other, Gloria's face set in a determined grimace and she steered the vessel as far over to the right as she could. She wasn't sure how wide this tunnel was and, in the gloom, the shadow of the wall on her left looked perilously close, but once the two fore-ends were alongside, she turned her attention to listening for a fateful bang.

'Mornin'', a deep voice said from the other boat.

All the girls breathed a huge sigh of relief. There was just enough room for the boats to pass, something the more experienced boatman had always known. Gloria saw a flash of yellow teeth as he grinned at their panic before she let rip.

'Why didn't you tell us there was room?' she shouted angrily but her words were lost in the sound of his engine as he chugged past.

The girls emerged into the daylight and they all sighed with relief. There was so much to learn about the Grand Union and they were all still novices.

* * *

'I can see Jake and Dolly ahead, they've not made much ground,' Gloria said, pointing to the familiar Spencer boat in the distance. Both Elizabeth and Maggie found it hard to use the first names of the boating families, as was the custom on the canals, but Gloria managed to say them with a respect that sounded natural.

'Maybe they've had a problem,' Maggie said.

'Hmm, could be, this stretch is notoriously full of weeds at this time of the year, as we know only too well, don't we, Mags?'

As they turned around the next corner, they saw the full extent of the Spencers' difficulties. The boat was stuck on the far side of the canal, not moving either forward or backward. Maggie cocked her head to listen.

'There's no engine,' she whispered to Gloria.

'You all right?' Gloria shouted across. Dolly Spencer glared at the chugging vision of the *Nancy May*, approaching them from the rear. She had her arms folded defensively over a noticeable bump in her stomach.

'Yes, thank yer,' she replied sharply but her husband muttered almost to himself, 'Engine's kaput, bloody thing's packed up.'

Standing looking down towards the engine room like a disappointed parent, he shook his head again and said to his wife, 'Been spluttering for days. Dunno what's up with it.'

Maggie, with her recent experience of weeds around the propellor, was about to make a couple of what she thought might be helpful suggestions, but Gloria nudged her and shook her head.

Signalling to Elizabeth to let go of the snubber line and wait at the side of the canal, Gloria gradually slowed the *Nancy May* while Maggie made her way along the side of it, stepping carefully on the gunwale – the thin ledge along the whole length of the boat – which she was beginning to manoeuvre like a pro, with her hand holding onto the roof and one turned-out foot carefully placed in front of the other. Once at the fore-end, she handed the rope to the Spencer son, who hardly acknowledged her but took the proffered line in submission.

'Let's see if we can tow you,' Maggie said gently. She knew how much pride this was costing the Spencers. The lad glanced fearfully at his father next to him, who grunted, before taking the rope.

Maggie stood ready to warn any oncoming boats of the little convoy that would soon be taking up most of the canal. There was complete silence apart from the gentle thrum of the girls' boat while Gloria expertly moved onto the other side of the water to pass while the Spencer lad walked slowly along the ledge on the side of their boat, keeping pace with the stern of the *Nancy May* until he got to the triangular prow of the Spencers' *Buffalo*. The two boats moved in silence towards the moorings in the distance where the young son could go off to get help.

Once the two boats were clear of a stone bridge spanning the cut, Gloria moved in towards the left bank and slowed again. The lad, whose name none of them knew, threw the line back towards Gloria. She made sure she caught it to prevent it tangling in the girls' propeller, gave a brief nod and studiously ignored Jake, who was letting out a string of expletives, causing his wife to scurry below to get a mug of tea and maybe a precious biscuit to calm her furious husband.

There was no word of thanks or acknowledgement while the girls re-manoeuvred the *Nancy May* out of the way to carry on their journey.

'I can't believe they didn't even say thank you,' Maggie complained.

'Oh, not a chance in the world,' Gloria said, as usual her superior knowledge of the ways of the canal community coming to the fore. 'To have to be rescued by us would really gall them.'

'Well, they haven't said a pleasant word to us all the time we've been trailing them,' Maggie said with a pout. She so wanted to be accepted by the seasoned boat people.

Gloria smiled. 'You wait,' she said, 'we may not be their favourite people but what we did today'll earn their respect.'

'Hah! I'll be surprised,' Maggie said and went below to make a cup of tea.

* * *

Elizabeth hummed quietly to herself. Back on the butty boat, she welcomed the isolation that had initially irked her, especially when she'd heard laughter from the *Nancy May* in front, but after a few days, her own company had begun to suit her, leading her to volunteer more regularly to be the one to steer the little boat behind. Without a gunwale and an engine room, there was more space for her to spread out her things, she could get dressed in private and she also loved being able to snuggle up in the little bunk without Gloria's chatter disturbing her. When she remembered it wouldn't be long before she would have to return to that big Cotswold stone house with its imposing porticos and latticed windows, the thought made her shudder. She longed to see her boys, though, that was sure. Michael must be growing fast, she thought, judging by the requests for a new blazer and Edward seemed to be coping better with the older boys in his dorm. She hated the rule that parents should limit their visits to the boys during term time to avoid unsettling them, but it had at least allowed her to take on this job, which she needed; no one knew how much. Her strait-laced husband, Christopher, serving with the Royal Navy in the Mediterranean, thought she was sitting at home, dutifully dusting and making recipes out of the National Food Campaign's war-time recipe books and hopefully, she thought, she'd be back home before he found out what she was really doing. To begin with, when she first spotted the advertisement in *The Lady*, she'd laughed at the prospect of all those upper-class women living on dirty boats doing a strenuous job but when this twenty-nine-year-old received yet another threatening telephone call from the man in the grubby trench coat, she decided that the canal network was exactly the place a woman could disappear.

Chapter 5

Maggie replaced the receiver slowly, hearing the familiar click as the pennies ran out. She suddenly felt weak and struggled to push the heavy, glass-paned door of the red telephone box outside Braunston. Angrily shoving it with her shoulder, she stumbled onto the patch of grass outside. The telephone box had that familiar smell that all of them had – a mix of metal, damp and urine – and it was threatening to make her feel sick, so she gulped in the fresh air outside. There was a small wooden bench to one side with a metal frame and her hand reached out for its cold solidity.

She wasn't crying; the shock was too great for that. In her head, she kept hearing her brother's voice over and over again: 'I'm sorry, Mags, I'm sorry.'

It had a been a short, grim telegram delivered by a young lad on a bicycle from the Braunston office. He was full of resentment about the amount of mud on the towpath and how he'd had to check every boat on his route until he found the *Nancy May*, but Maggie had had no time to listen to his litany of complaints. She'd simply ripped open the envelope and then tore off to find the nearest telephone box where she'd fumbled to insert enough coins into the slot until she heard the officious voice of the telephone operator at RAF Cranwell at the other end. Mumbling out the name of her elder brother, there had been a short pause before she heard Patrick's bleak voice.

'We only heard yesterday, Mags, it was quick. I promise you, she didn't suffer. Grandad went to wake her with a cup of tea and . . .'

Her brother's voice was muffled as he huddled in the corner of the admin office at Cranwell where he operated as ground crew for trainee pilots. Patrick assured her he'd got a separate telegram to Billy who was performing a similar role at Lossie-mouth in Scotland, too far away to get back to Manchester for the funeral.

'All right, all right,' he was saying to the telephonist who was pointing to her watch. 'I've got to go, Mags. I'll leave it with you and hope you and I, at least, can get there.'

Maggie's ears had heard the words, the arrangements for the funeral and her brother's concern for their grandfather but her heart had heard nothing but the screaming in her head. Sitting upright on the bench outside the telephone box, her eyes were drawn towards the canal in the distance. Birds were flying, trees were rustling in the breeze and there were even some children playing in the streets nearby. A burst of anger shot through her. *How dare life go on as normal when her lovely grandmother . . . that cuddly, warm woman . . . how could . . . that soft, gentle voice be . . . silent?*

Distraught, Maggie tried to concentrate on what Paddy had told her, and she quickly calculated the amount of time left on her own journey, fervently hoping they would be able to reach Tyseley in time for her to catch a train to Manchester for the funeral but she knew it would be a rush.

She jumped to her feet. Crying would have to wait; she had a load to deliver and the timescale had just shrunk.

* * *

Maggie was exceptionally quiet over the next few days; her whole being concentrating on rushing the load along the canals to get to Birmingham in time. The other two worked silently alongside her, doing everything they could to speed the process along. Seeing her distress at the loss of her grandmother, they tacitly did everything they could to make sure she got to the funeral.

It was a Wednesday evening that the girls finally unloaded the steel at Tyseley with a communal sigh of relief. They were only half a day late and their pay had not been docked by much. It annoyed them all to see the Spencers sitting smugly on the wharf, Mr Spencer puffing contentedly on his pipe and his wife smoothing out her grubby skirt over her distended stomach whilst sitting on a small stool. They had arrived on time and Jake Spencer wanted to make sure the girls knew that.

'Let's get fish and chips tonight,' Elizabeth said, checking her watch. She needed to get the first train in the morning to get to the railway station in time to pick the boys up and had to do some washing before she went.

Gloria tipped out the earthenware jar where they kept the kitty and passed some money over so that Elizabeth could cycle off to the nearest fish and chip shop.

When she returned, the three girls sat quietly in the little cabin, all sense of achievement overshadowed by Maggie's obvious anxiety.

'Well, we did it,' Elizabeth ventured.

'Yes, we did, and we did it well,' Gloria said and then in an effort to lighten the mood, added, 'Only a squashed tunnel, a damaged prop and a war with the Spencers. That's not bad for our first trip.'

'I wonder what the next one will have in store for us,' Maggie said quietly. She looked pale and her fingers were twitching.

'Why don't you tell us about your grandparents?' Elizabeth said in a kinder tone than the other two were expecting.

With paper shortages increasing, Maggie folded the outer layers from the tea-time treat to keep for next time and looked at them both wondering how much of her story she could share with them. Glancing round, she realised that, despite having spent the last three weeks in close proximity, they really knew little about each other.

From childhood, Maggie had dreamed of becoming a teacher and one of her first memories was of twirling a globe in her grandparents' house in Didsbury, trying to learn the countries that made up every continent. The ill health of her mother and the sullen introspection of her father permeated her childhood home with the atmosphere of a library, and it was no wonder the three children would spend as much time as possible at their grandparents' house, where the boys, in particular, could let off steam. But then, when her mother died, leaving two sons, aged twelve and ten and eight-year-old Maggie, all dreams for the future seemed destined to come to nothing. Their father, a survivor of Gallipoli in 1915, struggled to cope for six months before leaving nothing but a desperate, apologetic note on the oak sideboard with a suggestion that the children should go down the road to live at their grandparents' house.

Maggie would never know how the vision on their doorstep of three children, clutching a small, battered leather suitcase each, had prompted an anger in her mild-mannered grandfather for which he had never forgiven his son. Her grandparents hid their shame by turning their well-ordered lives upside down to try to provide a family home for the three siblings but a bitter twelve-year-old and a bewildered ten-year-old proved a tough challenge for their rusty parenting skills and they couldn't help but heave a sigh of relief when Patrick left school at fifteen to go and train as an engineer for the Crosville Bus Company, followed by his younger brother two years later.

At first, the quiet house seemed strange for all of them but then, with only one child to care for, her exhausted grandparents were delighted to discover a little girl who drank in knowledge like the milk she devoured from the scullery. When she got to Fallowfield High School, Maggie was the sort of pupil every teacher dreamed of and with her increasingly long legs tucked under her, she would curl up on an uncomfortable bench in the library to start at the letter 'A' of book titles, gradually working her way through the alphabet while her grandfather coached her in the evenings. With their heads bent together, Charles Carpenter would trace countries in the atlas with his finger, grudgingly giving in to her demands to be told about her father's Great War travels through Europe. Still furious with his son's weakness in abandoning the three children, he was surprised that he became equally absorbed in finding information about the awe-inspiring Alps or the beautiful cities of Europe his son, Jim, might have passed through. It was as if, through their 'travels' he was rediscovering his own son. One night, after looking along the Dardanelles to find Gallipoli, he crept into bed next to his wife, Winnie, remembering a night so many years earlier when Jim had first returned home from the disaster of that campaign to sit at their kitchen table, head bowed and his hands shaking. Charles, a proud man for whom self-analysis was a weakness, had sworn in exasperation and left the room but his wife had stayed. He'd always meant to ask her what their son had revealed about his time in Gallipoli but, somehow, couldn't bring himself to mouth the words. His wife, meanwhile, kept her lips tightly shut; sometimes, however, Charles would find her sobbing into her pinny.

Maggie had no idea about the thoughts that continued to spiral around in her grandfather's mind throughout her childhood, but instead, tortured herself about what had prompted her father to walk out of their lives without a backwards glance.

She was unable to escape the thought that it was she who had done something terribly wrong. She looked up now at the expectant faces of Gloria and Elizabeth and realised she didn't have the courage to tell them the whole story.

'My mum died when I was eight. My dad, well, he left my brothers and me, so we went to live with my grandparents. They were wonderful to us . . .' She tailed off and Gloria passed her a grubby handkerchief.

Maggie looked up pathetically.

'I'm dreading tomorrow. I'm just dreading it. I can't imagine putting my lovely granny in the cold ground.'

Her head dropped and her shoulders started to shake.

Elizabeth took charge. Emotions embarrassed her.

'Come along now, Maggie. There's a war on out there and people are dying all the time. At least your granny lived to a ripe old age. You must be thankful for that.'

Maggie wiped her eyes and nodded.

'I know, I know. It's just, I don't remember my mum very well and Dad, well, he had his own war to deal with and we've no idea where he is. He just vanished.'

'Well, I think you should eat up those chips, you've got a long journey tomorrow and you'll need your strength for your grandad's sake,' Gloria said, pushing a fork towards some soggy remnants that were hiding in the creases of the newspaper. Maggie was thinking it would take more than a few chips to get her through the following day but dutifully raised them to her mouth.

Chapter 6

Maggie walked through the familiar front door and could have sworn she heard her grandmother's cheerful, welcoming voice, but then the clock struck twelve and the echo seemed to resonate throughout the small rooms, mocking her.

A small voice called from the back room, 'Is that you, Margaret?'

'Yes, Grandad. I'm coming.'

She quickly put her coat and hat on the wooden coat-stand in the cold hallway and walked through to the morning room. It was even colder than the hallway and sitting in the old armchair was a man who used to be her cheerful grandad, she thought, only this man was shrunken and grey.

Maggie went over to him and enveloped him in her arms, leaning her head in as she felt him shake with tears. Longing to join in, she braced herself and stood up.

'Come on, Grandad, this won't do. We're due at the church in a couple of hours and we need to get organised before I grab a quick bath and wash my hair. Now come on.'

Looking around her, she asked, 'What about the tea? Are we having it here?'

His granddaughter's practicality seemed to have the desired effect and Charles Carpenter got to his feet and gave an embarrassed cough.

'Yes, yes, the tea. Well, actually, I mean no. The Ladies' Guild is putting it on at the church hall.'

Maggie, who had been viewing the dirty dishes on the drainer in the back kitchen in dismay, gave a grunt of relief.

'Oh, thank heavens for that. There might be quite a few from the Red Cross and all those other organisations she was involved in. Now look, Grandad, Patrick's going to make it but, as you know, Billy can't, so let's get these pots washed and then at least we can offer Paddy a cuppa when he arrives.'

And with that, she rolled up her sleeves and got to work on the plates and cups, silently tutting at the congealed mess that had obviously been there for days. While she worked, she couldn't help but smile at the amount of room there was in this kitchen, that she'd always thought of as being tiny. Compared to the *Nancy May*, it was huge.

'Mrs Harper's been wonderful,' her grandfather was saying from the doorway, 'she's been dropping off some soup and . . .' he waved his arms vaguely in the direction of the pantry '. . . things.'

Maggie looked suspiciously at him and went to open the pantry door.

The smell hit her and she reeled back.

'Gracious, Grandad, haven't you eaten *any* of those casseroles? Some of these have been here for days.'

Charles Carpenter looked surprised, as if he hadn't realised the pantry door led to anywhere.

'Oh, well, some of the soup, perhaps, and a bit of cut loaf, but I've not been hungry.'

'Right, well, I'll get these sorted and then we'll find something among this lot that you *can* still eat,' Maggie told him and immediately set about separating the mouldy dishes from the ones that still looked edible.

Her grandfather slumped against the door. 'I didn't know, I didn't know,' he said pathetically.

'No, well, it doesn't matter. There are still some bits that look OK,' Maggie said in a muffled voice from inside the pantry.

'No, not that.' He stopped and then, his eyes glistening with tears, 'About your dad . . . about my son. I didn't know.'

At this, Maggie whipped around, almost banging into the door. 'Didn't know what? Didn't know what, Grandad.'

Before Charles could answer, they heard Patrick's voice from the front hall.

'Oh, that's good, my key still works,' he shouted and then his reassuringly sturdy figure appeared in the doorway.

Maggie flew into his arms with a cry. 'Oh, Paddy, I'm so glad you made it.' The familiar hug wrapped around her like a warm blanket.

'Well, nearly didn't. Missed the transport and had to hitch a lift. Do you know how many service people there are on the side of the road with their thumbs out between here and Cranwell? Anyway, eventually, an army truck took pity on me, and I piled in with some squaddies.' He gave his sister a squeeze and then looked carefully at the scene in the familiar little morning room.

'Hmmm, hello, Grandad. Good to see you . . . well, um . . . you know what I mean. Sorry about Granny and all that. Terrible shame.'

Faced with another man, Charles seemed to pull himself together and stood up to shake hands in a formal manner.

'Yes, well, she was a good wife – and grandmother – and we all have to be thankful she didn't suffer.'

Paddy turned to Maggie, blinking to disguise his damp eyes and said: 'Grief, Mags, did you bring the canals home with you?' His wrinkled nose broke the tension and his sister went over to pick up a towel from the drying rack near the fire.

'I know, I know, I'm going up to the bathroom now. You stay and have a chat with Grandad. It'll do him good.'

When Maggie came back downstairs, rubbing her hair with the towel, she found the two men discussing anything that related to the world outside the four walls of the house in Didsbury and Maggie was left puzzling as to what on earth her grandfather had been about to say when her brother had walked in.

The funeral was a rushed affair; there were too many of them to fit in these days and the vicar looked worn out when he greeted the mourners at the church door. He barely got through the service, needing to catch his breath all the time. At his side was a young army chaplain who Maggie realised was the nephew her grandmother had written about. Maggie looked curiously at the tall young man, who turned and smiled and then blushed. Maggie went a deep red in return; she hadn't expected a man in a dog collar to be so attractive. He had such an interesting face, full of compassion, but the lines around his mouth suggested he could be as full of mischief as Paddy. She found herself comparing his shining dark brown eyes to the best conkers she'd proudly collected in autumn and, realising she was staring into them, Maggie turned quickly to Reverend Moore, whom she had known all her life, to get her breath back. The elderly vicar's face was pale, but his hands were warm when they grasped Maggie's.

'Ah I see you've met my nephew, Harry. This is Maggie, Harry, Maggie Carpenter, Winnie's granddaughter.' He was surprised to see both of them nod nervously and then turn away. He spoke directly to Maggie. 'Your grandmother was a good woman, Margaret. She kept more secrets and had more humanity about her than anyone ever knew.' With that, he glanced crossly over towards Charles and then hurried on to the next in the queue.

His words brought Maggie's thoughts back into focus and she frowned, puzzled. It was as if he knew something about the Carpenter family that she didn't. A deep, rich voice spoke from behind her.

'Are you all right?'

She looked up to see the padre's gentle brown eyes assessing her with genuine concern. The intensity of his gaze took her aback and her mouth went dry.

'I'm, umm, fine. I just . . .'

Maggie tried to concentrate on the white band around the incredibly strong, tanned neck in front of her and forced her eyes to look beyond the toned physique and the warm breath she could feel from this padre's generous mouth to search for her grandfather. Latching her eyes onto Charles Carpenter's familiar dark overcoat and trilby hat, she felt more stable but then she saw her grandfather wipe his eyes and she blurted out to the young clergyman:

'No, actually I'm not fine. I mean, look at that coffin – it's so unfair and now it seems there's so much I didn't know about her and I can never ask.'

She waved a hand vaguely at the undertakers' horse and cart.

'My granny, she was just the kindest, most wonderful woman and I can't . . . I just can't imagine life without her and I don't know how I can leave Grandad – he can hardly boil an egg.' She suddenly felt overcome with emotion and gave a heartfelt sob.

Maggie immediately felt ridiculous and gave an embarrassed smile through her tears.

'I'm so sorry, you're just a stranger.'

Glancing up through her glistening eyelashes, she reeled back in surprise, wondering what on earth had come over her and muttered a goodbye before scurrying away to talk to the ladies from the Women's Institute.

The vicarage housekeeper was patting a distracted Harry on the arm. 'Padre, Padre . . . the telephone . . .'

Maggie didn't see him twist round to catch a glimpse of the departing swirling skirt of the girl in the black hat before he followed Mrs Hennessey out of the room.

* * *

By the time the spam sandwiches had been eaten and everyone had complimented the carrot biscuits made by the Women's Institute, it was almost time for Maggie's bus. She searched the room, ostensibly looking for her grandfather, but when there was no sight of a tall man with tousled, light brown hair, she felt her shoulders drop in disappointment.

'Grandad, I've got to go in a minute,' she whispered, pulling him away from Mrs Winter who was only up to her third grandchild in her long catalogue of family news. He looked relieved to be rescued and turned willingly towards Maggie.

'Will you be all right?' she asked him, biting her lip.

'Yes, yes of course,' he replied, sounding stronger. 'Patrick's got three days' leave so he's staying on a bit and he's promised he'll take me to the Old Cock for a pint; maybe it'll do me good to see some of the old bowls crowd.'

Maggie interrupted his thoughts. 'Grandad, what did you mean about dad?'

'Hmm? Oh nothing. Never you mind.' And he gave her a hug.

'Now, you take care on those boats and particularly on those towpaths; they can be nasty places at night.'

'Yes but . . .' she started but he'd already turned away to talk to Herbert Parsons, whose marrows at the pre-war harvest festival had always been a source of envy.

'Paddy, Paddy,' Maggie hissed.

'What's up, sis?'

'Grandad. He said something strange – that "he didn't know". It was to do with dad but I've no idea what. Can you try and find out?'

'Is that all he said?' her brother asked. 'Nothing else?'

She shook her head.

Patrick gave a bitter laugh. 'Well then, I'd be surprised if it's anything interesting about that man. He abandoned all of us and poor old granny never got over it. If I never hear his name again, it'll be too soon.'

Then, seeing his sister's face drop, he relented. He knew how his younger sister had spent her childhood creating endless excuses for their father's behaviour.

'OK, OK, I'll ask, but don't hold your breath. You just take care of yourself.' He stepped back and really looked at her for the first time.

'I have to say you look a bit less peaky than when I saw you before you left, but make sure you're eating, won't you, Mags?'

She wondered whether it had been the encounter with the young clergyman that had given her pink cheeks and to hide her embarrassment, she gave her brother a hug, holding on for longer than he expected. There was never time in this war for anything but the briefest of conversations and it was with reluctance that she stepped back, blew him a kiss and left.

Two minutes later, a puffed Harry Moore roughly pushed open the church hall door but he was too late, there was no sign of Maggie Carpenter.

* * *

On her way back to the bus station Maggie tried to ignore the tingle that Harry Moore had induced in her. Convinced she had no right to feel attraction for anyone, especially a man of the cloth, she concentrated on looking around her at all the landmarks that had taken on a Hollywood glow just a few years earlier. She had a sudden vision of a room at Salford Training College for Teachers where she had started out so optimistic and excited about helping young people discover the joys of learning but then she shuddered. It had all gone terribly wrong, and it was all her own stupid fault.

She stumbled and gasped for air, clutching her chest. *Was this feeling ever going to go?* she wondered. *Was she ever going to forgive herself?*

Maggie gulped at the memories that flooded in yet again. It had all started when Roger Anderson had swaggered into the classroom on that first day and from that moment on, all her aspirations of being the best student were overtaken by her obsession with this older man.

She kept her head down and pushed her hands firmly in her pockets while her feet stamped on the pavement, trying to erase the memory of Roger. Amidst the trams, the cars, the rushing pedestrians she had a sudden longing for the peace of the canals.

Chapter 7

'Oh, thank God you're back,' Gloria shouted from inside the boat when she heard the familiar thud of Maggie's shoes on the deck. 'We have to go on the "bottom road" to get to Coventry for loading and Elizabeth's going to have to meet us there. I've sent her a telegram.'

Maggie dropped her bag down the steps into the cabin. It seemed a million miles away from gorgeous clergymen and perfidious lecturers.

'That'll be really hard with just the two of us and I've heard there's loads of narrow locks.' She sighed. 'I suppose I'm bow hauling the butty then. Trust Elizabeth not to be around when you need her. So, what are we getting this time?' Maggie asked, reaching out to get the rope she was going to have to tie around herself to pull the butty into the locks.

'Coal,' Gloria said with a groan.

'Why, what's wrong with coal?'

'You'll see.' And with those ominous words, Gloria started up the engine to set them on their route to Griff Colliery, six miles north of Coventry.

Maggie steered the butty along the pound, as the canal stretches were called, but the need for concentration precluded any conversation. She couldn't believe how tired she felt. Gradually, her shoulders dropped and she willingly immersed herself in the smell of the smoke from the houses' chimneys on each side, the plop of water as a moorhen dropped in from the towpath and the relentlessly optimistic sound of the birds in the bushes. She knew the canals could provide a tempting target to enemy aircraft if they caught sight of the channels through industrial areas but most of the time, their passageways created a swathe through the death and destruction of a war that had already lasted three years. Travelling back to Manchester for the funeral had made Maggie gasp. The devastation of the Blitz was still evident and as recently as August, there had been yet another bombing raid on the city.

Her own grandparents' house had seemed so cold and so quiet and even when she had lit the fire with their meagre coal allowance, the whole building had seemed, well, just wrong, she thought. Her grandmother had been the heartbeat of the house and without her there, the walls seemed to resonate with her spirit, but it was a hollow sound.

'Dammit,' Maggie said quietly. She'd taken to swearing quite a bit recently. There just hadn't been enough time and she was trying not to think about the pile of washing in the back kitchen, the dirty tiled floor and the sad figure of her grandfather sitting all alone in the morning room. At least Patrick would be there for a few days, she thought but, as the only female left in the family, she felt a huge responsibility and wondered, yet again, whether she had been right to sign up.

It occurred to her that while she felt all this guilt at abandoning her grandfather, as far as she knew, her own father had felt none when he walked out of her childhood home in Didsbury and she thrust the tiller angrily to one side to steer around the corner behind the *Nancy May*.

It was quite a way out of Coventry that Gloria yelled to her to pull over.

'There's a really low bridge coming up and we're going to have to dismantle the cratch,' she said, heading below for the tools. Maggie looked perplexed. She had no idea what the 'cratch' was, but Gloria was already down at the front of the boat where she was starting to prise the nails out of the wooden frame that held the tarpaulin. It was a fiddly job and while Maggie held the ropes to both boats, she smiled at the colourful expletives that were coming from the front of the boat. There was no doubt where Maggie was learning all her best swear words.

'What about the butty?' she asked Gloria when she walked back along the towpath rubbing her hands on a bit of cloth.

Gloria looked pensively back at the smaller boat, gauging the height of it.

'We're just going to have to risk it,' she said finally. 'I'm not doing another one,' she said with a pout, 'that was bloody hard work. We'll be all right on the way back, though, the coal'll put us deeper in the water. Anyway, there's only one winding hole near here for us to turn both boats round and that's past this bridge.'

The approach was incredibly narrow with dense woodland on either side. Maggie had been told to remove anything on the roof and when they reached Griff Bridge, she understood why. The entrance looked more like a hole for a water pipe than a bridge and she shook her head, wondering whether they would be able to get through it. Slowing to a snail's pace, Maggie followed Gloria's lead in front of her by edging through the hole with her fingers while they both ducked down as much as they could. It was a claustrophobic experience but neither of the girls noticed, they were too busy holding their breath.

When they arrived at the wharf, Gloria skilfully moved them into position so that the coal could be shovelled aboard. No sooner had she manoeuvred the boat correctly than the foreman yelled at them to clear the 'tarp'.

They jumped ashore to manhandle the heavy tarpaulin out of the way just as the first load was dropped onto the *Nancy May*.

Gloria had a handkerchief wrapped around her mouth but still had the one in her left hand.

'Sorry,' a muffled voice told Maggie. 'Should've given you this. Don't breathe in.'

Maggie leaned forward to grab the handkerchief and held it to her mouth, spluttering as the black dust rained down from the shovels in the air above. She couldn't believe how it pervaded everything – her hair, her clothes, even her shoes had taken on a mottled grey appearance. She nodded at Gloria in understanding.

Gloria shrugged. 'Told you,' she said, 'I've done a couple with my dad and it's the worst thing. I hate it. Now grab this shovel, they're not going do it all for us and we'll need to even it all out.'

It took two hours to secure the load and sheet up, which involved scrabbling on hands and knees to get the beams, rigging chains and stands into position before unrolling the heavy, black, tarry canvas to sheet up and cover the heaped mound at the front of the boats. By this time, Maggie and Gloria were covered in soot and their knees were red raw.

As they tied the last knot, they heard Elizabeth's horrified squeal from the wharf.

'Oh, my goodness. What on earth do you two look like?' She unexpectedly let out a girlish giggle and, taken by surprise, Gloria and Maggie joined in. There were no mirrors on the boat but when they studied each other's blackened face, they knew what they looked like and started to rub their cheeks with their sleeves.

'Get these bloody boats out' t'way,' an angry foreman yelled. 'We ain't got no time for you lot to' ave a fashion parade. We got more boats to load. Now'op it.'

Maggie jumped aboard to start up the motor and Gloria untied the mooring ropes to head for the winding hole to turn around.

'See you in a few weeks,' she called to the foreman, who just waved his arm dismissively and turned to the next boat in the queue.

Once they'd turned round, there was silence for the first couple of miles back along the canal as first Maggie then Gloria went below to try to clean up. Left alone on the stern, Maggie looked around her. It all looked so different going back the other way. She suddenly felt at home.

Gloria appeared with a welcome brew.

'Oh, my throat's so dry,' Maggie said, taking it gratefully.

'I know, it's the load my dad hates. That coal dust gets everywhere – it's grimed into the pillows, the water in the kettle tastes gritty and every bit of food tastes of it. Still, it pays well, and I've got our last load's wages too so maybe we can get to the pub tonight and celebrate.'

'I'm not sure they'll let us in,' Maggie laughed, brushing more coal dust off her shoulder.

'Aw, we'll pick a pub that's used by the boats. They won't care. They've seen worse.'

But by the time they moored up at Braunston, all three girls were too tired to venture over the threshold of the Admiral Nelson. Maggie's journey back from Manchester had worn her out; Gloria was exhausted from the morning trip when she'd worked the boat on her own and Elizabeth was unusually quiet, claiming a headache before retiring to her own bunk on the butty.

It was only the next morning that Maggie inspected her hands, holding them up to the daylight.

'Ugh!' she exclaimed. 'Look at my fingernails. They're filthy.'

'Well, you'd better get used to it. We've got days of this before we can offload at Alperton,' Gloria said from under her blanket.

Maggie tumbled out of her bed to put more coal onto the stove and fan it into life before putting the kettle on for some hot water.

'Well, I'm not going anywhere until I've cleaned up a bit,' she said and she unearthed a small piece of valuable soap and stripped off, no longer embarrassed in front of Gloria.

'Save me some, nature calls,' Gloria said, climbing out of her bunk and heading out to run towards the hedge.

Thinking how a drop of hot water can soothe all ills, Maggie luxuriated in rubbing her flannel all over herself. As it moved across her naked body, she felt a frisson of longing and cursed Roger Anderson for awakening feelings in her that previously she had been blissfully ignorant of.

Hearing Gloria jump back on board, Maggie fiercely wiped her face before starting to use a small scrubbing brush on her fingernails.

'Move over, it's my turn,' Gloria said to Maggie who had turned away to hide her blushing cheeks.

Chapter 8

Harry glanced across the altar at his uncle whose mind seemed to be far away from the candlesticks in his hands.

'You all right, Uncle?'

The two of them were cleaning the brasses, something the women of the parish normally did, but this morning, the loyal parishioners were busy preparing yet another funeral tea. Peter was rubbing the candlesticks far too furiously and Harry was concerned. It was only a few months since his uncle had suffered a heart attack.

'Yes, lad, of course I am. I'm just thinking about the Carpenter family – you know, that funeral we had the other week.'

The name jolted Harry. Maggie Carpenter had been in his thoughts ever since.

Reverend Moore carried on tackling the large brass stems with gusto, but his nephew was not fooled.

Putting down his duster, the younger man went over to steer the stooped figure to the front pew.

'Come on, you know the golden rule. A problem halved is a problem solved. Stop being so stubborn.'

Peter Moore smiled with affection at his favourite nephew, remembering how hard he had prayed that Harry would return safely from serving with the British Expeditionary Forces in Northern France. He had never married and his brother, Norman and his wife, Enid had only had one child so he'd always thought of young Harry as the nearest thing to a son he would ever have.

Glancing around the church to make sure it was empty, he leaned forward, talking partially to Harry and partially to the cross above him.

'I've just had a telephone call from a veterans' centre in Salford. They've found Jim Carpenter – you know, the son of Winnie and Charlie Carpenter. I don't know if I told you but, years ago, he abandoned the children to be brought up by their grandparents. He's just been found living on the streets by the Salvation Army and they've managed to secure him a place at this centre If only I could have told Winnie – she spent her whole life trying to track him down.'

He paused.

Harry sat quietly and waited. As an army padre, he special-ised in being a sympathetic listener to all ranks and it pleased him to think those skills might come in useful for such a beloved relative.

'Oh, Harry, I feel so angry with both Charlie and Jim Car-penter for causing all that hurt for the family.'

'Go on,' Harry said, his thoughts turning to the beautiful young girl with her tear-filled eyes who had unearthed more than a clergyman's compassion in him, and he wriggled uncom-fortably in his seat before making himself focus on his uncle's words.

'Well, before he left all those years ago, Jim had told his mother what had happened in Gallipoli, something it's not up to me to tell you but know he could never forgive himself for it. Winnie watched as her son slowly disintegrated before her eyes and then he disappeared. She came to see me a few months ago to ask whether she should share her secret with her husband, Charlie. I agreed she should – it was eating her up, Harry.

'On that day in the vestry, just before she died, she was in such a state after telling Charlie; instead of sympathising with what their son had been through, her husband's's furious response had been to forbid her from mentioning the subject ever again.'

Harry leaned over to cup his hands over his uncle's; they were freezing cold.

Peter wearily went on: 'What haunts me, Harry, is should I have advised her to tell him and . . . could I have done more? I mean, if they argued about it, is it possible that brought on the seizure?'

Harry was about to utter some reassurance but his uncle brushed him off and got to his feet to speak. He didn't need answers, it was too late for that.

'I have to admit,' he added, 'I find it difficult to talk to Charlie just now, but I wonder whether you could visit him occasionally in the hope that he finally sees sense and maybe we could arrange a visit between father and son. I think young Maggie, in particular, deserves that chance; for some reason, she's always felt it was her fault her dad left them.'

Harry sat upright; an excuse to become involved with this family and perhaps the daughter was exactly what he had been hoping for.

'Anyway, Peter said, 'I must get on, got another three funerals this week. This war is not only killing those fighting but those left behind too. They may have survived the Blitz, but they're scarred and sometimes those scars finish them off; they're buckling under the weight of all that worry.'

'Let me finish these brasses,' Harry said kindly. 'You go and put the kettle on.'

Peter Moore reluctantly handed over the duster and went, head bowed, towards the kitchen.

Harry stared at the drooped shoulders of the retreating figure. *Talk about people buckling under the worry of it all*, he thought, turning to rub furiously at the candlesticks.

As an army padre, his career so far had taken him to train with other soldiers at Woolcott Army Training Camp, the only difference being that instead of carrying a gun, he carried a Bible, a copy of the army prayer book and a Communion kit. After joining the Expeditionary Forces in France, which resulted in the Dunkirk Evacuation, he'd been preparing to go to help with Operation Torch – the Allied landings on North Africa – but then his uncle had been taken ill. Harry didn't hesitate to accept the compassionate leave he was offered to come home to help but he still felt he was abandoning his men. He'd been longing to get back to the army and thousands of miles away from yet another committee meeting about who was making the tea after evensong. Now, it occurred to him, there was a new reason for him to stay.

Harry glanced up at the beautiful stained-glass window above the altar in front of him. In the past it had always given him solace but now, he just saw the figure of an agonised man hanging uselessly. Brushing away the unsettling thoughts that had been keeping him awake recently, he went back to his cleaning.

Later that day, Harry fulfilled two tasks: the first was to call on Charles Carpenter. There he found two women from the Red Cross in the Disbury kitchen, vying with each other to provide casseroles and stews to this new widower, who seemed to be enjoying the attention. Harry gave up any thought of having a sensible conversation and left them to it.

The second was to creep to the telephone in the cold hallway of the rectory later on, while his uncle was ensconced in his study, composing his sermon for Sunday's services.

He asked the operator to find the number of Broughton House Veterans' Centre in Salford and waited.

* * *

The two canal boats moored up and Maggie went below to grab some paper and a pen to write a letter to Patrick. Her brother had returned to Cranwell without a word, leaving her to turn her grandfather's enigmatic words over and over in her mind. They'd brought back the familiar anger, disappointment and resentment she'd felt as a child when she'd watched her childhood friends being taught how to ride their bicycles by their parents while she stood on the pavement, watching enviously. Her own father had shaken his head sadly when she had asked him if he would show her how, as if doing anything practical was beyond him. Angrily, she had grabbed the old bike that used to belong to Billy and tried to teach herself. It was only after both knees were streaming with blood that her two brothers had taken pity on her and, one on each side, had steadied the bike until she got the hang of it, but all the time, Maggie had longed for her father to be the one to show her.

Once she had shouted at him through furious tears, her pigtails bobbing up and down in indignation.

'Why can't you be like a normal daddy?'

'I just can't,' came the pathetic response. 'I don't deserve any of this,' he'd said, waving his arms vaguely towards his three children and then he'd almost run out of the door, his shoulders heaving.

Maggie's brief letter simply begged Paddy for more information from his visit and with the post collection due any minute, she jumped onto the girls' bicycle they kept on the roof and pedalled along the towpath almost bumping into Elizabeth who was scurrying along in the dark ahead of her.

'Where are you off to?' Maggie asked, pulling the bike to a standstill.

She had never seen Elizabeth nonplussed before but there was a decidedly flustered look on her face.

'I . . . um . . . just going for a walk.'

'Oh, OK,' Maggie said with a shrug. 'Well, I'm off to the office with this letter, see you in a min.'

And she pedalled off into the twilight.

There were three letters to be picked up from the Inland Waterways office, one for each of the girls. Maggie scanned the envelopes: Gloria had her regular letter from her mother, there was one for Elizabeth that was obviously from her husband in the Mediterranean and a third was from Maggie's grandfather. She tore her letter open to check he was all right only to read that 'that nice padre' had been calling round to check on him. Surprised to find that the mention of Harry Moore made her toes wriggle in her boots, she got back on her bike to return to the boat while furiously telling herself and every hedge she passed that she could never, ever, have a relationship with one of God's representatives on earth.

*   *   *

While Maggie was remonstrating with herself, Elizabeth was hiding in the doorway of the local pub, talking to a man in a peaked cap and a raincoat. He was moving threateningly close to her and his face, which caught the light when someone opened the door, held an ugly expression.

'That all you got?' he said, stepping even closer.

Elizabeth nodded, biting her lip.

'That's all my wages but,' she said encouragingly, 'there'll be more when we do our next drop off.'

The man stepped back again and counted the money in his grubby hands.

'Well, it'll' ave to do for now, but—' and here he moved towards her again, his finger pointing in her face '—we want the rest by the end of t'month, yer'ear me? Or that posh school'll know about it and then maybe yer'usband: you wun't want that now would yer?'

Elizabeth went pale. The thought of that strict headmaster hearing the truth about the mother of two of his pupils, let alone Christopher, was too much for her to contemplate. Somehow, she had to get more money.

* * *

The girls' kitty was collected regularly by Gloria who demanded payment every Friday. The little jar of coins was mounting up and was kept on the shelf next to the three ration books and it meant that every now and again, Gloria would allow them a treat of some beer and even though they all moaned about the strength of it since they had rationed sugar, it made a welcome change from tea. By the time they got back through the Blisworth Tunnel to Stoke Bruerne on their next trip, Gloria had decided they needed that treat.

'Hand me the jar, will you, Mags?' she said. 'I'll pop into The Boat.'

'Uh-huh,' Maggie replied. 'Just going to check if a certain RAF man from Bletchley is around, are you?'

Gloria gave a guilty grin. She'd already checked her dungaree pockets to make sure she had some change for the telephone.

Tipping the money out of the jar, she separated the pound and ten-shilling notes from the coins and then frowned, turning back to bang the earthenware jar upside down on the little ledge above the fire before peering into it.

'I thought there was more.'

Maggie shrugged. She left the finances to Gloria but Elizabeth, who was perched on the step, almost fell forwards onto her knees to have a look.

'No, that looks about right,' she said with a dismissive wave of her hand. 'We had those fish and chips on Tuesday, don't you remember?'

Gloria shrugged. 'Perhaps you're right, well, it just means we'll have to share one bottle between us.'

'Or,' Maggie put in mischievously, 'we get those servicemen of yours to buy us a drink.'

With that, Gloria laughed and said: 'Better doll up then.'

Gloria pushed Maggie out of the way to peer into the brass kettle to see her reflection and then grabbed the one hair-brush to vigorously attack her long, auburn hair. Maggie, seeing how Gloria's eyes were shining in excitement, shrugged in submission and made do with running a comb through her own tangled locks.

Maggie, who'd been brought up with two brothers, was surprised how much she was enjoying this shared existence with another girl. Gloria dealt with every challenge with equanimity and good humour. The young girl was disarmingly straightforward and thought nothing of putting the older two in their places if she felt they weren't working efficiently enough, but she never held grudges and would shout at them one minute and then joke with them the next. Elizabeth, however, was another matter, Maggie thought. They really didn't know any more about her than they had on that first day.

* * *

Betsy looked up suspiciously when the door opened to the Boat Inn but then beamed with delight. She'd been wondering how these three had been getting on, especially after the last lot of girls who had passed through Stoke Bruerne had been stand-offish and full of themselves. It hadn't taken long for the judges and jury who gathered at the bar every night to pronounce that anyone who would stop to help a boat in trouble, especially if it belonged to Jake Spencer, must be all right and, one by one, the boatmen raised their pints to give a small salute to the three in the doorway.

Elizabeth and Maggie were completely unaware of the significance of that little gesture, but Gloria gave a disarming smile to the men who turned back towards the bar with embarrassment.

'Hello, you three,' Betsy said, looking the coal dust covered girls up and down. 'Well, you're looking a bit more like yer belong on the canals than when yer came in last time. Not so pristine now, are yers?' And laughing, she held back the wooden counter to jerk her head towards the scullery.

'Hope yer've brought yer own soap. We ain't got none left.'

Elizabeth brandished a small bit of soap in the air and Gloria grabbed it off her to elbow her way through to the back first.

After they'd washed, Gloria started to look nervous.

'Do I look all right?' she asked, standing on tiptoes to peer at her reflection in the window.

'Me thinks our Gloria has a date,' Maggie said with a smile, admiring the fresh face and distinctive curls in front of her.

'Oh, maybe – I don't know if he'll come. After all, he's so posh and I'm . . . well, a girl off the boats.'

As she uttered those words, Elizabeth strained to listen to the sudden increase in chatter in the bar.

'I think you're in luck, Gloria, that doesn't sound like a crowd of boatmen to me.'

* * *

William Nicholson was fiddling with his tie. He'd been surprised, and delighted, when his landlady had given him the message from a telephone box in Stoke Bruerne, but he could hardly remember what the girl looked like and wasn't actually sure of her name. To disguise his nervousness, he'd asked three of his friends to join him, not mentioning his possible 'date'.

They'd approached the bar and ordered their drinks just as the girls emerged from the back room. Every serviceman turned to see the three lovely girls emerging from the back but Will's eyes immediately picked out the pretty, deep-auburn-haired girl behind the other two.

Betsy was struggling to cope with the number of people waiting for drinks and was trying to hustle the girls through, but Elizabeth spoke in a low voice into her ear. 'Would you care for some help?'

Betsy was astonished. She'd have put this one down as being used to giving orders at The Savoy not serving a bar full of grumpy boatmen but before she could protest, Elizabeth was already expertly pulling a pint to hand over to one of the Bletchley visitors.

Narrowing her eyes, Betsy said, 'You've done that before.'

Elizabeth gave a knowing smile and moved on to Will, who was far too captivated by Gloria's face to notice he still did not have a drink.

Maggie took Gloria's arm and steered her towards Will. She'd seen how he was staring.

'Hello, it's Will, isn't it?' she said breezily. 'Well, here we are again, aren't we, Gloria?'

Gloria, Will thought, *that's her name* and he stepped forward to flash a perfectly white smile at the young girl.

In the noisy bar, the girls hardly noticed when the door opened and Jake Spencer and his son walked in to be greeted by gruff comments about what took them so long but then

Maggie looked up and felt a glow of pride as Mr Spencer gave a condescending nod towards them. His son was too busy glowering at Will and Gloria, she noticed. Aged about eighteen, she wondered why he hadn't been conscripted. His head was bowed as usual but out of the corner of his eye, he was watching every move that Gloria made. It made Maggie smile.

Chapter 9

Later that evening, Elizabeth and Maggie left Gloria and Will huddled in the corner of the pub. As they were making their way back to the boat, they heard raised voices emanating from *Buffalo*'s small cabin and then Mr Spencer said loudly in a sneering tone, 'For Christ's sake, just forget it, she wunna look at a dolt like you. Now, get out my way.'

Maggie nudged Elizabeth, who had slowed down, to listen.

There was suddenly the sound of yelling and pots being broken and then as they heard Mrs Spencer's muffled scream, the two girls hurried along the edge of the towpath towards their own boat.

Both girls were unnerved. They came from homes where the deepest anger was expressed by a firmly shut door; there had never been any violence, and they suddenly felt like strangers in this alien world.

Maggie was still awake when she heard Gloria humming with happiness as she stepped aboard, oblivious to the drama that had unfolded on the quayside. Knowing that Elizabeth had made sure she locked her door from the inside and that her own heart was still racing, Maggie pretended to be asleep to avoid spoiling Gloria's evening by recounting what had gone on at the Spencers' boat. After hovering for a while, hoping for a confidante, Gloria took in the prone figure on the bunk and gave up;

she climbed into her own bed ready to replay every moment of her magical night in her head.

* * *

The Spencers had already left when Gloria emerged from her cabin the next morning. She rubbed her eyes, wishing she hadn't had that second beer. Elizabeth, who had spent the whole evening pulling pints and delighting the customers with some unexpectedly funny retorts to their raucous comments, was now finding fault with everything from the mooring ropes to the state of the cabins.

'Hope you got paid for that bar work, Elizabeth,' Gloria called over the roofs of the boats as their irritable colleague meaningfully held up yet another piece of rope that needed splicing, but there was no reply.

Gloria shrugged and started up the engine. Maggie was struggling back along the towpath with a paper bag in her arms. Her trip to Flecker's Merchant Grocer at the Gate of the Moon was a highlight of calling into Stoke Bruerne and she loved the array of ropes and lines hanging from the ceiling or coiled in the corners. It had always been a welcome port of call for boaters, selling tea, jams, liniments and salves for bruises and cuts, clay pipes and sherbet suckers for the children but as rationing took hold, the shop seemed much emptier than usual.

'I had to take my own bag,' she complained, pushing gently past Gloria. 'They've run out of paper, apparently and, it seems, just about everything else. Honestly, this war will leave us with nothing. I could only get some more Marmite, a cabbage and a couple of potatoes so dinner's going to be interesting. At least we've got some porridge left.' She thought longingly of her grandmother's stove and the pre-war stocked larder and went below to put the paltry supplies away.

Gloria dipped her head behind her into the cabin. 'Did you notice anything strange about Elizabeth?'

Maggie chuckled. 'What, apart from the fact she's even more like a fish out of water here than I am?'

'Yeah,' Gloria said, reaching over to put the porridge in the pan, 'she seems so rich and posh but she knows how to pull a pint, and is always short of money and – oh, I don't know, I sometimes wonder if she's a spy. She's a bit odd.'

Maggie burst out laughing. 'Ah yes, the Mata Hari of the waterways. That'll be her.'

'Well, you mark my words, there's something odd going on. I'm going to keep my eye on her.'

The next stretch before Slapton was relatively free of locks so Maggie took over the tiller while Gloria took some time to clean up below and put on the kettle for a cup of tea.

Gloria noticed the shelf next to the jar of money was covered in dust and started to wipe it down, tutting to herself. Then she stopped. There were marks on the wood behind the jar and when she pressed her fingers against it, the planks gave way to reveal a hollow space behind. Reaching her first finger into the hole, she pressed her shoulder against the side of the boat and prodded.

It seemed empty and she was about to withdraw her finger when it touched something round and hard. Using her nail to pull it towards her, she saw it was a half-crown and behind it, she found several more.

Gloria stared at the coins, turning them over and over in her hand. She was puzzled but eventually popped them back in the jar, her face troubled.

'Are you making that brew or not?' Maggie's voice came from above.

'Yeah. Won't be a min,' Gloria said, leaning over to fill the kettle and put it on the stove.

She popped her head out of the hatch while it was boiling and said, 'Have you been in the kitty jar?'

Maggie, who was concentrating on a sharp turn in the canal, shook her head. 'Nope, why?'

'Nothin'. Just found a few half-crowns stuck behind. I've put them back.'

It was later that night when the three girls had finished their dinner of mashed potato and cabbage and were curled up on the little bunks in the *Nancy May* that Gloria brought the subject up again.

'Elizabeth, you been in the kitty jar?'

For a split second, Elizabeth's eyes flickered but only Gloria noticed. Maggie was too busy spreading the left foot of a sock she was darning over a saucer.

'No, of course not. Why on earth would I do that?'

'Just wondered,' Gloria said in a vague voice, but her eyes were examining Elizabeth's face keenly. 'It's only that I found a few half-crowns near the jar, but I've put them back now. They must have fallen out.'

'Have we got enough money to get some more wool?' Maggie asked, thinking wistfully of the constant supply of socks her grandmother used to knit for her. 'I've run out of old socks to unravel for re-knitting and these are on their last legs. She chuckled at her own joke and wiggled her finger through the hole. The other two ignored her.

Gloria got the jar down and counted the contents.

'No, we haven't. We won't have enough to get diesel at this rate. We're all going to have to put more in.'

'I thought you wanted to be in charge of the kitty,' Elizabeth said tartly. She thought she'd been so clever to only take a few coins at a time, hiding them behind the jar until the coast was clear for her to put them in her purse. 'Doesn't seem to me you're doing a very good job.'

'I'm doing fine,' Gloria replied, frowning. 'I just don't understand. It goes down quicker than it should.'

Elizabeth jumped up and said quickly, 'Well, maybe I should take over.'

Gloria shook her head more vehemently than she meant to.

Elizabeth gave a sharp snort and said, 'I'm off to bed. I'll wire for some more money; it doesn't matter to me.'

'Must be wonderful to be so rich,' Gloria muttered, but she was puzzled. This woman seemed to be so wealthy and yet . . . There was something that didn't add up, she thought.

* * *

Adding up was something Elizabeth spent every evening doing and when she got back to *Florence*, she got out her little notebook that she hid under the mattress and moved her finger up and down the columns. The money that Betsy had slipped her after her night on the bar had helped but she had another instalment to pay and her allowance from Christopher's Royal Navy pay was never enough. Now, the carefully hidden haul of silver coins had been discovered and she would be late with the next payment. She shivered at the possible consequences of Gloria's find. The other problem was passing the odd telephone box knowing that a certain number was etched on her brain.

It had been a slow and painful process for Elizabeth to admit she had a gambling problem. Bored to tears alone in her house outside Oxford, she'd seen an advertisement for help in a pub. It was on the wrong side of the river, so far enough away from anyone she knew. She had applied and been amazed to be given the job. It had been the start of a double life for the Honourable Mrs Elizabeth Stillings and she'd loved the excitement of her racy existence, relishing the lively atmosphere and coarse comments, knowing it would scandalise the Country Club and her moralistic husband. Rather than suppressing her accent, she'd refined it to keep her safe from the drunks who would weave their way out of the pub at the end of the evening, but it was there that she first saw the men playing dominoes. They would stack up their earnings to one side of the board and as the bone pieces clicked into place, she would feel a rising tension and her eyes would fix on the little piles of coins as they grew. One quiet evening, she asked to join and from then on, she would race to get her work done so she could play. The excitement of winning was like nothing she'd ever experienced and then one of the men, Ted, told her about a horse that was running at Newmarket, one of the few racecourses not requisitioned by the military. He offered to put a bet on for her and when he counted out the dirty pound notes into her hand the following day, she was hooked.

Elizabeth knew she was becoming increasingly nervous and tetchy with the girls. She had to beat this she told herself for a whole ten minutes before pulling the *Sporting Life* paper from under her mattress and checking the horses she had put a ring around. This product of a traditional upper-class upbringing and a 'suitable' marriage shook her head in shame and then put on her coat before quietly creeping out to find a telephone box.

Chapter 10

'I'm sorry, most of our men are confined to bed,' David, the chaplain at Broughton House, told Harry as the two men walked down a dark corridor towards the first ward. The long room had originally been painted white but was now a nicotine-stained yellow and along each wall were men in neatly made beds, some pale and still, others flushed and twitchy. The meals in front of them demonstrated an effort by the cooks to tempt their appetites but the tinned offerings of rationing had none of the pre-war freshness about them and the dull meals seemed to merge into the stained walls and brown bedside tables.

Harry tried to smile encouragingly at the men but there was that familiar blank expression that hid a turmoil of thoughts and memories. He noticed that many of the beds had flat areas where legs should have been and some of the patients were struggling to eat with one hand.

He turned towards Reverend Phillips.

'David, how on earth do you bring them back from . . . this?' he asked registering the dull eyes in front of him.

David gave a grimace. 'It's hard and it takes time, but you'll see, I'll take you in the garden later to meet the ones who are almost ready to go home. Many of them do get a chance at having a future when they've been here.'

Harry gauged the ages of the men in front of him; obviously some of them were Great War veterans and to be honest, he thought ruefully, many of them would probably never go home but there were others who had been the victims of this current war and perhaps might learn to live with their disabilities and find a meaning to their lives again.

'Would you like some dinner?' David asked, moving over to the serving trolley where a large woman in a pinny was hovering, waiting to collect empty plates. She seemed to be on edge, so Harry gave her an apologetic smile.

'I don't want to take anyone's rations,' Harry said hurriedly, surprised how the smell of potatoes was making him hungry.

David smiled. 'Let's ask the boss. Any extra for us, Mrs Lewis?'

'Oh, I think we can spare yer a bit,' she said and then in a quieter voice, she whispered to Reverend Phillips, 'Is he someone important?'

David shook his head and whispered back, 'No, he's just a padre, nothing to do with the authorities.'

'All right then, I think we could find some'at for 'im. Albert and Fred din't want theirs. They're feeling a bit ... well, yer know.'

'I'll pop back and see them later,' David said. 'But let me introduce you to Reverend Harry Moore, Mrs Lewis. He's come to visit us.'

'Oh lovely,' Marjorie Lewis said half-heartedly but the look she gave him was full of suspicion.

'I'd better see if I can find yer both a bit of sponge pud as well then.'

The two men sat opposite each other at the far end of David's office, tucking into their spam and mashed potatoes.

David spoke in a hushed voice, forcing Harry to lean forward to hear. 'So, you want to know about Jim Carpenter, do you?'

Harry glanced back towards the corridor they had just left. 'Was he in that ward?'

'No, he hardly eats enough to keep a sparrow alive. He doesn't have dinner, just a small sandwich at teatime.' David sighed. 'That man has so many demons chasing him I'm not sure we'll ever get him out of here. Mind you,' he added, 'it's such a bright day, we have managed to get him in the garden today and I'll take you to meet him in a bit. What's your connection?'

'Well, you know he abandoned three children years ago and went on the road . . . ?' Harry said, remembering the conversation he'd had with his uncle in the church.

David nodded. He'd read Jim Carpenter's file thoroughly and knew the whole story.

'I gather something happened in the Great War that played on his mind and once his wife died, he couldn't cope but, um, the daughter . . .' Harry stopped and gave an embarrassed cough which was greeted by slight lifting of the older man's eyebrows '. . . I don't really know her well – yet – but apparently, she's haunted by the fact her dad disappeared and somehow feels it was her fault.'

'Uh-huh. Pretty, is she?' David grinned.

Harry tried to look affronted but then smiled in capitulation.

'Hmm, very, now you mention it . . .' He rushed on: 'But anyway, it was the grandparents who took Maggie and her two brothers in after their dad left, and now the grandmother's passed away as well. I just feel that if I could help them reconnect as a family, it might help. They've no idea he's here yet. It was my uncle, their parish vicar, who told me. You know,' he added thoughtfully, 'too many people are separated by death; to be separated by a mind that's still reliving the memories of war seems unnecessarily cruel.'

The two men stopped talking while Marjorie Lewis came in to clear their plates and replace them with jam sponge; this time, reassured by the vicar's explanation, there was a gentle indulgence in her smile. It was good to see Reverend David having such a good chat with a fellow clergyman; she knew how much weight he was carrying on his shoulders.

'So how are you liking parish life?' David asked.

Harry winced and the older man laughed. 'I could have guessed. Somehow, I can't see you worrying about how you're going to find enough candles for the altar or whether the verger has fallen out with the WI again.'

'No, you're right,' Harry said with a grin and added in a conspiratorial whisper: 'It's unbelievable how heated people get about stupid little things, David. There's a war going on out there, for heaven's sake. They have no idea.'

'They probably have,' David said, 'but at a time like this, it's concentrating on the little things that stops you caving in because of the big ones.'

Harry nodded, reminded of a conversation he'd overheard between the secretary of the Women's Guild and one of her friends about the state of the tea towels in the vestry. He knew the woman's two sons were serving in Africa and while there was nothing she could do about Rommel's tanks, boiling tea towels was something she could concentrate on.

'I know you're right,' he said, quietly. 'People must feel so useless, no wonder they get so het up about the minutiae of everyday life.'

By the end of the meal, the men had got the measure of each other, and both nodded in satisfaction as they talked through a plan of action. The first step was to introduce Harry to the patient.

It was in the garden that David pointed out Jim Carpenter, but Harry would have known him anywhere. Like Maggie, he had blonde, wavy hair, although his was streaked with a few strands of grey, but it was his green eyes that mirrored his daughter's completely.

'Will he mind me talking to him?' Harry asked.

'No, I don't think so, but I suggest you don't mention his family, not yet anyway. Let's take this slowly. He's having a good day; I think helping in the garden heals more than anything we can do, and I don't want to distract him from that.'

David walked over to the man who was wearing an old boiler suit and bending down awkwardly by the vegetable patch, digging out the weeds.

Harry noticed how a simple touch led to a jerked response and a panicked expression. It was as if he'd been stung.

'It's all right, Jim,' David reassured him, 'we just wanted to say hello and see how you're doing.'

Jim looked dubiously towards the stranger hovering in the background.

'Who's he?' he said in a low voice.

'This is Harry Moore; he's visiting his uncle at Emmanuel Church, but he's a padre with the army. He's come to have a look round and I wanted to introduce him to some of our residents. Perhaps you could come and walk with us a minute, if we're not disturbing you?'

Jim looked extremely reticent but wiped his hands on his overalls and stretched. The man had once been tall and by the look of him, strong, but now his hands were sinewy and his body was barely visible inside the voluminous brown boiler suit. He kept his head bowed and hung back while they waited for him to slowly walk around the garden with them.

'What are you planting?' Harry asked in an encouraging voice.

'Beans, for the spring. If there's going to be one,' Jim muttered.

The two clergymen caught each other's eye over the veteran's head. Harry knew that hopelessness. He'd heard it so many times before.

David ignored the comment and went on: 'Perhaps you'd like to tell the padre about what we do here? Maybe we could start with what else you're planting.'

A sigh was followed by Jim reeling off a few plant names, like a child repeating a times table at school.

Harry stepped forward to examine the tiny shoots that were beginning to emerge from the dark soil. He grinned encouragingly at Jim, ignoring the bland expression he got in return.

'They're coming on grand, Mr Carpenter. My uncle would be jealous. His haven't sprouted yet.'

For a split second, Jim's face brightened. He found a tiny shred of hope in the little plants' efforts to break through the ground. Harry took it as a sign he could risk another question.

'I hope you'll forgive me, but I deal with a lot of vets like you in my army work and I wonder whether I could ask if working in the garden is . . . Helping – you know – with forgetting?'

Too late, he realised his mistake as the mask came down again and a shrug was the only answer he got. Harry could have kicked himself.

David broke the silence and in a very gentle voice said, 'Jim had a lot of issues when he first arrived, didn't you, Jim? But I think we're getting to the bottom of them and hopefully, we'll be able to get you better enough to leave one day, won't we?'

Jim looked around him, wide-eyed, as if surrounded by an invisible fence. Harry put his hand out to touch the man's shoulder and smiled into the green eyes that reminded him of so much of the girl he had seen at the church. An electric shock ran through him.

'I'm sure no one's going to make you do anything you don't want, Jim,' he said in an uneven voice.

David quickly agreed and the three of them turned back towards the vegetable patch. Jim quickened his pace with every stride to reinforce the fact that the conversation was over.

* * *

Back in David's office, a cup of tea in hand, the two chaplains were subdued.

Harry was pondering how David coped with negativity surrounding him day in, day out and as if reading his thoughts, the older man started to explain.

'It's very small steps, Harry. These men are like Ypres after the Great War. They've been completely destroyed and brick by brick we have to rebuild them, but they'll never be the same. We may be able to recreate some of what they were but there's the danger that only the façade is left. What we try to do is delve deeper and see if we can unearth any of the vestiges of the person they once were.'

'Do you feel you can tell me what happened to Jim at Gallipoli? My uncle's the family's vicar so can't reveal a confidence.'

David put his head on one side and then said, 'Yes, I think it's time that man was helped and it's in his records. It was in that dreadful battle in the Dardanelles. He was the sergeant and led his men around a corner where there was a trap. The enemy waited until the whole troop was in the gully before opening fire. Because he was at the front near to a rock, they never spotted him. He watched as thirty-five of his men were plundered – shot to ribbons – and he was unable to do anything. He was hopelessly outnumbered and all he could do was hide until the Ottomans had gone. Jim was found three days later cradling the body of one of his men; he was dehydrated and at the point of madness. He's never forgiven himself.'

There was a moment's silence as Harry took in David's words. Feeling guilty for surviving was one thing but to feel responsible for your whole platoon's deaths was taking that guilt to another level.

When Reverend Phillips shook Hary's hand at the door of Broughton House, there was a real warmth between the two men.

David spoke first. 'I . . . I don't know to say this . . . but your visit today has given me a strength I've been losing,' he said, looking guiltily at the picture of Christ on the wall.

Harry followed his gaze and nodded. 'I know, I know. It's hard to keep believing there's anyone there with a divine plan.'

David looked cheered and his shoulders visibly untensed.

'I hope you're going to come back and see us again. This is going to take time with Jim and, to be honest, it would be so good to chat more with you. I feel we understand each other. And,' fingering his dog collar, he added, 'sometimes this is a lonely job.'

Reaching to grasp the other clergyman's hand again, Harry said enthusiastically, 'I'd love to.'

David turned to leave but called over his shoulder, 'Great, let's not leave it too long.'

Chapter 11

The bus journey back gave the young padre time to examine his conscience. He had been, frankly, getting bored to tears with the endless fund-raising tea parties organised by the Women's Guild and the Women's Institute. Chatting about how many biscuits would be needed really wasn't this active man's forte and, as practically the only eligible male left in Didsbury, there had been many an occasion when he had bitten back a retort to yet another older woman's query as to his marital status. Briskly walking the streets near the church had been his only refuge and often, late at night, he would head towards Fletcher Moss Park to sneak in through the broken fence on Millgate Lane and walk the dark paths that meandered in all directions. He never got lost, his navigational skills having been honed as a youth on holiday in the Lake District and Wales, and while walking a park in Manchester couldn't compete with Great Gable, it was the only time he felt like himself. The latest quest to track down Jim Carpenter had given him a purpose he had been lacking and the fact that it might, in the future, give him an excuse to see that lovely young woman again put a spring in his step.

'Sorry?' He realised the woman in the scarf on the seat opposite him had said something.

'I said, it's a nice day, isn't it, Padre?'

'Oh yes,' Harry replied, surprised to see the sun shining through the bus window.

She was obviously settling in to find out more about the good-looking young man in the seat opposite, but Harry suddenly jumped up, relieved to see it was his stop.

He felt uncomfortable that he had been rude but honestly, did every mother have to home in on him like Cupid's arrow? Harry had a longing to be back with his men, facing the enemy – these women were far more terrifying.

Later that evening, Harry braced himself to confess to his uncle that he had taken the Carpenter case into his own hands. He wasn't sure how his uncle would take it so, in his usual forthright manner, he plunged straight in.

'Went to see Jim Carpenter today.'

His uncle swirled round, his eyebrows raised. Then a flash of anger erupted. 'I didn't expect you to do that. Or ask you to.'

Harry hung his head for a moment but then raised it to defend his actions.

'I'm sorry, Uncle, but you needed help. You have so much to deal with here and I *have* been sent to support you. I've been calling on Charlie as you asked but, I thought if I could get to see his son, it might help the whole family.'

Ignoring his uncle's disapproving expression, Harry went on, 'He was having a good day and was out in the garden.'

Peter Moore frowned but then gave a reluctant smile.

'OK, well, thanks for going. You're right, I really don't know how to help that family. I mean, I did try to talk to Charlie about what Winnie had told him before she died, but he refused to discuss it. Somehow, he needs to lead the way for that family because the two boys have shut out all memory of their dad and Maggie, well, she's just desperate to find a father she can love and respect.'

He looked across at his nephew and noticed his expression softened at the mention of Maggie's name.

'She's very lovely, isn't she?'

Harry pretended to look surprised and then laughed.

'It seems I'm not doing very well at hiding this but, yes, now you mention it, I think she is. Perhaps I'm not being completely altruistic in wanting to help this family.'

'In that case, maybe I'll forgive you for interfering,' Peter said with an indulgent smile. He tried to ignore the delightful thought that he might one day officiate at his nephew's wedding.

'OK, what can I do to help?' Peter asked, grinning.

Harry had been thinking about his next move and leaned forward with enthusiasm.

'I'd like to go to Broughton House again, but I don't know whether to mention that to the family.'

'Hmm, don't think I would, not just yet. Um, Harry,' he faltered, 'did you happen to hear the whole story – about Jim?'

'Yes, Uncle, the chaplain there told me.'

To know that Harry finally understood was a huge relief and Peter felt the tension drop from his shoulders.

'Nice chap, David. He does an amazing job,' Harry was saying. 'But yes, he told me all about the ambush. It's a terrible story and, you know, that guilt's like a millstone dragging Jim down into the depths of despair.'

He paused and then went on, 'David thought that maybe, just maybe if we could track down some of the relatives of the men who were killed in that gully . . . well, do you think some of them might have forgiven him?'

'Oh, now that's an idea,' Peter replied. 'To be honest, we have nothing to lose. Let's make a list of people and organisations you could contact and see if we can find any of them. Forgiveness is a great healer, as we know.

'Oh, and maybe you could write to Maggie,' he added innocently, 'just to, well, let her know how her grandfather's doing. I've got a note of an address for her somewhere, in case of emergency, you know, so you leave it on the side for me and I'll find it and send it.'

Harry wanted to ask so many questions about Maggie Carpenter but didn't dare. He had vowed at the beginning of this war not to start a relationship he might not be alive to finish but there was something about this girl that suggested a mix of strength and frailty and he was finding that combination irresistible. A man who had avoided relationships to put his men and his vocation first, Harry had always used the white collar around his neck as a barrier. This time, however, it seemed to be choking him.

He decided to ignore the chuckle coming from his uncle and instead led him over to the desk in the study. The pair sat late into the evening planning their next actions and then a galvanised Harry spent the next few days sending off letters to the army to check records. There was one letter, though, that he couldn't wait to write. He just didn't know what to say.

Dear Maggie,

I really hope you don't mind me writing to you, but I thought you might be interested to hear how your grandfather is doing.

Harry looked at his opening lines with satisfaction – perfectly plausible, he thought, and carried on.

I've been calling round to see him on a regular basis and he seems to be doing quite well. Both the Ladies Guild and the Red Cross, who worked with your grandmother, seem to be organising a rota to keep him fed and their visits – and I hope my own – will keep him engaged with life. He looked in good health and I thought, quite good spirits, considering. I hope you find that reassuring.

My uncle said he has an address for you so will forward this letter for me as I'm afraid I didn't even get a chance to ask you what you're up to during this war or where you are, but I'm sure it's something terribly impressive!

Too much? he wondered, pausing his pen. He decided it might be better to stop now, before he said anything he would regret.

Anyway, I must go, there are brasses to clean, sermons to write and Mother's Union cakes to enthuse over – surely, I'm winning this war single-handed?
Sending best wishes
Harry Moore

To prevent himself from rereading the letter and then rewriting it, he put it straight in an envelope and sealed it, leaving it on the sideboard for his uncle to find in the morning.

With so little time left before he was due to return to the British Expeditionary Forces, the young padre attempted to put Maggie to the back of his mind, using a strategy that had always worked in the past where he had thrown himself into practical tasks to dispel any emotions. Unfortunately for Harry Moore, this time the plan failed, and he was subjected to constant flash-backs to her tear-stained, heart-shaped face.

He slept little and ate even less as he rushed to pursue his investigations into the massacre at Gallipoli while supporting his uncle's parish work. The housekeeper at Emmanuel Church rectory, Mrs Hennessey, tutted disapprovingly as she watched him, once again, go to the bread bin to grab a piece of bread rather than sit down to the potato pie she had baked.

She barred the door, a plate in her hand.

'Look 'ere young man, it's Sunday and I've already got the vicar fading away before me very eyes, and I don't need you competing wiv 'im. You'll not step one foot out o' this door till you've eaten this pie. Do yer 'ear me?'

Harry knew he was beaten and reluctantly took the empty plate from the woman's hands and headed towards the table to sit down.

It was as she was insisting on ladling out a huge helping to him that his uncle came in. Harry glanced up and then looked again. Mrs Hennessey was right.

'Uncle Peter, come and join me. Mrs Hennessey won't accept anything less.'

Peter pushed back his sleeve cuff to check his watch and wavered, but Mrs Hennessey was there already, her ample body pushing him towards the table.

'There now, that's better,' she said, standing back triumphantly. 'I won't let either of you out of here until those plates are good an' empty. I slaved all morning to make that potato pastry taste some'at like and you're going to eat every bit.'

The two men gave in and silently began to eat. Harry took a bite and realised it was a very good pie indeed and grinned gratefully at the matriarch towering over him, but Peter played with his fork and ate very little.

'Are you feeling OK, Uncle?' Harry asked.

'Yes, fine, just got a couple of parishioners to see before evensong.' Peter Moore pushed his chair back and then wobbled.

Harry jumped to his feet.

'You just sit there; I'll see the parishioners and then do evensong.' He turned around. 'Mrs Hennessey, I wonder if you would be kind enough to do a hot cup of tea for my uncle and then bundle him off to bed? I think he's done enough for one day.'

'Enough for one lifetime,' Sybil Hennessey muttered but gently took the vicar's arm to help him into the armchair on the other side of the room. She frowned as he dropped heavily into it, noting his pale face.

'He's done in,' she whispered to Harry while she put the kettle on. 'He'll be 'aving another of them 'eart attacks if he's not careful.'

Harry looked across at the man slumped in the tapestry-covered armchair and couldn't help but agree with her.

Over the next few days, he watched carefully as his uncle rallied himself to listen sympathetically to the constant stream of people who 'happened to pass' the rectory and pop in for a chat. Their need for some sense for all the disaster that was surrounding them was blatantly obvious and Harry became increasingly concerned as to how long this overburdened vicar would be able to go on finding the energy and the words to offer them comfort. The young padre knew he was becoming increasingly impatient with how the flower group were going to find foliage for the Christmas service when the ground was frozen and all spare soil had been dug up for vegetables anyway, but lying beneath his intolerance, a greater struggle was keeping him up at nights.

Giving up on sleep on one occasion, he went for a walk. He had to concentrate on not tripping up on the pavements of the pitch-black streets of Didsbury as he made his way back carefully across to the familiar portal of Emmanuel Church.

The old wooden door creaked as he pushed it open to go and sit in a back pew where he glanced at the familiar symbols of the Church of England, heaving a long sigh.

'Are you there? I mean, really, are you there?' he said out loud to the altar. 'I don't mean to be critical but to be honest, you're really not doing a good job are you?'

The silence echoed.

Harry knelt down and banged his fist on the pew in front.

He had been so sure of his vocation, standing up to his parents who had suggested one clergyman in the family was enough, but he'd always looked to his Uncle Peter as someone who had found a mission in life and a contentment he lacked. Harry was a young man who always felt on the edge of something exciting he couldn't quite grasp, using climbing the Lake District and Welsh mountains to try to capture the adrenalin he craved. So, he'd determinedly ignored his parents' suggestions he should follow his father into the law, instead reading every book on religious philosophy that he could until he was offered a place to study at Wycliffe Hall, Oxford. In the heated debates and deep learning, he found a passion and a conviction that helped to assuage his yearning for excitement. He loved the fact that Christianity had endured and prospered over nearly two thousand years and was almost evangelical in his confidence that there was a divine plan. But all that changed at Dunkirk.

A small vessel that had valiantly made it across the Channel to help rescue the stranded soldiers in France hovered in deeper waters, anxious to avoid the strafing fire from the planes targeting the beach and a group of dejected, soaked young men looked hopefully to their padre as if he could part the waters in front of them for them to reach it. Just as terrified as they were, the young chaplain had headed out as confidently as he could into the cold, heaving waves but was soon knocked off his feet with the strength of them. Clambering back to his feet, he'd yelled to the little trail of men behind him to hold onto the shoulder of the person in front and slowly, they made their way to the boat. Once Harry reached the hull, he'd turned to help the others but when he tried to grab for the hand of one young man, who couldn't have been more than eighteen, the thin, white fingers slipped from his grasp. The anguished face had glared accusingly at him as it disappeared beneath the waves and as much as Harry had tried to pull the soldier back to the surface, the boy had become a dead weight and the waves sucked him out to sea. It was that soldier's face Harry saw at two o'clock in the morning – a face that had turned to a man of God to explain why his young body did not have the will to hold on, why the waves were stronger than he was and, most of all, what the hell he was doing on a beach in France being shot at. Since then, Harry had found himself acting a part – performing all the duties expected of him with a sympathetic expression but like with that young soldier, he had found himself without any answers.

Standing up from the pew, he shook his head angrily.

Chapter 12

It was a Sunday morning and the girls were almost at Boxmoor near Hemel Hempstead. Gloria glanced at her watch. If she ran, she could make it to church.

'You two coming?'

Elizabeth replied instantly. 'Nope, I need to mend these ropes.'

Maggie tilted her head to one side, thinking. She felt a duty to her late grandmother to make one more effort with a God she was no longer sure she believed in; there was no doubt in her mind, however, that God didn't believe in her anymore. She'd often given in and gone to church with her grandmother just to avoid awkward questions, but these days, the liturgy had a hollow sound.

'All right, give me five minutes,' she said, and she popped below to see if she could find anything vaguely smart to wear. Her leather gloves, given to her by her grandmother for her birthday three years ago, were smeared with oil and her coat was threadbare. She unearthed her velour hat from the back of the cupboard and tried in vain to squash it into some sort of shape.

'My grandmother would have a fit if she saw me looking like this,' she said as she emerged onto the counter with an apologetic grin but then her eyes misted over; she had moaned so many times when her granny had dragged her to church and now, she would give anything to have her next to her, tucking her arm in hers.

'Come on, Mags,' Gloria said, 'we need to say a prayer of thanks for those people in Malta; I heard they had to eat sparrows and rats to survive that dreadful siege but now the whole island's being awarded the George Cross.'

Maggie braced up and sniffed.

'You're so right, I have a cousin who was on a ship trying to get fuel through to them so, yep, that's one thing we can celebrate and while we're there, let's go and bombard heaven with our instructions about the rest of the war from here on.'

Maggie's grandmother had clung to her faith after her son had walked out of their lives but complained regularly to God that He had let her down and that He was going to have to do better in the future. On the day the three youngsters had arrived on the doorstep, the children's grandfather determinedly took the cross off the wall and put it in the drawer. Maggie had spent her childhood kneeling by her bed begging God to bring her father back. By the time she went to college, she'd given up all hope of a response and once she'd met Roger Anderson, she was convinced only the devil would be interested in her.

Maggie bowed her head as the vicar at Boxmoor repeated the familiar words, thinking firstly of her grandmother, then of her grandad. She exhaled, looking at the domed archways, and shrugged, deciding she had nothing to lose by sending a quick prayer skyward for her brothers and thanks for the deliverance of the people in Malta, but when she looked at the back of the vicar in his robes, it was the figure of the young army chaplain at Emmanuel Church she was imagining instead. She jerked backwards making Gloria glance with concern at her. Maggie squirmed in embarrassment, but she felt her cheeks turning red. A chaplain? She almost laughed out loud but stuffed her fist in her mouth, wondering if everyone around her could read her thoughts. The shame was more than she could bear and there was a moment when she contemplated running out of the church.

After that, the service was interminable. By the time the two girls finally emerged into the weak sunlight, Maggie wanted to get as far away from the beautiful church as possible and she put her hands in her pockets to determinedly march back towards the canal and the sanctuary of the *Nancy May*.

Running to keep up with her, Gloria panted, 'What's your hurry? It's as if the devil himself is chasing you.'

Maggie couldn't help herself; she looked round fearfully and then gave a bitter laugh.

'I think he's already caught me,' she said dismally and quickened her pace.

*　*　*

They took time to stop at Hemel Hempstead to do some chores, so while the other two spliced the ropes, cleaned out the mud box and did some washing, Gloria rushed off to the local company office to pick up the post. She was delighted to find a letter from Will telling her he was heading home to London on a three-day pass but could divert his journey to find her at Watford if she wanted to see him. Bundling the rest of the post into her pocket, she ran to the nearest telephone box to ring Will's landlady. A formidable woman, disapproving of a female caller, haughtily told her that Will had just come in and Gloria found her fingers were shaking, making it difficult to put more coins in the slot to delay the pips.

'Hello, Redhead,' a cheerful voice greeted her. 'You got my letter then? Where are you?'

There was never enough time to talk on a public telephone and in any case, Gloria treated them like a hand grenade, holding the receiver away from her as if it could harm her. She breathlessly told him they would be at Hunton Bridge near Watford the following evening.

'No idea where that is but I'll get a train to Watford and then try and hitch a lift. Hopefully see you at seven,' he managed to say before her money ran out. Gloria stood looking at the receiver with new affection until a knock on the window made her jump.

'Got to ring me nan,' a woman outside said impatiently. 'Come on, out o' there.' She tutted at the girl who held open the heavy door for her to push past brusquely, but Gloria didn't seem to notice her rudeness.

With a smile pasted to her face for the rest of the day, Gloria was the first to offer to run and prepare the gates along the cut so their boats could pass swiftly through, ignoring the furious shouts as she pretended not to see a boat waiting patiently at the side of the lock.

It was only when they were waiting outside Kings Langley heading into Watford that Gloria remembered the rest of the post.

'Oh, I forgot, here are your letters,' she said and threw them onto the roofs for Maggie and Elizabeth as she went up to the next lock.

Maggie reached to pick hers up and frowned at the unknown writing. She opened the envelope, puzzled, and then scanned down to Harry's signature, which immediately prompted a sharp tug in her stomach. The words were bland enough, but they were warm and even, at times, humorous. She felt goosebumps on her arms, wondering whether the young padre was hoping to open up a correspondence between them, but then she remembered:

You can't let a religious man be interested in you, Margaret Carpenter, you just can't.

She sadly put the envelope in her pocket, thinking of the short, unemotional reply she would make and got on with steering the boat through the lock gates.

Reaching Hunton Bridge couldn't come quickly enough for Gloria and even before they'd moored up, she was checking the towpath for Will in case he was early, but seeing it was empty, she went down into the cabin to get ready.

Unceremoniously, she demanded the whole space to herself to do so, making Maggie sit on the stern in the cold.

'It's more important I impress Will than you keep warm,' she said unsympathetically, pushing a coat through the hatch for Maggie to put on.

It hadn't taken the others long to realise that when the diminutive Gloria's mind was set on something, arguing was a waste of time, so Maggie went along the towpath towards Elizabeth who was still securing *Florence*.

'Gloria will land this Will if she gets a chance,' she told Elizabeth. 'I wonder if he knows what he's up against.'

Elizabeth stood up from the mooring rope and twirled the mallet in her hand. 'I just hope she knows what she's doing. I'm not sure Will's family will be too thrilled to find out he's going out with a girl off the boats.'

Maggie reluctantly agreed.

'Yes, perhaps we're all hiding behind secrets,' Elizabeth said, almost to herself.

Maggie coughed and then blushed making Elizabeth look keenly at her.

'Got something to share have you, Maggie?'

'No, not at all,' Maggie said briskly and marched back along the towpath.

Elizabeth stared after her. Gloria was so uncomplicated, she thought, but Maggie . . .

Looks like I'm not the only one with a past, she thought.

* * *

A couple of days later, the noise of the 'plop' on the doormat in the vicarage made Harry drop his toast back onto the plate and walk briskly to the front door, trying not to run. The buff envelope on the doormat suggested answers to some of his questions about the families of Jim Carpenter's platoon, but it was the other letter he ripped open first.

The initial joy at hearing from Maggie was tempered by the cold tones of her reply. It simply thanked him for his kind letter and for taking the time to visit her grandfather and was signed 'With regards, Margaret Carpenter'.

Harry perused the other letter but walked dejectedly back into the kitchen, putting Maggie's letter on the side table. *Perhaps it's for the best*, he thought sadly, *I'm due back on duty soon and it really isn't a good idea to have any complications.* Somehow, that reasoning didn't make him feel any better.

'Is that it?' his uncle called. 'Is that the letter from the Records' Office?'

'Yes,' Harry looked again at the other envelope in his hand. 'They've sent us two addresses, but one's in Surrey and the other's in Watford. I can't travel down there, and I really don't think this is a conversation I can have by letter.'

His uncle peered over his shoulder.

'Hmm,' he said musingly, 'well, let me check the diary and see if we can enlist some help. In the meantime, why don't you start by writing these good people a letter and we'll see where that gets us.'

Harry had gone back thoughtfully to his toast. He looked disapprovingly at the beef dripping spread, hoping the family they had donated their butter ration to would appreciate the sacrifice and chomped into his toast thinking how the revolting taste mirrored his misery perfectly.

'Oh, could you pop round to see Mrs Wellings this morning?' his uncle was saying. 'She's received an MIA telegraph about her son who's with the navy and has been with the Atlantic Convoy.'

A 'missing in action' telegram was a particularly cruel thing to receive, leaving a mixture of despair and desperate hope and Harry knew it was a fine line the clergy had to tread when dealing with the recipient between allowing them that hope and preparing for the years of emptiness ahead. The headlines had been stark in their assessment of what life was like for the sailors in the Atlantic protecting supplies on their way to Britain, and there had been constant reports of sinkings and deaths.

'Of course, I will.' Harry made an effort. 'She's a widow, isn't she? And just the one son?'

Spotting the letter on the side, Peter Moore added with a gleam in his eye, 'While you're there, perhaps you could call in at the Carpenters' again; it's not far away and it's been a while since you've had time to go.'

Peter expected to see Harry show some enthusiasm, but instead, his nephew's whole demeanour was one of sadness. Remembering the little boy who had wanted to run the fastest, climb the biggest hill and take the biggest risks, he'd always known Harry wasn't meant to be parish vicar and it had been his idea for his nephew to join the army where he would be a spiritual guide, yes, but also where he could be at the forefront of the action. After witnessing the chemistry between him and Maggie Carpenter at the funeral, he'd hoped that an interest in the delightful girl would distract Harry from the mundane life of a suburban vicar but now, he wondered whether he'd made a mistake. Determining on a little bit of old-fashioned matchmaking, he went off into his study to scan the books on his shelves. When he came to a map that showed the canals of Britain, he followed the Grand Union Canal with his finger until he found Watford. The elderly vicar gave a delighted little chuckle. All he had to do now was telephone the Inland Waterways to see whether God was on his side and whether a certain young lady's boat was going to be anywhere near.

* * *

The first visit was as gruelling as Harry had anticipated. Mrs Wellings was sitting in her morning room, without a fire lit. Her face was blank and although he did what he could to give her some hope, they both knew that the freezing waters of the Atlantic left little chance of rescue for a desperate sailor. Eventually, he resorted to washing up and putting a match to the few paltry bits of coal from the ration in her coal shed but it was little comfort and as he walked out of the front door, he felt completely defeated.

'Hello, it's Reverend Moore's nephew, isn't it?' A woman with a rosy complexion, wearing a paisley scarf, crossed the road to meet him.

Seeing his blank expression, she went on: 'I'm Dorothy Harper. I met you at Winnie Carpenter's funeral.'

'Of course,' Harry replied, vaguely.

The woman grinned and prodded his lapel with her finger. 'No, now, don't you pretend, young man. I know you don't remember me. I mean, why should you? There's a lot of us in this parish but I certainly remember a good-looking young man like you. I'm just on my way to see Charlie Carpenter, I've made him a potato casserole.'

Perked up by her directness and the twinkle in her eye, Harry told her he was headed that way too and they fell in beside each other to walk the few streets to the Carpenter house.

By the time they got there, Harry had warmed to this cheerful, kind soul who seemed to be offering time and practical help to anyone in the community who might need it and as they reached the Carpenters' front door, he turned to face her.

'I wonder, well, I hope it's not asking too much . . .'

'Ask away,' she said encouragingly.

'Mrs Wellings, she lives at the house you saw me coming out of, she's not good and could do with a bit of cheering up.'

There wasn't a moment's hesitation before Dorothy Harper agreed to call on her the very next day. Her willingness gave Harry an insight into how his uncle managed to survive parish work; it was the generosity of people like Mrs Harper who provided the scaffolding around his crumbling building.

She reached into the Carpenter letter box and pulled out a key on a piece of string to unlock the door with a familiarity that took Harry by surprise.

The morning room seemed cold, but Harry thought it was perhaps just that being here reminded him, far too brutally, that there was no room for him in Maggie's life.

Charlie Carpenter was still in his dressing gown, even though it was three o'clock in the afternoon. Mrs Harper strode straight up to him and pulled him out of his armchair onto his feet.

'Right, up you go, Charlie, I'm not telling you one bit of gossip until you're dressed with your hair combed and I'm sure you've got some Brylcreem somewhere you can put on it to make you look respectable.'

Charlie shuffled quickly out of the room, knowing resistance was a waste of time, and Mrs Harper turned to Harry.

'If you've got time, Padre, I could do with a bit of help here.' And after taking off her coat and placing it on the back of the chair, she rolled up her sleeves and headed towards the sink. 'I'll wash, you dry.'

Harry started to chuckle and she looked at him quizzically.

'It's all right, Mrs Harper, it's just that we have a Mrs Hennessey at the vicarage and I'm beginning to think Hitler has no idea what he's doing when he takes on the women of Britain.'

She shrugged her shoulders and turned on the tap.

'I bet there are a few Fraus in Germany who'd give him short shrift for taking their menfolk off to war too,' she laughed.

By the time the pots had been washed and dried, the pair were fast friends. A sheepish Charlie Carpenter appeared in the doorway, his hair slicked to one side.

Harry wiped his hands and stepped forward. 'I hope you're keeping well, Mr Carpenter, I just thought I'd call again and see how you were doing but,' he added, turning to Mrs Harper, 'I can see you're in good hands.'

Charlie leaned forward to whisper with more sense of humour than Harry was expecting, 'She's terrifying! I have to do as I'm told, as you can see,' and he moved to one side of Harry towards the woman who was now leaning down to reach to the back of the cupboard, a carrot in her hand.

'What are you after, Dorothy?'

'A baking tin,' came the muffled reply. 'I'll knock us up some scones if you've picked up your rations. I can add this carrot instead of butter, that'll make them moist enough. They'll only take a tick. You two sit down and have a chat; it'll do Charlie good to talk to another man. He's had enough of my nattering about the knitting group, haven't you, Charlie?'

'Never, you know I love hearing all about Mrs Thompson's endless grandchildren,' Charlie replied, and Harry was pleased to see another glint of humour in his eyes.

Mrs Harper happily prepared the tea and mixed the scones, humming softly. A confidante of Winnie's, she knew everything that had gone on over the years within these four walls and had been watching Charlie closely since her friend died, noting that as he sorted through family photographs, he lingered over ones of his son. Taking a small posy to Winnie's grave earlier that week, Dorothy Harper had whispered to her friend that she thought there might be a chance her family could finally start to rid itself of ghosts.

Later, when Mrs Harper served the tea and warm scones, Harry walked over to the mantelpiece which showcased memorabilia of a happy life – a china doll from a holiday to Wales, photographs of Charlie and his wife and smiling photos of the three children in school uniform. Harry sidled up to the fireplace and fingered the picture of Maggie. He couldn't help smiling at the pigtails with one ribbon missing and the toothy grin on her face.

'A grand looking lass, isn't she?' Mrs Harper said from behind. He turned to face her and she watched the embarrassment seep up his cheeks but there was more; she realised it was regret.

Dorothy Harper knew far more about Winnie's granddaughter than anyone could have suspected and, at that moment, she decided that a stable young man like this was exactly what that young madam needed – if he could accept her past. The thought of exorcising yet another demon from this family cheered her and, with a determined pursing of her lips, she chuckled that this padre would need more than God's help if he thought he could escape Dorothy Harper's plotting.

Chapter 13

'You see, I don't actually know either of them,' Gloria was telling Will, who was trying to listen without being distracted by her lovely mouth.

'Are you listening to me?' she asked abruptly.

He sat forward at the wooden table in the King's Head and tried to concentrate but this girl had no idea how alluring she was and how much he had been thinking about her since their last date at Stoke Bruerne.

'I was saying that I've been bundled in with these two posh girls and I really don't know anything about them.'

Will looked perplexed. He was completely at a loss.

'What do you mean? They seem nice enough.'

Gloria leaned in and whispered that she suspected Maggie 'had a past' and that Elizabeth was a spy.

At that, Will burst out laughing and she looked immediately affronted and then panic-stricken. She so wanted to appear sophisticated and here she was rabbiting on like a schoolgirl in a playground.

She took what she hoped was an elegant sip of cider to hide her embarrassment.

Will reached across the table and took her hand. 'You are the most enchanting girl I've ever met.'

She looked up and felt almost faint. He was so good-looking, and his eyes were full of affection for her.

'Let's get out of here,' he whispered, and she shivered with excitement.

Blackouts were a welcome restriction of the war for many a young man and Will hardly managed to get a few paces from the pub front door before turning to wrap his arms around Gloria's small frame.

He was torn between wanting to ravish her beautiful young body and feeling he needed to protect her. It was strange, and he wasn't sure what step to take next.

Gloria seemed to decide for him. She pulled his face towards hers and fiercely pressed her lips against his, wriggling in to fit exactly against his chest, and heaved a sigh of pure delight.

'Have you ever . . .' Will panted.

'Ever what?' Gloria asked, distracted by the feel of his hands on her waist, which was sending a tingling up her spine.

'You know, done it?'

'Done what?' And then she reeled back with shock and said firmly, 'No!'

Will immediately regretted his words.

He gently moved back to take her in his arms again.

'I'm sorry, I just, I mean, I'm just not sure what you want.'

Gloria felt ashamed. She had so little knowledge of any of this sort of thing and she wasn't quite sure what 'it' was but her sister, Molly, had written on many occasions to warn her against it so she had decided it was something really quite terrible.

'I don't know what "it" is, Will. How could I?'

She looked so forlorn and so young that Will's passion dissipated in a moment.

He pulled her towards a bench on the edge of the canal and gently pushed her to sit down.

'Gloria, how old are you?'

'I'm just eighteen,' she said with a proud toss of her head.

'Oh, that grown up.' He smiled. 'Well, I'm twenty so I'm much older than you. Tell me, have you had any boyfriends before?'

Gloria frowned, thinking, and then her face cleared and she said triumphantly, 'Yes, yes, I have. There was Albert Finks. He was fourteen and I was twelve so yes, I have.'

Will couldn't help it, he gave a loud guffaw, partially in relief that he hadn't taken things any further.

'I'll have you know he kissed me. Twice,' Gloria was saying with indignation.

'Oh, well, that makes you practically an old married woman then.'

Gloria prodded him and he fell off the end of the bench.

She giggled and offered her hand to help him up.

'OK, I admit, I'm new at this, Will, and I don't know how to behave but I want you to know you're the nicest man I've ever met, and I really like you.'

Her words made the thoughts that had been going through Will's mind even more inappropriate, and he felt ashamed.

'OK, Gloria. I don't even know your surname.'

'Smith,' she replied.

He reached out his hand to shake hers and said, 'How do you do, Miss Smith, I'm Will Nicholson and I'm very pleased to meet you.'

Gloria giggled again and then he took her arm and announced he was going to see her safely back to her 'abode' and the two of them walked arm in arm along the towpath, feeling they had started something that might be worth having.

* * *

Harry walked down Watford High Street from the station. He fingered the piece of paper with the address written on that was in his pocket, fearing he could be on a wild goose chase, but his uncle had, for some reason, insisted he make the journey in person. The letter from the family in Surrey whose son was killed on that fateful day in Gallipoli had been brief and unequivocal. There was no hope of forgiveness there and the family of Private Arthur Baines . . . his second hope . . . had not replied to his letter.

The last few weeks had been exhausting and Harry had not had a single day off. One of his main concerns was his uncle, who was losing weight and looking worryingly pale. Harry had been trying to take on as much work in the parish as his uncle would let him but today, an old clerical friend from a neighbouring parish was calling in, leaving Harry free to pursue his investigations.

He checked the piece of paper and headed towards Shakespeare Street where he found the bay-windowed terrace he was looking for. It didn't look very hopeful with its peeling paint around the door and faded patterned curtains hanging off the hooks in the front room. Taking a deep breath, Harry knocked on the door and waited.

He was about to give up when the door finally opened a crack. A woman in a floral pinny peered around the door. 'Yes?'

Harry tried to give his best padre-reassuring smile and said, 'Mrs Baines?'

'Who wants to know?'

'I'm Harry Moore, I'm here about your son, Arthur.'

Her face visibly brightened for a brief second and Harry panicked that he had given her false hope.

'I wrote you a letter,' he said hurriedly. 'Do you remember? I told you I'm trying to help his sergeant, Jim Carpenter, who is ill.'

'Why should I help him?' the woman replied, visibly crest-fallen.

Harry's shoulders sagged. He couldn't really think of a reason now he was faced with this bereaved mother.

'I honestly don't know, Mrs Baines.' A long pause ensued until he said, 'But what I do know is that Jim Carpenter has been carrying the guilt of what happened in Gallipoli all his life. It's haunted him and to be honest—' he breathed out heavily '—it's destroyed his whole family too, nearly as much as yours, I suspect. There was nothing he could do that day; he just feels fate was cruel not to kill him alongside your son and the rest of his men that he cared for so much for, but it's his children who've suffered. They've lost their father just as much as you've lost your son.'

He hoped his words would appeal to the mother in her and it seemed, as she opened the door a little more, he might be succeeding.

She eyed him up and down, noting the sincerity in his eyes and eventually said, 'You'd better come in.'

The early spring air outside was almost warm in comparison with the dark entrance hall but when he walked into the back parlour, the light was flooding in, which made it look more cheerful, even if it didn't make much difference to the temperature. In one corner there was a neatly made bed and a bedside cabinet with a tasselled lamp on it, a small table, an upright chair and two armchairs next to the range, one hardly used with a pristine piece of lace draped over the back. There was a small table next to it with a pipe and ashtray on it. It looked like a shrine, Harry thought.

Mrs Baines turned to face him. 'So, what is it you want then?'

Harry was a great believer in the balm of a cup of tea in difficult situations but didn't dare suggest one even though he was

parched after the train journey. He looked around questioningly at the hard-backed chair behind him and begrudgingly,
she waved her arm towards it.

Shuffling in his seat, Harry began his tale, explaining how
the events in Gallipoli had affected Sergeant Jim Carpenter so
badly that he had almost lost his mind and was now in a special
home for veterans.

'You see, he cared deeply for his men, including your son,
and was unable to save them and he's lived with that for years.
Not long after it happened, he decided he just couldn't cope and
deserted his three children, leaving them in the care of their
grandparents and disappeared off the face of the earth. His two
sons and a daughter were distraught. I've only recently discovered he's in a home for veterans, but he isn't in a good way, Mrs
Baines. He can't forgive himself and I was hoping you might be
able to help with that. He and his family don't deserve to live
under this terrible cloud. His two sons are angry and bitter and
his daughter, well, she just wanted her father to love her, but he
couldn't; he felt too guilty to let any love in.'

Suppressing the vision of Maggie that popped up, unbidden
as always, he looked up hopefully.

Mrs Baines got to her feet.

Harry held his breath; he had no idea how the rest of the visit
was going to go.

'Right, I'd better put the kettle on then,' she said.

While she made the tea, Harry looked around him. It may
have been cold in Mrs Baines's home, but it showed signs of
a happy family life with pictures above the range including
a photograph of what must have been Mrs Baines and her
husband on their wedding day, looking full of optimism and
excitement. Next to that was one of a soldier standing proudly
and grinning. He got up to have a better look. This juxtaposition

of a photograph of a young man with so much to live for and the scene he'd imagined in that gully in Gallipoli filled him with sorrow and, he couldn't help it, anger.

A voice behind him said, 'Yes, that's my Arthur. Good-looking lad, wasn't he?'

Harry nodded, took the proffered tea and sat down again, cupping his hands around the mug for warmth, prompting an embarrassed glance from Mrs Baines. 'I'm sorry it's so chilly in here,' she said, 'it's just me now, you see. My husband died when Arthur was little, they said it was an infection from the water. I try to keep this room warm but there's not much money coming in.'

She scanned his face and saw a deep understanding there. 'So, what's a young man like you doing bothering with this family?'

Harry blushed and her mouth tilted into a slight smile of understanding. He was nice-looking, she decided, and not unlike her Arthur. Perhaps he deserved a bit of help.

She slowly reached up to the mantlepiece and took down a faded letter, which she handed to Harry.

The words in the letter were a loving message from a son to his widowed mother, telling her he was fine, that the bully beef was dreadful but keeping them alive and that the sun was far too hot. His spelling was erratic, but it was a letter like so many others Harry had seen – full of reassuring words that hid the terror and the despair of a soldier on the front line. At the end of the letter, there was a paragraph that made coming to Watford worthwhile.

We've got a great sergeant, he's really one of the lads, Ma, and really tries to look after us. You'd really like him, Ma, he reminds me of Dad. Not as old as Dad would have been, obvusly, but a great laf and yet, I dunno, sort of caring. He wurries about us all the time and thinks he can save us all from this war, but he canna, can he, Ma? We know that cos of Da but don't you worry yerself, Ma, I'll be all right. You just take care of yerself.

With all my love, your loving son, Arthur

There was silence while Harry turned away to wipe his eyes. He passed the letter back to Mrs Baines and she examined him closely, finally saying, 'I'll get you a biscuit with that tea.'

Chapter 14

By the time Harry left the house, he felt brighter than he had done in weeks. In his pocket, he had two pieces of paper – one was the copied words of Arthur Baines about his superior and another was one from Arthur's mother to Jim Carpenter. He had no idea what it said but he hoped it might start a road to recovery for the whole Carpenter family and maybe Mrs Baines too. Checking his watch, he saw he had three hours before his train and, remembering his uncle's random comment that the nearby canal was an ideal place to have his sandwich, he made his way to Cassiobury Park. It felt like a real treat to be out, and he was delighted to see the daffodils already peeping their heads out. As always, the fact that nature plodded on despite everything that was happening around it, gave him hope.

'Surely, it can't be . . . it's Reverend Moore, isn't it?'

Harry jumped and then, he couldn't help it, a radiant smile spread across his face.

It was as if a film that had replayed in his mind on numerous occasions had suddenly stepped out of celluloid and into reality.

'Miss Carpenter? I don't believe it, what on earth are you doing here?'

Maggie frantically tried to adjust her shopping so she could smooth her hair into place while rubbing the dirt off her fingers.

'I work on the canals, you know for the Inland Waterways. Maggie was puzzled. 'I thought you knew – well, with the letter and everything.'

Harry looked embarrassed: 'I didn't, well, my uncle, he found your address and sent the letter for me.'

Maggie tried to hide the disappointment that he obviously hadn't been interested enough to ask. 'We've just stopped here to get supplies,' she told him, at a loss for something to say. 'Um, it was so kind of you to write . . . and to visit Grandad.'

Taking in the pink glow on Maggie's cheeks and the way her tattered jumper hugged her neat figure so perfectly, Harry's determination to avoid romantic entanglements vanished in a second and he ran through several perfectly plausible reasons as to why she might have written such a cold, short letter, but none of them bore any relation to the girl standing in front of him now, emanating a warmth that threatened to set him on fire. He tried to concentrate on the words she'd spoken and was genuinely astonished. He had had no idea women worked on the canal boats and certainly, such a tough, dirty life seemed incongruous with the lovely girl standing in front of him.

She pointed to the little badge on her sweater and said defensively, 'See the letters IW, well, we deliver goods on the inland waterways between London and Birmingham. Our engine's playing up so one of the girls has gone to find a spanner'

Harry didn't know whether to be impressed or horrified.

'But isn't all this, well, you know, too dirty and physical for a girl like you.'

A flash of indignation spread across Maggie's face, and she rubbed the dirt on her cheek furiously.

'Certainly not, we women have to do our bit for the war, you know, and I, well, I just love the freedom of it all. The canals are wonderful.'

Harry looked over to the canal; it was bustling with activity.

'I don't suppose you have half an hour for a sandwich, do you?' Harry said, holding out the paper bag with his Marmite sandwich in.

'I can do better than that, I can make you a cup of tea to go with it,' she told him and started to stride off towards the towpath.

As the two walked over to the canal, thoughts were swirling in both their heads. Maggie was hoping that Gloria had left the little cabin in a reasonable state before cycling off to get a new spanner, and she also prayed that Elizabeth wouldn't rush back from the telephone box so she could have this moment to herself. Harry was almost skipping with excitement.

'But it's huge,' his astonished voice said when they approached the long, sleek lines of the *Nancy May*. 'Surely you don't drive that thing.'

'Yep, with Gloria and Elizabeth and we've got the one behind as well; it's called a butty,' she said with her head held high, pointing to *Florence*.

Harry was completely lost for words and looked at Maggie with a new respect. He walked along the towpath pacing out the length of the boat with his long legs and then peeped under the tarpaulin to look at the cargo of coal.

'And I suppose you loaded this as well, did you, Miss Carpenter?'

She giggled. 'Yes, I did – well with the men at the wharf and the other two – and it's Maggie.'

She led the way into the cabin and breathed a sigh of relief, everything had been neatly packed away during the automatic morning tidy-up. This time, as she watched Harry's face, she knew she was impressing him, especially once she showed him how the little bunks worked, explained the cooking facilities and pulled down the little table to expose the packed shelves behind.

'I can't believe you live in this? With . . . Gloria . . . is it?'

'Yes,' she replied, 'and Elizabeth sleeps in the butty and look, Reverend . . . um . . .'

'Harry, please' he said, delightedly shifting his weight on the little bunk and settling back to lean against the side of the boat. 'Oh Maggie, it's wonderful. I can see why you love it. It's a world away from the war, isn't it? I think I'll move in!'

They both immediately blushed at the implications of his words, and she quickly interrupted. 'So, what are you doing here? In the middle of Watford?'

He paused for a moment but knew he would have to talk to Jim before he revealed anything to the family.

'I had to follow up on something for my uncle. One of his parishioner's family lives down here and wasn't replying to any letters.' He suppressed a grin as he realised he'd been the victim of his uncle's plotting.

'And did you find them?'

'Yes, I did, and I think the Didsbury family will be very grateful.' He didn't dare look at Maggie in case he gave away which family he was referring to.

'Good, now let's have that tea, the kettle's boiled.'

The next hour passed far too quickly for the young couple. In the privacy of the cabin, the outside world with its sensible reasonings that such a relationship could never work was shut out as firmly as the shouts and noises from the canal around them. Maggie was surprised at how easily she chatted to this man and how, far too easily, she forgot that he was wearing a dog collar.

She told him about Gloria and Elizabeth, confessing that she still didn't feel she knew either of them very well and then regaled him with stories of the cill episode, the tunnel and the Spencers, leaving out the signs of violence they'd heard.

He told her about his uncle's health and how he was due back to his detachment in another week.

'So where were you before Didsbury?' Maggie asked.

'Oh, you know, here and there. I was at Dunkirk though.' His face darkened and Maggie couldn't help it, she didn't know if it was the fact that they were sitting in such close proximity or whether this man made her feel as if she'd known him all her life, but she leaned across and put her hand on his.

Harry jerked back, banging his head on the wall and she immediately dropped her arm feeling ridiculous.

'No, I'm sorry, that was a lovely gesture,' Harry said, mentally kicking himself. 'And you're right, it was tough but not as tough for me as it was for so many of the other blighters.'

Maggie immediately started to babble. 'So, will you be able to leave your uncle? Is he going to be able to cope? Where will you go?'

'So many questions and unfortunately, Maggie, I don't have any answers for you.'

Aware something had changed between them, there was a brief silence broken by the welcome sound of Gloria jumping on board.

'I'm back. I finally got the right sized one and I passed Elizabeth on the towpath so we can get going as soon as I've sorted the Lister out,' she called from above but then stopped in the doorway in surprise.

'Oh, hello, I didn't realise we had a visitor.'

Harry jumped to his feet and then yelped as he bumped his head again.

Gloria laughed. 'Yep, you learn that one pretty quick. So, who are you?'

Harry ducked to shake hands, rubbing his head with his other hand and smiling. 'I'm Harry Moore, well, I think I am if the concussion hasn't confused me. I know Maggie's family from Didsbury.'

'And just happened to be passing, did you?' Gloria asked suspiciously.

'No, he's been on parish business in Watford and, unbelievably, we bumped into each other just over in the park,' Maggie said quickly.

'Uh-huh. Well, nice to meet you, Rev. I'm Gloria. We have to get off now, got deadlines to meet you know. I just need to tweak the engine now I've got this ...' and she triumphantly held up her new spanner.

'Yes, of course,' Harry said, in awe of these women who knew their way around an engine. He awkwardly made his way past her to get to the steps. 'And I've got a train to catch. Nice to meet you, Gloria and er ... Maggie ... it was lovely to see you again.'

'I'm ... um ... well, I'm going home when we've delivered this lot,' Maggie blurted out, immediately embarrassed at the hopefulness in her voice.

'Oh, well maybe I'll see you before I go back to duty then,' Harry said, his spirits lifting.

Maggie waved a feeble goodbye and then as she felt the boat lighten as he jumped off, she fell back on the bunk.

Gloria didn't speak, she just folded her arms and waited, one eyebrow raised, but Maggie simply got to her feet and moved across the cabin to give all her concentration to tidying the cups.

Chapter 15

That night, as Gloria and Maggie were getting ready for bed, taking it in turns as usual in the limited space to wash and do their teeth, Gloria asked the question that Maggie had been dreading all day.

'So, who's the handsome vicar then?'

'Oh, he's not a vicar, well, I don't think he is, I'm not quite sure how it all works. He's a padre with the army, so he's a soldier. He does everything they do except kill people, I think; you know, listening to their problems, doing services, that sort of thing.'

'Oh right . . .' the sceptical voice replied, 'and how exactly do you know him.'

Maggie tried to explain about her family's connection with his uncle's church. It was all beginning to get a little complicated without revealing all her family's history, but Gloria's sharp intellect was gradually piecing together the bits of conversation the girls had had over the past few weeks.

'Look, Maggie, I've got more skeletons in my family's cupboard than you can imagine,' she said, immediately thinking about Molly, her sister, who had joined the police force and was serving in an internment camp in the Isle of Man. There were certainly secrets there, she acknowledged.

It took until the light was turned off and the girls were in bed for Maggie to finally tell Gloria how her grandparents had taken the three siblings in once her father had abandoned them.

The pain in her voice was obvious, even in the dark, and at the end of her tale, Gloria hoped that, at last, the barriers were coming down between them.

In response, she started to tell Maggie about Will.

'I've never felt like this before, Mags, oh, when he kissed me, I thought I was going to melt.'

Maggie tensed under the blanket. She remembered that feeling so well. Her body immediately started to tingle but she felt fear for her young friend.

'Just you be careful, Gloria. He's totally different to you, his background is nothing like yours. I'd hate to think he would just use you for, well, you know and then drop you.' Her words came out more bitter than she had intended and as soon as she'd spoken, she could feel the wave of animosity emanate from the other bunk.

'Oh, so I'm not good enough for him, eh? You know what, Maggie Carpenter, you're nothing but a snob.'

And Gloria turned over noisily in disgust.

Maggie spent the next few hours worrying that she had hurt Gloria but aware that the young girl had no idea about the real world and finally, she recalled every caress, every false word of affection spoken by Roger Anderson. It was almost daybreak before she remembered instead the warmth of Harry Moore's hand under hers and she cringed with regret at what could have been. Finally, a vision of her grandmother's disappointed face made her sob, and she stuffed the blanket into her mouth to stop Gloria hearing.

* * *

Gloria was ostentatiously humming to herself on the tiller, ignoring Maggie, who was standing next to her looking at the map. They'd hardly spoken for days and Maggie was struggling, thinking how she could improve matters. She wanted to explain her reasonings about Will but couldn't without revealing her own experiences. They were both oblivious to the rain that was pounding down on their heads as they approached Bull's Bridge. Elizabeth was in *Florence* behind, wrapped up in her own world, as usual. Suddenly, Gloria stopped mid-hum and peered suspiciously into the dark edges of the bridge ahead.

'I'm pulling in,' she said curtly and signalled to Elizabeth to follow while telling Maggie to jump off in readiness for the rope.

As soon as the boat was near enough, she cut the engine and threw the stern rope to a bemused Maggie before leaping onto the towpath to run towards the bridge. At that moment, the girls heard a splash and a shout from Gloria demanding another rope – and quickly.

Elizabeth, furious that she'd nearly run into the back of the *Nancy May* thanks to the abruptness of Gloria's instructions, steadied the boat as best she could, then ran forward to hold the *Nancy May* line while Maggie grabbed the second rope and ran to join Gloria under the bridge. In the water was a young man, flailing his arms in panic.

'Put your feet down, you idiot,' Gloria called to him and with that the splashing stopped and the man swayed and then stood up, looking rather foolish in the middle of the canal.

'What the hell are you doing?' she shouted to him, but he was frantically looking towards the other bank to see if he could escape that way.

'Don't even think about it,' Maggie warned. She noticed the filthy army uniform and the young man's distraught expression. 'We can help you. Here, take this.'

She threw over the rope and he automatically reached out to catch it.

Gloria was about to let loose with a torrent of accusations, but Maggie shook her head and moved in front of her.

'Here, lad, give me your hand and I'll help you out.'

A bedraggled figure emerged from the canal, shivering. He was a young man in his early twenties his face was haggard and his eyes were darting from one direction to the other.

As soon as he got his feet onto the towpath, he tried to run but his legs gave way under him, and he fell to the floor.

Maggie took one look at the threadbare trousers and the worn-through boots and said quietly to Gloria, 'Go and get a blanket.'

By now, Elizabeth had tied the boat up and she came running towards them. She pushed Maggie out of the way and said, 'Let me see.'

There was a moment's irritation at Elizabeth's peremptory tone before Maggie gave in and stepped back.

Elizabeth moved forward to kneel down and gently examine the prone body, turning the young man's head from side to side.

'Hmm, no injuries. I think he's just on the point of starvation. Let's get him on the boat.'

Gloria glanced at her watch; they were already behind and did not have time for this.

'Can't we just leave him and tell the next lockkeeper?'

A weak but well-spoken voice haltingly said, 'Please . . . no . . . please.'

The girls exchanged glances. Questions could come later but right now all this young man needed was some warm food and dry clothes. They shepherded him towards the *Nancy May* and gently pushed him down the steps to the cabin. Elizabeth immediately took charge, put the kettle on and then wrapped him in a blanket; the other two held back on the towpath to whisper to each other.

'What are we going to do?' Gloria asked, turning hopefully to Maggie, ignoring their squabble the night before.

Maggie was already pacing up and down, her brow compressed in concentration.

'He's a deserter, I'm sure of that,' she said at last.

'Hmm,' agreed Gloria but then: 'Do they still shoot deserters?' Her eyes widened.

'No, thank goodness, but they do court-martial them. He's in deep trouble, that's for sure.'

'We can't get any more behind; this trip's already been a catalogue of disasters.'

At this point, Elizabeth came out to join them and overhearing their conversation put in: 'There are more deserters than they're telling us. I know someone, he . . . well, he operates an organisation . . . well, that's all you need to know, but he might be able to help.'

Maggie looked up with surprise. They knew so little about each other. She and Gloria had speculated about Elizabeth's high-class social life and how she moved in influential circles and here she was, admitting she knew people in an underground organisation that could help a deserter. Maggie blew out her cheeks; she thought her life had taken her down unexpected paths but she was beginning to suspect that Elizabeth's had taken even more twists and turns.

Elizabeth had already moved to the top step to the cabin, saying, 'Let's see what he has to say, and we'll take it from there.'

Maggie glanced at her watch; they were well behind schedule. 'We need to get moving,' she shouted to Elizabeth, but it was too late, she was already inside.

'Now, what can you tell us?' the older girl was barking at the terrified young man. 'We need information, and we need it now.'

The solider was clutching an enamel mug of tea and had a half-eaten biscuit in his grubby hand. He rammed the rest of it into his mouth, fearing it might be his last bit of food before he was handed over to the authorities. His face was flushed and Elizabeth leaned over to put her hand on his forehead; it was burning. She stepped back thoughtfully but he was looking at Maggie for sympathy, feeling she, at least, might be on his side, then to Gloria, and finally to the daunting figure of Elizabeth standing with her arms folded in front of him. He clutched the plaid blanket around him with fingers that were filthy, but, Maggie noticed, his nails were neat and tapered and his hair may have been matted but it was thick and curly.

The man was struggling to swallow his biscuit and slowly, a tear started to fall, leaving a track down his dirty face, and his shoulders sagged; this was likely to be the end of the road for him.

Maggie turned to the other two and whispered, 'Let's just leave him here for a bit to gather his thoughts. We're way behind schedule and we need to get to be at Alperton by tonight, ready to offload tomorrow morning. We can decide what to do with him later.' Then she turned back towards the sunken figure on the bed. 'Perhaps you could at least tell us your name?'

At that, the young man quietly muttered, as if the information was being tortured out of him, 'It's Leonard, well Lenny really.'

His eyes looked from left to right to see whether there was any way of escaping once the girls had gone back up on deck but with the only exit up the steps past them, he sank back.

A quick whispered discussion on the stern ensued, which initially got the girls nowhere. Gloria was adamant they should hand him in immediately, Maggie was aware they were already late and suggested it wouldn't harm to let him sleep a little while they got on their way. But it was Elizabeth's solution that surprised them.

'He's ill,' she said, her tone softer than earlier. 'I think we need to let him sleep and see how he is when he wakes up. After all, we're in the middle of nowhere and at least if we decide to hand him over when we get to Alperton then we'll be back on target with our delivery and, to be honest, trying to get the authorities out here would take hours. I mean, we're nowhere near a phone box.'

The logic was indisputable and eventually Gloria went to drive the butty while Maggie took the tiller on the *Nancy May*. Elizabeth went back below to watch their charge and, perching on the end of the bed, pretended to fill in delivery forms. After waiting anxiously for a few minutes, the young man's eyelids started to droop, and he fell asleep.

Gradually, Elizabeth's face softened as she took in the unlined skin and the emaciated body. He looked so young and, as a mother, it took all her efforts not to reach over and smooth his tousled hair. The impulse made her think of her own boys and home, which somehow seemed more real with the arrival of this young man. Elizabeth put her pencil down to assess her own situation, which was only marginally less precarious than that of their new passenger. It had all seemed so exciting; to rebel against the expectation of duty and societal norms with that job in the bar where she found an intoxicating liberty and, like a child forbidden to climb a high wall, she found herself craving more risks. It was as if the bored housewife with her diary packed with good works and country club functions had opened the cover of a banned book and she'd been loving every minute of it.

By the time Elizabeth's lust for adventure had lured her into gambling, it was too late; the demands for repayment had turned into threats and now she was at the mercy of debt collectors and a shadowy boss. That man's henchmen, some of whom she suspected were deserters like Lenny with nothing to lose, made it very clear that they had no respect for her status at the country club or the fact that her husband was a captain in the Royal Navy. Christopher's protective arm around her now seemed a long way away and it occurred to her that this new freedom came at a price. The advertisement in *The Lady* had come just at the right time.

'Oh darn it,' she muttered. 'I've been behaving like someone of Gloria's age, not a woman in her late twenties.'

It had all happened so quickly; her 'fall into disrepute' as she called it. The annoying thing was, though, there was a part of her that really needed that excitement in her life. She shook her head; Christopher had no idea of this side of his wife's character but the one thing she was sure of was he wouldn't like it.

Now, the three of them had somehow found themselves in charge of a fugitive and her first thought that she knew someone who could help a deserter hide out was soon replaced by a fear that she would just be leading one more lamb to the slaughter.

* * *

Once the girls had moored up just outside Alperton, they gathered on the towpath.

'He's still asleep,' Elizabeth told the other two. 'He's exhausted. God knows how long he's been on the run.'

'We have to hand him over to the authorities,' Gloria said. For her, the rules and regulations were not subjects for debate and the strict principles of right and wrong were non-negotiable, especially when it came to harbouring a deserter.

Maggie nodded. 'We'll lose our jobs and . . . we could be imprisoned.'

The simple truth of her statement made them all pull up sharply. Elizabeth, in particular, thought how little she needed this complication in her life but then, remembering how young he was, she said, 'I think we need to hear his story first.'

'OK, he has one chance,' Gloria stated without hesitation, 'and then I'm off to the police station.'

* * *

The three of them squashed into the *Nancy May* that night, limbs crossing and shoulders bumping, to interrogate Lenny. The young soldier still looked very flushed and there were beads of sweat on his brow. Every time he spoke, the words came out in a rush and even though he had eaten some food, he'd immediately vomited it up into a bucket. He pulled himself to sitting, but it was an effort. Elizabeth decided he looked less like a deserter and more like a scolded youth and a rather poorly one at that.

'So . . . ?' Gloria began uncompromisingly.

Lenny weakly assessed his judge and jury and blew out a sigh. It was either these three or the police, he thought.

'I was at Dunkirk,' he began.

'So were many others,' Maggie said, thinking of Harry, 'but what happened to make you desert?'

'It was my pet mouse. It died.'

There was silence for a moment then Gloria burst out laughing. 'Your . . . what?'

'My mouse, Whiskers. I'd found him in France in a barn where we bivouacked. He'd been through everything with me. I'd managed to keep him alive here,' he said, patting his breast pocket. 'I fed him scraps and somehow he survived, but then, at Dunkirk . . . well, his little body didn't feel warm anymore and when I took him out, he was . . . stiff . . . and cold and . . . dead.'

Gloria suppressed a giggle, but the other two looked more sympathetically at the young man opposite, especially Elizabeth, who had created a large plot in her garden for the family's dogs and cats.

Maggie was surprised to see tears welling up in Elizabeth's eyes.

'I'm not sure the authorities are going to see . . . Whiskers did you say 'is name was . . . as being a justifiable reason to desert,' Gloria said dismissively, and Elizabeth and Maggie had to agree.

'You don't understand' Lenny said plaintively. 'My mum and dad – they were killed in the blitz in Manchester, the whole house blown up and my brother, Bill, well, he went missing at Tobruk. Whiskers was the only friend I had because everyone else I served with was blown to smithereens in an air attack on that French beach. I was the only one left from our company.'

He started to cry, and Elizabeth automatically folded his wasted frame into her arms, noting how hot and sweaty his body was.

'Whiskers was such a brave little thing,' he said into her shoulder, 'never squeaked when the enemy was near, never panicked in the gunfire. I only knew how frightened he was when I found the little pellets he'd passed at the bottom of my pocket. Poor Whiskers . . .'

None of the girls knew what to say.

* * *

Later that night, Lenny had been put to bed in the butty boat and the three girls bunked up together in *Nancy May*. They were all half lying, half sitting in the cramped space but none of them felt like sleeping. The enormity of their young charge's plight was beginning to sink in.

Gloria was still determined he should be handed over to the authorities while Elizabeth's maternal instinct made her more compassionate. Maggie had no idea what to do.

'You know what they do with deserters,' Elizabeth said to the pitch-dark cabin. 'They lock them up and throw away the key. No one's got any sympathy for them. He'll get a long prison sentence and then when he does get out, everyone will shun him.'

'What if we get him to give himself up?' Maggie put in.

They all thought about this option but, remembering the boy's desperate yet determined face, they doubted he would comply with this suggestion.

'I think he'd rather die,' Elizabeth said, thinking of his plunge into the canal.

'Well, he's not very bright, is he?' Gloria said dismissively. 'I mean, to think you could end it all by jumping in the cut? Bleedin' idiot.'

'You know, one day, you might have cause to temper your sharp tongue,' Elizabeth told her. 'Life's not as black and white as you think; people make mistakes you know.'

Maggie looked closely at the tall figure crouched at the end of the cross seat and wondered what was lurking in Elizabeth's past; certainly, she had her own errors of judgement to deal with and, for a brief moment, she longed to confide in someone older and perhaps wiser, but Elizabeth's next comment put paid to that idea.

'Anyway, I'm certainly not sleeping here with you two for more than one night, this is horribly uncomfortable. I want my butty back, so we need to make a decision and soon.'

She turned towards the wall on the side of the boat and hunched down with a grunt. The discussion was at an end.

Chapter 16

When Harry arrived back in Manchester, he almost skipped along the road towards Emmanuel Church, unable to to believe his luck that he had bumped into Maggie Carpenter and he whistled as he made his way along the pavement, but when he got to the vicarage, there was a small crowd of people outside and an ambulance. As he approached, Mrs Harper ran up to him.

'Oh, Padre, I'm so glad you're back . . . a terrible thing, your uncle's being taken to hospital. Mrs Hennesseyfound him writhing on the bedroom floor. We think he's had another heart attack.'

Harry's face paled and he ran towards the house.

The ambulance men were just bringing the stretcher out carrying his uncle. His eyes had been closed but he opened them when he heard his nephew's voice.

'Ah, you're here, that's good,' he said, and he reached out a weak hand to clasp Harry's. 'How did you get on? Did you get anywhere with them?'

Harry tutted. 'There's no need for you to worry about that now, Uncle, just you get yourself better.' But then, seeing his uncle's disappointed face, added, 'I've got letter from her for Jim and I think it might help, now don't you worry.'

As the ambulance men went past him, he called out, 'And don't worry about the parish, I'll sort everything,' then muttering to himself, added: 'Although, God knows how.'

Mrs Hennessey tapped him from behind and handed him a cup of tea with a biscuit in the saucer.

'You're going to be needing this, Padre.'

An hour later, Harry had to agree with her. The red leather-bound diary in front of him was packed with lists of the tasks that needed doing each day. The office floor was covered in a mass of tumbled files and the shelves above packed with books, documents and boxes. He could hardly see the door. Sorting through this lot to even get to today's jobs was going to take some time.

Searching around, he found some notepaper and unearthed a pen from the drawer and started to write.

Dear Sir,

I regret to inform you that my uncle, the vicar of Emmanuel Church in Didsbury, has been taken ill again and that leaves the parish without a pastor. I realise I am due back on duty next week, but I wondered whether there might be any leeway so that I may stay and cover his work for a while. I have no idea how long he will be incapacitated but I am going to talk to the diocese in the hope they will be able to provide some cover quickly to leave me free to return to my duties.

I realise this is an unusual case, but I know the detachment is being well looked after by Padre Potter and I am hoping my compassionate leave can be extended. This parish is huge, and my uncle's flock need the guidance and practical help of the Church at this difficult time, so I am hoping you will be able to accommodate my request.

Yours truly,

Revd Harry Moore

He sat back and, as always, felt conflicted. The anxiety of not being with his men was enormous and yet, the needs of the parish right in front of his eyes were overwhelming. Besides which, there was a new pressure – that of wanting to help the Carpenter family, and especially Maggie. His training had always led him not to question decisions made at a higher level, so he reached over and picked up the first document on the top of the biggest pile in front of him to start work until someone told him to do something different.

* * *

Lenny didn't dare emerge from the cabin on *Florence* in case anyone saw him and, in any case, when he stood up his legs wobbled, forcing him to sit down again quickly. He had been called up as soon as he turned eighteen and in the three years since, he had been thrown from front line to front line, somehow dodging the bullets and surviving the onslaught of bombs, grenades and mines. His face showed signs of unrelenting worry and the once-innocent expression had been transformed into a permanent frown. After escaping Dunkirk on a small fishing boat, he'd arrived at Dover to be taken in an army truck to Birmingham for reassignment to duty, but there he'd spotted a canal boat and had made an instant decision to flee. Hiding under the tarpaulin, he had no idea whether the boat was going north or south, but the gentle lapping of the water was a balm to his soul, and he found the tremors he had been experiencing since Dunkirk begin to subside, but then he was discovered and had to jump ashore to run along the towpath to escape his older, puffing pursuers. The hopelessness of his plight had finally engulfed him near Cassiobury and the dirty water seemed like a shroud he could entomb himself in.

'Are you up?' he heard Maggie's whisper from the deck.

In panic, Lenny jumped up and locked the door.

'I'm not coming out,' he said, putting his mouth to the little wooden door.

'Don't be ridiculous, you can't stay in there . . . and we need to get on, we're due to unload,' Maggie told him, sounding cross.

The dark of the cabin seemed like a good place to hide, Lenny decided, so he sat back firmly on the bunk.

'He won't come out,' Maggie told the other two, pushing her hair back in frustration.

Gloria huffed and marched back towards *Florence*, her arms folded across her chest, but returned five minutes later with a furious expression at his refusal to negotiate.

'We'll just have to get the police; we can't be late or we'll be in trouble.'

Maggie was about to offer to go to the telephone box when Lenny's head emerged slowly, his knuckles gripping the top of the hatch. They all automatically checked no one had seen him and then followed him back down into the cabin.

'We're going to have to get the police, you know that,' Maggie said.

He grabbed her arm and with a wild-eyed look said, 'No, please, I'm begging you. They'll lock me up.'

'Well, what do you suggest we do, then?' She was completely torn. She knew the consequences of desertion, but he looked so like her brother, Billy.

'The police, that's the only option,' Gloria repeated.

Elizabeth took in Lenny's flushed face and the way his hair was sticking to his head with sweat. 'I'm not sure he's well enough. What if we could hide him for a bit and get this load off at Alperton, then we can make a decision.'

Lenny reached out his clammy hand to grab hers and she found her eyes moistening thinking of her own two sons. She couldn't help it, the face in front of her had been superimposed with her younger son's expression when he'd pleaded a cold to

escape the first day back at school and she smiled sympathetically at him.

'We have to all be agreed about this,' she said to the other
two and raised her eyebrows questioningly.

Maggie nodded but waited until Gloria finally gave in. 'All
right, all right, but for God's sake, stay out of sight, especially
when we're unloading at Alperton.'

'After we've unloaded,,' Elizabeth said, 'I'm going to see if I
can get some sulphonamides for him. I'm worried that he might
be getting pneumonia.'

Her comment drew blank expressions all round, but
Elizabeth was too busy wondering whether this treatment for
pneumonia was actually available and how much it would
cost. It occurred to her that her 'associate' in the gaberdine
mackintosh would probably be able to get hold of a supply but
revealing they were harbouring a criminal would only open
her up to more blackmail.

She huffed in frustration. This criminal underworld was a
minefield.

* * *

The wharf at Alperton was busy and the girls nervously uncov-
ered the load and started to shovel at twice their normal speed,
hoping that none of their helpers were peering in through the
windows of *Florence*.

'Blimey, you girls are fast,' one old-timer said. 'I don't think
I've seen men unload this quickly. You'll be doing us all out of
a job at this rate.'

Normally, such praise would have delighted the girls but,
desperate to get out of the wharf, they simply gave weak smiles
and carried on shovelling.

It was an even dirtier job than loading and seemed to take forever to get the cavernous, long holds on both boats clear of the filthy cargo, by which time the girls were as black as the coal that was piled up behind them. Previously, Maggie would have felt proud of her muscles that rippled in the pale April sunlight, marvelling at how fit she had become since her sedentary life in a classroom, but today she had no time for anything except getting the hell out of there.

While Elizabeth was getting their delivery note signed and receiving their wages, Maggie spotted a telephone box just along the wharf. The memory of a certain padre's story of Dunkirk made her wonder whether she could possibly ask for help and before she could think of a myriad of reasons why she shouldn't make that call, she found herself running to dial a number she could unfathomably remember off-pat.

*   *   *

The telephone at the vicarage was constantly ringing so Harry took no notice until he heard Mrs Hennessey calling him.

'There's a young woman on the telephone,' she said, holding the receiver out towards him. She still treated the modern black Bakelite machine as if it were a poisonous snake.

Harry sighed; he had three visits to make that morning and a funeral in the afternoon but when he heard the voice at the other end, he cheered up enormously.

'Maggie,' he said in delighted surprise. 'How lovely to hear from you. Are you all right?' and then, 'Slow down, slow down and tell me again.'

As Maggie's garbled story continued in the background, Harry bit his lip. He was a military man who had been taught to obey the rules, but he was also a priest and the story she was telling him would be a test for any conscience.

Finally, he got a word in.

'OK, calm down. I think you have no alternative but to tell the authorities; it could put you in a really difficult situation, but I do know they are being a little more understanding than they were before with this kind of thing. I did hear there's some work being done in America on the long-term effects of combat but . . .'

He listened for a moment and then burst out laughing. 'His what? His mouse? You have to be kidding.'

He heard the defensive tone down the line and had to suppress a grin to pay attention to the rest of her tale of this young man's experiences at Dunkirk.

Immediately, the noises of the gunfire, the lap of the waves and the screams of men came back to him and he again felt that familiar anger.

'I hate this war, Maggie, it's destroying people on all fronts but . . . let me think if there's anything I can do to help.'

Harry heard the emotion in her voice at her dilemma and wanted to get on the first train out of Manchester down to the Grand Union Canal.

'OK, well, you're right, you can't turf him out if he's that ill. I'll talk to a few people, see what I can find out about what's happening to deserters to see what alternatives there are.'

He then blurted out: 'You know, I . . . umm . . . think you're doing an amazing job; I couldn't believe the hardships of the life you're living and I think . . . well, I think you're incredible.' Harry was taken aback at the words that came out of his mouth. He hadn't meant to say that much.

The pips started to beep and Maggie said hurriedly: 'I just needed to talk to someone I trust. Oh, I've no more money . . . I'll let you know what hap—'

And then the line went dead.

Chapter 17

Maggie went back to find that the other two had moved the boats along the wharf, away from prying eyes. Wandering along the towpath to find them, she thought how every word that Roger had uttered had been about Roger and she had drunk in every single one like a parched man in a desert. He had seemed so clever and so in control of everything and she had been just a child at the feet of a master.

It had been so unexpected to find someone who actually wanted to hear what she had to say that she scuffed the grass beneath her feet in frustration. She'd heard the admiration in Harry's voice, but it was like a dream where she was trying to call out, but no sound emerged from her throat. He would never be interested in her, not once he knew.

Maggie picked up a pebble and threw it furiously into the canal, sending a squawking duck scurrying to the reeds.

Ahead of her, she heard loud voices, arguing.

'You've nicked it, haven't you? Admit it.'

'No, I haven't,' Elizabeth retorted. 'It's all there.'

'No, it isn't,' Gloria said and was about to say more when she spotted Maggie.

'She's stolen our money,' she yelled to her.

Maggie quickened her pace and told them both to calm down.

'We don't need attention drawing to us, you idiots, now shut up. Whatever discussion we need to have can be done inside the boat, not here on the towpath.'

She ushered them into the cabin and shut the door behind them.

'Now, what's going on?'

This unleashed a tangle of arguments and Maggie couldn't make sense of any of them. Both girls were purple with indignation and fury.

'One at a time,' Maggie said as calmly as she could, and turned to Gloria.

'The pay we've just got, you know, that Elizabeth picked up this morning? Well, she should have put it all in the pot as usual but it isn't all there,' she said, pointing to the jar on the shelf. 'I was about to head off to the shops with our ration books. I know she said she needed some of that sul . . . sulf . . . medicine for Lenny but when she got back, I counted it and we're missing more than just that.'

'No, no we're not,' Elizabeth protested. Her visit to the chemist had unleashed a catalogue of lies about a sick child and the pharmacist had asked too many questions, which she had only been able to answer by pretending to have nursing training. Her limited knowledge and haughty voice had finally convinced the chemist that she knew what she was talking about. However, faced with this challenge from Gloria, she was less convincing. 'Well, if we are, you must have dropped some when I gave it you just before at the wharf; it could easily have dropped out of your pocket. I mean look, there's a hole in it.'

She reached forward to examine Gloria's trousers and with a flourish, put her finger through the bottom of one of her pockets, waggling it in the air.

Momentarily, Gloria shut her mouth that had just opened to argue but then her face brightened.

'Good try, but no, I held the money in my hand until we got back here.'

Maggie moved to sit down on the bunk. She felt like the adult amidst two squabbling children.

'OK, enough's enough. Elizabeth, we need to know what's going on. We know money's been disappearing from the pot and we're all in this together so come on, tell us what's wrong.'

For the first time, the three girls sat together like a family – in the throes of a bitter argument, yes, but a family nevertheless.

'Look, we undress in front of each other,' Maggie said in as reasonable voice as she could muster, 'we even use the bucket in front of each other. Surely, it's time for us to be honest.'

As soon as she said this, she regretted her impulsive words. The last thing she wanted to do was own up to her besmirched past but from Elizabeth there came a sudden sob.

'I'm in such a mess, I'm in debt . . . and I think I'm being blackmailed,' she said in a whisper.

Gloria was stunned. How could this posh woman owe money?

'I got addicted to gambling,' Elizabeth was saying. The other two had to lean forward, she was speaking so quietly.

'How?' Maggie said simply.

Slowly, Elizabeth explained about the boredom of being in a big house on her own, her husband, Christopher, and boys both away and how she had been desperate for some excitement.

The ensuing tale took Gloria's breath away. She had completely been taken in by the pearls around Elizabeth's throat and the clipped tones that reminded her of a newsreader off the BBC. As Elizabeth explained how she had taken a job in a pub on the other side of town to her, the ability to stand in as a barmaid at The Boat and the rushed trips down the towpath began to make sense, but it was the description of the man in the raincoat and his threats that made the two girls gasp.

There was no doubt of Gloria's condemnation, but Maggie was thinking how differently she would have reacted to Elizabeth's story before the fiasco with Roger and she wondered whether the whole experience might actually make her a less judgemental human being.

At the end of her tale, Elizabeth looked up with a challenging air.

'So, not the person you thought I was, I suppose? Just a common thief with an addiction to, well, the more unsavoury side of life. I am so sorry to have let you down but, honestly, girls, I intend to pay you back every penny, I promise.'

Gloria was unequivocal in her reply.

'Yes, you will and now. We can't manage on the money we're making so you're going to have to sell something to pay all this off. What about those pearls?' She'd made so many jokes about the fact that Elizabeth wore pearls under her sou'wester.

There was a bitter laugh. 'They're just for show. Paste, my dear. I flogged the real ones a year ago.' She fingered her necklace sadly and said wistfully to Maggie, 'You can hardly tell, can you?'

Maggie stared blankly; she had never owned a set of pearls and her grandmother had not been the sort to wear them anyway, preferring to spend what money she had on a bike or a doll for her grandchildren.

'Well, you're going to have to do something, I'm not living on cabbage and Marmite just 'cos you think horse number three is going to come in first,' Gloria said. 'We need supplies and we haven't got enough money to pay for them.'

Maggie went to the back of the cupboard where she stored her clothes and brought out a small purse. Elizabeth was shocked to find her first thought was that she wished she'd known earlier that it was there.

Doling out two half-crowns, she told Gloria to go and get the tea and bread they needed before the little shop along the canal closed. The younger girl cast a withering look at Elizabeth and stomped up the steps to stalk along the towpath before slowing down to wonder at her own temerity to challenge this posh housewife. So much younger, she had been in awe of Elizabeth and was unable to understand how someone who seemed to have so much could risk everything for gambling. She thought that was something only poor people did. It reminded her of how her uncle Albert had been forced to hand over his weekly pay packet from the docks to her aunt Mildred to stop him betting on the greyhounds. At the time, she hadn't thought deeply about it, but now she remembered the family had been evicted by their landlord and had to move into the tiny terrace in Limehouse with Gloria and her family. There had been rows and even fights between her aunt and uncle prompting Gloria and her sister, Molly to hide in the understairs cupboard to avoid the blows. However, it was a revelation that rich people had their problems too. It made her feel strangely superior, and she raised her head and started to whistle.

Back in the cabin, Elizabeth, her cheeks smeared, was looking at Maggie. 'I'm sorry, I really am, I feel so ashamed, but I don't know, Maggie, I just don't seem to be able to help it. I mean, have you ever done something that you know you shouldn't, but you just can't stop yourself?'

Maggie busied herself putting the purse back behind her jumper in case her face gave her secret away.

'Hmm,' she murmured non-committally and then turned to add with more certainty than she felt: 'But this needs to stop. We need to think how we can help you, Elizabeth.'

Now she had unburdened her soul, the effort seemed to have exhausted her and Elizabeth's whole torso deflated, making her shoulders hunch forward. The despair was evident.

Maggie immediately longed for Harry's kind face and gentle voice and then chided herself; just because he was a good listener, didn't mean he had all the answers. She shook herself. She didn't need a man telling her what to do anymore and anyway, this was one relationship that wasn't going to happen. She already regretted telling him they had a deserter on board, not only because she couldn't bear the thought that he might think badly of her but also because she knew it had put him in a difficult position.

'All right,' she said, taking matters into her own hands. 'How do you actually gamble? I mean, do you buy a newspaper, or do you telephone that dreadful man?'

Elizabeth explained how she found it hard to pass a telephone box and that somehow, the man at the other end always had a top tip that he'd got from a trainer, he knew all the gossip of the track, she said almost with pride, and really did know the best horses.

Maggie exploded. 'You have to be kidding, Elizabeth! He's playing you for a fool. Of course he's got a top tip for you, he wants you to lose just enough so he can blackmail you!'

Elizabeth looked genuinely astonished. It had never occurred to her that he wanted her to lose and, all of a sudden, she felt a complete idiot.

'Right, you are not going in one more phone box. We are going to watch you like hawks. I will lend you the money to pay this man off and you are never, never to contact him again after that, do you hear me?'

* * *

The argument had delayed the girls and now they were in danger of not reaching Maida Vale tunnel entrance before nightfall. Gloria insisted on going back to steer *Florence* with their stowaway so that Maggie could keep an eye on Elizabeth, but within two minutes, she was racing back along the towpath.

'He's gone,' she said, 'Lenny, he's just vanished.'

The three of them ran back to the butty and Maggie searched under the cushions as if he could be hiding somewhere.

'He's not here,' she said, straightening her back.

'Well, obviously not,' Elizabeth said tartly, sounding more like herself.

Elizabeth and Gloria jumped off the boat and one ran in each direction along the towpath while Maggie followed and then climbed over a gate into the adjoining Kensal Green Cemetery.

She shielded her eyes from the late afternoon sun and peered from side to side.

Gloria came up behind her.

'I can't see him anywhere. I mean, he could have been gone ages. We were so busy arguing with Mrs Fancy Pants we wouldn't have seen him go.'

Elizabeth joined them, puffing at the exertion of racing down the towpath.

'No . . . sign,' she said, 'he could . . . be miles away . . . by now.'

Maggie was staring at the ground beneath them and then bent down to examine it more closely. 'Is that a footprint?'

Elizabeth crouched down next to her. 'Yes, I think it is. And look, there's another one.'

They followed the prints along the boundary of the cemetery until there was a break in the early spring foliage where some of the branches had been broken off.

Gloria was beginning to feel like a character in a detective novel and she narrowed her eyes as she ran her fingers over the severed twigs and clambered under the hedge.

'He went this way,' she said with the certainty of Sherlock Holmes.

'We won't get through here; we're not as small as you. We'll go to the next gate and meet you there,' Elizabeth said.

Picking the young leaves out of her hair on the other side, Gloria looked from left to right. 'I can see more footprints,' she called through. 'I'm going to follow them.'

And with that she disappeared to make her way along the cemetery side of the canal,, looking carefully at the ground for signs of disturbance. She was grateful that there had been rain during the night and that any prints would surely be engraved into the mud. Concentrating on the ditch in front of her, she edged along the boundary until she almost fell into a pair of legs that were splayed out across her path.

'He's here,' she shouted. 'I've found him.'

'Is he conscious?' Elizabeth's voice came over the hedge.

'Oh help, I'm not even sure he's breathing,' Gloria replied, her voice rising in panic.

Elizabeth and Maggie ran along the towpath until they found an opening. After pushing through, they raced towards the kneeling figure of Gloria.

'Stand back,' Elizabeth ordered and immediately started to feel for a pulse in Lenny's neck.

'It's very weak,' she muttered, mainly to herself. 'We need to get him off this cold ground and back on *Florence*.'

The three girls worked together to try to move the prone figure but even though Lenny was emaciated, his weight was still too much for them.

In the distance, they heard an engine and Gloria peered over the hedge towards the canal.

'It's the Spencers,' she called in relief. 'They don't give a damn about the authorities. We can't lift him on our own. They'll help us.'

Elizabeth, remembering the row they'd heard coming from *Buffalo* at Stoke Bruerne, hoped she was right.

Chapter 18

Joe Spencer gently laid the young soldier on the bed in *Florence*. His father's assessment of the filthy uniform had rapidly been followed by an instruction not to touch that 'bloody deserter' but for once, Joe had defied him and had gone to the girls' aid. It was worth the beating he knew would follow just to see Gloria's grateful face.

Elizabeth gently manoeuvred Joe to one side and opened Lenny's collar. She felt his forehead, which was worryingly hot, but his pulse had strengthened slightly which made her heave a sigh of relief. His breathing was very erratic though.

'Thank you so much . . . I'm sorry, I don't know your name,' Gloria was saying to their rescuer.

'Joe,' was the embarrassed reply.

'Well, thank you, Joe. That was really nice of you.'

Joe flushed and he started to back away, but Gloria put out her hand to stop him.

'At least let us get you a cup of tea, by way of a proper thank you.'

Joe shook his head. He knew his furious father would be waiting at the side of *Buffalo* for him.

Elizabeth saw his distress and said quickly, 'Maggie, put some cold cloths on Lenny's forehead, I'll go with Joe.'

This wasn't what Joe had wanted at all and he wasn't sure who he was most scared of – this commanding, well-spoken woman or his father – but ended up following Elizabeth meekly onto the stern and along the path.

'Thank you so much, Mr Spencer, for lending Joe to us,' Elizabeth called to the man waiting on the towpath with his arms folded, puffing fiercely on his pipe.

Completely taken aback, Joe's father found himself telling the posh woman in front of him that it was no trouble at all.

'You see,' Elizabeth went on, putting on her most concerned face and lowering her voice, 'that young man tried to kill himself, and we are putting our trust in you, Mr Spencer, because you must know he's a deserter. We've been waiting to report him as one to the authorities, but you know what these deadlines are like, Mr Spencer, we had to get our load to Alperton and then he fell sick. I mean, we'd have been penalised if we hadn't unloaded in time and to be honest, what could a Christian woman do? He's no older than your lad and I know how you would feel if your Joe was in that state.'

Jake couldn't think of a word to say; his mind was too busy processing the thought that he wouldn't care one jot if it was Joe, but from behind him, he heard his wife's voice.

'That's all right, your ladyship, um . . . Mrs . . . Joe's a good lad and his dad likes him to help where 'e can, don't you, Jake?'

There was a momentary look of understanding between the two women as they pursued the same tactics with this difficult man.

Elizabeth continued: 'I mean, we've learned so much from you, Mr Spencer, and one of those things is that the load comes first. We're so new to this but that's one lesson we have had to come to terms with. Your family are so fast with these deliveries and we're only just finding our feet.'

She leaned forward to whisper conspiratorially, 'To be honest, a deserter was the last thing we needed, and we had no idea what to do so now perhaps you could help us. We'd really appreciate your advice. He's so ill and so young and the story he told us of Dunkirk would make you weep, Mr Spencer, it really would. It's so awful what these young men are facing, don't you think? I mean it could be your Joe in that cabin, what would you want us to do then?'

Jake was thinking that he would hand over his useless son to anyone who asked but then he caught Dolly's eye. There was only one person who could quell Jake Spencer's anger and that was Dolly. She fought for her family like a tigress defending her cubs and all his bullying didn't stand a chance against the ire of the solid frame of a woman standing behind him.

'S'pose so,' he said with reluctance. As far as he was concerned, the boy was useless and the fact that he'd been turned down for conscription because he had flat feet was tantamount to an excuse for cowardice. That soldier on board *Florence* may be a deserter but at least he'd served.

'So what yer goin' to do with 'im?' he asked, jerking his head in the direction of the butty boat.

Sensing a slight conciliation, Elizabeth opened her mouth to speak when Gloria interrupted from behind. 'I don't care what we do with 'im, all I know is we need to be in Limehouse by the weekend. We've got a break in our schedule and I'm not wasting it worrying about some deserter.'

She had her own reasons for wanting to get to London; Will was going to try and get a three-day pass and come down to meet her. Maggie, too, was due a few days off and wanted to get back to Manchester to check on her grandfather and, maybe, she hoped, see Harry. Elizabeth looked from one to the other and finally said, 'OK, well, I'm not going anywhere this weekend, so I'll stay on board and look after him.'

Mrs Spencer stepped off *Buffalo* and said quietly to Elizabeth, 'I'll 'elp you. It sounds like that pneumonia with all that sweating. My da had that. I know what to do so if you want, I'll come on board while we all get to Limehouse. We just got t'get 'im through the crisis, then wiv a bit of luck, 'e'll be right as rain. Then you can decide what yer gonna do with 'im. We'll say nought, you can be sure o' that.' She turned to her husband who gave a reluctant incline of his head in agreement and Dolly turned to have a hushed discussion with him which resulted in Mr Spencer shrugging and starting up the engine while his wife went below. She emerged two minutes later with a small cloth bag. Dolly Spencer paused on the towpath to ask the customary permission to board *Florence* before putting one foot on her deck.

Maggie and Elizabeth heaved a sigh of relief. They really did not want to turn Lenny over to the authorities and it seemed as if the Spencers were going to keep their secret so Gloria cranked the *Nancy May* into life, leaving Maggie to untie *Florence* and Elizabeth and Dolly to go below.

While the little convoy of boats made its way along the Grand Union towards Limehouse, Elizabeth and Dolly Spencer took turns placing cool cloths on Lenny's hot forehead. He tossed and turned, talking gibberish; sometimes about his parents, sometimes about the guns but always with eyes wide with terror. His words came out in gasps and he was struggling to get his breath.

'They always do this,' Dolly told Elizabeth, who was looking increasingly worried. 'It's the fever, yer see. He'll be all right when it dies down.'

Either that or when he dies, Elizabeth thought, noting the difference between the burning cheeks and the cold hands of the young lad. She knew that explaining a dead deserter might cause more problems than a live one and for once, her own worries about being blackmailed went to the back of her mind.

Dolly Spencer stood back, assessing the situation. She had given birth to three children but after Joe, one had died in childbirth and the other had died of scarlet fever. She stroked her swollen belly and sighed. Already in her forties, she had not wanted this baby and was all too aware of the risks she was facing. Her sister's unequivocal warnings about another pregnancy echoed in her ears but refusing a man like Jake was even riskier than bringing a baby into the world on the cut.

'When are you due?' Elizabeth asked, wishing Gloria was there to guide her in the fine line between showing interest and being nosy with these canal people.

'About ten weeks,' Dolly answered in a bland tone. All her children had been born on the *Buffalo*. This time she'd had more pain than usual, and she was very anxious. Elizabeth leaned over and covered the woman's gnarled hand with hers. The gesture brought tears to Dolly's eyes but, taking a big breath in, she looked away to take in her surroundings and nodded her approval.

'You've done a good job 'ere. Made it all 'omely like.'

Her warmth and matronly air made Elizabeth relax and she realised how long it had been since she had spoken to her own mother. The thought made her wince at the shame her parents would experience if they knew what their daughter had been up to.

Dolly noticed it all and for the first time, it occurred to her that these newcomers to the cut were actually just young girls. The realisation surprised her; she had thought of them as something from another world.

Lenny groaned and his head flopped to one side.

'This is it,' Dolly said, 'this could be the crisis. Take that pillow away, it'll 'elp him breathe.'

'Oh my God,' Elizabeth suddenly yelped and jumped up. 'The sulphonamide, I completely forgot!' She delved into her trouser pocket to unearth the package she'd managed to get from the pharmacist.

Overwhelmed with guilt that she had forgotten the one thing that could save this young man's life, she quickly grabbed a cup and a spoon.

Dolly was suspicious of any new developments in medicine and taking in her sceptical face, Elizabeth took on a confident tone she did not feel.

'If we grind them up, they'll be easier for him to swallow,' she said, reaching for a spoon and flattening the tablets with the back of it, then she leaned forward to hold Lenny's head so she could get him to sip the liquid with the squashed tablets. He spluttered but then she was pleased to see him swallow some.

She checked the time on her watch so she could give him the next dose in four hours. The pharmacist had been very exact in his instructions.

Dolly was willing to be impressed, but her own experience had taught her to not expect much from someone who looked as ill as the young man in front of her. Her uncle had died of pneumonia, and it was an illness that took far too many people in the boating community, but maybe this girl from the outside world knew more than she did. Looking at their patient's face, she hoped so.

Chapter 19

It was hard work operating the locks without the help of Elizabeth, who was too busy dealing with Lenny. Maggie and Gloria struggled to moor up long enough to race ahead and set the lock up, but again Joe came to their aid. Once *Buffalo* and their butty had gone through, he then ran between the lock gates to fill the lock ahead to get *Nancy May* and *Florence* in side by side. With Jake Spencer in front, there was no doubt that anyone waiting for the locks on the other side was not going to hold them up and he even got off the boat to make sure the transitions worked smoothly, yelling obscenities at anyone who dared to argue with him. He wanted his wife back on board where she belonged and if that meant he had to help these girls, help them he would.

By nightfall, the four boats arrived at Limehouse. It was going to be more tricky to keep their stowaway hidden, Maggie thought, knowing that the Spencers would be welcomed by friends and family. She also wondered whether Gloria's parents might turn up to greet their daughter. Suddenly, a plan that had seemed a simple one on a towpath in the middle of nowhere, took on huge risks.

It seemed Gloria was having the same concerns and as soon as they approached the end of the journey, she called out:, 'Let's find somewhere down the end, away from everyone.'

Mr Spencer was already skilfully manoeuvring his way past all the moored boats to a corner on the far side of the wharf. He too had unloaded at Alperton so was due to reload in Limehouse. His cargo was ready so he needed to get to the bay where the steel would be waiting for him. But, first of all, he wanted to get Dolly off that boat with the deserter. He didn't need the police or authorities anywhere near his family.

''Ere, pass me yer rope,' he shouted to Maggie and he quickly tied it round an iron ring that was on the side of the wharf. Joe had done the same with the butty boat behind and then Jake moved towards *Florence* looking fearfully from side to side.

'I want my missus back,' he said in a quiet voice to Maggie. 'She 'as to come now.'

Maggie nodded and opened the hatch door.

Mrs Spencer already had her coat on and her bag on her arm but, before she went up the steps, she turned to Elizabeth.

'I think he's goin' t' be all right, luvvie. You've taken grand care o' 'im. You're a clever one, you is. Now I don't know what yer gonna do wiv him and I don't wanna know but I wish you all the luck in the world.'

And then she leaned forward and gave Elizabeth a peck on the cheek. Reaching to touch the spot, Elizabeth stroked it gently.

'Thank you so much, Mrs Spencer, I wouldn't have been able to do it without you.'

'It's Dolly,' the older woman said and as she went up the steps called out, 'I'm coming, I'm coming, Jake Spencer, just keep yer 'air on.'

* * *

Gloria and Maggie squeezed into the cabin where Lenny was propped up on a pillow. He had more colour than they had seen in his face for days, but his eyes were still closed.

'Is he, you know, is he all right?' Maggie asked fearfully.

'Yes, I think so.' Elizabeth sat down heavily on the bunk near Lenny's head. She wiped the back of her hand across her damp forehead.

'I was so scared, though,' she told the other two in a whisper, 'I thought he was going to die. Mrs Spencer – Dolly – she was wonderful; she was so calm. It's like life and death are an everyday occurrence on these boats and she accepts whatever comes. I don't know how she does it.'

'That's like my grandmother was,' Maggie said. 'Whatever happens is God's or whoever else's will; it makes life so much less complicated.'

Any next thoughts were interrupted by a shout from the wharf.

'Glor . . . are you there, love?'

'Hell's bells, it's my mum,' Gloria said, jumping up. 'We can't let her see Lenny.'

Gloria's family all lived near Limehouse Basin and were a *tour de force* and not long after her mother arrived, her father, three cousins and an aunt turned up. It meant there was such a crowd there was fortunately no chance of them all fitting onto either of the boats so, after a thorough, expert inspection of the two vessels from the outside and cheery introductions to the other two, Gloria steered them all back towards her parents' house, where she knew tea and carrot scones would be served. As she went, she gave a relieved smile over her shoulder.

'So now what do we do?' Maggie said.

Elizabeth thought for a moment. 'Well, I had promised to stay on board with him, but I don't know, Maggie, the longer he stays, the more we're implicated. I mean, we had an excuse to begin with but now . . . I just don't want any more problems in my life.'

She was already worrying about being left to her own devices, especially as she had felt that familiar tug towards the red telephone box on the corner. Maggie's words came back to her then, and she really was trying to beat this compulsion, but it was harder than she thought and to be harbouring a deserter as well was a situation she didn't want to face.

'Do you want me to stay?' Maggie asked her.

After a moment's pause, Elizabeth shook her head. 'No, you need to go and see your grandfather and,' she added with a grin, 'maybe that nice padre that Gloria told me about?'

It was disturbing how often Maggie had been thinking of Harry Moore and she knew she was hoping the trip home might offer an opportunity for her to meet him again but taking a sideways look at Elizabeth, she caught her glancing towards the telephone box.

'You can't stay here,' she said. 'You know what'll happen; I can see you eyeing up that telephone box, Elizabeth. Anyway, Limehouse isn't safe. It's right in the firing line for any bombers. It's too dangerous.'

'No, I'll be fine,' Elizabeth assured her and taking in Maggie's concerned face, she inhaled deeply and said: 'I really will. I promise I won't let you down and, to be honest, I'd rather be here risking an odd random bomb than going back to that empty house in Bourton. I could do with a quiet weekend.'

The next load wasn't due to be picked up until Monday morning, which would give the girls a much-needed break. Each trip involved twelve-hour days, seven days a week and every muscle in their bodies ached, the blisters on their fingers stung and, with the drama of Lenny and then his illness, they were all exhausted. Hoping that Elizabeth knew what she was doing, Maggie went off to pick up their post and register their arrival.

There were two letters for her; one from her grandfather and one with handwriting that made her quiver with excitement.

Like someone wanting to savour a teatime treat, she made herself open her grandad's letter first.

Her grandfather was surprisingly chirpy and regaled her with stories of how Mrs Harper and her friend, Mrs Mullins, had been calling in regularly with casseroles and soups. He was very enthusiastic about Mrs Mullins's potato pies and casually mentioned that Mrs Harper had invited him to a Red Cross fundraising event, which made Maggie raise her eyebrows. Mrs Harper was a widow and a very capable woman. Maggie made her way to a bench, wondering with a wry smile, what else Mrs Harper was capable of. Then, smiling to herself, she opened the second letter.

Dear Maggie,

I hope you get this letter OK. I finally managed to find an address where I could get in touch with you directly. I've been thinking about your predicament and may have an idea that could, at least, offer a way forward.

I have been in contact with a home for veterans and the chaplain there is so knowledgeable and helpful, I thought, with your permission, I might talk to him and see if he has any suggestions.

I would say that I am concerned about your involvement in all this, but I fear you would give me short shrift at such a patronising comment! I hope you won't think of this as interference but more as a genuine desire to help.

Life here is very busy; my uncle's been taken back into hospital. I think he was trying to do too much too soon and to be honest, he isn't getting better as quickly as we hoped, so I've asked to delay returning to my unit. It makes it difficult for me because I'm torn between being of use here and helping my men with whatever dangers they're facing. At the moment, though, there's very little choice because there

*is no one to run the parish except me and believe me, I'm
not cut out to be a parish priest!*

*I really enjoyed bumping into you and couldn't believe
my luck, although seeing you on that boat was an eye-
opener for me – I had no idea women could do all that
physical work but somehow you keep surprising me,
Maggie.*

*I know you said you might be home on leave this week-
end so do please call at the rectory if you get the chance, it
would be lovely to see you.*

With all best wishes,
Harry

* * *

Harry had hovered over the last part of his letter debating how
to sign off. He worried he had already said too much by confessing his delight at seeing her at Cassiobury and he had the
evidence of the different versions where he had tried in vain
to sum up how he felt crumpled up on the floor next to the
study waste-paper bin. There was a part of Maggie that made
him wary of making a move; she was friendly, that was certain,
but he sensed an invisible wall around her – one that he wasn't
sure she wanted breached. Eventually, at midnight, with early
service the next morning, he'd been so tired he just folded the
latest offering to prevent any more prevaricating and sealed the
envelope, wondering whether he had sealed his fate too.

An uncompromising reply from his superiors had made it
clear that they expected the diocese to find a replacement for the
incumbent vicar as soon as possible so that Harry could rejoin
his men. Remembering his talk with the archdeacon, Harry
wasn't as convinced as they were that it would be an easy task.
There were so few men left at home to fulfil the roles the church

demanded of them and the archdeacon had given unveiled hints that a young man like Harry was too valuable to give up lightly.

Meanwhile, the frustrations of dealing with the minutiae of everyday life in Didsbury were wearing Harry down and he thought he would scream if one more well-meaning parishioner asked him how they were going to rustle up any Easter flowers. His suggestion that cabbages and onions might be more suitable than any spring flowers they could find had earned him more than one scandalised frown and he feared he'd unleashed a grass-roots rebellion when he heard members of the Women's Institute discussing in despair how on earth that 'ridiculous young man' thought they were going to fit cabbages into the cut-glass vases stored in the vestry.

Harry's war so far had been on the front line, dealing with death, destruction and dysentery and no matter how hard he tried, the efforts of this little congregation in the leafier suburbs of Manchester to try to maintain pre-war standards left him feeling irritated.

His other problem was praying. Firstly, there was no time, and secondly, he suspected he was avoiding any opportunities as the words seemed to be nothing but an echo in his head. Without his uncle's solid presence, Harry was beginning to feel claustrophobic in a faith that had ceased to have any meaning to him.

That gnawing feeling nagged away at him for several days until he had a couple of hours off and took himself on a bus to Salford.

* * *

'Harry! Oh, it's so good to see you again.' David greeted him with delight when he popped his head around the chaplain of Broughton House's office.

'Do you want to see Jim?' David immediately asked.

'Yes, I do, but in good time. Do you have a minute in the meantime?'

A cup of tea was provided by Mrs Lewis, who looked as nervous as ever, and the two men settled down in the leather armchairs.

'Oh, I long for the day when we can indulge all the time in proper milk, don't you?' David said, leaning forward to pour a small amount of Carnation milk into his cup.

Harry had almost forgotten what milk tasted like as he usually gave his ration away to anyone in the parish who looked as though they needed more flesh on their bones but, savouring the sweet, sickly taste in his mouth, he couldn't help but agree.

'Here,' David said, delving into the desk drawer next to him, 'we can at least have an oat biscuit. These were only baked yesterday, and Mrs Lewis insisted I keep them for visitors. I wish we had confession—' he smiled '—I could at least do some penance for the indulgence. I've had two already today. So, what is it I can help you with?'

Now it came to it, Harry felt a moment's qualm. He was about to admit that he knew of a criminal who was being harboured by three girls on the Grand Union Canal and he paused.

'You can tell me anything, you know,' David said, laying a strong hand on Harry's arm. 'I don't judge, and I don't condemn.'

Harry made the decision to dive straight in and, bit by bit, told the story of Lenny. He didn't mention who the girls were, but David had made his own assumptions.

At the end of it, Harry put his cup down on the small table next to him and waited.

The agonising silence made his pulse race, and he wondered whether he had made a terrible mistake sharing Maggie's secret but then David spoke.

'We've got one here,' he said in a soft voice.

'What? A deserter?'

'Yes, he's only twenty-one and he's Mrs Lewis's son.'

It was rare for Harry Moore to be shocked, but to discover that such a respectable establishment as this veterans' centre was harbouring a criminal left him speechless for a moment.

'Mrs Lewis found him shivering and starving in her coalhouse,' David said. 'She was distraught and didn't know what to do so asked me for help.'

Harry waited while David collected himself before continuing with his tale.

It transpired that Mrs Lewis had two sons and both had been at Dunkirk. The older one, Alfie, had promised his mother that he would take care of the younger brother no matter what and that he would make sure he brought him home but as the two of them hid in the sand dunes on the beach in Normandy, a Messerschmitt 109 flew over and strafed the ground below. Alfie had tried to shield George but then when the plane had passed over, he realised his brother had been hit and the blood from his head was seeping into the sand beneath them.

'He did everything he could to save his brother,' David said, 'and screamed for the medics, but there was nothing they could do – their priority was the living.

'Alfie may have escaped without injury but knowing he'd have to explain to his mother that he'd abandoned George's body to rot amidst the marram grass, the poor man had to be manhandled by his fellow soldiers to get him on a boat out of there. Once he got to Dover, he had lost the power of speech and since then, Harry, he hasn't spoken one word.'

Harry felt himself getting angry. He remembered that in the Great War, a young Winston Churchill had been blamed for abandoning soldiers at Gallipoli and, almost in defiance of the newspapers, as prime minister he had made a speech at the time of Dunkirk reminding the country that 'wars are not won by evacuations'. The newspapers had heralded the 'little ships' rescue as a triumph but Harry's own experiences told a different story and now, he wondered whether Churchill and families like the Lewis's felt the same.

He turned his attention back to David who was saying that while many soldiers were sent on to continue fighting, others were sent home to recover, and Alfie was one of those. He was seen by a rather unsympathetic doctor who signed him off fit for duty, confident the traumatised soldier was simply suffering from LMF – lack of moral fibre. At the end of his leave, his mother waved him goodbye with a sodden handkerchief clutched to her mouth, but he then doubled back, and it wasn't until three days later that she found him huddled at the back of the coalhouse.

'But . . .' Harry began. He knew the answer to the question before he asked it. There was no mother on this earth who would give their only remaining son up to the authorities, even if he was a deserter.

'So how have you kept him hidden?' he asked instead.

David explained that they found Alfie a job working in the kitchens, washing up and being a general dogsbody. No one suspected he was Mrs Lewis's son and as he didn't speak, there was no danger of him saying the wrong thing to the veterans at the home.

'They'd turn him in in an instant,' David admitted. 'They've all fought bravely – as did Alfie to be fair – but they'd have no sympathy for a man who deserted. But how long we can keep the truth hidden, I have no idea.'

Having unburdened his soul, David seemed to relax. The subterfuge happening in plain sight in a home for veterans had been a huge weight he had been carrying and he had spent night after night wrestling with his conscience. He sat back in his chair and said, 'So, what are you going to do now with *your* runaway?'

The options were discussed in detail until at the end of their cup of tea, David tentatively said, 'There's more of these men than we know, but I've heard they're so desperate for troops they're looking for other ways to deal with them such as treating desertion as AWOL, which would allow them to give short penalties and then get them back into service. They don't want to admit that there are some men who are so traumatised that they're ill.'

The suggestion that being 'absent without leave' might be an alternative to the long imprisonment doled out to deserters cheered Harry up and he suddenly remembered a senior padre who had been doing some work with the recruitment officers on some of these men and felt more optimistic than he had since Maggie's telephone call. The thought that he might be able to see her this weekend and tell her he had a solution for her gave him a little shiver of excitement and he had to stop himself from imagining the scene where she would fall into his arms with relief.

'Let's go and find Jim,' David said, standing up. 'I'm afraid I've got some news there too that might give you another headache.'

As they walked along the corridor, David explained that there had been a medical meeting about Jim; his physical health had been reassessed, and it had been decided that he was capable of living on his own.

Remembering the frail man he had seen in the garden on his last visit, Harry was appalled.

'But how can they discharge him from here? Where will he go?'

'Well, it seems we may have to talk to him about getting in touch with his family after all,' David said. 'The problem is these beds are full, and we have so many more who need to come here. We can no longer keep those who are not completely incapacitated.'

With that, they reached the ward to find Jim sitting on the edge of his bed, his head bowed. He didn't even look up when they walked over but just stared at the four shiny shoes on the wooden planks in front of him. Harry wondered how much he knew about the impending change in his circumstances.

'Hello, Jim,' Harry said in a gentle voice.

'Hah,' came the dismissive reply that seemed to answer Harry's question.

David pulled up two chairs and they both sat down.

'So, they're turfing me out,' Jim said, pulling his head back. His eyes were on fire.

'Not exactly turfi—' David started to say but Jim interrupted.

'Well, what would you call it? I may as well finish myself off now. I've got nowhere to go so it's the streets or the Ship Canal. Doesn't matter to me. I'm no use to anyone anyhow.'

It was so tempting for Harry to remind this broken man that he did have a family, but he couldn't without David's lead, so he kept quiet, letting the more experienced veteran chaplain reassure and cajole the patient he had come to know so well.

It was only when Harry produced the letter from Mrs Baines that Jim looked at the padre properly. At first, he was furious that Harry had interfered but when he read the letter and the young, innocent soldier's words to his mother, his anger started to dissipate. He read it over several times but didn't say a word, then he put it ever so carefully in the cupboard next to him as if he were gently closing young Arthur Baines's eyes for the last time.

Chapter 20

Maggie walked briskly along Barlow Moor Road. She was so used to the speed of the boat, it felt like a luxury to be able to walk at her own fast pace. It also suited her mood not to dawdle. She had always grabbed at life like the candy floss she would mither for during a visit to Belle Vue as a child but since Roger, she had lost confidence and hated herself for it. Now Harry's letter had given her a glimmer of hope that she might, finally, be able to leave all that aside. Today, the sun was shining with the tentative tendrils of spring and she was looking forward to seeing her grandfather, who was sounding so much more positive in his letters than she had expected – a bonus, she thought, that might be due to the indomitable Mrs Harper. She was realistic enough to know that her grandfather was not a man who could survive on his own and Mrs Harper was, after all, a widow, Maggie thought with a slight smile. That she also hoped to see a certain army padre this weekend bore no relation to the fact that she was humming to herself as she hurried along.

Maggie had been congratulating herself on having survived life on the cut for more than six months now – so much longer than many of the girls who'd trained when she did. Most of them had got the bus or train straight back home once they had tried to cook on the tiny stove, had suffered muscle aches and blisters or spotted the rats running along the towpath. Working on the canals was not for the faint-hearted.

Lenny, of course, was a problem they needed to face but Harry's letter had given her hope that all was not lost as far as that young deserter was concerned.

She slowed as she approached Emmanuel Church and found herself looking around in all directions to see if she could see a familiar tall figure.

'Looking for anyone in particular?' a voice behind her said. She jumped and then her face broke into a wide smile when she turned to see Harry's beaming face.

'I could pretend to be terribly nonchalant but, now you mention it, yes, I was looking for you.' Maggie didn't pause and reached forward to give him a kiss on the cheek.

Harry put his hand up to touch the spot, his expression full of wonder.

'Well, that's a good start; now we're on such intimate terms, I think I could be so bold as to invite you in for a cup of tea,' he laughed.

The women from the Mothers' Union, who were polishing the pews, excitedly nudged each other when the couple walked past them towards the vestry and as soon as the door closed, the noise level increased with animated chatter.

'You do realise you've started a riot, don't you?' Harry said, putting the kettle on the stove in the corner.

Maggie grinned and then said more seriously, 'I hope it gives them something to talk about other than the terrible events in Poland we keep hearing about.'

'Yes, the Germans seem intent on driving all the Jews out. We're never far from this terrible war, are we? But no, you're right, most of those women's husbands are serving and anything that distracts them can only be a good thing. So, how are you? How's that extra passenger of yours doing?'

By the time Maggie had filled Harry in on the latest developments with Lenny she looked so forlorn that he longed to reach out to her but, as if anticipating his move, she folded her arms defensively .

Harry sucked in his breath and quickly said, 'So, what are you going to do?'

Kicking herself for her automatic reaction, Maggie concentrated on the the question that had been churning around in her mind- the one she had failed to find any solution for and she shrugged.

There was almost a boyish excitement that melted Maggie's heart as Harry leaned forward to reveal the plan that he and his friend had come up with to get Lenny accepted back into the army.

'David came up with it really,' he said. 'He's the chaplain at a centre for veterans in Salford. He's such a nice man, you really feel you can trust him. He too thinks they're beginning to take deserters back, Maggie, and, between us, we're going to see if we can find out more, so don't you despair.'

He risked a pat on her hand and she reached to cover it with her own. They both felt a warmth that came from more than just their hands but when they looked into each other's eyes, the silence between them was deafening until Harry lurched to his feet and suggested a walk, feeling if they stayed any longer in the safe haven of the vestry with a wooden door between them and prying eyes, he might not be able to hold back any longer. She looked so beautiful – a capable woman and yet a young girl. He knew that, despite all his own protestations, he was falling in love.

* * *

With the reassuring bustle outside, Harry's shoulders relaxed and Maggie breathed in deeply. The intensity of her own feelings in that small room had been stifling.

Harry tucked her hand in his arm, and they walked along Barlow Moor Road, oblivious to the nudges and meaningful glances of passers-by, so much so that Maggie hardly heard when one stopped and said, in surprise, 'Maggie? Maggie Carpenter, is that you?'

In front of her was Roger Anderson, his blue eyes twinkling with mischief.

He raised his eyebrows with surprise at the clergyman next to Maggie.

Pulling her hand away from the crook of Harry's arm as if it were on fire, Maggie blurted out, 'Roger . . . what the hell are you doing here?'

The anger in her voice made Harry look again at the man staring far too knowingly at Maggie. There was an intimacy in his expression that prompted an automatic defence in Harry, and he felt aggression bubbling inside him.

'Aren't you going to introduce me to your friend?' Roger said, turning with a pleasant expression that belied the impression that Harry was being sneered at.

'Um,' Maggie started, 'this is Har—' Then she stopped and felt a hot anger sear through her.

'No, no I'm not going to introduce you,' she said, her face burning. In a chillingly quiet voice she said, 'Would you excuse us a moment, Harry?' And she stepped away, leaving Roger no option but to follow her.

All the shame, all the hurt and all the anger erupted as Maggie remembered that the last time she had seen Roger had been at Manchester Piccadilly railway station when she had clung to his mackintosh, begging him not to leave her. Instead of clasping her in his arms, he had peeled her fingers away one digit at a time and then briskly walked off, after announcing to the stunned Maggie that instead of marrying her, he was going back to his wife. The memory of crumpled sheets in a back-street hotel near Piccadilly was vivid, but instead of being a romantic finale to a beautiful love story, it was simply a sordid disaster. As he'd walked away, she hadn't cared who had seen her wrap her arms around herself in despair and start to sob, but onlookers had no idea that this was an illicit affair that had come to a tragic end; only Maggie knew that.

Reluctantly, the padre stayed where he was but within reach, like a guard dog ready to pounce. Roger held his superior stance and looked down, almost pityingly, at Maggie's distraught expression.

Seeing her shoulders suddenly heave with a sob, Harry moved forward.

'I think it might be better if you left us now,' he said, coming eye to eye with Roger.

'Really?' Roger replied. He was enjoying every minute of this uncomfortable meeting. Little Maggie had been fun, oh, he remembered how much fun she could be, and to see her arm in arm with a man wearing a dog collar seemed like a good joke.

'Yes,' Harry said, determination fixing his mouth in a hard line. 'You're upsetting Maggie, and I don't like that.'

'Oh, don't you?' Roger said, stepping forward so the two men's noses almost touched. His eyes were flashing, and all semblance of friendliness had vanished. He remembered Maggie's warm body and her soft skin and the thought that this man was now enjoying her affections led to a knowing sneer in Maggie's direction.

Maggie pushed between them. 'Let's go, Harry, he's not worth it.'

She pulled his coat and Harry stumbled backwards, prompting a smirk from Roger. For one whole minute, the soldier in Harry thought how satisfying it would be to wipe the smile off that smug face but catching sight of two of his astonished parishioners on the other side of the street, instead, with icy calm, he said, 'You're right, Maggie. He isn't. Let's go.' And with that, he turned on his heel and with her rushing to catch him up, he stalked away, leaving Roger Anderson looking slightly ridiculous.

*　*　*

'Harry, Harry, wait for me,' Maggie called from behind, but Harry kept walking; so many thoughts were swirling around in his head he couldn't even look her in the eye.

There had been no doubt of the relationship between those two, he realised with a sinking feeling and, right now, he didn't know what to say to her.

The footsteps behind him faded and it was only when he got to Fog Lane Park that he slowed down, calmed as always by the green of the trees.

There was a bench ahead of him and he went to sit on it, forcing himself to breathe slowly. All his training in counselling and dealing with people's problems had been eradicated in one moment of blinding jealousy and he felt mortified.

'Harry?' a quiet voice said. He looked up to see Maggie's tear-stained face in front of him. The desire to blot out the last twenty minutes and take her in his arms was enormous but then Roger's face came back to him and he couldn't help it, it was that man's arms that he imagined around her and he closed his lips firmly in case he said something he regretted.

'Give me a minute, Maggie,' he said quietly.

She went to sit down next to him, her hands folded in her lap.

'So,' he eventually said, 'did you have an affair with him? Do you want to tell me about it?'

At that, Maggie reared up like a defensive tiger, her whole demeanour changing.

'No, I don't. I mean, you and I, well we're not even going out with each other. You have no rights over me. Roger is in my past and I don't want to talk about it. You're in no position to demand answers from me.'

She couldn't tell him. She was too was riddled with guilt at the history between her and Roger and seeing the two men together had made her regret every single stolen kiss, every embrace and, especially, that dreadful night of passion in a seedy hotel in Manchester. Their two faces, sized up against each other had been like the two faces of Janus, one representing her past and the other, a future that she had now shattered.

Her gaze focused on his dog collar and the impossibility of it all overwhelmed her, and she stood up.

Harry watched in shock as she stalked away from the bench, just as a cold wind whipped down the pathway. He shivered.

*　*　*

The visit to her grandfather's may as well not have happened as far as Maggie was concerned. She went through the motions of tidying the kitchen, checking his ration book, going to the shops and doing his laundry but she was like an automated figure wandering through the house. She did, with mild surprise, notice that the house was in a better state than she had expected and wondered vaguely whether her grandfather had found a home help or whether Mrs Harper had been coming round more regularly than she had realised.

Fortunately for Maggie, Charles Carpenter was too absorbed with a conversation he'd had with Dorothy Harper the day before to notice how distracted his granddaughter was. After her visit to Winnie's grave, Dorothy had been unequivocal about Charlie's behaviour as a husband and had intimated that, if he wanted their relationship to continue, then he was going to have to find a way to forgive his son, Jim.

It was only when Maggie served him an empty cup instead of the tea he'd asked for that he seemed to notice she was not quite herself.

'You all right, Maggie?'

For a brief second, she longed to unburden herself, but to tell her grandfather she had had an affair with a married man would be too humiliating, so she just gave him a weak smile and blamed the wet weather.

Assessing her slumped shoulders, Charles realised with some remorse that his wife would have known what to do. A doorbell broke the silence and Mrs Harper's bright voice called from the hallway.

'Only me. Is Maggie here yet?'

Looking at her grandfather properly for the first time, Maggie took stock of his appearance. He was smartly dressed and his hair was combed. She suspected it was all due to this formidable woman who swept in wearing a faded tweed suit and with her handbag tucked firmly under her arm. Maggie's glum expression was immediately spotted by the eagle-eyed Mrs Harper. She'd heard about the altercation in the street and had come round with the sole purpose of seeing if Maggie was all right.

She opened the cake tin in her basket and said briskly, 'Right, you put the kettle on, love, and I'll get some plates. I've made some nice oat biscuits for us.'

Charles's face lit up; Dorothy Harper's oat biscuits were legendary. He settled back in the chair, relieved of responsibility and allowed the warm, nurturing glow of Dorothy's competence to seep into his body.

Mrs Harper's keen questioning yielded nothing but bland replies from Maggie and, taking in her bleak appearance,

Dorothy made her a cup of Horlicks and gently suggested she should have a bath followed by an early night.

'I'm just going to listen to the wireless with your grandad for a bit, then I'll be off,' she told Maggie, who gratefully took the cup and fled to the sanctuary of her bedroom.

It was a long night during which Maggie tossed and turned, seeing Harry's face turn into Roger's and then Roger's turn into Harry's. She woke late the next morning with her hair all over her face and her eyelids stuck together with dried tears.

There was a noise from downstairs as the front door opened and she heard her grandfather and the now familiar voice of Mrs Harper resound up the stairs.

Gracious, Maggie thought, quickly brushing her hair. *That woman is almost living here.*

Making her way downstairs to the hallway, she realised with some guilt that the pair of them had been to church without her. However, the thought of seeing Harry there was too much for her to contemplate so she mumbled her excuses.

Dorothy Harper interrupted her: 'It was better you had a good night's sleep, dear. Now, don't you have to get the bus soon?'

Maggie looked down at her watch with surprise. It was eleven o'clock. If she was going to make the bus back in time to catch the train down to London, she was going to have to hurry so she raced upstairs again to get her small bag and gave her grandfather a quick hug but when she headed for the door, she found Mrs Harper was there before her.

'I'll walk with you, lass. I'm going that way. Bye, Charlie, see you tomorrow,' she called.

There was something about this woman that made Maggie think of her grandmother and she was almost glad of the reassuring figure walking in step beside her to the bus stop. They had just missed a bus and the next wasn't due for ten minutes.

Mrs Harper turned to her and put her warm hand out to clasp Maggie's.

'So, love, I heard about the scene yesterday. Are you all right?'

She should have been affronted at the infringement of her privacy, but all Maggie saw was understanding and sympathy. It made her well up with tears and she dropped her head in submission.

Mrs Harper went on: 'You know, your grandmother told me all about what you were going through at college. She didn't want to interfere, but she would have liked you to have known, she understood. I mean . . .' Here she paused, noting Maggie's stunned expression; she didn't want to reveal her friend's secrets but, then again, Winnie was dead and here was her granddaughter needing advice.

'Your granny, well, she knew how you felt. There was a time, when your grandad closed off from her when your dad left that she . . . well, let's just say, she had a friend. She knew what it was like to fall for someone unsuitable and she promised me she'd talk to you, knowing how you were suffering, but, well, she didn't get the chance did she?'

For the first time since she'd walked away from that bench in Fog Lane Park, Maggie was jerked out of her misery.

'Granny?' she said in disbelief.

Mrs Harper laughed. 'Oh, you young people, you think you invented love. Yes, Maggie, your granny. It came to nothing of course. She couldn't just leave your grandad now could she? Anyway, the point is, she wanted to tell you that as long as you didn't, well, you know, get into trouble, you had to just make sure any mistakes you'd made didn't define your future. She was definite about that.'

At that moment, the bus came and Maggie only had a moment to give Mrs Harper a desperate hug and say, 'Thank you, thank you so much. I don't know what to say.'

As she stepped onto the platform at the back of the bus, Mrs Harper called after her, 'Just think what you're going to say to that nice padre. Don't let him go, Maggie.'

Chapter 21

Maggie was deep in her own thoughts as she approached their boats but seeing the butty boat all locked up and then finding Elizabeth curled up on the bunk of the *Nancy May*, reading Hemingway's latest novel, *For Whom The Bell Tolls*, she jerked out of her reverie.

'Hello, where's Lenny?' she said, suddenly becoming fearful. She wondered whether they had entrusted too much responsibility to Elizabeth by leaving her with a patient who was certainly not fully recovered when she had so many of her own issues to deal with.

Elizabeth grinned and touched the side of her nose. She was obviously very pleased with herself. Maggie started to feel alarmed.

'I'll tell you when Gloria gets here,' she said and was about to go back to the library book that she'd picked up from the post office but with a sigh, closed it and asked, 'So how was your weekend?'

Maggie had no intention of telling her and in any case, at that moment, Gloria's cheerful voice could be heard calling from the towpath.

'I've had the most amazing weekend, I can't wait to tell you both all about it,' she called and pushed open the hatch door.

'Where's Lenny?' she asked, echoing Maggie.

Elizabeth sat forward and said with a smug voice: 'I've sorted our little problem, and we don't have to worry anymore.'

Both girls looked very nervous, but Elizabeth was still talking excitedly. 'I had a brainwave. I mean, we needed to get rid of him but we didn't want to hand him over to the authorities, so guess what I did?'

She didn't wait for a reply.

'I told you I knew someone who could help. I've found him a job! Somewhere where he can lie low.'

Gloria came down the steps and sat down next to Elizabeth with her arms folded.

'What the hell have you done, Elizabeth?'

It was at this point that Elizabeth started to look slightly embarrassed.

'You just need to know he's OK, not quite better, obviously, and still weak, but he'll be looked after and he's in no danger.'

But Maggie and Gloria were not content to leave it there and they both leaned forward until their heads were just inches from Elizabeth's.

'I repeat,' Gloria said, almost menacingly, 'what the hell have you done?'

Bit by bit the story came out and Elizabeth admitted she had received a visit from the man in the gaberdine mackintosh. He took the money that Maggie had lent Elizabeth to pay off her debts but then spotted a pair of soldier's boots under the bed, which obviously told their own story. What she didn't tell her friends was that the man's mood had turned ugly and he had threatened her with letting her husband and her sons' school know about what he called 'her dirty little secret' unless she told him why they were harbouring a deserter.

'He offered us the perfect solution; he was looking for someone who could do the "collections" and we needed that boy out of our hair,' she said, but her voice weakened as she realised the perfect story she had practised was not having the effect she had hoped for.

'What you're saying is that you've sold that poor lad to pay off your debts,' Gloria said, her face contorted with anger.

'Well, you couldn't wait to get rid of him, so I thought you'd be glad,' was the only response she got.

Maggie stretched out her arm to the middle of the cabin like a barrier to make sure the distance between the other two was maintained. She didn't need this drama; her head was too full of her own thoughts, but Gloria was already perched on the edge of the bed like a rattlesnake about to strike.

'Do you know where they've taken him?' Maggie said in a calmer tone than the one screaming in her head.

Elizabeth shrugged. 'He'll disappear, I'm sure of that. They'll keep him out of sight.'

Maggie was thinking that might be true until he turned up dead behind a dustbin. *Honestly*, she thought, *for an intelligent woman, Elizabeth could be remarkably naïve sometimes.*

She was inwardly seething. All the way back, she had tried to prepare for a conversation with Harry, but each version had left her feeling more hopeless by the minute. However, he had come up with a solution for Lenny that might, just might, allow him back into the army, and now here the lad was, becoming embroiled in an underworld that just reeked of violence, crime and danger.

In silence, she got up and went to the door. Turning at the last minute, she went to say something to Elizabeth but then just shook her head and went out. She desperately needed to clear her head.

Walking slowly along the towpath, she pulled her scarf around her ears to block out any thoughts of Harry. It was May but the air had turned very cold and despite the bluebells on the side of the towpath, it felt more like winter. There may have been a very small part of her that was relieved 'the Lenny problem' had been taken out of their hands but she didn't believe this was the answer. The thought of that lad's pale face brought bile into her throat. She felt like Judas.

*   *   *

By the time she got back to the boat, the other two had obviously carried on their row and were now launching into an icy silence that was colder than the chilly wind outside. As she entered the room, Elizabeth pushed past both of them and made her way back to *Florence*, deciding that the cold cabin there was preferable to spending one more minute with this censorious pair. She had been so convinced that she'd found a way to solve their problem, but their reaction had taken her by surprise and was making her question her motives. It was true that the man in the gaberdine had hinted that this would act as a trade-off for all her problems and with a letter in her pocket from her husband, demanding to know why so much money had been withdrawn from their bank account, she'd welcomed the opportunity to push that particular episode in her life under the carpet. In addition, the man – she'd never known his name – had seemed to suggest that Lenny would be cared for by a kind of brotherhood and she'd been so willing to believe him that it was only now that it occurred to her that she hadn't asked enough questions.

*   *   *

None of them slept that night and it was hardly light when they needed to get the *Nancy May* moving the next morning and Elizabeth automatically untied *Florence*'s mooring ropes to join the long line of boats waiting to re-load. Seeing the other two with their heads together, she had no doubt she was the topic of their conversation so, in defiance, started to hum and then increased the volume until she was singing 'Manhattan Serenade' at the top of her voice.

'Just listen to her,' Gloria said, pushing the tiller sharply right and left so that the butty boat behind would find it hard to steer. Maggie gently took it off her.

'That won't help. If we damage these boats, we'll have to pay to repair them and, as you know, we haven't got any money left.'

Gloria stepped back to lean against the hatch so she could glare in Elizabeth's direction. Her frown was so fierce it almost made Maggie laugh. It was hard to let any joy in; her night had been spent worrying about Lenny, being furious with Elizabeth and being beyond angry with Roger. But, when daylight came, the person she hated most in the world was herself.

'She can't see your expression from here,' she told Gloria, 'but I'm sure she can detect your animosity – I can certainly feel it from here. Anyway, let's get to the depot, pick up our orders and get out into the open fields again.'

She looked around at the industrial landscape of the London skyline. It was like a Meccano set but with bits of buildings that were actually partially destroyed by bombs. This part of the journey made her feel very uncomfortable and, standing in the open air at the back of a boat, quite vulnerable.

There had been fewer raids on London since the Battle of Britain but following the bombing of Berlin there had been a flurry of attacks on the east end of London, including two at Poplar, which seemed frighteningly close to their current location. Even the underground wasn't safe, Maggie thought, remembering the one hundred and seventy-three people who had been crushed in a panic at Bethnal Green tube station the previous month. The government had tried to hush it up, knowing the high death toll would threaten morale, but everyone on the cut was talking about it. Attempting to take in a deep breath to calm the jumble of thoughts that were milling around in her brain, her chest constricted and she spluttered.

'You OK, Mags?' Gloria asked.

'Hmm, yes,' she said unconvincingly. She felt utterly miserable, despairing at how ironic it was that the first time she had actually started to like someone, really like them, it had to be a man of God who would certainly never entertain a relationship with a Jezebel like her. Maybe she could buy a boat and spend her whole life evading real life on the canals of England, she thought, feeling very sorry for herself.

Realising Gloria was waiting for a reply, she mumbled, 'I was just thinking about how our pilots use the waterways to navigate. These canals make an ideal target. I just hope the Jerries don't decide today's the day to pay London a visit.'

Gloria, as someone who had so far survived the attacks on the docks around Limehouse, shrugged. She still had the optimism of youth and an unshakeable belief in her own immortality.

'Stick with me and you'll be all right,' she said cheerfully. 'They've managed to miss me so far, so I'll be your lucky charm.'

Maggie gave a weak smile, but her grandfather had told her how the local telegram boys had been seen far too often cycling furiously around Didsbury, carrying the dreaded telegrams from commanding officers in the Mediterranean, the Atlantic or even in the English Channel, let alone the casualties that had occurred in the streets of her own home city. Nowhere was safe. A blackbird was singing its lilting, tuneful melody in the trees at the side of the canal and the purity of the sound lifted Maggie's spirits, prompting her to look at the skies above and to wish away any huge dark wings of the German Luftwaffe and the memories of meeting Roger. Shivering, despite the sunshine that had broken through, she wrapped her arms around herself, suddenly imagining how safe she might feel if those arms belonged to Harry.

The thought made her wobble and Gloria reached to grab her, always mindful that the murky waters of the canal were only inches away from them both.

'Sorry,' Maggie muttered. Gloria took a keen look at her friend. Despite her youth, she was beginning to piece together the thoughts that went on in both her friends' heads. She opened her mouth to speak but then Maggie spotted the warehouse ahead where they were to pick up their cargo.

'There, over there,' she said. 'We need to go to the left.'

This part of Limehouse Basin, was, as always crowded with boats, and it took all the girls' concentration to manoeuvre into a position where they could fit the *Florence* in too.

From that moment on, the afternoon was a frantic schedule of getting to the cranes on time, uncovering and covering the hold at the front of the boats and being yelled at by impatient staff who had no time for inefficiency or dawdling, but by the time the girls had finished and placed the last piece of rope around their load of timber, they received a nod of approval from the brawny man in charge of the depot.

'Not bad, girls, not bad,' he said, mopping his brow. His heart had sunk when he'd seen the three women queueing up behind the more seasoned boat handlers, but he'd been pleasantly surprised by their speed and strength. 'You're certainly better than many of the other girls we've had through,' he told Gloria.

'Pah, that's because I've been brought up on boats,' she retorted, unimpressed by his reluctant praise, but Elizabeth gave him a grateful smile, which sent him home to his dour wife with a spring in his step.

Once they'd slid the butty in behind the *Nancy May* like a jigsaw piece, they were able to ignore the tirade of instructions yelled through the loudspeakers above them. Maggie, who had been thanking her lucky stars all day that the foray into central London had been without incident, was feeling magnanimous.

'Let's go to the pub,' she said. 'Isn't The Grapes where Dickens wrote one of his books?'

Elizabeth nodded. Gloria looked perplexed.

'Call yourself a London girl and you've never read Dickens?' Maggie said, pushing her gently. 'Right, we need to improve your education.'

Gloria thought of Will and how he had casually talked about writers, artists and cultural centres.

'Yes, yes, I'd really like that,' she told Maggie. 'I think it's time I made the most of having a teacher on board.'

* * *

The Grapes was packed and there were no tables free, so the girls were forced to stand at the bar, much to the disapproval of the locals, but just as they'd ordered a cider each, three more girls came in, looking as dishevelled as they did. One of them squealed in delight when they spotted Maggie, Elizabeth and Gloria.

'Ooo, look, there's more of us.'

'Bloody 'ell, are we going to be taken o'er by women?' one old-timer grumbled, spreading his legs as wide as he could to take up as much of the bar as possible, but one of the new girls was having none of it.

'Move over,' the same girl said with a beaming grin, 'the women have arrived. You're going to have to get used to it. Times have changed, you know.'

'Over my dead body,' the man retorted but by then all six girls had forced their way to the front of the bar and he had been unceremoniously pushed out of the way. Assailed by a sudden rise in the excited chatter of the newcomers, he took his pint off the bar and begrudgingly moved to a seat in the corner, chuntering on his way that this war had a lot to answer for.

By now, the latecomers had introduced themselves as Mavis, Polly and Vera and unaware of the atmosphere that hung over the men in the bar, they all started to chat happily on about their cramped conditions, the lack of a toilet and where the best places on the Grand Union were to get a wash.

Their enthusiasm at meeting fellow female boaters broke through the ill feeling and gradually the sharing of experience was too good to resist and even Gloria started to enjoy the chatter. On the way back to their moorings, with two ciders inside her, she took Elizabeth and Maggie's arms.

'Come on, you two. We've no idea where they've taken Lenny so we can't help him. We're just going to have to hope Elizabeth is right and the outfit's some sort of brotherhood where he can sit out the war. At least he isn't on the front line. Anyway, for better or worse, we're in this together, so we may as well make the most of it. After all, my sister's having to deal with lots of petty stuff like who's in the bathroom next in this Isle of Man internment camp, and here we are, under the twinkling stars, heading back towards our little havens on the water. Who could ask for more?' And she started to sing 'Somebody Else is Taking My Place', doing her best to sound like Peggy Lee.

Finally, the other two joined in.

Chapter 22

Harry looked back at the entrance to Emmanuel Church and the pale figure of his uncle on the step. He was waving encouragingly.

'I'll be fine, now off you go, lad. You've done a great job but it's time for me to take back over now. I'm feeling much better.'

Harry waved back but looked doubtful. His uncle had lost weight and his hair had definitely gone greyer, but the doctors had declared him able to come back to 'light duties' and a curate from Stretford was going to help out so Harry had no choice but to leave him to cope and go back to his unit. Despite feeling that he shouldn't be leaving his uncle, it was a return he was actually looking forward to. He needed the distraction of a real war to quell the war that was happening in his head. He knew now that he loved Maggie with all his heart, but he had been horrified at how jealous he'd felt when he discovered she had a past. His own youthful experiences, when he had been initiated into the joys of sex by a rather energetic girl at a hostel in the Lake District, he dismissed as being something men were expected to do. He'd never thought about it from a woman's perspective.

Every woman with blonde hair on the platform, on the train and when he got off at London, reminded him of Maggie.

'I need a unit full of men,' he said out loud.

A girl with dark curls passing him grinned, tossed her hair and said, 'Oh, so do I, ducky.'

He burst out laughing. This was what he needed, to put distance – and a sense of perspective – between him and the churning thoughts in his head.

Later on, he was pleased to find that the nauseous feeling in his stomach had almost completely subsided. He had been touched by the home-made banner that had been erected in the barracks in Suffolk. And while the pints were lined up on the bar for him, men clapped him on the back, joked about how he was beginning to look like a country vicar and that he needed knocking back into shape.

He felt he'd come home.

* * *

It was the gentle ripple of the water and the June sunshine that was finally calming Maggie down. She'd volunteered to go ahead to prepare the locks, pedalling along the towpath, relishing the quiet. While she waited for the locks to fill, she blotted out any thoughts of Harry and concentrated on the birdsong from the trees, the whoosh of the water as it powered through the gates and the buzzing of the bees. It helped her to breathe and was a welcome relief from the nightmares that were plaguing her. She was forgetting to eat and her skirt was feeling loose around her waist.

Getting astride her bike to cycle on to the next lock, she looked back enviously at Gloria, who had been wearing trousers ever since they had met her, but somehow Elizabeth and Maggie couldn't quite bring themselves to dress like men. It seemed so unladylike, Elizabeth had said, and hearing her own grandmother's shocked reaction in her head, Maggie had agreed, but now she began to wonder whether it was time to give in.

By the time they got to Hemel Hempstead, she'd shared her radical thoughts with Elizabeth, who, rather than looking scandalised, was also contemplating the joy of being able to jump ashore without the restrictions of a straight or A-line skirt.

Gloria took the advantage.

''Bout time you saw sense. OK, you two, we're off to find a jumble sale. We'll get you kitted out, then you'll look like real boaters.'

An hour later, the three girls were rifling through piles of old clothes at the Red Cross jumble sale in the village hall at the familiar Boxmoor. It was raising money for the troops so they all felt they were helping the cause. As they picked out bits of material or an odd jumper or skirt, dodging the unruly hordes of evacuee children who still hadn't returned home, they held them against themselves to see what the others thought. Gloria found an old woolly hat and plonked it on her head.

'Perfect,' she said in delight. 'This'll stop my head getting cold at night in the winter.'

Elizabeth said dubiously, 'I've found some.' She held up some corduroy trousers that had obviously belonged to a man. 'Maybe I should buy these, if I'm actually going to wear this sort of thing.'

It made the other two laugh to think of their posh friend cavorting around in a pair of men's trousers.

'I wonder what the country club would say,' Maggie chuckled, but Elizabeth was already on her way to pay the lady in the pink cardigan by the door.

'Right, Maggie, just you now,' Gloria told her, steering her towards some overalls.

Walking back to the boat, their purchases under their arms, the girls were in high spirits.

'Nothing like a good shopping trip to lighten the soul,' Elizabeth said, and the other two agreed.

* * *

Dressed in their new trousers, Maggie and Elizabeth felt liberated. They had both grown up living the lives they were expected to live but in recent years, each of them had broken rules. Maggie looked at the others that night over tea and decided now was the time.

'I had an affair with a married man,' she blurted out.

She waited for their shocked reactions, but they just glanced at each other and then Elizabeth nodded.

'We guessed as much,' she said, not pausing eating. 'Well, we guessed some of it, we just didn't know he was married.

'Oh!' Maggie exclaimed. 'Umm . . . how . . . how did you know?'

Elizabeth summed it up in her usual forthright manner. 'Well, you're obviously not a virgin.'

'What? How can you tell?' said Maggie, horrified, looking down at herself as if she had it emblazoned on her next to her Inland Waterways badge.

'Oh, little things, like the way you fold your arms across you whenever you talk about Harry in case somehow your body gives it away.'

'Come on, Mags,' Gloria said, 'we're fed up trying to work it out for ourselves, spill the beans. You know you can trust us.'

It was strange to feel at such ease in a tiny cabin with two girls Maggie would never have met if it hadn't been for the war.

'You're right;' she gave in., 'I do. Even if Elizabeth did sell Lenny down the river,' she smiled. 'I think we've been through so much together, if we don't have faith in each other, who can we trust?'

And, bit by bit, the story came out.

Halfway through, when she got to the part about meeting Roger, Gloria decided they needed another cup of tea and put the kettle on. She sat down again for the second instalment; this was better than her stories in *People's Friend*.

Instead of outright condemnation, the end of the story was greeted with an understanding nod from both of them.

'Sounds to me like he's the one who's at fault, not you,' Gloria said, going pink at how she was part glad Will was proving to be such a gentleman and part disappointed. 'He sounds like a complete cad.'

'He told me he loved me; that we'd get married,' Maggie moaned. 'I didn't know he was already married. How could I have been so stupid, so naïve?'

'It's not unusual, you know, Mags,' Elizabeth said, using her shortened name for the first time. 'A man in power often uses it to his own ends and you shouldn't feel bad. You were his pupil and young, what, about eighteen?'

Maggie nodded.

'Well, that just sums up what sort of a swine he is. You were used, Maggie, completely used. You were simply caught up in the words you longed to hear.'

They waited for a reply from Maggie, but it was a long time before she could utter, 'You don't think I'm a fallen woman then?'

Gloria giggled and pushed her off the bed.

'A bit wobbly maybe, but fallen, nah.'

'But Harry's a padre,' she said feebly.

'Huh! I just saw a very dishy young man,' Gloria said, her eyes sparkling. 'Didn't know God made them like that.'

'Hmm, sounds like he is dishy from your description, Gloria,' Elizabeth agreed with a grin. 'But don't worry, Maggie, he'll get over it, they always do. They have to; they need us. And you are such a catch, Maggie. I mean look at you: perfectly manicured nails, beautiful, neat hair and did I mention, wearing the latest fashions?'

The three of them started to laugh.

That night, as Maggie lay down on her bunk, she listened to the regular breathing of Gloria. Telling the whole story about Roger first, and then how she was beginning to feel about Harry, had worn her out. She thought back to the young girl who had gone off to college so innocently with so many aspirations. There were parts of her that couldn't believe she was the same person who had put on a cheap ring to try to convince the man on the desk at the hotel in the centre of Manchester that she and Roger were married. Now, she realised, he couldn't have cared less as long as Roger paid the money, and that she was just one of a trail of young girls who crept up the faded maroon carpet on the stairs to a seedy hotel room with some man who had lied to get them there.

Elizabeth's wrong, Harry will never be able to look at me again, she thought, a sob suddenly emerging from her throat. It made Gloria stir.

Stuffing the edge of her blanket in her mouth, Maggie rocked backwards and forwards while Gloria settled again. Desperate to distract herself, Maggie thought back to Mrs Harper's revelation about her grandmother. With the innocence of a child, she'd never questioned her grandparents' relationship, but now a scene came back to her. She must have been about twelve, she thought.

Her grandfather had been sitting in his chair, drinking his cocoa when news had come on the wireless about former soldiers who, unable to cope with civvy street, had been involved in crime. She'd known he was thinking about her father when he jumped to his feet, upsetting the cup in anger. His face contorted as he shouted at the wireless that they were all the 'lily-livered cowards' and deserved to be locked away forever. Instead of reacting verbally, she'd watched as her grandmother's face froze and the look she gave her husband was one of pure hatred. Taking herself out of the room, Maggie had heard her muttering something about 'And so should those who can't forgive.'

At the time, Maggie had taken no notice and had simply gone to get a cloth to mop up the cocoa, but now she recalled that it had been several days before her granny was able to look at her husband and talk to him about anything more intimate than the fact that his tea was on the table.

She shook her head in disbelief; how could she have missed the atmosphere between them? Too busy examining whether it had been her fault that her father had left, she now wondered how happy her granny had been married to a man who was unable to show affection.

It was three o'clock in the morning before an exhausted Maggie fell asleep.

*　*　*

'She was looking for a father figure,' Elizabeth told Gloria the next morning when they went to get some supplies.

Gloria jerked round in surprise. That had never occurred to her.

Elizabeth elucidated. 'Don't you see, Gloria? She's spent her whole life feeling like her father left because of something she'd done and when an older man like Roger came along, all she wanted to do was please him.'

'Well, she certainly did that,' Gloria said with a grin. 'Who'd have thought our Maggie had it in her? And then to fall for a man of God, well, that puts the cherry on the cake.'

Elizabeth tutted. 'Come on, Gloria, don't tell me you haven't fallen for Will? It shines out of your eyes. You know as well as I do how powerful passion can be.'

Both girls fell silent. Elizabeth was thinking of when she met her own husband, Christopher. He'd been so handsome it hadn't taken her long to climb into his bed, not even knowing how babies were conceived. She soon found out, though, when Michael was born nine months later, just seven months after a hasty wedding. Gloria, too, had gone quiet as she thought back to how it had been Will who had insisted on separate rooms when they met up in London and how she had sulked when he wouldn't let her in his bedroom. She was beginning to feel deeply for Will, but her pragmatism made her wonder whether they could ever be a match. The more he talked about his family's large house in the country and their flat in Mayfair, the more her own family, with their back scullery, their dirty fingernails from working the cut and her father's tendency to sup too many ales in the pub, seemed from a different universe. She wondered whether his insistence on keeping her at arm's length was because he knew that too.

A shuffling noise behind them in the queue for the butcher's made them both look up.

'Hello, Joe,' Gloria said cheerfully, welcoming the opportunity to brush her worries about Will under the carpet.

'How are you?' Elizabeth said kindly. She liked this young lad and felt irritated that he was so cowed by his father.

'All right, s'pose,' Joe replied, not looking up from his feet.

'Who's next?' the butcher called from behind the counter.

The girls were next in the queue, but Joe was looking nervously back towards the canal. His father would be pacing up and down the towpath and he knew he would be for it if he was much longer.

'You go in front of us,' Gloria said generously, and Elizabeth reached back to take his arm and push him forward.

Joe looked grateful but then flummoxed as he glanced at the bits of paper sticking up from the scarce meat on the shelves in front of him and Elizabeth stepped up next to him.

'What about a nice bit of scrag end for tonight?'

He nodded. Yes, that was what his mum had asked for, but he couldn't tell one bit of meat from another and the names on them were a jumble.

Gloria was about to speak but Elizabeth shook her head and let Joe mutter out his order to the butcher before hurrying off.

A couple of lambs' hearts wrapped in brown paper bought for their own tea, Gloria and Elizabeth made their way back to the boat.

'He can't read, can he?' Gloria said.

'No, I don't think he can. Mind you, his mother and father can't either. I've seen them peering at signs trying to work out the shapes. Right, I know someone who can help with this.'

Once they got back on board, Elizabeth announced, 'Maggie, we think you should teach Joe to read.'

Maggie was puzzled until the girls patiently explained to her how Joe had struggled in the butcher's.

'We thought it might make his father respect him,' Gloria told her. 'I think he knows his ABC, I've seen him pointing to letters and trying to work them out, but he can't read words, I'm sure of it.'

Maggie's face lit up and she felt a little excited shiver creep up her spine. It had been so long since she had used her teaching skills and anything that might help Joe stand up to his father could only be a good thing.

'But how am I going to do it without his father knowing?' she asked.

While the lambs' hearts cooked on the stove, the three put their heads together to think of a way.

'I think we try to follow them up the cut and then talk to Joe at locks,' Elizabeth said. 'I'm sure he'll be very happy to keep a secret from his dad.'

Delighted to have something else to think about other than Roger and Harry, Maggie started by writing out some letters for Joe to copy.

'Tomorrow, while you two get ready to go, I'm just going to nip back to that church hall where the jumble sale was,' she said, 'I'm sure I saw some children's books there. They might not have sold them all.'

* * *

Maggie spent the next few evenings gathering reading tools, writing out simple exercises and keeping a sharp eye on the Spencers' two boats in front. It wasn't long before they reached Marsworth and Maggie raced ahead to try to catch Joe, who was setting up the very lock where Maggie had nearly sunk the boat so many months before. She glared at it but then called out, 'Joe, Joe, wait for me.'

A slow smile spread across the lad's face. The fact that the two older girls were so close to Gloria made him anxious to please them, and he'd seen them glowering at his father and the way he shouted at his wife and son. In fact, he thought incredulously, they didn't seem frightened of his dad at all.

'You know your alphabet, do you, Joe?' Maggie said bluntly, puffing as she ran to catch him up.

He was taken aback but nodded proudly.

'Would you like to learn to read and write properly?'

Joe drew in a sharp breath. As things stood, the chances of him ever escaping his father's clutches were slim but if he could read, he thought, could the future be different for him? 'More than anything,' he blurted out.

Maggie delved into her pocket and drew out some papers she'd folded up in there. Hearing the chug of the engines approaching behind them, she stuffed them in Joe's hands and said in a quiet voice, 'I've done drawings, so you'll understand the words. Practise them when your dad isn't watching and see how you get on. And here's a couple of children's books too. I suggest you keep them hidden from your father.'

Joe smiled conspiratorially and put the books and the paper into his overalls before turning back to use the windlass on the lock gates, his face aflame with excitement.

Chapter 23

After that, every time Joe had a spare minute, he would take himself off and study the books and the pieces of paper. To begin with, they were just a jumble of lines but then, looking across at the drawings, he began to mouth the sounds. Every time the little convoy reached a lock, it was Maggie who raced ahead to join Joe while they waited for them to fill or empty and go through the sheets of paper he'd been practising on. With regular help, Maggie was surprised that the lad really did have a good brain and was working hard to use it. On the day that Joe, while pretending to service *Buffalo*'s engine, realised the letters CAT actually described the picture that was opposite it, he whooped with joy, making his mother call down to him to see if he was all right.

'I'm fine, Ma, just caught a rat.'

A woman who hated the four-legged vermin that plagued the canals, his mother was so pleased she served her son an extra potato at teatime.

'What's 'e getting that for?' Jake demanded.

''E caught a rat today,' Dolly said with a smile.

'Oh, bloody 'ell, first time 'e's done anythin' useful all week. M'be he needs remindin' of 'is place around 'ere.'

Joe looked with bitter dislike towards his father but then lowered his head quickly when he saw him reach for his belt.

'Joe, go and clean out the mud box,' his mum said quickly.

Joe didn't have to be told twice and he fled back to the engine room, stuffing the potato in his mouth as he went. It was a job he hated, but tonight it meant he could close the door onto the engine room behind him and while he poked around to clean the series of holes in the intake on the hull, he used the time to mouth the letters he was obsessed with learning. A young man who had been told he was useless all his life, Joe had no idea he was actually an expert in fixing engines, maintaining the water and outflow pipes and making sure everything worked on the boat, but learning to read and write was already making him stand a bit taller.

Dolly passed over her own potato to her husband and looked thoughtfully towards the engine room; she was also noticing a difference in Joe, and it made her heart leap to see him looking more like the good-looking young man he was. Listening to Jake grunt as he slurped his tea made her sigh and turn away. She would do anything to help Joe escape this life.

* * *

Harry felt his foot squelch beneath him in the mud. He pulled at his boot but knew it was stuck. An arm came from behind and yanked him backwards and the foot gave a sucking noise as it was released.

'Don't you worry, Padre, we've got your back – or in this case, your foot,' a voice said.

He glanced around to look gratefully at the young soldier who was still holding on to his arm and grinned.

'I know, but it's my boot I'm worried about!' He gave a weak laugh. All around him, the devastation of Sicily and the filthy uniforms of himself and the men around him made him shake his head in wonder. *Why on earth did he feel more at home here than anywhere else?*

As always, his thoughts turned to Maggie and he pictured her dirty fingernails, her unwashed hair and her mud-splattered clothes and his heart lurched; even that image made her look beautiful to him.

'Come on, Padre, you're going to have to get a move on, we need to bivouac soon,' the young man behind him said in an anxious voice. They were a moving target and needed to get to shelter soon. Since they had arrived on a choppy crossing to Sicily, the summer heat had been relentless, but a torrential downpour this morning had turned the dry, cracked earth into a quagmire. Harry glanced up at the skies, which were beginning to clear, and he couldn't decide whether he was relieved the rain had stopped or whether he was dreading the eighty-degree temperatures that would follow. They were on the Catania plain and the whole troop was being plagued by mosquitoes, which, ironically, seemed to be attracted by the compulsory mosquito repellent they had all been issued with. The Allies had taken Augusta but the advance to Catania had been slow and far too cautious for an impulsive man like Harry. He kept his complaints to himself but he couldn't understand why it should take what looked like being three weeks to get to the town of Catania. However that was the problem of being with the Seventh, he supposed – when you're trailing machine guns, progress was bound to be slow.

He looked up at Mount Etna, awed by its size.

'You've seen a few goings-on, here, haven't you?' he muttered to it.

Sicily was a place that made him nervous and not just because of the Germans, who could be around any corner. He'd already witnessed two fights involving knives between rival factions, who were more concerned about a feud with their neighbours than the hundreds of troops trailing through their villages. However, every now and again, he spotted a shrine with a few dried-up flowers and a statue of the Virgin Mary and the fact that everything stopped for mass on a Sunday indicated there was a huge heart beating throughout the country; he just wasn't sure he was going to have time to discover it. He turned to the young man behind him.

'You all right, soldier?'

A weak nod suggested Harry's skills as a padre might be needed so he dropped back to fall into line next to him.

'Tough going?' he asked.

'No, Padre, it's just . . .' The lad paused. Harry waited.

'Well, it's just my girlfriend, I think she's found someone else. She's joined the ATS you see, and her letters, well, they're all about this mechanic. I don't think she loves me anymore.' His head dropped.

Relationships were held together by a thread and a flimsy piece of writing paper in war and Harry knew how hard it was for these soldiers to hold on to the dream of a dimple-faced girl when there were so many miles between them. Those girls had their own problems at home – he was the first to appreciate that – and to remain faithful to a man they hadn't seen for four years was asking a great deal.

'Um, you know, you think everything's just as you left it at home, but, believe me, it isn't,' he said. 'The girls are having to do their bit and it's tough for them too.' The words sounded hollow even to him and he coughed in embarrassment before carrying on. 'This war's driving a wedge between everyone. But at least ENSA should put something on for us once we take Catania. They usually include some pretty girls.'

The Entertainments National Service Association, or ENSA as it was called, was a bit of a joke among the men. It was supposed to provide entertainment but, more often than not, the 'females' were men with their trouser legs rolled up and bits of cloth around their heads. But every now and again, some brave girls made the journey to the front line to sing or dance and it was always noticeable how morale lifted when they'd been.

The lad's face brightened. 'Yes, p'raps I should move on. I mean, I wasn't sure when I left. I was feeling a bit trapped, to be honest, Padre. You know, she wanted marriage and children and I'm not sure I'm ready for that.'

'No, maybe we all needed to grow up a bit,' Harry told him. 'She's now learned skills in the ATS she never expected and you, well, you won't be the same after all this. What's your name, Private?'

The soldier stopped and stood up straight. 'Private Ted Keyes. Thank you, Padre, you've really made me feel better,' and his march took on an almost jaunty speed.

Harry should have felt better himself but didn't. He had so many conflicting thoughts in his head. Unable to talk to God in the way he always used to, he was struggling with thinking at all. Most of the time, he decided it wasn't worth the effort so blocked out any reasonings or debate that plagued his mind, concentrating instead on simply putting one foot in front of another alongside the men, but that didn't stop his brain switching to a time in England.

He wasn't even sure whether Maggie knew he was abroad, but every time he thought of how her eyes reflected the colour of the sea on a summer's day, the next instant would be ruined by the sneering expression of that Roger. Harry was beginning to have some very un-religious thoughts about Maggie Carpenter and his nights were being plagued by passionate desire. As an Anglican padre, marriage was an option for him but somehow, he felt it should be a measured decision dictated by duty, not this heady compulsion that was engulfing him.

'You all right, Padre?' his friend and assigned carer, Paul, asked from behind. Paul Murphy was a private and had been at Harry's side since before Dunkirk. His freckled face nearly always had a grin on it and even in the more dire circumstances he would find some humour to lighten the men's gloom.

'Hmm? Oh yes, fine,' Harry replied.

Paul doubled his speed to catch up and walk alongside Harry.

'Oh yeah?' he said, 'still thinking about that girl back home? Had a falling-out?'

Harry gave a deep sigh. 'Sort of,' he admitted. 'She was seeing someone else, you see, before I met her, and I just can't let it go. I should write to her but, to be honest, Paul, I need to sort it out in my head first. Anyway, she won't want to hear from me in any case.'

Paul thought for a moment. 'This war has buggered everything up, oops, pardon my French,' he said, his jaunty smile suggesting he didn't want forgiveness at all.

Harry smiled and signalled for him to go on.

'Well, we all thought we knew how everything worked but now, I really think there's no going back. One of my sisters has gone to be a WAAF and from being a shy, wouldn't-say-boo-to-a-goose girl, I think she's, well, shall I say, found her feet, and has even been jitterbugging with GIs.'

Paul came from an Irish family in Liverpool and Harry had given up months ago trying to keep track of his numerous siblings.

'Hey, do you know,' Paul went on, 'I even heard some women are becoming pilots, delivering planes all over the country. I tell you, Padre, a man's world isn't safe anymore. These women are taking over, you mark my words.'

Before Harry could reply, they heard the drone of planes above and he yelled to the men in front of him, 'Take cover, at the double.'

As he crouched in a ditch, Harry covered his helmet with his hands. There was no time to shake any more, no time to feel the fear that Dunkirk had left him with when he first rejoined his unit in Egypt. A certain pride made him slowly nod his head in approval. He was finally one of the men again.

All he had to do now was to expel the visions of a certain Inland Waterways employee from his head and stay alive.

Chapter 24

Joe was running along the towpath towards the girls' boats, shouting.

Gloria was the first to emerge onto the counter deck, her fork still in her hand. She had been enjoying the spam fritters Maggie had prepared on the stove.

'What is it, Joe?' she called.

The other two came up behind her, Elizabeth daintily wiping her mouth with an almost clean handkerchief.

Joe's face was ashen. 'It's Da,' he spluttered. 'There's some'at wrong with 'im.'

The three girls ran towards him and then followed him quickly to the *Buffalo*. When they got there, they all paused, aware of the etiquette of entering someone else's boat without permission but Joe nodded frantically and gestured Elizabeth towards the cabin while the other two stayed on the small deck.

Elizabeth knocked on the side of the entrance, and called, 'May I come in?'

Dolly's reply was high-pitched and resonated with panic. 'Yes, yes, please.' E's gone all funny. I dunno what's up wiv 'im.'

Blinking in the gloom, Elizabeth saw Dolly leaning over her husband, trying to put a wet cloth on his forehead but he kept pushing it away with his left hand and grunting. The side of his face had fallen and his right arm was hanging uselessly at his side.

'What can we do?' Maggie asked from the hatch above. She and Gloria were staying out of the way; there certainly wasn't room for anyone else in the cabin below.

'We need some help,' Elizabeth said. 'If I'm not mistaken, he's had a stroke.'

'That's serious, isn't it?' Dolly asked fearfully.

'It's a sort of seizure, like an apoplexy,' Elizabeth said. Normally calm in all circumstances, the condition of the man in front of her made her frown with concern. There was obviously no money for a doctor, and she certainly wasn't qualified to deal with this.

At this point, Jake started making groaning noises and thrashing his left arm about.

Elizabeth pulled Dolly to one side.

I'm not sure but I think there's always a chance of another, bigger stroke coming along. If we don't get some help . . . well, he could die, Mrs Spencer.'

Dolly tipped her head to one side. The boat was their livelihood and without Jake, she didn't see how they would go on but there was a guilty moment when she thought how peaceful life would be without him. Then she patted her taut stomach. For better or worse, this baby needed a father and this boat needed him too.

She looked pleadingly up at Joe, who was peering anxiously from the hatch knowing his father would blame him for this, without a doubt. 'There's Sister Anne . . .' his mother said.

His face cleared. Everyone on the cut knew Sister Anne; she was the only medical help available to the people who worked the canal, and she would help first and worry about payment later.

'But, Ma, she's at Stoke Bruerne,' Joe said haltingly, realising that the distance of about ten miles would take him over two hours to travel.

'Borrow our bike,' Maggie said. 'Take it off the roof. It's old but it'll get you there.' Then she stopped. 'You can ride a bike, can't you?'

Jake was making noises like an angry bear. 'N . . . n . . . no use,' he said, attempting to shake his head. The scorn in the left-hand side of his face made Joe flinch for a moment but then he nodded with more confidence than he felt. He'd only once tried riding a bicycle, when they were moored up at Limehouse, and had ended up in the canal but when his mother's face looked so desperate, he knew he had to try. Any remaining doubts were dispelled by the look of pride that Gloria gave him and he took a leap onto the grassy bank. The next minute, he was purposefully wobbling along the towpath. He didn't care about rushing for help for his father, even though he knew that without him, they would struggle to survive, but he did care that Gloria believed he was a hero. That was enough.

Jake, meanwhile, was struggling to stand up but unable to do anything but drag his right foot, he was powerless, and he knew it, so sank back onto the bunk.

Maggie looked at Elizabeth for a signal as to what they should do next, but Elizabeth was concentrating on Dolly. She'd become very flushed and was leaning over the bunk, one hand holding onto the side wall of the boat.

'Are you all right, Dolly?' she asked, then she saw a wet trickle dripping from between Mrs Spencer's legs onto the wooden floor below.

'I think the baby's coming,' Elizabeth said, more calmly than she felt.

Dolly looked up. 'It can't, it ain't time yet.'

'Well, the baby doesn't seem to know that,' Elizabeth said, rolling up her sleeves as Dolly bent over double, groaning.

'We have to get her out of here. Come and give me a hand, Maggie. Gloria, you stay here with Mr Spencer.'

Dolly was about to protest but then groaned in pain again, making Elizabeth rush on.

'Maggie, go to *Florence* and get that clean sheet I washed today. It should be dry now. Lay it out on my bunk, she'll have to have the baby in there. And put some water on to boil. Gloria, there's nothing you can do for Jake at the moment except wait, but you can help me find some clean cloths.'

She sounded doubtful but then took in her surroundings for the first time. Joe lived in the butty boat behind, desperate to put some space between himself and his father but here, the brass on the walls shone, the little lace curtains that hid the pans were amazingly white and the stove was polished to perfection. Gloria pointed towards a small drawer under the drop-down table.

'Yes,' huffed Mrs Spencer, 'that's where we're gonna put the little 'un but there's my ma's best linen in it at t' moment.'

Elizabeth opened the drawer and gasped. She couldn't believe the shallow box was destined to be a 'cot' for a baby and once again, she wondered at the secret world of these canal dwellers. The linen was beautifully folded and neatly piled. She hesitated, hardly daring to use these precious items that were obviously Dolly's treasured possessions but then Dolly panted: 'Yes, yes, them. They'll wash up . . . after.' Elizabeth helped the stricken woman to her feet and then Gloria helped push Mrs Spencer up the steps of *Buffalo*, saying, 'You'll both be fine, your man's in good hands and you, well, Elizabeth is good at this sort of thing.' She looked across at the woman they were all relying on and thought to herself, *Well, I hope she knows what she's doing 'cos Mags and I haven't got a clue.*

Dolly's face was screwed up with pain but she managed to stutter, 'I've . . . lost two already . . . don't let me lose this 'un . . . please, miss.'

'It's Elizabeth and no, Mrs Spencer, you're going to do just fine, we're all here to help you.'

Once on the *Florence*, Maggie was standing uselessly to one side, so Elizabeth said, 'Here, Maggie, you massage her feet, they're a bit swollen.' At this Elizabeth frowned. She had only once helped the local doctor when her own cook was giving birth, but she knew that swollen ankles were not a good sign. Above all, she now wished she'd stood her ground when her husband had talked her out of training as a nurse. She now knew it was all she'd ever wanted and had realised that if she'd been able to take her qualifications, she'd never have become bored enough to get involved with gambling, but pushing such thoughts out of her mind, she again concentrated on the tiny cabin on the Grand Union Canal.

'Now we've got more room,' Elizabeth said, 'let's see if we can make you a bit more comfortable.'

Time seemed to tick by slowly, but the contractions were coming faster and faster. Elizabeth suspected that Dolly wasn't dilating as quickly as she should.

Gloria's head appeared in the hatch.

'Jake's sleeping, I think. I did check and he is breathing. I didn't know if you still needed it, but I've boiled up some more water.'

'Good,' Elizabeth said, then paused. She didn't like to suggest she should clean up the private parts of this woman she hardly knew but Dolly was already hitching up her skirts. She'd done this before.

Smiling gratefully at her, Elizabeth turned to Gloria. 'Come here behind her and rub her back,' Elizabeth said.

Glad to have something to do, Gloria edged her way around the side of the cabin to perch behind Dolly.

'That's it, now you keep massaging her ankles and legs, Maggie.'

The contractions were coming every three minutes and Elizabeth glanced around the limited space. She had no idea how she was going to manoeuvre round to deliver this baby but then Dolly took the decision for her.

'I need to crouch, it's coming,' she said, her face contorted with pain.

The three girls moved out of the way to allow Dolly to shuffle off the bed and crouch on the floor. Elizabeth looked with a sigh of relief at the polished floor she'd mopped only that morning. Carefully placing one of the clean sheets down under the doubled-up woman, she got down as low as she could to see what was happening.

It was at this point that the door flung open and a woman with a round, flushed face bustled in. She had a crisp white headdress on and white cuffs.

'Right, out, you lot, I'll take over now.'

'My man?' Dolly spluttered between contractions.

'There's nothing I can do,' the nurse told her, 'he won't let me near him and to be honest, Mrs Spencer, it's just a matter of time; he may improve . . .' She shook her head.

Joe was hovering at the top of the companionway, but his face blushed with pride when Gloria rushed up to give him a hug. He clung on as long as he dared but then moved back to let the other two women out.

'Wait a minute,' Sister Anne said, 'yes, you, the one who was on the floor, come back and give me a hand. Looks like this one's coming out back to front.'

Maggie closed the door behind Elizabeth as she went back down and left the cabin to the experts. She'd seen the look of relief on Elizabeth's face at the sight of Sister Anne and knew that her skills had reached their limit.

Standing at the end of the nearby lane was the bread van and its driver, a man in a cloth cap. He'd taken out the bike from the back and was standing holding it.

'What about your da?' he asked Joe.

'He wudna let her near 'im; he 'ates anyone in uniform so she went straight on to see my ma.'

'She gonna be all right?'

'Yeah, thanks to yer letting us hitch a lift, I think she might be,' Joe said, taking the bike and giving the man a warm handshake.

'Well, anything for Sister Anne. She's a good 'un. I'll be off then, got me deliveries to make and I'm a bit behin' now but glad I could 'elp.' He looked with affection at Joe. 'You know, I've always liked you, Joe, you just need to stop letting that da of yours bully you. You're a fine lad.'

Joe was so embarrassed he almost stumbled but then he heard a baby's cry. Maggie and Gloria gathered in delight and put their arms around him, which left him speechless. His father certainly never gave him any affection and with her husband watching every move, his ma only ever dared to brush her arm against his. Between Gloria's earlier hug and now this, he was feeling valued for the first time in his life.

The canal was as busy as ever with boats and one of them was being driven by a man of about Jake's age, wearing the obligatory red neckerchief and cord trousers. He shouted over to the scene on the towpath, 'One girl not 'nuff for yer, young Joe Spencer. Do yer da know 'bout this?'

Joe stepped back as if stung but then the man chuckled. 'Good on yer, lad. 'Bout time yer stood up for yerself.'

Gloria glanced across at Joe, noticing his clear blue eyes for the first time. When he stood up straight, he was much taller than she'd thought.

'He's right, you know, Joe. You're a man now. And, if your da's going to be, well, different, you're going to have to take the lead. Your ma's going to need you.'

'Won't 'e get better?' Joe said, hope rising in his voice.

Maggie butted in. 'Well, I think a stroke can take a long time for someone to get over, if they ever do.'

Joe pulled his shoulders back. This could be the miracle he'd been praying for.

Elizabeth emerged from the cabin brushing her hair out of her eyes. She looked flushed and exhausted but exhilarated.

'It's a boy and your mum's going to be all right,' she said to Joe, and then vanished back inside.

Joe stared at the space left on the stern by Elizabeth and at that moment swore that his whole life would be dedicated to protecting his little brother and that no bully of a father was going to get within a belt's buckle of him.

Chapter 25

The days went by in a haze of loading, unloading, maintaining the boats the three week schedules seemed to merge. One night on the stretch before Watford, Maggie was deep in thought. On evenings like this, Maggie could walk along the towpath and forget the dramas that played out on the waterways or even that there was a war going on all over the world. It gave her hope, and she paused to appreciate how the water seemed to gleam in the twilight sunshine, masking its murky depths while the chug of the boats passing was a magical symphony that harmonised with the sounds of ducks in the reeds and birds in the trees.

She had never thought she would find such peace after the turmoil that had made her join the Inland Waterways. If only she and Harry hadn't bumped into Roger that day, she thought regretfully.

'No,' she said out loud, 'if only I hadn't been dazzled by that deceitful, lying toad. How could I have been so naïve?'

Letting out a deep sigh, the familiar shame consumed her and then a deep sense of loss for what she could have found with Harry.

She'd tried so many times to put her feelings for him into a letter but then she remembered his shattered expression and screwed the paper up to burn in the fire. The fact that no letters came from him supported her opinion that Harry Moore wanted no more to do with her.

She remembered every feature of his face and the thought of the touch of his hand still burned her skin. During the day, she obliterated the memory of lying in that bed in a Piccadilly hotel, but at night, in her dreams, when the person next to her was Harry, she experienced a completely different sensation and she would wake tingling with desire.

Scuffing her feet on the grass beneath her in despair, she headed into the dark shadows of a bridge and almost fell over something.

It was a pair of legs, clad in torn trousers and spattered with mud. Maggie screamed and the figure jumped to its feet. She focused and then yelped, 'Lenny! Is it really you?'

The filthy face of the young soldier was even more gaunt than she remembered. In the gloom, the whites of his eyes shone out and she recognised the same panic he'd had when they rescued him from the canal.

'What the hell are you doing here?' she demanded.

He grabbed hold of her arm and pulled her into the arch of the bridge, checking on both sides to see if there was anyone there.

'Oh, thank God it's you. Where's the boat? Where are the others? I've been hiding out here for days in the hope you'd come past. I'd almost given up.'

Knowing that each trip between London and Birmingham took three weeks, Maggie wondered how long he had been waiting for them.

'But how? What?' she started and then, gathering her wits, looked back along the direction she had come. She'd walked further than she'd intended and now she had to think how she was going to get Lenny back to safety without being seen.

Coming so soon on the back of the crisis with the Spencers, she couldn't help but think of the other girls they'd met at

Stoke Bruerne. Their journeys seemed to be such a normal mix of loading, unloading and dealing with bad weather and a lack of soap while the *Nancy May* was turning out to be a magnet for drama, and she wondered what on earth they'd all done to deserve it.

Looking at Lenny's expectant face, it was obvious now was not the time for introspection and she went to the edge of the bridge to peer down the cut. It was empty.

'OK, follow me, but make it fast,' she told him and the pair of them started to run along the towpath, Lenny tripping up every now and again.

Maggie had no idea when he had last eaten or whether he was in a fit state to run but she couldn't stop to ask him and, instead, increased her pace.

'Oh, there you are,' Elizabeth's voice called out when she heard the footsteps running past *Florence*. 'I was thinking we might have potatoes and spam for tea, what do you think? I'll bring them over.'

Maggie paused to lean over the hatch and whisper, 'You'd better bring some extras, we have a guest.'

She carried on quickly towards the *Nancy May* in front leaving Elizabeth to emerge then gasp and clasp her hand to her mouth at the familiar figure of Lenny. She almost tumbled back down the steps to grab the food.

Gloria was even more shocked.

'What the bloody 'ell are you doing here?' she screamed.

Then, noting the state of his clothes and dirty appearance, her look turned to one of concern.

'Oh my God, Lenny, what's happened to you?'

Maggie interrupted. 'I think he needs a cup of tea and something to eat. He looks on the point of collapse.'

Elizabeth had come up from behind, taken one look at the boy and immediately climbed down next to him to feel all around his face and examine his arms. Pushing up his tattered sleeves, she breathed in sharply. There were bruises all over him.

'But you're hurt' she said gently.

Lenny started to weep, and she put her arm softly around him, ignoring the wince as she touched him.

Gloria handed him a mug of tea and a slice of bread with Marmite on, which he munched ravenously.

A look of unease passed between the three girls. They didn't want to admit that Lenny's sudden departure had lifted a cloud of anxiety and now, here he was, back with them. What on earth were they going to do?

Pushing that thought to the back of their minds, their first priority was to get him cleaned up, put some ointment on those bruises and get some food in him, so they crammed into the tiny space and held their tongues.

Questions could wait.

* * *

Harry crumpled up yet another letter and threw it into the bin. It was the fourth one he'd written to Maggie that night and he was strangely finding it much harder than the 'if I die' letters he'd just written to his parents and uncle for the lieutenant colonel to store away until necessary.

Everyone around him had their heads bent over the flimsy paper that served as their stationery. Some were sobbing softly; others had their knuckles clenched and the rest had that blank expression that accompanied this regular exercise the night before a battle.

None of them ever knew how to put a lifetime of advice, love or support into letters that would be read weeks after they had been killed. Some were struggling with regret, realising this was their last chance to salve their consciences for mistakes made, words said in anger, or a love not returned. Those with children found it especially hard and Harry was aware it was up to him to give a good example to them all.

He put his own letter to one side and left it to the fates – or maybe a higher power – to help him survive and one day be able to say what he needed to, to her face. There certainly wasn't enough space on the single sheet of paper he had left in his pack to explain his remorse, his guilt and, above all, his love. Moving around the tent, Harry stopped to put a hand on a soldier's shoulder here, give an encouraging smile there and generally try to be a reassuring figure amidst the despair and dread that was hovering over every single soldier.

When he got to Paul, he found him leaning forward on a stool, his head in his hands. It was so unlike his friend to give in to feelings of gloom that Harry pulled up a chair next to him.

'You OK, Paul?'

'Yep, sure, I mean, we all saw the bodies of the parachutists at Primosole Bridge in July and then the way the River Simeto turned red with the blood of the poor chaps from the Ninth but yeah, I'm fine.'

Harry searched for words that would help and eventually, simply laid his hand over Paul's and gave it a squeeze.

'It's all right for you, Padre,' Paul said with uncharacteristic bitterness, 'you've got those Pearly Gates to welcome you. You'll be all right.'

Paul got up and went out to go to the latrines, leaving Harry to sink down on the stool where his friend had been.

'If only I had, Paul, if only I had,' he said to himself.

Since arriving in Sicily, Harry had taken any opportunity he could to provide the men with an ad-hoc church service – anything to give them comfort and support. He'd made an altar out of empty paraffin cans, a sick-bay bunk and even a pile of rough blankets that he propped the Bible on top of, but he felt he was letting everyone down because the words he was saying sounded empty to him. The advance had been so slow, so costly in lives and unbelievably dispiriting, especially because of the poverty, dirt, dung heaps and disease. Everywhere they went, starving locals pestered the troops for food, which they were forbidden to give out. He'd witnessed food riots in the streets and, like many of his fellow soldiers, he'd found it difficult to follow the advice given in the 'New Country' guidelines – that the Italians were known for their hot tempers and it was advisable not to engage with them but rather to offer them a smile to convince them how much nicer the Allies were than the bad-tempered Nazis. However, he found it difficult to smile when he was being yelled at by a distraught mother thrusting an emaciated child in his face. He thought of the medic he'd met last week who'd told him how the fraught atmosphere was getting through to the commanders too and how General Patton had had no sympathy with a wounded carpet-layer from Indiana who'd told him he couldn't take it anymore. Any weakness was being stamped on ferociously but events like that did nothing to improve morale among the troops, Harry thought. The commanders seemed desperate, the people were desperate and the countryside was in a desperate state. He sighed: it would take more than Saint Peter to sort it all out and it was at times like this that he missed praying the most.

Outside, he found Paul having a cigarette. His face brightened with an embarrassed smile when he saw Harry.

'Sorry, Padre, I just needed some fresh air,' he said, and he handed Harry a battered packet of Woodbines. 'Here you go, a ciggie always makes you feel better.'

They stood side by side, smoking the untipped cigarettes.

'These been in a battle?' Harry laughed, turning the little squashed box over in his hand.

'Yep, been through it all with me, Harry. They're battle-scarred treasures, them are.'

'Well, they're certainly doing the job,' Harry said, taking a deep inhale and beginning to feel calmer.

Paul looked sideways at him. 'You're not yourself, are you? You've not been the same since yous come back.'

Harry hadn't spoken to anyone about his crisis of faith but standing there, between the latrines and the men's quarters, he felt an enormous need to unburden himself to the man who washed his clothes, made sure he was fed and tended to his most personal needs.

As if sensing his friend's hesitation, Paul piped up, 'That girl? Or is it God?'

'It's both,' Harry sighed. He turned towards Paul and stubbed out his cigarette, keeping the dog-end for later.

'I think I've fallen in love with Maggie and out of love with God.'

Paul gave a chuckle. 'Oh, nothing serious then?'

Harry gave him a friendly shove and his mouth turned upwards into a reluctant grin. Paul always cheered him up.

The two men turned to look at the landscape in front of them, preferring to have deep discussions shoulder to shoulder rather than face to face.

'Maggie's amazing,' Harry started. 'She's a wonderful mix of vulnerability and strength and what she's doing is just incredible.'

Paul inwardly chuckled at his friend's obvious enthusiasm. 'Yeah, my missus is making ammunition. She works all day in a factory and then picks the kids up from her mam and does everything else in the 'ouse.' To think, I used to tell 'er I didn't like 'er working. Well, it seemed wrong that a man couldn't support 'is family, but, bloody 'ell, Padre, these women are certainly showing us. I'm not sure they'll need us back,' he added gloomily.

'Your Doris adores you,' Harry said, 'those letters you showed me prove that. Yes, she's doing what needs to be done, but you mark my words, she'll be waiting at the door for you with her arms open wide.'

'Maybe,' he said, then: 'Oh, hang on, I know your game – we're supposed to be talking about you. Typical bloody padre, always having to give everyone else advice.' He changed to a sonorous tone and said, stroking his chin, 'OK, now tell me your problems, young man.'

It made Harry laugh but then he started to talk, haltingly to begin with, but then the words came out like a torrent. He told Paul how he'd started to worry whether his faith was strong enough when he came back from Dunkirk. He couldn't understand how a benevolent God could inflict such misery.

'When I went home to help Uncle Peter, all the women in the parish seemed to be worried about was what flowers they could muster to put on the altar. I mean, honestly, Paul, would any God care?' His voice exploded into anger. 'People have no idea what's going on out here. Just look around us.'

As always before a major battle, there was an unnatural stillness in the camp that descended like an invisible mist. It seemed to hang in the air above the mix of mud and dust while men in various states of undress silently washed in small bowls, shaved or made their way back from the latrines. Some were stripping and cleaning their guns with bandages wrapped around their heads or limbs, others had bloodied uniforms they were trying to scrub clean.

'Yeah.' Paul nodded. 'But yer know, those women in Didsbury, they're too old to go to war, but if they think a few flowers can 'elp their men, then they'll look for the best blooms they can and who'd blame 'em? And I agree, we're a motley crew but yer know what, Padre, I'd rather have any of these men by me side tomorrow than anyone else in the 'ole world. And if God has got any sense at all, He'll be there too.'

A smile slowly spread across his face and Paul added, 'And all right, if yous behaves as well, you can come too.'

'Well, the pub's closed so, yep, I may as well turn up.' Harry gave a reluctant grin.

Chapter 26

Lenny's appetite hadn't diminished and Gloria had twice checked the rations wondering how long they could feed an extra mouth. He was tucking into a cabbage sandwich in the cabin while Maggie was steering and Elizabeth was on the butty boat. Gloria sat opposite Lenny. She'd been primed to find out the full story.

'So, what happened to you after you left with that man?' she asked.

Lenny stopped mid-bite. 'Umm, I don't want to say.'

'Well, that's tough, 'cos we're not looking after you and feeding you until we get some answers.'

The conversation was interrupted by Maggie's shout of 'Locks ahead' and Gloria gave a disgruntled sigh and went up on deck to jump ashore.

Lenny heaved a sigh of relief believing he had escaped the interrogation but then he heard Maggie's voice from above, her body moving around the tiller to expertly manoeuvre the boat into the narrow lock.

'Go on, Lenny, you carry on, I can listen while I get us in here.'

He gave in. Somehow it was easier to talk to an empty cabin.

'Well, I was taken in a van to a warehouse somewhere, I've no idea where. They showed me a mattress in a back room and told me that was where I'd be staying. They gave me some food; it wasn't bad actually and I thought I was going to be all right. But then, the next morning, they sent me on my first job.'

His voice had gone quieter and Maggie had to lean in to hear him over the gush of water.

'What was that job?' she called down.

Lenny faltered. He didn't know how to tell these girls, especially the one who'd owed the boss money. She'd been so sure he'd be safe if he went with her friend.

'I'm waiting,' Maggie said from above.

'I was sent with Arthur; he wears a smart suit but honestly, he's a nasty piece of work. He "visited" a man in a pub who owed him money and . . .'

'Go on,' the patient voice drifted down the hatch.

'He shot him.'

Maggie gasped. 'What . . . dead?'

'Yeah, right there in front of me. I think it was to warn me not to mess with them as much as getting revenge on that poor chap. They knew they had me over a barrel; first, I was a deserter and second, I'd been party to a murder.

'After that, they became cocky, thinking I wouldn't dare try to escape, and I was taken as backup for when things got, well, difficult. That's where all these bruises have come from. I became the heavy.'

Maggie almost laughed. Lenny was such a slight figure, she couldn't believe anyone would feel threatened by him.

'I know you don't think I've got it in me, but you forget, Maggie, I'm a soldier, I'm trained to fight.'

'What were they dealing in?' she asked.

'Anything really – drugs, alcohol, ammunition and . . .' he hesitated '. . . gambling.'

The two of them became silent, thinking what a lucky escape Elizabeth had had. Maggie was beginning to learn more about the seedier side of life than she had ever wanted to know.

As the boat emerged from the lock, Lenny heard voices and, as instructed, tucked himself down to hide under the blankets while Maggie kept the nosey lock-keeper talking and well away from the boat.

Relieved at the break, Lenny breathed easier. Maggie would never know what it had cost him to recall the gruesome scenes he had witnessed. He was already shivering.

'And I thought Dunkirk was bad,' he whispered to himself.

* * *

Later that evening when they all, including Lenny, squashed into the *Nancy May*, Maggie filled the others in on what he'd told her.

'Your man in a suit. Did you say his name was Arthur, Lenny?' He nodded, and she continued, 'He's a murderer and now Lenny's seen it, he's an accessory.'

It was Elizabeth who was the first to recover her voice. 'So how did you escape, Lenny?'

'They were all out on a job but I'd been sick that day. Actually,' he said, quite proudly, 'what I did was I ate some raw potatoes on purpose. I remembered it had made our dog sick. Arthur said he didn't want the "hit" to think I was spewing up because I was scared, so they locked me in, but I'd found a crowbar hidden in an old oilcan they'd forgotten about and prised open the metal shutter and got out.'

His look of pride was cancelled out by the look of horror on the girls' faces.

'But that means . . .' Gloria started.

'They'll come after you,' Maggie finished.

'Lord, Lenny,' Elizabeth said, looking around the cabin as if Arthur and his friends could break in at any minute, 'they'll come straight here to look for us. They'll know we're the only people who will help you.'

Lenny suddenly paled. He hadn't thought of that. He jumped to his feet, banging his head on the roof.

'I'm so sorry, I'm so sorry, I'll go at once.'

Elizabeth took hold of his hand and pulled him back down onto the bunk.

'No, it won't make any difference; they'll still come looking for us. You go – carefully – onto *Florence* now and lock the door. Don't open it for anyone. We need to talk about this.'

Gloria went onto the counter at the back to check the coast was clear, cursing the bright summer evening light. When she nodded, Lenny quickly sprinted along the towpath towards *Florence*. Having watched his head disappear, Gloria went back inside.

'Anyone got any idea what we do now?'

* * *

The discussion took the girls into the early hours of the morning, and they still couldn't find an answer. Gloria thought they should make Lenny leave now and take his chances; Elizabeth felt a responsibility towards him as she was the one who had let Arthur take him in the first place, and Maggie just kept kicking herself that she hadn't talked to Harry earlier. If she had, Lenny might have been back in the army by now and certainly, the three girls wouldn't be in so much danger.

First thing in the morning, the girls started moving the boats up the canal towards Birmingham, feeling that every mile along the cut took them nearer to Arthur and his friends. The familiar territory of Cassiobury gave Maggie a pain in her chest, making her think longingly of that shared cup of tea there with Harry. It was as that feeling swept through her that she remembered that chaplain at the veterans' centre. He might know where Harry was, she thought with a jolt. No matter how he felt about her, Harry was the only one who could get Lenny out of this mess. She ran to find a telephone box, armed with coins from the kitty jar, looking right and left in fear.

On her way, she passed *Buffalo* and waved nervously to Joe, who was on the helm, looking more confident than she'd ever seen him. She knew she really should have asked how his father, mother and the new baby were but didn't have time.

The operator put her straight through to Broughton House and a kind man's voice answered with 'Hello, Reverend Phillips here.' Maggie started to gabble, remembering the name but wondering what Harry had told this person.

'Oh, I'm sorry to bother you, Reverend Phillips, but my name's Maggie Carpenter and I need to get in touch with Harry Moore urgently,' she said, and then embarrassed, added, 'I, um, haven't heard from him in some time but I need to know how to telephone him or write to him. I don't want to bother his uncle; he hasn't been well, you know, and Harry told me you might help me.'

'Yes, of course, I wish I could, Miss Carpenter but I'm sorry, Harry is back with his unit and well, he's abroad, that's all I know.'

'Oh, well, I'm sorry to have bothered you, thank you, good-bye.' Maggie was desperately disappointed.

'Please, wait,' the man on the other end said. 'I think I can help you if you're ringing for the reason Harry and I talked about.'

The pips started to beep and Maggie hurriedly put more pennies in. Was this stranger really offering her a lifeline?

'I've been wondering how you've been getting on, Miss Carpenter. I've heard a lot about you and I really think I can help. Now, maybe you start by telling me where you are and whether your friend is still with you.'

When Maggie breathed the word 'yes' in relief and told him the boats were heading north from Cassiobury, David took charge and outlined the plans he and Harry had prepared all those months ago.

'Can you hide him for a bit longer? I need to see the bishop in Birmingham next week and could drive a little further on to find you on the canal. I happen to have a spare curate's cassock that would, I'm sure, fit your friend very well.' He then told her he would take Lenny somewhere safe but that perhaps it would be better if Maggie didn't know where – just yet.

By the end of the conversation, Maggie felt a load had been lifted off her shoulders and then asked the question that had been plaguing her since she'd been told Harry was no longer in Didsbury.

'Um, Reverend Phillips, can you tell me, is Harry all right?'

David was delighted to hear the break in her voice. If there was anything he could do to help these two patch up their differences, then he would be delighted. And if, he thought, he could then reunite a father and daughter, then his prayers would have been answered.

He decided to go out on a limb. 'Yes, but he misses you. I know he does.'

Chapter 27

Joe Spencer watched Maggie hurrying back from the telephone box, noting that she looked more cheerful. He looked down the cut to see the back end of *Florence*. The last few weeks had been like a weight lifting from his life. The frail, weak man in the bunk below no longer had the power to dominate or threaten and even his mother was growing confident enough to ignore the grunts and jerked, threatening movements that came from her husband. To begin with, Dolly would dream he had got out of bed and was coming towards her with the boat hook, and she would wake in terror to see nothing but a man sleeping fitfully next to her, slobbering out of the side of his mouth. Gradually, as the strong muscles weakened, she suspected it was only anger that was keeping her husband alive. Sometimes, Jake caught her looking proudly in Joe's direction and would thump the table with his left hand and make a howling noise, but without being able to manifest that anger, his eyes were starting to dim. Up on deck, Joe read the signs on the side of the canal out loud, delightedly sounding out the words to himself. He was reading everything he could and, without his father's bullying, was openly reading the books from the girls on the *Nancy May*. He took a real delight in seeing his father's face go red with indignation and fury, knowing that his right hand could no longer reach to unbuckle his belt.

Mrs Spencer came to join her son up top and tied little Thomas to the cabin chimney, according to boating custom. Despite still being pale from the traumatic birth, she had a bright expression on her face and smiled with pleasure at Joe. Her fears that they wouldn't be able to manage without Jake had been unfounded as Joe had stepped up to somehow manage all the chores, the loading and the maintenance on his own.

'Is Da awake?' Joe asked but his mother was too busy looking ahead down the pound.

'Those girls look nervous.'

Joe followed her gaze. 'You're right, Ma, why do think that is?'

They looked at each other in realisation and a shadow of fear passed over both their faces.

'That deserter's back. You mark my words,' Dolly said. 'Those girls are in deep trouble.'

Joe's hand gripped the tiller, his knuckles white. He revved up the engine to catch the girls up. He didn't want to be out of calling distance.

* * *

David found Mrs Lewis in the kitchen, making Woolton pie for the patients' dinner. The recipe of vegetables and potato pastry suggested by Lord Woolton, the Minster of Food, had become staple fare on the Broughton House menu.

She'd lost weight, David noticed, and then spotted her son cleaning out the pantry behind her. There was no one else around.

'Mrs Lewis, can I have a word with you?' David said quietly.

She wiped her hands on her pinny and joined him by the door.

'We may be having another "guest" in Salford.' He said the word carefully, nodding meaningfully over at Alfie.

She looked shocked then worried. 'But surely that'll be dangerous for . . .' she said, jerking her head towards her son.

'Hopefully not and he's not coming here,' he said. 'You see, I've been thinking, your Alfie really can't stay here much longer in any case; Ken Perkin's dad is a policeman and now Ken's been moved here from the hospital, his family'll be visiting him and we can't risk him bumping into Alfie and asking questions. The flat where we've put Jim Carpenter has enough room for another couple of mattresses in it. It's dirt cheap because the man who owned it left it to us in his will. No one would know the pair of them are even there and maybe they could help each other.' He didn't mention that a distraction might help Jim as well and if, in time, he found out about Maggie's connection with their new 'guest' then maybe . . . A delighted chuckle started in his throat at his own ingenuity but catching sight of Mrs Lewis's frown, he checked it.

David's thoughts were racing but so were Mrs Lewis's.

'But they can't stay there forever,' she said. 'If Alfie can't work, then there's no money for them to live. I can't support him.'

'No, but I'm trying to pursue another option. The war isn't going well. Thousands are being killed. They're desperate for men and are beginning to take deserters back. There is a chance that the opportunity to re-enlist two trained soldiers might be too good for them to miss.'

'Yes, and Mr Churchill's going to join us for Woolton pie tonight,' Mrs Lewis scoffed.

'Well, we've made enquiries and it does look promising,' David said, his confidence wavering. 'We can only see.' He patted her arm and then said, 'That one does smell good, Mrs Lewis. Mr Churchill doesn't know what he's missing.'

'Oh, my pies' she yelped, 'they'll be burning.' She ran over to the ovens to grab a cloth. David left her to it but as he walked out, he glanced back to see Alfie looking over. His expression was a mixture of terror and hope.

* * *

Harry looked up and down his body; no blood, he thought with surprise. All around him, men were either scrambling to their feet or lying chillingly still. The air raid had seemed endless, and the strafing of the ground beneath had been purposeful and, in many cases, sickeningly accurate. Harry had dived into a ditch but some men, his beloved men from his unit, had not been quick enough and their red-stained bodies bore witness to their fate. Harry stood up shakily and almost fell over again. An arm grabbed his and he heard the wonderful Scouse tones of Paul reverberating in his ear.

'Come on, Padre, let's get yous out of here. You look like yer need a bit o' help.'

Harry shrugged off the arm and with more anger than he meant and said, 'No, no, I need to do something. Look at them . . .' He tried to stumble away from Paul, who grabbed hold of him again.

'No you don't.' He then shouted to the men with the red crosses on their arms. 'Hey, over 'ere.'

Harry looked down, wondering why his left foot wouldn't go where he wanted it to. Seeing a dark stain seeping over his newly polished army boot, he swayed, and a medic caught him, calling to his colleague for a stretcher. Harry started to speak. 'My men, I have to get to my m—' before he collapsed unconscious.

* * *

Paul spent the next two days constantly calling into the hurriedly erected field station to make sure the nursing staff were tending to his friend's wound, changing his dressing and getting fluids into him through a drip. He'd heard stories about medics having to use coconut water because they had run out of saline, so he was just checking the bag when a nursing sister marched over to him and demanded that he should leave her nurses to do their job and go back to winning the war.

Dismissed like a naughty schoolboy, Paul pouted, making a passing nurse laugh. She looked a bit like his sister, Sheila, so he gave a rueful grin and shuffled out of the ward. On his way out he spotted their commanding officer marching towards Harry's bed and he darted around the corner. After all, he was supposed to be getting ready for the next assault. It was all right for Harry, he thought, army padres were separate from any rank system but a private like him had to be much more careful.

Harry felt a warm hand on his shoulder and dragged his mind back from the deep space the morphine had immersed him in. Seeing the company commander, he tried to sit up, but the hand firmly pushed him back down again.

'If you don't want that foot to turn gangrenous, I suggest you stay put, Padre.' Lieutenant Colonel Colin Forsythe pulled up a chair and asked kindly, 'Now, how are you feeling? OK to talk?'

Wishing his head didn't feel like a bag of cottonwool, Harry tried to concentrate.

'Yes, I'm fine.'

The Lieutenant Colonel smiled at the false bravado he'd heard so many times from this man and swallowed down the lump that had arisen in his throat. A padre's role was such a difficult one. The men all knew they could call on Harry whenever they needed some guidance, support or simply someone to listen. He wondered who the man in front of him relied on; he hoped God was enough.

'Well, I do need to talk to you,' Forsythe said, 'doc says the infection should clear in a couple of days but you're not going to be able to march on with us. You're going to have to grab some transport when you're signed off and catch us up. Shame though, these lads are going to miss you.' He smiled.

'How many did we lose?' Harry asked.

'Too many,' was the muttered response.

'We need to get some more men from somewhere but, to be honest, Harry, we've conscripted everyone who's capable of holding a gun.'

In his drugged state, Harry vaguely knew there was something he needed to say. He frowned and then it came to him. He wriggled to lean up a little.

'Deserters, Lieutenant Colonel, we need to get them back in the field.'

A soldier of many campaigns, Forsythe's expression hardened. He had no time for those yellow-bellied cowards, but they did desperately need more men.

He sighed. 'I have the awful feeling the bigwigs agree with you; there's been talk about that and while you may be right, I don't know where the hell we're going to find them. Once they go on the run they vanish into thin air.'

Fortunately, his gaze was focused on the blank wall behind Harry's bed, and he didn't notice the slight flush that crept across the patient's face and simply carried on talking. 'I have heard there are amnesties being offered to anyone who rejoins their unit. God knows how their men are going to feel when these bastards turn up looking all fresh from their "holiday" but I'd rather they were on the front line than the poor buggers who've been there all this time.'

A man who had been taught the power of forgiveness, even Harry could understand the commander's attitude towards deserters. The war had certainly been relentless since Alfie and Lenny had deserted, and many men would find their absence hard to forgive. Harry put his hand to his head. It felt like it was splitting open.

A nurse approached and said, 'I think that's enough for now, sir. He needs his rest.'

Standing up, Forsythe gave Harry's arm a final pat. 'Well, you see if you can get a lift with the chaps travelling north when you're ready and . . . Padre, if you happen to know where we might find a few deserters, perhaps you'd better let me or one of the other COs know. I did hear the police are rounding some up and taking them back to the recruitment offices. We'll have them back in their nice clean uniforms in no time,' he added with a bitter laugh.

*   *   *

When Harry politely informed the medical team by his bedside that he was well enough to be discharged, the young doctor took one look at the stubborn face in front of him and knew arguments would be futile so he sighed and signed the form allowing Harry to limp off to cadge a lift with anyone in a uniform heading north up through Sicily.

At every turn, the padre felt mortified that he had missed the obviously fierce fighting that had gouged its way through to Italy through Salerno. By the time the Italians had surrendered, he was near Caserta but still hadn't caught sight of any of the Cheshires, so was delighted to see some of the huge transporters parked up at the side of the road. The tanks were always just behind the action, ready to be brought in to give weapon power to the infantry and Harry knew he was getting nearer the front line. He hobbled towards the huge vehicles that were waiting to follow the action. One soldier was leaning against his cabin, having a smoke.

'Hello, Padre,' the soldier said cheerfully. 'Been in the wars, have you? Or just this one?'

Harry smiled; it was an old joke but a favourite. 'Any chance of a lift north, soldier?'

'Sure. Strangely, I do happen to be going that way so, if you don't mind another terrible joke, hop in.' He laughed, looking down at his passenger's bandaged foot.

The journey was likely to be arduous with potholes, blown-up surfaces and, worst of all, a trail of dead bodies that lined the route. They were also on constant alert for the sound of planes approaching from above, so some company was welcomed by both of them.

'Danny Jackson,' the soldier said, holding out one hand away from the enormous steering wheel. Harry shook it as quickly as he could to allow the young man to put both hands back where they belonged.

'Harry Moore. Padre with the 6th Cheshires, if I can find them.'

Danny's face lit up. 'Oh, my home area. I'm with the 8th but a Manchester lad. Stretford. Where are you from?'

By the time they'd chatted for another five minutes, swapping knowledge of their local haunts, they found they had a great deal in common and kept interrupting each other in their excitement of shared memories. Danny was delighted to hear that Harry had been in Manchester so recently and plied him with questions – not about bomb damage or empty shops but what the trees looked like in the parks and whether he'd still been in Manchester when the spring bluebells came out in Fletcher Moss. After another few miles, Harry noticed his driver had started to grimly clench his teeth. It was something he had seen so many times when his men received letters from home. To recall their previous life was almost too painful to bear.

'Left a girl back there, have you?' he said, in an attempt to distract Danny.

'Yep, well, I've left her but I'm not even sure she's noticed I've gone. She's a wireless operator with the WAAF and all she keeps talking about is the Yanks.'

'What's her name?' Harry asked.

'Lily, Lily Mullins,' Danny said with a tinge of pride in his voice. One day, he'd make it Lily Jackson if he could.

Harry thought hard. 'Mullins, Mullins,' he said. 'Oh, I know a Mrs Ginny Mullins, it isn't her daughter is it?'

Danny nearly swerved across the road before taking a moment to right the juggernaut that he was driving.

'Yes!' He almost squealed with delight.

'How are the Mullins family? I love them, they're wonderful.'

Harry filled him in with as many details as he could remember while Danny listened intently.

'Has Mrs Mullins ever mentioned her daughter?' he asked as casually as he could.

'Umm, no, I don't think so. Oh, hang on, she might have mentioned she's dealing with Lancasters.'

Danny's chest rose and fell rapidly. The bleak scene in front of him was suddenly superimposed with a vision of Lily tossing her hair back in indignation at one of his cheeky remarks and hearing she was dealing with such huge bombers filled him with pride. To be sitting that close to someone who had been in touch with her family so recently had prompted an electrical charge in his body. He shuffled in his seat and quickly changed tack.

'Lily's dad, John, was at Gallipoli, you know. He doesn't talk much about it because, well, as you can imagine, there aren't many of them left.'

Harry swivelled around towards the man at his side.

'Gallipoli you say? Oh, that's amazing, I've got someone I know who really could do with some help getting to grips with the memory of that terrible battle. I wonder if he could provide some assistance?'

Danny assured him that if anyone could get through to a man battle-scarred from such a dreadful ordeal, it was John Mullins. 'I've never met a wiser, more measured man.'

After that the two men settled into a thorough examination of their backgrounds, the pubs they frequented, the streets they walked down and then they started to talk about the Lake

District, a place they both knew well. Danny had climbed many of the same summits that Harry had and they shared their love of the wild, open outdoors and the freedom it offered. It was almost dark when they realised the convoy in front had stopped and it was time to bivouac.

Their farewell handshake had so much warmth in it, Harry felt more cheered than he had done in ages, and he whistled as he limped over to find a Cheshire unit.

Chapter 28

The last few days had been stressful for the girls on the *Nancy May* and *Florence*. They were slightly behind schedule and had to race to catch up, all the time checking at every bridge to make sure there were no men in gaberdines lurking, ready to jump aboard as soon as the boats came within reach. Their equilibrium wasn't helped by Lenny, who was taking out his nerves on their rations and seemed to need to eat every five minutes to take his mind off the predicament he had put himself and the girls in.

As they approached Fenny Stratford near Bletchley, Gloria was on high alert. She had written to Will when she left Limehouse but now she was almost hoping he hadn't received her letter. Her visit to see all her relatives had left her with a sickening feeling that she was trying to reach the moon by having a relationship with someone as rich as Will, but now she could almost feel his presence, the same prickly sensation rippled up and down her skin.

Further up the pound, Will was waiting anxiously, peering down the canal. Every time he heard the chug of an engine, his heart raced. He'd had a very uncomfortable chat with his father on his last leave when he was left in no doubt that, firstly, his parents were very disappointed in a son who was apparently sitting at a desk doing admin while other chaps were fighting bravely, and secondly, his father had bluntly told him the least he could do was start to think about providing the family with an heir who would inherit the estate. Will had bristled at the accusations about his job, thinking how the cracking of the Enigma Code at Bletchley had saved thousands of lives but his next words about an heir had hit a nerve. the memory of Gloria's shapely body and her infectious giggle was vivid, especially when he tossed around in his bed at the digs, but every time he tried to imagine her hosting a garden party or joining him at the country club, he would come out in a cold sweat.

Still, when he finally spotted the *Nancy May* making its way towards him, he leaped forward to put out his thumb with a delighted laugh.

Gloria took a much bigger leap than anyone would have thought those little legs could manage and landed awkwardly into his outstretched arms.

'I've been coming down here for two days,' Will complained with a grin. 'What kept you?'

'Never you mind,' Gloria said, snuggling into his chest. 'Just hold me now. Oh, I've missed you.'

For a brief moment, the two young people clung to each other, both wishing the war, society rules and their families to hell.

Elizabeth, drawing level with them, called over, 'We'll moor further up the pound, come and find us when you're ready.' And then the two boats disappeared around the corner.

* * *

Elizabeth gave a sad smile. It was so lovely to see the affection between two young people like that and it reminded her of when she'd first met Christopher. He had looked so dashing in his naval uniform and she had fallen in love in an instant. Now she wondered whether she knew him at all. He didn't know her, that was for sure.

A whisper came from below. 'Will Gloria tell him, you know, about me?'

'I hope not, Lenny,' she said, 'I hope not.'

* * *

Harry reread the letters to his uncle and to David Phillips, checking to make sure the censors couldn't redact too much. Suggesting that John Mullins might visit Jim Carpenter to help him deal with the aftermath of Gallipoli was fine but trying to ask questions about one deserter on a canal boat and another at a veterans' centre without giving the game away required more ingenuity. He ended up relying on them both to recognise the coded references to the Prodigal Son and Noah's Ark to ask questions about Maggie, the deserter and Alfie. The censor would think he was having some sort of divine revelation, he thought with a wry smile.

He took out another blank airletter, thankful that the limit of one letter per man per month had been relaxed and finally started a letter to Maggie:

Dear Maggie,

He stalled. He had no idea what he was going to say. He'd tried so many times to write to her and so many times he'd given up. Every time he thought of their last meeting, a hot flush of shame spread up his body to his face making him fan himself with an envelope like he'd seen some of the matrons at Emmanuel Church do. He was beginning to realise what an idiot he had been and how insignificant the normal rules of society were when you were facing death every day. All he wanted now was to survive long enough to tell her how he felt. He realised that his obsession with her affair was because he was insanely jealous that someone else had held her, loved her before he'd had the chance. Now, sitting in yet another devastated Italian village, none of that seemed important. Pragmatism had always been Harry Moore's strongest asset, but even that was now failing him. He normally never agonised, looked ahead with dread or back with regret and it had all been so easy when he had a higher power to allocate that responsibility to, but recently it had occurred to him that he might be on his own.

He put his pen back on the paper and continued writing:

I do hope you and the girls are well and that life has calmed down for you on the waterways. I realise our last meeting did not go as either of us had hoped but now, with thousands of miles between us, I realise what a complete fool I made of myself and I hope you can find it in yourself to forgive me.

Every time I think of your lovely face, I'm transported back to Manchester and to our meetings there and near the Grand Union Canal. Maggie, you were absolutely correct, I have no right to judge you or anyone and perhaps if I tell you my anger came not from indignation but from jealousy, you might find it in you to think more fondly of me.

I daren't say too much in this letter because I'm scared you hate me, so I'll just plead with you to write back and let me know how you're feeling.

He had to stop writing. He was imagining her fingers touching this piece of paper, maybe holding it to her chest. He realised this surge of warmth that was flooding his body was prompted by a completely different feeling from the embarrassment he'd felt earlier; one he knew his men suffered from when they raced towards the cold showers and it took several seconds for him to finger his dog collar before he could calm down again enough to carry on writing.

There's so much I want to say to you Maggie but perhaps this short letter could be the start of a new relationship between us? I would really like that. I hope you've been able to find a solution to your problem by now but if you haven't, just know that I've put measures in place that could help you if you're still stuck . Do you remember me talking about Reverend David Phillips at Broughton House? Do call on him if you need him. Notice, I'm not presuming you do need any help – I know you're perfectly capable. See, I'm being much better behaved these days!

I can't tell you much about life here but just know I'm OK and the thought of the burnished autumn leaves on the trees in Britain and those chilly, misty mornings on the canals keeps me going. By the time you get this, it will be winter for both of us and if it's anywhere near as cold and wet as it is here, you'll need that little cosy burner. I wish we had one. As ever, the men I serve are being incredible and I have no idea whether I'm making any difference at all. Sometimes, it all seems so useless, but they appear to value my services and it's that that keeps me going.

I have to go now to catch the post – it's a bit intermittent, but the Postal Service is doing its best. I'm going to send this to your grandad's house to make sure you get it. I'm in awe of the fact anything at all reaches us out here but it would be wonderful to hear from you, if you feel you can write.

With fondest love,

Harry xx

It had taken him half an hour to write the letter and he looked at his watch, realising he had yet another burial to do so he put the flimsy letter in the provided envelope, sending a fervent prayer that his confessions weren't going to be in vain. It was possible she just didn't want to write to him, but it was also possible she had no idea he had gone back to his unit. He veered between worrying about the huge risk Maggie and her friends were running in harbouring a deserter, to concern that a random German bomber or fighter might decide to strike at a highly visible industrial highway that threaded through England. Harry cursed the war for taking him away from her but they both had their wars to fight and he needed to be back here, alongside his men.

Finally, he put the letter in the tray for the censors. Now it was up to fate.

'Am I disturbing you?' Paul said from the door flap of the tent.

Harry jumped up in delight. 'There you are. Where the hell have you been? I've been looking for you ever since I got back. You missed all the fun getting into Italy. Good job you're back in time for the onslaught on the Gothic Line. I'd have hated you to have missed that party.'

Paul touched the side of his nose: 'None of your business but I'm expecting a medal for it.'

Harry laughed. 'It had better be worth the George Cross at least.' He looked Paul up and down, taking in his emaciated frame, his muddy clothes and the stubble on his chin and he frowned.

'Been sent ahead have you?'

Paul pulled up a stool next to the oil canister Harry was using for a writing desk and whispered to him how he had been looking for two soldiers who'd gone missing.

'I think they're gonners to be honest, their tank transporter was blown to smithereens, but Lieutenant Colonel Forsythe thinks there's a chance they may have headed for the hills. Apparently, one's a geography teacher and knows how to read the landscape and the other one, well, I wasn't sure why they had such faith in him, but the old man reckons he's a resourceful type, always done camping and walking and stuff.'

'What was his name?' Harry asked sharply. 'I got a lift with one weeks ago, a Danny Jackson. If it's him, I agree with the old man, he seemed as if he could deal with anything. At least I hope so.'

'Yeah, that's him. Fancy that. Well, anyway, I don't hold much hope for their chances, but stranger things have happened in this war.'

Harry immediately thought of the Mullins family and their daughter, Lily, and automatically sent a prayer skywards for a man he'd only spent a few hours with. Then he cursed. How could he pray to a God he was no longer sure was there?

'Padre, are you listening to me?' Paul said.

'Oh sorry, I was miles away.'

'Not still thinking about that girl, are you? Maggie?'

'For once I wasn't, well, not really,' Harry replied with a slight smile. 'I was thinking about those two men and if I'm honest, Paul, well, how I've always sort of relied on the heavens to take care of everything and now I'm not so sure that'll work.' He spun round to face Paul. 'How am I supposed to do this job anymore if I really *am* on my own and this is it?'

Paul tipped his head to one side and then said, 'Nope, my Irish da wouldn't have that. I mean the Virgin Mary . . . all those saints, are you telling me they're not up there looking down on us and taking care of us? Nope, not a chance, Padre, you're wrong.'

There was no option but to smile. Paul's belief was so innocent and so sure. Harry envied his friend.

That night, the young clergyman took himself off to the edge of the camp and sat down, propped up against a tree.

He tried to unjumble his thoughts using all the skills he had learned at the seminary. They'd warned that this day might come, and they had provided a sort of 'toolkit' to deal with it. He went through the logistical arguments for and against having faith but the phrase that kept coming back to him was his uncle Peter's. A young Harry had once asked him how he could be so unwavering in his faith. He'd answered, 'I just know that I'd rather be wrong with God than right without Him.'

Harry got to his feet, brushing off the dirt from his trousers and saying out loud, 'Well, that's one way of looking at it, I suppose.'

In his bunk later that night, Harry felt an uneasy peace descend on him. Was it possible, he wondered, that he didn't have to have all the answers after all? Maybe it wasn't up to him to proclaim there was a divine plan that would lead them to victory but it was up to men in Whitehall, the newly built Pentagon and the Kremlin to come up with a plan themselves, and all he and the men on the ground could do was to put one foot in front of the other every day? Pulling his rough blanket around him, he turned over and had the best night's sleep he'd had in months.

Chapter 29

Maggie, however, was struggling to get any rest and despite being exhausted, was lying in her bunk with her eyes screwed tightly to blot out Harry's reassuring face and she longed for him more than ever. Ignoring the uncomfortable shivers passing up and down her body, she tried to pretend it was his practical advice she was missing, but then she was engulfed by one single reality – he obviously wanted nothing more to do with her or he would have written. She opened one eye to see Gloria still brushing her teeth.

'I think those spam fritters have upset my tummy,' she said.

'Well, Lenny seemed to wolf them down,' Gloria said, whispering as usual whenever she mentioned his name. 'Talking of our stowaway, when did you say our rescue would arrive?'

'I think soon, oh, I do hope so. We're getting behind again and we're all nervous wrecks that someone will spot him and that his erstwhile "friends" could be looking for us.'

The last few days had felt especially long and every lock had seemed to take more time than normal. Keeping Lenny hidden from the constant flow of passing boats, inquisitive lock-keepers wanting to know everything about these three girls doing 'men's work', had put them all on edge and they just hoped that Maggie's vicar friend would be the solution to their problems.

It had been just after Marsworth that Joe finally caught up with them. His gentle probing had finally prompted Gloria to confess that Lenny was back on board. She was relieved to know that he would be behind them if they needed help and gave him a particularly warm smile. He answered her polite questions about his father and baby Thomas and then said with a new-found confidence, 'You get any problems, just you whistle, 'I'll be there before you can say Jack Robinson.'

Gloria reached up and gave him a grateful kiss on the cheek. He determined not to wash for a week.

As they got further north, they all felt tense and Elizabeth, in particular, was scanning every towpath, the bridges and the encroaching locks. She was terrified, knowing it wouldn't take much for a gang of dangerous criminals to find them on this long strip of water.

It was Maggie who heard an insistent cough as they approached a bridge just before Stoke Bruerne and she slowed down to check where it came from, her hand ready to flip round the speed wheel to accelerate away if necessary. Gloria grabbed the barge pole to ward off any boarding party but then Maggie saw the clerical collar and indicated to Gloria to help the man under the bridge on board. Neither of them spoke a word while the man was unceremoniously pushed down the steps into the cabin while they passed moored boats.

Once they had negotiated the little line of vessels, that were unaware of the drama unfolding on the boat gliding past them, Maggie handed the tiller to Gloria and went below.

'Reverend Phillips?' she asked.

'Yes, that's me, and you are?'

'Umm, Maggie' she said, suddenly confused. *Surely he knew who she was?*

'So, where is he? I'll take him off your hands.' The voice was gruff and not at all like the kind tones she had heard on the telephone, and she looked at their 'guest' more closely. The man's fingernails weren't clipped. It was a small thing, but it seemed odd that a clergyman wouldn't attend to such a simple matter of personal hygiene and care. She noticed as well that the dog collar wasn't fastened properly at the back.

'So, it's Eric, isn't it?' she asked, watching to see if he reacted to the wrong name. He didn't. 'What's your plan now?'

'Well, I'll just make sure he's taken somewhere safe.' The man looked around the cabin, peering under the bunks.

'OK, that's fine,' Maggie said brightly. 'He's not here, we had to hide him somewhere else but now you're here, I'll get him brought to you. Let me get you a cup of tea.'

'No,' was the abrupt response and then in a more conciliatory tone: 'Let's just get this sorted, you know how dangerous it is to have him on the loose. We need to get him somewhere where the authorities won't find him.'

Maggie attempted a relieved smile and said, 'It won't take long, let me get a message to where he's being hidden. We can have him with you in a jiffy.'

'OK, but make it fast, I've got to get back. I haven't got much time.'

Maggie turned to put the kettle on, hoping the man couldn't see how the hairs on the back of her neck were standing on end. Every sinew in her body was taut, waiting for a strike from behind. With one hand on the kettle, ready to swing it at him if necessary, she turned.

'Well, I'll just pop this on the stove; even if you don't want a cuppa, the others will, but don't worry, I'll nip out while this is boiling to give the signal to the boat following behind us; they know the plan.'

The man gave a suspicious look; he didn't need anyone else involved.

Maggie went on top and nudged Gloria to move to one side so she could whisper in her ear.

'It's not Reverend Phillips,' she confided. 'I think it's one of them.' Gloria was about to let out a cry, but Maggie clasped her hand over her mouth. 'We have to get help.'

The boat behind the *Florence* was *Buffalo*, as it had been all the way since Marsworth. Joe had been sitting silently on deck, clutching a large club. Maggie nodded her head towards it and Gloria slowed to let the boat come alongside. As Joe smiled at her, noting the way the wind was catching her auburn hair, she mouthed the word 'Help' and pointed towards the cabin.

Joe didn't need any more information. He'd prepared for this and, pulling the boat in front of the *Nancy May*, quickly secured a line and ran back towards Gloria. By this time, Maggie had gone back downstairs to tell her visitor that Lenny was being brought to them and should be with them soon.

Gloria jumped off and ran to meet Joe but as she raced past the little porthole, the man below saw her. He immediately jumped up and grabbed Maggie, spinning her round so that he had his arm around her neck. She felt something metallic poking into her side.

'Don't you get any ideas, missy. We're onto you and your friends. Now just give us Lenny and we'll go.'

Maggie stifled a scream, but it was cut off by a piece of cloth that was deftly tied around her mouth. This man was an expert, managing to keep the gun pointing into her side while using his teeth and left hand to tie the knot.

Joe, however, had heard the noise and leaped onto the boat. He flung open the hatch door and rushed down the two steps, before grabbing the man from behind and twisting his arm violently. Maggie immediately pulled free and then the sound of a gun resounded in the wooden cabin.

* * *

Tying up *Florence* at the back, Elizabeth had no idea what was going on but realised something was terribly wrong when she heard the noise of gunshot. Lenny struggled to get past her in the butty companionway, but she shoved him back down, saying, 'You stay right where you are, you're the last person we need to get involved here.'

Then she ran towards Gloria who was standing, frozen, next to the boat.

'I can't go in, I can't,' she stuttered. 'I don't know what I'll find . . . Maggie . . . Joe.' Elizabeth grabbed her by the shoulders.

'I'll go but we need help, Gloria, go and find help, NOW!'

* * *

Propelled into action, Gloria ran off. She had no idea who she was going to get or what she was going to say to them, but this was bigger than any of them could deal with.

It was typical that on the busiest canal in the country, the towpath was empty, Gloria thought, looking in all directions for a house, a road or another boat. She ran into the darkness of the next bridge and almost collided with a man slumped against the side of the wall, his top shirt button hanging on a thread.

'You must help me,' the man spluttered. 'I've been attacked.' As if to prove his point he pulled his hand away from his head and it was covered in blood.

'Oh, for God's sake,' Gloria blurted out, 'I need help, not another casualty.'

'The attacker, he must have heard me ask for the *Nancy May* and followed me . . . he took my collar . . .'

Gloria froze but then the man seemed to regain his composure and politely held out his bloodied hand in a greeting that would have been at home in a country house drawing room.

'I do apologise, I should have introduced myself. I'm Reverend David Phillips. And your name, young lady?'

'*You're* Reverend Phillips? Oh, well, that explains everything,' Gloria said, and she grabbed his arm and pulled him back the way she had just come. As he stumbled along the path, clutching his trilby, she noticed blood was now dripping down the side of his face.

'I am so sorry, Reverend, are you OK? It's just that I'm Gloria – on the boat with Maggie – oh, you must know who we are, you were coming to meet us.' Her words came out in a torrent. 'I think your attacker is holding Maggie at gunpoint in our cabin. At least—' she took a sharp breath '—I don't know; we heard a gunshot.'

Her rushed words made him lose hold of her arm and, despite the blinding headache he was suffering, he sprinted off in front of her.

'Wait for me,' she called and sped up to catch him, and the pair of them ran until they spotted the *Nancy May*, looking deceptively calm and quiet in the evening sunlight.

As they approached, they both slowed down and started to creep towards the bow of the boat.

David put a finger to his lips, a gesture Gloria dismissed with scorn. She was the one who was experienced at this particular drama, not this newcomer. He took her by surprise by smiling reassuringly at her indignation, a reaction that was made quite macabre by the red streaks that were covering the left side of his face. She conceded that this calm, controlled man might be exactly the person she needed right now after all.

They crouched down to listen at the side of the hull but could hear nothing. Occupied with trying to be as inconspicuous as possible, they didn't hear the sound of the hatch opening and the querulous voice of Maggie.

'It's all right, you can come in. Joe's got him under control, but we could do with some help to decide what to do next. You must be Reverend Phillips. How do you do?' Maggie was standing stretching her hand out in greeting.

Gloria nearly exploded. 'What is it with you people? We've just had a life-or-death situation and you two are chatting as if you're at a cocktail party.'

Shaking her head at the middle class's ability to make an everyday event out of a crisis, she pushed past Maggie and peered warily down into the cabin.

In the gloom, she saw the prone figure of the man in the dark suit; on top of him, with his knee in the man's back was Joe, looking rather proud of himself. Behind him was Elizabeth holding the gun and pointing it towards the man on the floor like a character in a *Miss Fury* comic.

'Joe!' Gloria said, suddenly shy. He looked so in command and, if the truth be told, a bit like one of those heroes from her own magazines.

He looked back at her sheepishly, not letting the pressure of his knee lessen for one second.

'I, um, well, I managed to get the gun off him.'

That understatement was greeted with a smile he had only dreamed about.

'What's going on?' Mrs Spencer shouted from the towpath.

Maggie and Gloria looked out to see Joe's mother standing like an Egyptian sentry to a tomb with a frying pan in one hand and a poker in the other.

Maggie started to laugh. 'He never had a chance, did he? Our professional criminal?'

'Where's my Joe?' Mrs Spencer said threateningly.

'He's fine, Mrs Spencer. A bit of a champion, actually,' Gloria told her.

''Course he is,' his mother said, tilting her head up, 'always 'as been. Just never allowed to be.'

'I could do with some 'elp, here, 'Joe called from within. 'We need to get 'im tied up and then decide what we're gonna do with 'im.'

Reverend Phillips gave a small cough and twisted a handkerchief into a long strip. 'If I may be allowed . . .'

They all turned expectantly towards the man whose bloodstained shirt had been ripped at the top where the imposter had grabbed the clerical collar from him.

Elizabeth moved into action.

'While you do that, let me clean up that wound, it looks nasty.'

She ran back to the *Florence* to bring a terrified Lenny up to date with events and get a clean cloth and some hot water from the kettle. By the time she returned, the cabin was so crowded, she had to stand with Mrs Spencer watching helplessly from above at the bizarre scene below her. Joe, still with his knee firmly placed in the man's back, was ignoring the strangled, groaning sounds that were coming from his throat. Reverend Phillips was straddled over the man's legs and was doing a rather proficient job of tying his hands while Maggie crouched above him on her own bunk as there was no room on the floor for her. Next to her, Gloria sat cross-legged wondering what her policewoman sister, Molly, would think of all this.

When she had joined the Grand Union Canal Company, Molly had mocked Gloria, superior in her position of dealing with four thousand internee women behind barbed wire on the Isle of Man. She'd suggested that Gloria was going to have the life of Riley pottering up and down lovely waterways while Gloria retorted that Molly would spend her life dealing with the theft of hairbrushes and sunning herself on the beaches, tucking into a lovely Manx ice cream.

Ha! Gloria thought smugly, determinedly ignoring her sister's last letter that had talked about problems created by making German Nazis and German Jews live side by side. *I bet she hasn't got anything as interesting as this happening!*

Nothing like a deserter, a beaten-up clergyman and a dangerous gang member that's for sure, she concluded.

Chapter 30

Once the man was securely fastened with a bike lock to the bed leg, the others all gathered on the towpath.

'So, what the hell do we do now?' Maggie asked.

There was silence and then Reverend Phillips spoke. 'Well, I came to get Lenny and I think my first priority needs to be getting him out of here.'

Lenny hadn't dared move at all and was still cowering in the cabin. Having heard the gunshot, it had brought back memories from war.

'Well, I think the police need to know about our mate on the floor in there,' Joe said, jerking his head towards the hull.

'We can't!' all three girls cried at once. 'How on earth would we explain it?'

'Besides which, our captive's got friends who will come looking,' Elizabeth put in.

Her words hung in the air.

Maggie immediately thought of Harry; he'd know what to do.

It seemed the reverend was thinking the same thing. 'I wish Harry were here. He'd have a plan.'

A blush spread across Maggie's cheeks and Reverend Phillips squeezed her arm in sympathy. She gave him an embarrassed smile and wished these clergymen were less proficient at reading minds.

While the pair of them were trying to work out what Harry's next step would be, Joe piped up. 'I had some recruiters 'ere yesterday, they were asking me about my . . . ummm, flat feet.' Now it was his turn to blush. 'Couldn't we 'and 'im over to them. I'm sure he's a conscription dodger.'

'Yes, but won't 'e tell 'em?' Mrs Spencer said. 'You know, about everything.'

Elizabeth's face cleared. 'No, he won't. His sort don't tell the authorities anything. Besides, Lenny was witness to a murder that was committed by this gang. If we let him know that one word would lead them all to the gallows our prisoner wouldn't dare.'

Gloria then said: 'That's a great idea but aren't the gang going to come looking for him when he disappears?'

This time it was Maggie who spoke. 'I think knowing one of theirs might spill the beans to the police about everything they've been involved with, will make them lie low.

'I think we have no alternative but to tell the police,' she went on. 'It's going to come out that Lenny's a deserter anyway and if we say we only found him yesterday, then we don't get into trouble for harbouring him but . . .' She stopped; this was all beginning to rely on too many 'ifs' and 'buts'. Besides, it was a huge thing for them all to lie to the police. She felt completely out of her depth.

'Leave it with me,' Elizabeth said mysteriously.

* * *

Later that night, when the blackout made it hard to see even a yard in front, the girls bid Reverend Phillips and Lenny, clad in a curate's cassock, a fond goodbye. They all knew what a risk this clergyman was taking by getting involved in their drama and they were very grateful. Lenny looked terrified but resigned. A life on the run had given him as many nightmares as the battles he had faced in the army and this final chance at redemption was actually beginning to feel ever so slightly appealing. He'd discovered that the world away from the front had its dangers too and now simply wanted to get as far from Arthur and his mates as he could. David had a bandage around his head which shone in the moonlight and at the last minute, Elizabeth pleaded with him to put his hat back on. The two men walked quickly off down the towpath to David's car, which had been abandoned at the side of the road. Maggie had no idea that the plan was for Lenny to be the house guest of her father and David had decided now was not the time to tell her.

'Psst,' a call came from *Buffalo* and Gloria went over to it. When she came back, she had three bottles of beer in her hand. 'A present from Joe.' They delightedly accepted a bottle each and went inside to wait for the police.

* * *

Sergeant Tomlinson was utterly perplexed by the three innocent faces in front of him. His men had already removed the man who had been so expertly tied up. Even with thirty years' experience in the police, he was beginning to feel this case was like walking through fog.

'So, tell me again what happened,' he said. 'This geezer jumped aboard your boat and threatened you with a gun? But why?' he asked, going back to the textbook advice to stick with the simplest questions.

He watched each girl carefully waiting for muddled replies that would lead him to the cracks in their story but all he saw were three completely innocent faces staring back at him.

'It was my fault, Officer,' the older girl said.

She was disarmingly attractive, if very posh, he noticed. Mind you, he thought, looking around, they were all lookers.

Trying to maintain his best law and order officer expression, Ernest Tomlinson licked his pencil and turned over a page in his brown leather notebook in readiness.

'You see,' Elizabeth was saying, 'oh dear, Sergeant, I partook in a few bets – so many of my friends have racehorses as I'm sure you appreciate. Everyone's so missing the proper Derby, aren't they? The new Derby at Newmarket just isn't the same.'

Ernest Tomlinson's pencil remained raised in the air and he found himself nodding in sympathy; he had absolutely no idea what she was talking about.

'You see,' she continued, 'I really didn't know what I was getting into and when I started doing this canal work, I completely forgot to pay my debts. You can imagine how silly I felt when this man started turning up and demanding money.'

She glanced at the sergeant's face. He was captivated. She had to look down at her feet in pretend shame to disguise her twinkling eyes.

'I tried to pay but they kept turning up and demanding more and then that dreadful man arrived, threatening me with his gun.'

Sergeant Tomlinson looked grave. 'I think he may be part of a bigger gang, miss, but don't you worry, we'll put the word out that we're onto them and they'll go quiet, you mark my words.'

Gloria caught Maggie's eye. She hoped he was right.

Elizabeth gave them both a reassuring nod; she had this under control.

'They must be very bad men; you see, they were going to tell my husband.' Clasping her hand dramatically to her chest, she confided in a whisper, 'He's a captain in the Mediterranean and far too busy to be worrying about his wife getting herself into a little bit of mischief.'

She gave an exaggerated shiver and Sergeant Tomlinson put out his hand to cover hers in a fatherly manner. It took a moment for him to take in her words.

'Which ship?' he asked.

Elizabeth leaned forward and put her finger to the side of her nose. 'Now you know I can't tell you that, but it wasn't long ago that he was helping Malta after that terrible siege.'

Sergeant Tomlinson bit his lip; his lad was on a frigate with the Mediterranean Fleet and had also been involved in the desperate struggle to get fuel and supplies to a starving Malta.

'My lad Frank's with a boat out there. I wonder if your husband is, well, you know, the captain he tells us about. He says he's a great bloke and a great captain.'

She leaned over and touched his arm, her eyes misted with tears. Gloria looked on in awe. *God, this woman was good*, she thought.

'Oh, I'm sure my husband or whichever captain he has, will take the best care of him and all the crew – those brave boys,' she said, using a dainty handkerchief to wipe her cheek.

Sergeant Tomlinson used the back of his sleeve to wipe his own eyes and gave an embarrassed snort. 'I'm sure, madam, I'm sure.'

There was a moment of silence in which Gloria didn't dare look at Maggie for fear of giggling at Elizabeth's superlative performance. Maggie was just thanking heaven for the Malta coincidence.

'Anyway,' the sergeant was saying, 'I'm sure we can hush up the part about your, um—' he coughed again '—little flutter, because the main thing is, this ruffian has been caught. I have to say, ladies, I'm rather in awe of your skills in subduing him. Just you and the lad in the boat behind you say.'

'Oh yes,' Maggie said quickly, 'Joe was wonderful. He deserves a medal.'

'Well, he certainly did a great job,' the sergeant conceded. 'He told me he's got flat feet; that's a shame; we need men like him in the army.'

Maggie gave him a smile that took the fifty-year-old's breath away. His wife, Mildred, used to have a smile like that he thought.

'Would you like a cup of tea?' she asked him. 'I think we might even have a few biscuits left; we save them for special occasions.'

After they had handed over a steaming cup of tea and a carrot biscuit, the girls relaxed. They were home and dry.

* * *

More relieved than she admitted, even to herself, Maggie was the first of the girls to wake next morning. She felt refreshed, but there was no time to relish it with limited time to get to Birmingham. They all quickly got on with their tasks, dealt with the locks efficiently and moved both boats through the water as quickly as they could. It wasn't until they stopped for breakfast after Braunston that they were able to take a moment to reflect on their luck.

'If his son hadn't been in the navy . . .' Gloria said, handing bowls of porridge to the other two.

'I know,' Maggie agreed. 'But, oh, Elizabeth, you were magnificent! Have you ever been on the stage?'

Elizabeth gave a girlish titter. 'It is possible my artistic talents have been overlooked. I do remember when I was eight, I did an exceptional job of convincing poor Mary and Joseph that my overflowing inn really was not suitable for them but that the stable would be far comfier. So, now you mention it, maybe I did miss my vocation.'

Gloria suddenly guffawed in laughter, spitting porridge all over her trousers. Maggie started to laugh too at this new, frivolous side of Elizabeth and soon, the three of them were doubled over in fits of giggles. It felt good and, slowly, the tension they'd all been living under for the last few weeks lifted.

A splutter in the engine when they set off reminded them how they'd been simply been going through the motions on board the boats recently and there was a flurry of maintenance, cleaning and sorting to be done. That night, when they moored up, Gloria went into the engine room and tutted in horror at the state of the Lister, resolving to do a complete service. As she scrubbed the air intake with a long-handled screwdriver, she was appalled to see the amount of black gunk that emerged, so she carefully wiped the area with a cloth and white spirit, cleaned out the oil filter and then gave an extra polish to the metal cover, delighting in the efficiency of this beautiful piece of engineering.

Maggie, in the meantime, did a thorough job of blacking the stove and cleaning the brasses, grateful that they didn't have as many to do as the Spencers. Behind them, on *Florence*, Elizabeth, a girl who had always had maids to clean, was discovering an unexpected visceral delight in seeing gleaming surfaces and swept floors.

The dry, sunny summer had been overtaken by a more unsettled autumn with storms that lashed the tops of the boats making driving difficult. Recently, though, there had been a brief lull allowing them to finally wash out their sodden clothes and bedding.

In between their chores, they moved efficiently up the cut, more confident now about battling with what everyone on the cut called the 'Jossers', the boats that raced up and down the cut in their recognisable green and orange craft, hardly stopping in their mission to deliver loads. Their boats could often be heard long after the girls had gone to bed, making them feel guilty for having moored up along the bank after a twelve-hour day. These Jossers gave no quarter to anyone else trying to take a more careful path up the Grand Union and girls in particular had, in the early days, earned their scorn, but even Maggie had now learned to deal with them, disarming them with a smile as she sneaked the *Nancy May* in front of them. She'd realised that quick thinking and determination was the only thing that earned respect on the waterways and was now trying to teach Elizabeth that her impeccable manners would not suffice and that a more robust approach was needed.

At their mooring spots at night, they would often invite Joe across for a meal and to progress his reading, giving Mrs Spencer time to spend with baby Thomas. Jake was losing even more weight and his thundering voice that used to emanate from their hull was now little more than a hoarse whisper.

On one of the last evenings of the run, at Black Boy Bridge just outside Birmingham, Maggie passed Joe her copy of *Swallows and Amazons*. 'You'll like this one,' she told him. 'It's by a writer called Arthur Ransome and it's about boats.'

Joe reached out eagerly. He was loving this new skill and was taking every opportunity to practise. He particularly loved the books that Maggie would lend him, finding a world beyond the cut that was full of excitement and adventure.

Clasping his book to his chest, he looked around the cabin, his eyes aglow. Every bit of these evenings was replayed when he climbed into his bunk at night, especially the way the paraffin lamp made Gloria's hair glisten, but tonight, he had no time for dreaming; he had something to tell these new friends of his.

'I'm joining the navy,' he said, with some pride.

'But I thought . . .' Gloria began.

'Yeah, I do 'ave flat feet but they need men and I volunteered. They've decided these plates o' meat ain't that bad after all. They're going to put me on guns. You don't 'ave to walk much doing that!'

Joe explained how he had run after Sergeant Tomlinson when he left the girls' boat and asked him whether there was any chance he could be accepted into any of the services. Shyly, he admitted he was fed up of not being able to serve his country and this morning, Joe had received a letter from the recruitment office.

'Thanks to you, Maggie,' he said with a tinge of pride in his voice, 'I could read it, imagine that. Joe Spencer able to read an official letter!'

To begin with, he went on, his mother had been horrified at the suggestion Joe would leave the cut; she needed him to operate the boat and had assumed he was safe, working in a reserved occupation, but once he'd revealed he'd already been in touch with his uncle, Ernie, to come and take over his role, she had gone very quiet and he concluded that his arguments had won her over.

'You see, Ernie was the only one who could ever keep Da in check,' Joe told the girls, 'but the two brothers fell out over some'at, never knew what, so we ain't seen 'im for ages. I found him though.'

Maggie grinned at the young man opposite her. He was nothing like the lad who wouldn't look anyone in the eyes a few months back. Between his new skills at reading and his father's incapacity, the figure sitting upright with his head touching the ceiling exuded a confidence that took them all by surprise – maybe Joe most of all.

'When do you leave?' Gloria asked, looking, Joe noted with satisfaction, rather crestfallen.

'Soon as we unload this next lot. I'm to join the lads at Portsmouth. There's some training then we're off.'

Gloria felt a shiver of alarm. She'd become very fond of Joe. The cut wouldn't be as interesting or as much fun without him, she thought, and they all knew of the dangers the British Navy was facing. It wouldn't make any difference where Joe ended up – the Atlantic or the Mediterranean – they were equally treacherous.

Elizabeth stood up as much as she could under the arched ceiling and announced, 'Right, that's it, we're off to the pub. We need to buy this young naval cadet a drink.' She'd already decided she would find out where Joe was going to be sent and see whether her husband could help with placing him somewhere relatively safe.

Chapter 31

Later, when a slightly tipsy Joe had left them to go back to help his mother, the three girls sat in the corner of the Black Boy pub, not noticing the wooden beams or the empty grate where cosy fires used to burn before the war or even the scandalised looks from the locals that three girls were now in a public bar without a man's supervision. They were too busy discussing how Joe's departure would affect them all. Their chatter included how much his mother would miss him, their fears that Ernie would be another Jake and finally, how much they would all miss Joe too.

'It'll be the making of him, though,' Elizabeth said, taking an unladylike swig of her cider. Maggie and Gloria followed suit; they agreed wholeheartedly.

'Who'd have thought being able to read would change a person as much as it's changed Joe,' Elizabeth said. Watching Joe study so seriously had made her wonder whether she had taken for granted all the opportunities she'd been given of a private school, a finishing school and a European tour.

Gloria was more aware of the advantages of education and had worked really hard at school, wanting to set herself apart from other boaters' children who bunked off lessons regularly. She and her sister, Molly, had determined that they would do everything they could to escape the confines of the East End and while Molly had led the way by becoming a police officer, Gloria felt she still had a great deal to learn, and seeing Joe's enthusiasm had inspired her.

'I've been listening to everything you've been teaching Joe, Mags, and I've been reading Dickens,' she said, 'but now *I* want to learn even more about the world, books, art – all of it.'

'With pleasure,' Maggie said. 'Every time we're on a quiet stretch, I'll teach you as much as I can. Being in charge of the kitty's helping your arithmetic.'

There was a slight noise from Elizabeth.

'I know you still don't trust me, but honestly, I'm over gambling. All that we've been through has really frightened me; I don't want to put myself – or either of you – at risk again.'

Her face darkened thinking of how her own concerns had led Lenny into dreadful danger, which had then followed him back to the boat and her two friends. She looked at them both fondly and felt a lump in her throat. The noise of that gunshot would haunt her forever. Maggie could have been killed, she thought in horror, and with a quiet 'good night' to the other two, she took herself off to *Florence* where she crawled into her bunk and hugged her pillow.

Maggie's own thoughts turned to Harry as she unfolded the bedding that night. Talking about Joe going off to join the action had made her wonder what dangers he was facing, and she shivered. When she had given a sincere thank you to David Phillips and watched him and his 'curate' disappear down the towpath, Maggie had given a silent thanks to Harry, too, for coming up with a plan that got them all off the hook, but allowing Harry into her thoughts had left her feeling empty and sad and she clutched her stomach and groaned.

Gloria put down her toothbrush, spat out into her cup and gave her friend a knowing look. She was beginning to be able to read Maggie's face and every time she gazed into the distance, she was sure it was Harry Moore that Maggie was thinking about. She knew because she'd been guilty of doing the same thing over Will, but somehow, that image in her mind's eye was fading.

'Get to bed, Maggie,' Gloria said unsympathetically, 'we've got Knowle locks to do in the morning and if there's any time at all, I would like to nip off and look at the old church in the village. Apparently, it's really beautiful and I could do with a moment to pray for Joe.'

Maggie climbed into her bunk and hid her surprise. She'd noticed how Gloria had become conflicted in her feelings for Will, but it hadn't occurred to her that Joe had caught her eye. Cuddling down to get as much warmth as possible, she decided she was rooting for Joe.

* * *

Their departure in the morning was delayed by two boats from the Ovaltine factory. Their dark blue background paintwork was emblazoned with the words 'Drink Delicious Ovaltine for Health' in orange and yellow and the factory had its own fleet to bring coal direct to its doors.

Elizabeth, in particular, was a fan of Ovaltine and was quite happy to let them go in front but Gloria was in a hurry this morning and had no patience with the smiling boatmen on the back of the two boats, looking, it had to be said, very healthy on their diet of free Ovaltine.

'I wish they'd shift over,' Gloria was saying crossly. 'We need to get in those locks first or we'll be all day.'

Maggie, however, was noticing with envy how immaculate the boats looked and immediately went below to get a cloth to clean *Nancy May*'s roof.

'We haven't got time for that, Maggie,' Gloria said crossly. 'You need to go ahead and set up the locks.'

At that moment Joe called over. 'Quick, move across. Thems were so busy smiling at you lot, they've taken the wrong line. You can sneak between if yer quick.'

Seeing her chance, Gloria manoeuvred straight into the empty water in front of her, taking great delight in the way the smiles faded on the Ovaltine boatmen's faces. She gave them a grin and a thumbs up and they reluctantly waved her on, impressed by her cheek.

At the top of the locks, Maggie took over the tiller while Gloria jumped off.

'Won't be long,' she called, 'I'll catch you up.'

Wistfully watching Gloria go, Maggie would have loved to have visited the fourteenth-century church, but for now, she was the one who needed to steer the boat to make their way towards Tyseley. The girls would be given a few days off when they offloaded this load of cement. They'd all be glad to get rid of it; it had been a nightmare to keep dry, especially when the bilge pumps were still clogged with coal. She realised how ready she was for her leave. They'd had to miss many of the nine-pence baths along the canal because of the danger of leaving Lenny on his own on the boat and she ran her fingers through her hair, feeling the knots and tangles. She thought she might bring a small compact mirror with her on her next trip but then thought better of it; it was probably best not to see what she looked like.

It had been a long trip, no longer than the others but this one had seemed interminable at times and the girls were emotionally drained and physically exhausted. When Maggie had signed up, the promise of leave at the end of every trip had sounded like a huge benefit; now it seemed like a necessity.

Word had reached them that the other girls they had met at Stoke Bruerne all those weeks ago had all given up and gone home, leaving only a few female crews who, like the girls on the *Nancy May* and *Florence*, were becoming quite famous for their tenacity and growing expertise. She glanced round to see Elizabeth singing into the breeze; her perfect appearance altered into a windswept tangle of hair and dirt. Her haughty expression had softened and she looked completely natural surrounded by the increasingly industrial landscape around them. Ahead, she spotted Gloria's short legs running full pelt to meet them at the next bridge, her face aglow with the sunshine from a summer in the open air and the satisfaction that she'd ensured someone up there would look after Joe. Maggie felt justifiably proud of them all.

* * *

Jim Carpenter frowned at the new room-mate in the borrowed black cassock across the room from him; Alfie was hovering in the doorway, unsure whether he was welcome at this gathering. David Phillips was talking about how cosy the three men would be together, but Jim was angry. He'd already agreed to accommodate Alfie but at least he didn't speak, and now another deserter had been forced on him.

A strong feeling of abandonment at being made to leave Broughton House had resulted in even more bitterness in him, so much so that he had forgotten about the letter from Mrs Baines and her son, which he'd stuffed at the bottom of his old suitcase. Without a ration book, their diet had been limited to little more than cabbage and Marmite and that was not helping Jim's temperament and now another deserter had turned up, meaning their supplies were going to be even more minimal. Parcels from Emmanuel Church were beginning to be dropped off at the door with no questions asked but, Jim still complained bitterly about the injustice of life at every opportunity. Lenny stood uncomfortably to one side, still wearing the curate's apparel that had allowed him to travel up from Watford without being challenged.

Jim lit up the dog-end of a cigarette to stave off his hunger pains. They may not have been rationed but they did cost money, and the small allowance sent by Reverend Phillips every week wasn't going to be enough to feed Jim's addiction.

Meanwhile, Lenny was looking askance at the mess around him. On the floor were three mattresses, one with springs popping out of it, a couple of blankets were strewn across them and an old towel was being used as a pillow on one of them. There was a distinct smell of urine coming from the tiny bathroom, which made Lenny wrinkle his nose, and the man in front of him had on a pair of dirty overalls and had obviously not shaved in a month. Lenny was trying hard to face life with more optimism so stepped forward to hold out his hand in greeting only to receive a cold, weak clasp in return.

'So, you and Alfie'll stay here while I get in touch with my contact in the army,' David told Lenny. 'I know it's not much but at least you're safe from prying eyes.'

He turned to Jim. 'You need to do some cleaning up, Jim, because if we get any problems with damp or mould or, heaven forbid, rats, we can't let you stay here anymore.'

Jim had spent the time since David brought him there fulminating on his inability to deal with the unfairness of life. Left with too much time to think and no garden to tend, he had withdrawn more and more into himself, hating every fibre of his being with a passion.

David looked at his watch. He had a service in half an hour so had no choice but to leave these three to muddle along as best they could.

Lenny ran his fingers over the black cloth of the cassock and held his head a little higher. It occurred to him that in the clean clothes in the parcel David had given him, he might begin to feel more like the trained soldier he was, and he smiled warmly at Jim before going into the bathroom to change and look for a cloth and, hopefully, some cleaning products he could use to tackle that toilet.

After an hour of hearing scrubbing and brushing, Jim and Alfie put their heads round the doorway. Alfie's eyes opened in surprise and even Jim gasped in shock; he couldn't believe the difference this newcomer had made. All the mould was scrubbed clean with the bath brick that had been on the windowsill, the floor was mopped and the toilet – Jim peered into the bowl and let out an involuntary huffing noise.

'I can almost see my face in the damned thing,' he said.

Lenny beamed. 'Now, I'm going to cook tea but you two can tackle the main room,' he said, handing Jim a cloth and Alfie the Old Dutch cleaning powder.

By the time a delicious smell of potato and corn beef fritters was emanating from the little two-burner stove in the corner, Jim had actually shaved and washed his face. He'd hardly noticed Alfie's silent presence but there had been a feeling of shame when he saw how Lenny had looked at the flat and, for the first time, he saw the mess with someone else's eyes. Lenny might have been a deserter like Alfie, but he looked almost enthusiastic about going back. It made the gnawing feeling of his own inadequacy grow in his stomach and he was about to slink off into the corner chair when Lenny broke the silence.

'Here, grab a plate. I have washed them,' he added smiling. 'Do you know, Jim, you really remind me of one of the girls I've been hiding out with on the Grand Union Canal. She looks a lot like you.' He shrugged at the blank expression that greeted him and went on to say, 'Anyway, I've got to admit, I've actually enjoyed doing all this; watching those girls doing men's work, then cleaning, cooking and even doing the engine maintenance all in a tiny cabin a quarter the size of this. Honestly, we men are going to have to pick ourselves up a bit – they're leaving us behind.'

* * *

The next time David came to visit, he was stunned at the change in the place – and in Alfie. It was as if having a fellow deserter around had galvanised him to rediscover a little of the person he had once been. Between them, they'd cleaned the flat and organised the kitchen so that the shelves were neatly stacked with crockery on one side and the meagre rations on the other. Alfie was actually tackling the job of making fish cakes with a tin of salmon he'd found alongside the usual morning offerings left by either his mum or someone else from Broughton House. Ushering David in, he immediately put the kettle on and pointed towards one of the two hard-backed chairs near the neatly stacked mattresses in the corner.

David glowed with delight. There had been more progress in one week than Broughton House had managed to achieve in the six months that Alfie had been hiding out there. He looked at Lenny and realised the process had been two-way. He too looked brighter than when he hurried away from the canal and David wondered whether the challenge of cleaning up this flat had helped him to feel he could face going back to the army.

'You two seem to be getting along all right,' he said, taking the proffered cup of tea and was pleased to see a warm smile pass between the men in front of him. 'But where's Jim?'

'He's outside. He sits on the step at the back all the time.'

This told David everything he needed to know. Once the three of them had a cup in their hands, Lenny patted Alfie on the shoulder and like a proud parent announced, 'He's been saying an odd word like "yes" and "no" haven't you, Alfie?' His protégé looked pleased with himself but alarmed too, as if that revelation might raise expectations.

'It's all right,' Lenny told him gently and then to David, said, 'My brother could be a bit like this. I think I can help him. Bit by bit, Alfie'll come round, won't you, mate?'

There was a doubtful nod but David noticed that the young lad's eyes were definitely a little brighter.

Lenny continued: 'I've told him that if we go back, we go back together, so I can keep an eye on him.' Alfie grasped the hand that was patting his and squeezed tightly.

David smiled with pleasure. 'And I have news,' he told them, taking a sip and wincing, as always, at the Carnation milk that made the brew so sweet.

Slowly and in detail, he explained how he had been in touch with a friend of Harry's in the army who was prepared to meet Lenny and Alfie and hear their cases.

'We won't go to prison, will we?' Lenny asked.

'I don't think so,' David said. 'As far as Alfie's concerned, I think the fact he's lost his voice might help explain his desertion and, once they hear about the gang's role in all this, Lenny, I bet you've got a good chance of being taken back. And don't worry, we can make sure the girls aren't implicated.' He'd seen the shadow of anxiety that had crossed the lad's face.

'We mustn't,' Lenny spluttered. 'I won't let Elizabeth, Maggie and Gloria get into trouble because of me. They were so wonderful.'

There was a noise behind them and David turned to see Jim, standing on the threshold of the living room. His fingers clutched at the handle and he had gone very pale.

'Maggie?' he mouthed silently.

Oblivious to the implications of his words to the man hovering in the background, Lenny chattered on. 'They were all so pretty; Gloria, well, she's just a bundle of fun and Elizabeth is a bit scary but she knows a lot about medicine, but I think Maggie's my favourite,' he confided with a blush. 'Well, she had something special about her – she's from round here and is so clever but then she's a teacher so she would be, I suppose.'

Jim backed away like a retreating snake out of the room, watched carefully by David.

David turned his attention to the two young men in front of him. 'Don't worry, Lenny, I've already told this army chap you were being blackmailed to stay with the gang; the fact that you found refuge for longer than one night with the girls doesn't really need to be mentioned. To be honest,' he added thoughtfully, 'this chap was only interested in the training and active duty you'd both had; the rest didn't seem to bother him.'

Aware he didn't have a lot of time before he was due back at Broughton House for a new intake of veterans, David quickly told them both they would have to attend an interview the following morning and, bemoaning the fact that their uniforms were long gone, suggested they should just make themselves as smart as they could.

Leaving them to mull the information over, David went to find Jim, who was sitting on the metal step outside. His nicotine-stained fingers were shaking as he raised a cigarette stub to his mouth.

David hesitated, thinking of Jim's shock at Maggie's name, but then decided this wasn't the time to talk about it – Jim wasn't ready so he changed tack. 'I've got someone who'd like to come and see you,' David told him, noting the look of panic that spread across Jim's face.

'He's a vet like you and was in the Dardanelles,' he said quickly. 'I think you'll be interested in what he has to say.'

There was a slight shrug but nothing more.

Chapter 32

The battles for Monte Cassino were proving to be a bloodbath. The commanders knew it, the boffins in London knew it and the men certainly knew it, even without the gory display of the motionless khaki uniforms barely discernible amidst the blood and mud. Close to the Gothic Line, it was likely to be the last line of defence for the Axis powers and the Allies were determined to take it, but it had taken a heavy toll. A torrential downpour had caused roads to crumble, rivers to flood and mud to cake the terrain, bogging in troops and artillery, and the 6th Company were finding their weapons malfunctioned, their large vehicles were unable to move, and their boots sank with every step, adding to their frustration. On his weary way back to camp, Harry walked past bodies of men who had tried to claw their way up the hillside and would forever haunt the beautiful countryside under the monastery. Amidst the many Polish victims, he recognised familiar faces who had stepped forward only a few days earlier to receive Communion from his hands. He spotted one soldier whose frozen fingers were still clasped around the stone cross he had struggled so hard to reach and at such a cost. The cross seemed to represent an ideal to aspire to, overlooking the surrounding countryside, but with that dead soldier next to it instead there was a mockery about its towering solidity.

While the medical team struggled to keep up with the physical damage to the soldiers, Harry concentrated on the emotional and spiritual scars. To see the relief that spread across their faces when he turned up at their bedsides in those last moments reminded him why he had done this job in the first place and the clutch of a man's hand as he left this life touched him deeply.

The doctor and the medical orderlies were all tired and sweating and, if they got five minutes, they would lie on the straw on the floor to catch a short nap, ignoring the fact that some of the sheaves were moving with fleas. Harry was exhausted too and found a corner where he could lie down, trying to ignore Tommy Sinclair's toes that threatened to wriggle up his nose. His dreams, however, were a disturbing tale of his flea bites from the straw spouting fountains of blood. After what seemed like seconds, Tommy shifted his position, and Harry woke up to get to his feet and immediately carry on giving what help he could to the medical staff.

'You really do give them peace,' Lieutenant Colonel Forsythe said, pausing in his passage down the aisles of injured men. He had been standing behind watching the padre clasp the hands of a nineteen-year-old with a gurgling chest wound, blood mixing with spittle as it slowly spread across his uniform. When the rasping noise suddenly stopped, Harry tenderly closed the boy's terrified eyes with his fingers before placing the still muddied hands across the dead soldier's wounded chest.

Harry got to his feet. His eyes were moist. 'He was from Cheshire,' he said quietly. 'A farm, I think. Could have been excused in a reserved occupation but no, had to come and do his duty. God bless him.'

The words were said simply but, in his heart, Harry was fervently hoping his benediction would be heard by some higher power. The boy deserved that at least.

Lieutenant Colonel Forsythe pulled Harry to one side.

'Go and get a hot drink. I can't give a padre an order, but I can give some very strong advice. You've been here all night.'

Harry glanced around the room. It was emptier and a little quieter than the turmoil that had accompanied the constant influx of men through the early hours.

He nodded and took himself off to find the tea truck. He was scratching, confirming that the straw had been invaded by fleas.

'Post's here,' an excited private yelled to everyone within hearing. 'Post, come and get it.'

There was a stampede towards the truck that had just drawn up and a beleaguered 8th Army sergeant was trying to sort out the letters from large sacks that had just made their way up from Naples. The delivery had been a long time coming.

Harry strolled over, letting the men get to the truck first and after standing in line for twenty minutes, he was handed a total of four letters, which brought a delighted smile to his weary face.

He scanned the writing on the envelopes. Three were familiar, one from his parents, one from his uncle and the third from David at Broughton House but one, with the simple address of his number, name, rank and unit and the ubiquitous c/o APO England, was written in a hand that took him a moment to recognise. Clutching the letter in his fist, he raced back to his tent where he kept his precious letters in an old Huntley & Palmers biscuit tin. Scrabbling to the bottom to find the letter he had received from an office on the Grand Union Canal, he gave a little yelp of delight. Yes, it was Maggie's writing. He was about to rip it open but then paused, suspecting he might want to keep this letter forever, so he very gingerly edged the envelope open, just stopping to note it was dated from September. *She hasn't had my letter,* he thought. He took a deep breath, not sure he wanted to know what she had to say.

Dear Harry,

I hope you're well. I know it's been a long time since we've talked but I hope you don't mind my writing to you. I have no idea where you are but I do hope you're keeping well and safe. I think of you often.

We're still working hard but we've had a few dramas that I can't wait to tell you about, but for now, let me say, your friend, David, has been incredibly helpful and has relieved us of our 'package' who may be joining you and your friends again soon. I do hope so.

I'm writing this in early autumn but suspect you may not receive it until the weather has turned much colder, but just to let you know, the blackberries are out and providing us with some lovely fresh fruit from the hedgerows. The summer's been mixed but has cheered up over the past few weeks. I even heard some late swallows before they head south for the winter. I hope they don't get caught up in the fighting on their travels.

The girls are well and I've become very fond of them. We've been through so much together, I'm sure we'll be friends for life.

I do hope you can find it in your heart to write to me. I do know how you were feeling about me when we last met and I can't tell you how sorry, and ashamed, I am about all of it.

I would love to know how you are; I've really missed our talks. Keep safe.

With fondest regards,

Maggie.

X

Harry smelled the letter, clasped it to his breast and did a very unpadre-like dance around the tent.

A hoot of laughter came from the flap of the doorway.

'Time for a ballroom dancing lesson is it, Padre?'

Harry ran towards the weak sunlight that the open tent flap had allowed in and grasped his friend, Paul, by the shoulders.

'She's written, Paul, she's written!' And he twirled him round with a joyous laugh.

'From your mum, that letter, is it?' Paul joked and then spun Harry round at twice the speed.

'Careful, you'll make me fall, I haven't eaten all day,' Harry said, gasping for breath. 'I wrote to her months ago, but I don't think the letter's reached her, so she won't know how I feel but maybe she doesn't hate me after all.'

'Well, sounds like we've got lots to celebrate. I've just heard those two fellows, you know, your friend the intrepid tank transporter driver and his mate, well, they've just turned up. Who'd 'ave thought it? Bet they've got a few tales to tell.'

Paul saw Harry's face light up and then went to grab his arm to pull him towards the hastily erected NAAFI tent where the tea urn was always bubbling, but Harry was already running ahead like the young man who'd once raced up Scafell.

The letter burned like a hot coal in his jacket pocket all day until he was able to climb into his bunk that night. Every time he would say the familiar words over a dying soldier, he would now have the warmth and comfort of those simple lines – *I think of you often* – to give him strength. Life as a padre could be lonely and to know that Maggie cared gave him a renewed determination to deal with the Bruegel scene that surrounded him.

Snuggled under his rough blanket, Harry read and reread her letter using a torch he kept in his kitbag for emergencies.

The batteries were precious and after committing every word to memory he finally turned the torch off and tucked the letter under his kitbag, which he used as a pillow.

* * *

'Someone's been having a nice dream,' Private Paul Murphy thought, noticing the contented smile on the padre's face before putting the customary morning mug of tea on the floor. He stood over Harry for a moment, hesitating to wake him. He looked like his younger brother, Walter, and while Paul didn't really know where his brother was, the padre had been trying to get information for him, knowing that Paul was fretting. They all took this young chaplain for granted, Paul knew that, and often his wisdom, his caring and his solace was the one spark of sense in this whole war.

The batman put a gentle hand on Harry's shoulder to wake him, but it took a sharper shake to get him to open his eyes.

'Oh, I'm sorry, Paul, I was well away there,' Harry said, gratefully reaching for the tea. A haggard look had replaced the smile.

'You looked better in dreamland, Padre, not sure this real world's suiting you,' Paul said. 'In fact, if you don't mind me saying so, you look worse than many of the lads.'

'Hah, thanks a lot,' Harry laughed, 'but you wait till I've got my Yardley's face powder on. I'll look a lot better. So how are things this morning?' He hesitated, waiting to hear the answer but Paul had other news for him.

'You might be getting out of here. The old man wants to see you.'

Harry jumped up to go to the ablutions, handing his empty tin mug to the private on the way out with a smile.

'I just hope that doesn't mean I'd have to manage without your cuppas, Paul.'

* * *

Lieutenant Colonel Forsythe was pacing up and down when Harry was shown into the CO's tent.

'Ah, there you are, Padre. So, how do you feel about aeroplanes?'

Chapter 33

'Hello, Grandad,' Maggie called cheerfully from the front hall of her home in Didsbury. Her grandfather pushed open the door from the kitchen to greet her.

'Hello, lass, I weren't expecting you. How lovely.' He looked flustered and from upstairs came the sound of rustling.

Maggie raised her eyebrows. 'Got company, have you, Grandad?'

'Um, yes, Mrs Harper is, um, sorting some of your granny's things out upstairs.'

Leaning forward to give her grandfather a hug, Maggie noticed the smell of the new American craze, Old Spice.

'Uh-huh,' she said with a grin and went past him into the kitchen to put the kettle on. In the hallway, she heard the clatter of heels and some urgent whispering.

'Hello, Mrs Harper.' She turned to greet the woman who'd come in behind her grandfather. There was a smell of fresh face powder and Maggie noticed she was wearing a pair of slightly tattered pink, fluffy slippers. She and Mrs Harper exchanged a knowing look and Maggie decided to tackle the situation head on.

'It's so nice to see you here, taking care of Grandad,' she said warmly.

'I'm glad you approve, Maggie,' Dorothy Harper replied, as if to close the subject once and for all. 'It's been lonely for both of us and, well, in these times of war, we none of us know, do we?'

Maggie's grandfather looked on bemused. He had been so embarrassed wondering how he was going to explain the relationship he and this widow had started, fearful that Maggie and her brothers would condemn him for finding someone so soon after their granny died, but here was Maggie, pouring water into the pot as if it were a normal Sunday afternoon teatime.

Mrs Harper moved across the room and opened the biscuit tin on the shelf.

'It's as if I knew you were coming,' she said with a chuckle. 'I only baked these yesterday.'

Watching these two women bustle around his kitchen, chatting like his Winnie used to do with Maggie, Charlie looked from one to the other like a spectator at a tennis match. Handing the younger girl a tea towel to dry up the cups and saucers, Dorothy reached for the best plates from the walnut sideboard.

'Close your mouth, Charlie,' Dorothy said, 'you'll catch flies in it,' and with a smile, she gently pushed him towards his armchair and finally the three of them sat down.

'So, you'll be wanting a bath, Maggie,' Dorothy said, looking at the tangle that was haloing Maggie's head. 'I managed to save a bit of shampoo, it's on the shelf in the bathroom.'

It made Maggie laugh that she was now included in this woman's sort out of the little terraced house in Didsbury and imagined her taking a flannel to behind her ears if she didn't get upstairs and out of her reach fast enough. She wondered whether Dorothy Harper had moved in full time.

The toothbrush in the mug on the bathroom sink answered that question for her when, twenty minutes later, she went up to carefully fill the cast iron bath to well below the obligatory red line that was there to measure the water allowance for the household, which she now suspected numbered two.

Her grandfather looked so well – and happier than she'd seen him in a long time. It was sad her granny hadn't seen him like this in their later years together; that twinkle in his eye must have been what first attracted her to him when they were young, but it had been dimmed by anger for so long and she now realised their marriage had been tainted. Lying back, Maggie luxuriated in the warm water, until her hair fanned out behind her.

Maggie's thoughts, as always in a quiet moment, turned to Harry and she ran her hands over her body, feeling the tingling in her skin, but then it occurred to her that the two lovebirds downstairs might actually have shared this very bath and the thought was so disturbing that she sat up quickly and roughly scrubbed the precious shampoo into her scalp.

Lifebuoy soap had never smelled so good and when Maggie went back downstairs, her hair still wet, she felt renewed. His granddaughter's beaming smile seemed to allay any final concerns Charles might have had about the awkwardness of the situation.

They'd just sat down to catch up with all Maggie's news – or at least, as much as she was prepared to share with them – when her grandfather jumped to his feet.

'Oh, I completely forgot. This letter came for you Maggie; it looks as if it's been all round the houses.' He handed over a tattered envelope which made Maggie grab for the mantelpiece. Her grandfather continued: 'Anyway, I've got to get going, I'm meeting John Mullins; he was at Gallipoli you know and has been talking me through things.' There was brief pause that Maggie noted with approval. It was obvious that John Mullins was helping her grandfather finally to understand the tragedy of that terrible battle. Her grandfather went on, 'Anyway, he's going to Salford to talk to some chap who was there as well. John thinks he can help him.'

Dorothy hadn't minced her words when she told Charles that talking to people who'd actually been in the Dardanelles might help him understand what his son went through and get rid of his anger. Completely absorbed with so many regrets, Charlie failed to notice how Maggie was not listening to a single word.

'Actually, Maggie,' Mrs Harper was saying, a plan racing through her head, 'why don't you go with your grandad. I know he wants to spend as much time as possible with you while you're here. I've got some washing to do and it's not a bad day for November; I might be able to get it out.'

'Maggie?' she said again. 'Did you hear me?'

Maggie was staring at the letter in her hands but then couldn't stand it any longer and ripped it open. She read Harry's words that had been written so many months before and her eyes focused on the line: '*and I hope you can find it in yourself to forgive me*'. She emitted a slight squeak at the words that followed about her '*lovely face*' and looked round at the room in delight suddenly noticing how the weak winter sunshine from the back window shone on everyone.

Maggie got up and gave the new mistress of the house a delighted hug. 'Yes, of course I'll go with grandad. Sorry. I think you're going to prove to be a treasure, Mrs H., and I'm beginning to think we'll wonder how we'd have coped without you.'

Dorothy's eyes glistened. This morning's plan, which she and Reverend Phillips had come up with, was going to be a risky strategy before Maggie turned up but now, if Maggie was there as well, maybe, just maybe, she hoped, this circle of anger might finally be broken.

If only Winnie had been here to see this, she thought and then gave a snort. *Hmm, maybe not*, thinking of the warm bed she and Charlie had left upstairs that morning.

She watched Charlie and Maggie wander off down the road arm in arm and then turned back to tackle the washing.

* * *

Jim Carpenter was on edge. He didn't like visitors.

'I thought there was only one,' he grumbled to Lenny. 'Just the chap who was at Gallipoli; now it seems that he's bringing someone else. Well, I don't want to see either of them and that's that. You can tell them that, lad.' And he turned back to his copy of the *Manchester Guardian*.

At that moment, there was a knock at the door and Lenny jumped up to answer it. Jim couldn't hear the exact words, but he heard a yelp of delight from Lenny and then a woman's voice.

'Oh, for crying out loud,' he grumbled and stormed out to make his escape but then he stopped in his tracks. There were three people standing in the hallway: one was one tall man with a kindly face who must be that Mullins chap who'd been at Gallipoli, he thought, then there was an older man with the same eyes he saw in the mirror every morning . . . he couldn't possibly be, could he? And that girl . . . she looked so familiar.

Looking equally baffled, Maggie turned to her grandfather, who had gone a deathly pale and then to John Mullins.

'Anyone want to explain what's going on?' she said in a commanding voice that shocked even her grandfather and he looked sideways at her. He hardly recognised this new assertive Maggie.

Inspired by her confidence and with Dorothy's coaxing resounding in his ear, Charlie Carpenter hesitated for a split second before stepping forward with the words: 'Hello, son.'

* * *

Elizabeth had waited with excitement for the other two girls to return. Her trip home had been brief; the house had seemed so empty without the boys there and after walking round the empty rooms with an ineffectual duster to try to find bits that the maid, Marie, might have missed, she gave up and got the bus straight back to Birmingham. On her journey, it occurred to her that a tiny cabin on the Grand Union Canal was more of a home than the impressive, palisaded house in the Cotswolds.

With two days to kill until the other two joined her, she'd picked up their orders, collected the post and set to, cleaning both boats, washing as much bedding as the tiny bucket would allow and, with no one else taking up space, had been able to lay everything out to dry by the warmth of the stove. She'd been looking forward to seeing the looks on her two companions' faces at all her achievements but first Gloria then Maggie arrived. Within seconds, Maggie had stolen her thunder with the words: 'I met my father.'

There'd been no time for more questions as the shout 'next' came down the wharf and all the girls had to concentrate on the loading of the long lengths of timber that somehow refused to stack neatly in the allotted space. The task prompted a great deal of swearing from Gloria and even Elizabeth was heard to utter the odd 'damn'. It was only once the tarpaulin was sheeted up and neatly in place with the wood thoroughly protected from the rain that the hatch door was pulled shut and the interrogation could begin.

Maggie was bewildered by Elizabeth and Gloria's barrage of questions and blankly registered the expectant faces on the two girls sitting cross-legged on the bunk in front of her. She knew she had to tell them something but had no idea how to begin.

'Umm . . .' she stuttered. 'Well, I went with Grandad to this flat in Salford with his friend John Mullins who'd been at Gallipoli in the Great War. They were going to see someone else who'd been there. I didn't think to ask any questions; I'd had a letter from Harry, you see. I couldn't think about anything else.'

She paused, her mind going back to Harry's words.

'That's great,' Gloria said, 'but what else?'

Elizabeth took her hand and pressed it hard. 'Your father . . . how did you meet your father? You look in shock, come on, tell all and do calm down.'

Maggie was too tense to relax, preferring to sit upright with her hands clenched in front of her until she was ready to recount the events she'd played over and over in her head. By now, Elizabeth was tense with expectation while Gloria's eyes were sparkling with the drama of it all and she demanded to know where everyone was standing or sitting.

'What does it matter, Gloria?' Elizabeth asked, frustrated.

'I need to picture it,' Gloria said simply. 'This is what I do when I read a book, I imagine where the characters all are in the room. It's like in the movies,' she said, savouring the modernity of the American word.

'Oh, ignore her, just get on with it, Maggie,' Elizabeth huffed. Past experience had shown that Gloria's enthusiasm was hard to quell.

Maggie stuttered. 'I just went to keep Grandad company really – he seemed so much better and I think it's since Mr Mullins has been calling round. He's been helping Grandad to understand the way things were at Gallipoli – he's ever so nice.'

Gloria blew out a loud exasperated sigh. 'Oh for heaven's sake . . . and . . . and . . . ?'

'Well, you won't believe it but Lenny opened the door. Honestly, I was so taken aback – I had no idea he was there but apparently Reverend Phillips has put him there while he tries to get him back in the army, and there's another young deserter living there too, Alfie, I think his name was – he's hoping to get him taken back too.'

'For God's sake, Maggie, your dad . . . your dad?' Gloria butted in.

'Oh, OK, OK. So behind Lenny was another man. He looked vaguely familiar, but my grandad knew him immediately and stepped forward, his hand outstretched. My f-father, because I'd worked out that's who he was by then, stood stiffly and didn't respond; he just clutched his newspaper. Then . . .' Here Maggie paused and shrugged. This tale was getting more bizarre by the minute. 'It was the *Manchester Guardian* that changed everything between them. Mr Mullins pointed to it, telling them he was a printer there and that they should ignore the "darned cock-up" in the story on page twelve. It was such a random comment to make that it, well, it broke the tension. There was a brief moment before my dad and grandad just, you know, seemed to remember what caused the rift in the first place and started throwing accusations at each other. It was just like before . . .'

There was a catch in Maggie's voice and Elizabeth quickly intervened to prevent her from breaking down completely.

'And what about you, did you say anything?'

'Oh yes.' There was no doubt of the bitterness in Maggie's tone. 'I mean, I really went for them both. By the time I'd finished, neither of them had any doubt of the harm they'd both caused – to Granny, to me, to my brothers.' She sat back, exhausted, and Gloria started to clap. Elizabeth joined in and Maggie squirmed in embarrassment but went on: 'We all just stood there, but again, Mr Mullins intervened. He turned to me and explained that Dad's men had all been ambushed in Gallipoli and that because he'd gone ahead, he'd been forced to watch them from behind a rock while they were massacred.' Maggie took a long breath. 'I finally understood why he'd never been able to forgive himself.

'Then Dad went over to his suitcase and from the bottom brought out a letter. He passed it silently to Grandad who then gave it to me. It was from the mother of a man my father had held in his arms as he died and it talked of the respect her son had had for his sergeant and how she hoped her own forgiveness would allow him to forgive himself. I saw tears in my dad's eyes as he finally reached his hand out to Grandad, then as they touched, something seemed to connect them and they stared at each other, I mean really stared, but their hands sort of hung there – they had no idea what to do next. It was Mr Mullins who broke the silence. "I suggest it's time a father and son gave each other a hug. It's been a long time," he said, "and there are too many men out there in Gallipoli who would give anything to be here now and be able to reach out to put their arms around their mother or father."'

Maggie swallowed a sob. 'It was like time was standing still and then Grandad – I couldn't believe it – took another step forward with a gulping noise and clasped my . . . father . . . in such a tight hold, I wasn't sure he could breathe.'

'So how did the afternoon end?' Gloria was asking. The last pages of her books were always read and reread to make sure she hadn't missed anything, and she did like all the loose ends to be tied up.

But then, it was as if an open door had suddenly let a draught in. Maggie shivered and the other two noticed the colour drain from her face.

'Nothing. Nothing happened.' A bitter tone had been injected into her voice. 'I turned to my dad but he simply picked up the *Guardian* and turned to page twelve. It was just like always; it was if I didn't exist.'

The animation went out of Maggie's expression and her shoulders drooped as her eyes filled with tears. She simply shook her head.

Elizabeth leaned across and took her hand, but it was as cold as one of the towpath's metal rings on a frosty morning.

'Didn't he acknowledge you at all?'

'No, it was just that I brought up too many painful memories, I think.' There was a sad bitterness in her voice. Maggie had recognised the same mask that had hidden her father from her for so many years. She got to her feet and tossed her head.

'Well, I just left them all to it and went to get the bus back here. That's fine by me. He and Grandad can have a cosy reunion, I don't need to be a part of it. I've managed all these years; I can manage the rest of my life without a father.'

And she went out into the freezing evening air, closing the hatch door quietly behind her leaving her words hanging.

Chapter 34

There was little chance of sleep that night as Maggie recalled the gaunt face of a father she hardly knew. Shuffling her feet crossly beneath the blanket she remembered every slight, every blank expression and every tear she'd shed into her pillow at night throughout her childhood. There were so many times she'd read *Anne of Green Gables*, crying when Anne finally found a champion in her foster father, Matthew. It had made her wonder over and over again what that sort of support would have been like. She knew the boys had suppressed any emotion, cutting their father out of their thoughts, but to a little girl, desperate for the approval of the one parent she had left, she'd always held out a forlorn hope that one day he would wrap his arms around her and be the father she craved. At the school gates, her friends would race out to be embraced by their mothers or fathers, keen to hear about their achievements of the day, while she hung back. Her grandparents tried to fulfil the role, but their grey hair made them stand out and the bullying taunts from her smug classmates made the young girl retaliate with sharp words and, sometimes, fists.

It was hard to forgive the hurt of those years when she'd longed for a normal dad and one of the worst things was wanting him to share her love of books and learning, but then, sitting up in her bunk, one day, in particular, came back to her; she couldn't have been more than eight, when she'd found her father's English school books. Teeming with ideas, adventures and beautiful phrasing, she'd been entranced and experienced a brief moment when she suspected they might have more in common than she could have hoped for, but when she'd asked him about it, he'd just shrugged with that blank expression she knew so well. The way he brushed her off left her feeling crushed and it was up to her older brothers to wipe away her tears.

Patrick and Billy! She leaped out of bed realising they knew nothing about the weekend. She needed a pen and some paper.

On *Florence*, Elizabeth was having trouble sleeping too but she was thinking about Lenny. The news from Manchester that he was hoping to be taken back into the army had eased her conscience somewhat, but part of her unease was guilt that she had put him in such an impossible situation in the first place. She was also aware that seeing her own boys in him, she'd started to feel quite maternal towards the young deserter; to think of him going back to the army where they would undoubtedly put him on the front line, filled her with dread. The war was not going well in January 1944 and although there was talk of a 'big push' into Europe and the siege of Leningrad had finally given the allies victory, it had all come at a huge cost and now, in their struggles up to the Gothic Line in Italy, thousands were losing their lives at Monte Cassino. She didn't dare think about the Mediterranean where Christopher was, knowing he was telling her less and less about what was happening, but she suspected he was approaching Italy to bring more men to the front. Common sense meant she knew the Axis powers of Germany and its allies would do everything they could to stop that happening.

Working on the canals was satisfying and certainly challenging, but Elizabeth had an emptiness in her stomach that was only filled when she was helping people. She too got out of bed and started to write a letter; this one was to the Queen Alexandra Nursing Corps.

* * *

'Rise and shine.' Gloria's irrepressible cheerfulness penetrated Maggie's sleep and she groaned.

'Come on, we've got to get back to Knowle by tonight,' Gloria was saying, talking loudly over the bubbling of the kettle she'd already put on. She'd been hoping Will would be able to meet her at some stage but was struggling to remember his face; it had been so long.

Maggie forced her eyes open and pulled on her socks. It was freezing cold and the canal was frozen in parts. She'd hardly had any sleep.

'How are you feeling?' Gloria asked, aware of the noises that had emanated from the bunk across from her all night.

'I'm fine,' Maggie lied, but then she gave a weak smile. 'I'm just going to have to get on, aren't I? Like everyone else in this war. I mean, I've managed all these years on my own, Gloria, I don't need a dad – I need my breakfast!'

Once *Florence* was ready as well, they made their way as fast as four miles an hour would let them along the Grand Union. It was all becoming so familiar to them and Gloria and Elizabeth cheerily called back to the passing boaters, who mostly knew them by name by now.

The Spencers, however, hadn't been seen for a couple of weeks and they were all anxious for news of Joe so when, just before Gayton Junction, Maggie spotted *Buffalo* ahead, she shouted in delight seeing Dolly steering with a baby swaddled in a shawl around her chest.

Mrs Spencer's face lit up when she saw the girls and she waved enthusiastically as Maggie drew alongside to shout, 'How's Jake? And Joe? And you and the baby?'

Dolly looked taken aback at her directness: these girls were certainly not like boat people who guarded their privacy like they guarded their precious coal.

Gloria called from the gunwale ledge, 'You'll have to forgive her, Dolly, we've all been so worried.'

Dolly relented and in a low voice that was almost impossible to hear said, 'Jake's no longer with us. 'E was taken bad at Tyseley just after we arrived and, well, that were it.'

The words of condolence were hard to say and there was a silence for a moment while the girls thought of an appropriate response, but then they heard a man's voice from behind: 'Good riddance, if you ask me.'

Seeing the shock on the girls' faces, Dolly muttered to the man, 'Ah, shush now, Ernie, yer mustna speak ill of the dead.'

Ernie Spencer saluted the girls with a grin. 'I've 'eard about you lot. You've been proper good to my Dolly.'

Even Gloria looked askance. Tyseley was less than a few days back up the canal and here was this man talking proprietarily about Jake Spencer's wife, but Dolly looked anything but embarrassed; she looked positively radiant.

It was Elizabeth who called out, 'Good for you, Mrs Spencer. Life's too short.'

There was a real connection in the glance that passed between the two women who'd shared the birth of that little baby peacefully sleeping on his mother's breast, and Dolly gave a nod in Elizabeth's direction, knowing that this posh girl had seen the bruises on the insides of her thighs, the torn private parts and the strap lines across her buttocks. The man standing next to her now with his arm protectively around her had been her first love and – unbeknown to anyone except Jake – Joe's father. Dolly kept her lips tightly pressed together; these girls didn't need to know that a drunken brawl years ago between Ernie and his brother had resulted in Ernie being carted off to jail, during which time, Jake had forced Dolly to marry him to spite his brother. He'd never forgiven his wife, his brother or Joe. There was one more secret Dolly Spencer was taking to the grave and that was that Ernie had used a pillow to put an end to the slobbering, grunting man who had once been her husband. A broad beam spread across her face making Gloria think how she'd never looked prettier.

'Stoppin' down the road, are yer?' Ernie shouted over. 'I know Dolly'd be pleased to have a chinwag with you.'

'Yes. When we get to Stoke Bruerne,' Maggie replied, feeling the warm glow of friendship emanating from the boat next to them. She could never have guessed how grateful she would feel to be accepted by the people whose domain they were trespassing on and added, 'We'd love to catch up, I'll put a brew on when we on get there. We're dying to see the baby and . . .' she paused, nervous because fortunes could turn so quickly in wartime '. . . to hear how Joe's doing?'

A cheerful wave reassured her and then *Buffalo* deftly manoeuvred past them to get in the next lock first. Maggie shook her head and smiled; even friends didn't give any quarter on the cut.

*   *   *

It was dark by the time they moored up a few hours later outside the Boat Inn, but they gladly passed over a mug of tea to Dolly who was already there, waiting to take their rope.

Until this day, shamed by her husband's bullying, Dolly had given everyone on the canal a wide berth and she was more excited to see the girls than she admitted to anyone. With few friends and even fewer who knew the extent of the violence that had lurked behind *Buffalo*'s blackened hull, seeing the affection in these fresh, cheerful faces, dulled the memory of Jake's huge body leering over her and for the first time, she was daring to hope the future might offer a happiness she'd never envisaged.

However, she wasn't quite prepared for Elizabeth's gentle hug that enfolded her and the baby in her arms, and she felt tears starting to fall. These two were worlds apart but the unexpected kindness in her touch left Dolly bereft of speech. Gently, like a mother with a child, Elizabeth used a delicate lace handkerchief to wipe the teardrops away and then, pressing the beautiful linen object into Dolly's hand with a firm squeeze, Elizabeth read the story of this woman's life in her dark eyes. There was no shock, no condemnation, only a compassionate understanding that took Dolly by complete surprise.

'Come on, let's go and sit in *Florence* if you've got a minute, it's warmer in there.'

With her arm around her shoulders, Elizabeth led Dolly to the butty and down the steps.

Maggie and Gloria held back, not wanting to intrude and went towards the pub.

The men in the bar parted for them and some gave them pats on their backs or a welcome smile. Maggie couldn't believe it. She had no idea how much these boatmen knew about their dramas on the canal but somehow, even as rank outsiders, they'd had come out of it well.

A delighted Betsy called out from behind the bar: 'Ah, yer back are yer? Wondered when you'd turn up. Like bad pennies, huh? You'll be wantin' a cider then? Sit yer down then and I'll bring 'em over.'

When they were handed their drinks, Betsy bowed her head in towards them to whisper, 'There've been a couple of scum lookin' for you lot.'

Both girls went pale, the flush on their faces from the approval of the men in the bar drained to be replaced by looks of dismay; it could only be Arthur's friends.

'Don't you worry, I think they've been lying low after their mate was taken. Anyways, I told 'em you'd given up and gone 'ome like all the other girls, and then, to make sure they wouldna ask any more questions, we made a big thing about 'ow it was good riddance to yers and that we wouldna care if you'd disappeared off the face of the earth. That convinced 'em I think.'

She winked and looked so pleased with herself she didn't notice how dubious Maggie and Gloria were about her reassurances.

'That's really kind of you, Betsy,' Maggie said, 'but I doubt that's the last we'll see of them.'

'Well, if yer think they're gonna be a bother, we can get some of the lads to sort them out for yer,' Betsy said, more loudly, while fiercely wiping the table.

There was a general murmur from the men who'd been eavesdropping around them; this was obviously a subject that had been discussed thoroughly in The Boat and several men were clenching their knuckles threateningly. Maggie's neck tingled, wondering what their involvement with a danger-ous gang had unleashed on not only their own lives but on this close-knit community that had finally adopted the girls as their own.

'Let's hope it doesn't come to that,' Gloria said, her smile wavering between delight at the support around her and fright at what might be lurking in the shadows of the cut.

The girls lowered their voices to talk quietly.

'Those men won't give up that easily,' Maggie whispered, taking a sip of her cider. 'I think I've always known we hadn't heard the last of them and I don't know about you, Gloria, but I've been waiting to see them around every corner.'

'Yes, I have too. I wish my sister was here. As a policewoman, she'd know what to do.'

'Well, she's over on the Isle of Man and we certainly can't tell the police here,' Maggie said and the two lapsed into a glum silence. 'We won't get away with it a second time with Sergeant Tomlinson.'

'Well, you two look like a wet week.' Elizabeth pulled up a stool.

Gloria leaned in to bring her up to date and Elizabeth bit her lip in thought while Betsy brought over a glass of cider for her.

'Thank you,' Elizabeth said, and Betsy squeezed her arm with affection.

'You'll be all right, girls, everyone knows 'bout those men, we're all lookin' out for yer.' The change in Dolly Spencer had been like the sun coming out on the cut and Betsy knew a great deal of it was due to these young women.

Elizabeth glanced over at the men watching from the bar. Two of them raised their glasses towards the trio and she rewarded them with a smile that made them adjust their red scarves around their necks to wipe the perspiration.

'Hey, look at all your champions,' Maggie chuckled. 'Honestly, Elizabeth, you really know how to win a crowd over.'

'Hmm, I'd forgotten how good I am at flirting,' Elizabeth said, taking a rather large sip of cider.

'You certainly are,' Gloria giggled. 'Look at this lot, they're all in love with you.'

But Elizabeth wasn't listening; she had been putting off penning a letter to Christopher to confess her plans to train as a nurse.

'I'd like to see Sister Anne before we leave tomorrow,' she said mysteriously.

'Why? We can't wait for you, Elizabeth.'

'Oh, I'm just interested in how she manages to look after all these people on the boats,' she said, waving her arm vaguely. 'Don't worry, if Maggie could helm *Florence*, I'll run to catch you up.

'Let's have another drink,' she said to fend off any more questions. 'It's my round.'

It was incredible how the miles were eaten up on the canal now that the girls were so familiar with it. They convinced themselves that Betsy was right and that the gang wouldn't risk any more trouble by trying to track them down so they concentrated on tackling locks like a professional team, working in a harmony that was echoed by the birdsong in the trees or the gentle chug of passing engines. The appearance of life on the cut was one of calm control but in reality, every boat was constantly jostling for position to try to shave a few moments of their trip, anxious to get to the end point where they could deliver their load and claim their wages.

In that spring of 1944, the weather was chillier than normal but the news was hotting up. All over Britain, rumours were being circulated about 'The Big Push.' Everyone, including the girls, rushed to buy a newspaper at every opportunity. The customary canalside greetings were accompanied by crossed fingers or a look to the heavens that perhaps five years of war might finally be getting near the end but then reports of another bombing of London in what was being called the 'Baby Blitz,' would dash the optimism and heads would droop again. 'Do you realise we've knocked a whole day off this trip?' Gloria said as they approached the wharf to unload. 'I think even Joe Spencer would be impressed at that.'

Elizabeth glanced at Maggie, who was untying the tarpaulin. Both of them had remarked how often Gloria brought Joe into the conversation these days and how little she mentioned Will.

They all had a few days leave before they had to re-load at Bull's Bridge so they moved back up the cut to be ready. Maggie was desperate for a chance to nip home to Manchester, check up on her grandfather and have a bath. Elizabeth had managed to arrange to visit the boys at their school on the following Sunday and couldn't contain her excitement, while Gloria was staying with the boats until the following day when she was going to meet Will, who was combining a 'hush hush' visit to London with a chance to see her. She needed some space to sort out her muddled thoughts about him and was looking forward to having a whole cabin to herself for a night. She waved the other two off with a cheery smile and a screwdriver and oil can in each hand. There was nothing she liked better than a chance to strip the engine down properly.

Chapter 35

The ground below was like a miniature train set Harry had been given for his eighth birthday; everything looked so small from ten thousand feet and he peered down to spot the large cross marked on the ground for landing. It had been nearly a month since he had arrived back on English soil and, while others in the Second Battalion had been able to take advantage of the unheard-of three weeks' leave, his late arrival meant he had had to start training immediately. This weekend, though, he was finally due some leave. There were rumours circulating in the mess that the south coast was completely cordoned off to anyone except those training for the manoeuvres that would hopefully turn the tide for the war in the Allies' favour. Two hundred and fifty miles north of that area, Harry was only aware that his strengths as a padre were superseded by the fact that he was now a trained parachutist with the Airborne Forces. Thousands were being prepared for this crucial task and a shiver of excitement ran through him.

Others might start to worry as the time approached for them to be turfed out of the silent craft that was gliding through the air, but Harry Moore relished the excitement of it. He loved the adrenalin rush he got just before jumping and today, standing on the edge of the Horsa glider and noting the slight easterly breeze, he adjusted the straps of his parachute to compensate.

As he stepped out, coordinating his exit with a parachutist from the front to maintain the light craft's balance, he realised his trust in God had been supplanted by a trust in the young WAAF who had packed his chute.

With perfect weather conditions at last, this drop was going like clockwork and once he was floating through the air with a reassuringly perfectly domed canopy above him, he started to enjoy the sensation. It occurred to him that parachuting might be like dying, his soul hovering somewhere in an abyss where wars didn't exist and where he wasn't responsible for the souls of hundreds of terrified men who expected him to have all the answers.

'Bugger,' the clergyman suddenly exclaimed, seeing the ground beneath him rushing up to greet him. He automatically bent his legs to minimise the shock of the impending impact, tucked his chin in and grasped the parachute's 'risers' with his elbows bent to prevent injury. Pushing aside all thoughts of anything but that mark on the ground to his left, Harry executed a ragged landing and fell onto the tarmac, wincing in pain.

'Forget where you were then, did you, Padre?' the brigadier in charge shouted from his position lounging against a Tilly jeep.

'Yep, Brigadier, I think I might have done.'

The commander took a purposeful step forward, all remnants of a relaxed disposition gone. Having lost two men recently on practice runs that had gone wrong, he was not going to lose one more if he could help it. He came right up to Harry so that their noses were almost touching. It was rare for a padre to be admonished but Harry bowed his head in shame, knowing he deserved the censure he was about to receive.

'Never again, you hear me. You concentrate on that jump with every fibre of your body and mind. I'm not going to tell the troops that the man who was supposed to be offering them hope and a belief they'll be looked after, has reached the Pearly Gates before them.'

Harry spluttered an apology and then limped slightly to gather up his chute and get out of the way before the next soldier steered towards the same cross with perfect precision.

* * *

On the bus to Didsbury from the training centre at Ringway two days later, for a precious afternoon leave, Harry rubbed his sore ankle and reflected on how close he had come to being yet another casualty of war. It would have been ironic, he thought, if he had died just because of a lack of concentration. It had been the first lesson he had learned on his climbing adventures in the Lake District – to constantly assess and reassess – but somehow on that descent, it was as if he had tested fate, or God, to take care of him.

With the analytical mind of an educated man, he knew there was a fine line between fate and volition and for a bleak moment, he wondered whether he had wanted to die, to absolve himself from all responsibility of knowing whether there was an afterlife or not, but then he shook himself. His zest for life was too strong for that and besides which, there was a certain young lady that he intended to spend a very long life on this earth with first.

'Shove up, Padre,' a sailor next to him said, breaking in on his thoughts. 'We're almost at Withington and there'll be a pile getting on there.'

Harry shuffled along the seat and looked around at his fellow passengers. He recognised that hope in their eyes when they saw the dog collar, unshaken in their belief that he could provide answers to the turmoil that woke them at three o'clock in the morning.

He gave them the reassuring smile they were expecting and then saw he was being scrutinised by a child on his mother's knee next to him.

'Hello,' he said.

'Do you know God?' the child asked. He must have been about four years of age and the cap on his head was frayed at the edges.

'Well, not personally, but I do chat to Him a lot.' Harry smiled, aware that was something he hadn't done much of recently.

'Is He nice?' the boy persisted.

'Oh, yes, very, and He often asks about you,' Harry said with a wink.

The boy's face beamed for a minute and then clouded over. 'No, He doesn't. He doesn't care about me or He wouldn't have let my daddy die.'

Harry saw the anguished look in the mother's eyes as she wrapped her arms tighter around her son.

'I'm so sorry,' Harry said, but the woman and the child turned away from him. Harry's stomach churned. He wasn't sure he could do this anymore.

* * *

It was those haunting doubts that Harry really would have liked to have discussed with his uncle later that day when Mrs Harrison brought them both a cup of tea in the rectory but somehow, the words kept eluding him. The housekeeper had already confided to him in the hallway that the young curate from Stretford was proving to be invaluable, throwing his energy and organisational skills into making everything work much more smoothly and, Harry noticed, his uncle had more colour in his cheeks. The rectory office had benefited from a clear-out and for once, there was no need to move umpteen books and papers to be able to sit down on the green leather armchair. As always, Peter was more interested in his nephew's life than sharing his own concerns and wanted as many details as Harry could provide him with about his time in Italy. When it came to questions about what he was doing at Ringway, there was complete silence, and the young padre shook his head.

'You know I can't tell you anything about that, Uncle. But let's hope we're getting near the end.'

Peter put his hand on the cross around his neck and bowed his head in a quick prayer then he looked keenly into Harry's eyes.

'You still struggling with all this, young Harry?'

Taken aback, Harry spluttered, 'How did you know?'

'I haven't been in this job for as long as I have without recognising the signs. Have you talked to the boss?'

'No, I haven't been able to contact the DACG.'

'I didn't mean the Deputy Assistant Chaplain General.'

Philip got to his feet and reached his hand out to pull his nephew to his feet. 'Come with me.'

The two men sat side by side in Emmanuel Church and to begin with, Harry felt his feet twitching but with the stillness of his uncle and the familiar walls and pews, he began to relax. It had been a long time since he had felt the quiet of an actual church building rather than an altar made of an oil drum or a rock, where he was constantly alert for the sound of droning from above.

He realised he had nothing to say but somehow just being there seemed like a start.

* * *

It was a calmer young padre who later visited Broughton House to see David and find out whether he had any news of Lenny, Alfie and Jim – and – Maggie.

Bringing Harry up to date with the progress between Charlie and Jim gave David a great deal of pleasure and he told him in detail about their meeting with a satisfied smile, adding that John Mullins had persuaded Jim to actually visit his father again at the family home in Didsbury that very afternoon.

'But you say Maggie was there – at the initial meeting?' Harry asked. 'How did that go?'

David suddenly realised he didn't know. He'd been so pleased to see progress between the father and son, he'd failed to ask John Mullins whether there had been any warmth between Jim and Maggie.

'I'm sorry, I didn't think to find out,' he said shamefacedly.

'Well, did they acknowledge each other? Did they show any affection? It would mean so much to Maggie. Come on, David, you must know something.'

For the first time, Harry sounded impatient with his friend and David felt embarrassed.

'I can only think that nothing happened between them because, I'm really sorry, Harry, John Mullins didn't mention it.' He tried to change the subject. 'I can tell you a bit about Lenny and Alfie, though,' he said.

Harry tried to drag his mind away from Maggie. His first thought was that he should have been there to fight Maggie's corner for her and that was what was making him so cross. He knew it wasn't up to David to take that responsibility.

'I'm sorry,' he said. 'I'm not blaming you; you've done a great job getting Charlie and Jim on speaking terms again. I just know Maggie needs a dad as well as a grandad and if she was there as well, I had hoped she might have found some answers. But you've had enough to think about. So, go on, tell me about Lenny and Alfie.'

David pushed his remorse to one side. 'Well, Lenny and Alfie were both hauled up before a bunch of senior army ranks and were given a thorough dressing-down about their desertion, but, amazingly, it was decided that their punishments should be postponed. I think they need every man they can get but . . . I fear those two will be heading straight for the front line. It's cheaper than prison,' he added with a bitter tone to his voice.

Harry shook his head, lost for words. The war was on a knife-edge, and he'd heard a disturbing rumour that up to a hundred thousand men had now deserted their posts. From a commander's point of view, bringing those trained soldiers back into service could make the difference between victory and defeat.

'I had a letter from Lenny last week,' David went on. 'He's desperately trying to keep an eye on Alfie and stop him going back into his shell. It's my bet they're on their way to Italy.'

Harry's mind went back to the men who had been left on the road north from Cassino. They needed to be replaced and he feared there would be so many more who would join them before the allies finally secured victory of the Gothic Line.

Seeing dark shadows cloud his friend's eyes, David quickly changed the subject.

'But back to Maggie . . .' He paused and then smiled. 'I knew that would get your attention. Well, I did hear she's on leave so, if you're lucky, she might already be at home and you can ask her your questions yourself.'

Harry tried really hard to sound interested in the rest of the news about Broughton House but after a few moments of the latest developments with the new ward, how Mrs Lewis was coping and how the radio was playing up, David gave up.

'Just go, Harry.'

Chapter 36

When Maggie opened the door, the figure that was standing with a rueful grin on the doorstep made her reach her hand out to the door frame to steady herself. She had not been expecting her stomach to do a somersault at the sight of the tall man in front of her. In fact, she had not been expecting Harry Moore to turn up at her door at all.

For a minute, they both were silent, overwhelmed by the emotions that were racing through their bodies and then Harry reached his arms out and Maggie fell into them without hesitation. He held her to him with strong muscles that left her weak.

'Agghhh, Harry, I can't breathe,' she gasped and wriggled backwards only to hurl herself back into his embrace and with a muffled voice from his tunic, she said, 'Oh, I can't believe you're here. I thought you were in Italy.'

'Keep up, Maggie,' Harry laughed, 'you know how we padres get around.'

She grabbed his hand and dragged him into the hallway, but glancing towards the open door to the back room, hovered, looking for an escape:

'I've only just arrived but . . . Dad's in there.'

'I know, I heard he was coming.'

Shaking her head at how Harry seemed to know more about her family than she did, she pulled him towards the back room and then hovered by the door frame. Her father was standing across from her with his back to the fireplace, shifting nervously from foot to foot.

It had taken a huge effort for Jim Carpenter to accept Charlie's invitation to afternoon tea, but he hadn't expected Maggie to be there and since she had cheerily shouted hello from the front door just five minutes before, he'd been struggling to know what to say. Watching her face fall as she walked in the room was enough to make him retreat into the cave of shame he'd been hiding in since she was a child. He and his father might have come to an understanding but the way Jim had failed his own children would torture him forever.

After the stilted greetings, Harry and Maggie stood awkwardly to one side until they heard the front door open again and the cheerful face of Mrs Harper came in.

Taking in the little group in front of her and with a shrewd assessment of the situation, the older woman manoeuvred past Maggie and swiftly towards the side cabinet where she leaned down to peer into the gloom of the shelf at the back.

'I think it's time for some marrow brandy,' she said and, with relief at the arrival of some support, Maggie reached to get some of her granny's cut-glass sherry glasses from the corner cupboard.

When everyone had a drink in their hand, Mrs Harper held hers aloft and gave Charlie a meaningful look.

'Ahem, yes,' Maggie's grandfather said. 'It looks like Dorothy wants me to mark this occasion with three generations being together for a first time in years and I'd like to make a toast . . . .' Mrs Harper nodded to encourage him. 'In that case, I raise a glass to my son, Jim, who's come home to us, to Maggie, who's shown us that women can do anything men can do and to you, Padre, I know what you've done for this family.'

His granddaughter gave a weak smile but the small rag rug on the floor between her and her father stood as a testament to the huge divide between them.

As the cold glass touched Harry's lips, he thought Maggie had never looked more vulnerable and more beautiful. He longed to sweep down like an avenging angel and scoop her up in his arms and protect her from any more hurt. All of a sudden, he felt completely overwhelmed by love and his knees started to buckle, leading Mrs Harper to lean over and whisper with a chuckle, 'Think you'd better sit down, lad.'

The rest of the visit was excruciating for both of them; Maggie wanted to escape the anguished expression on her father's face that had dominated her childhood and then there was Harry – the proximity of his warm body was making her weak and she was desperate to be on her own with him, aware of the clock on the wall that was ticking away their precious time together. She didn't dare catch Harry's eye but could feel his longing with every hair on her arm when he purposefully brushed against her. Finally, when the men had finished discussing the finer points of the line-up for Saturday's match in the War League, Mrs Harper took the initiative.

'Do you know, I think we're a bit short of potatoes, Maggie, why don't you take the padre down to the shops and get us some. I hope you're both able to stay for tea.'

Dorothy smiled as they both leaped to their feet and sped out of the door.

As soon as they got far enough away from the house, Harry pulled Maggie into a doorway to take hold of her and give her a long, lingering kiss. This time it was Maggie's legs that went weak, and she responded by hungrily parting her lips and clinging to him.

'Careful,' he laughed, 'there might be some parishioners around. I've got a reputation to uphold, you know.'

'I don't care,' Maggie said with a delicious giggle. 'You don't know how long I've imagined that kiss.'

Taking hold of her shoulders, Harry took a long look at the girl he wanted to marry.

'Oh, Maggie,' he said breathlessly. 'Oh, Maggie Carpenter, have you any idea what you do to me?'

'If it's anything like what you do to me, then we're in trouble,' she told him, scanning the street to try to find a quieter corner where they could be alone but, in all directions, there were people scurrying about their business. Several had glanced over at the pair, some with pursed lips at the brazenness of their embrace and others who smiled indulgently. Maggie felt a shiver, she'd experienced the power of this longing before and it had caused so much damage.

'Can I trust what we're feeling?' she asked Harry in a quiet voice. 'It's just, well, you know, I've messed things up once already and I couldn't bear it if it happened again. And Harry – can you really forgive me . . . you know for, well, what happened before . . . ?' She still couldn't say the words. She didn't want to be forever wondering whether Harry had really forgotten her past.

Harry replied by taking her in his arms again.

'You are the only girl for me, Margaret Carpenter, and as long as I survive this war, I will come back and ask you to be my wife. I love you,' he added simply. 'As you are, here, standing in front of me, today and for always.'

Bereft of speech, Maggie looked deep into his eyes, trying to see into this man's soul. There was no subterfuge, no deceit, just love. There was such a gentle generosity of spirit there, surely, she could trust him?

'But can you forgive me, Harry, can you really?'

There wasn't even a moment's pause before Harry replied, 'I have watched many men being denied the chance to live out their lives, I have no intention of spending mine dwelling on the past – yours or mine, Maggie. If this war has taught me anything, it's that the time we have on this earth is short, too short for regrets. You did nothing wrong; you were used, that's all. None of it was your fault. In any case, I'm supposed to be a man of God, so forgiveness is etched into me. Let's just you and I move forwards to the rest of our lives together, if you'll have me?'

Maggie moved towards his outstretched arms and fell into them with a deep, satisfied sigh, but then, she registered his words and pulled back. 'What do you mean, *supposed to be* a man of God.'

Harry was furious with himself that he'd ruined the romance of the moment.

'Oh, nothing, just a turn of phrase.'

Maggie was not going to be fended off.

'Come on,' she said, standing stubbornly with her arms folded. 'If this relationship is going to go anywhere, we have to be honest with each other. After all,' she added with a wry smile, 'you know all about the skeletons in my cupboard.'

An irritated shadow came over Harry's face; this was the last thing he wanted to talk about when they had so little time, but Maggie was insistent.

'Well?'

'It's just, well, with all that I've seen in this war, I'm not sure anyone really is looking after us all and this, oh I don't know, Maggie, this feeling that I have for you, it just, well, it just doesn't feel very holy.'

He gave such a sheepish grin that Maggie burst out laughing.

She suddenly felt exhilarated. This was nothing like the sordid emotions she'd had with Roger, her whole body felt alive and when he took her in his arms, there was no guilt, no shame and no regret. It just felt completely right.

Seeing Harry's crestfallen face, she pushed her feet firmly into the ground, sure they would take off into the air if she didn't.

'Do you remember the Book of Genesis?' she asked him. 'And the words of the marriage ceremony?'

'Yes.' He was puzzled. Don't say this girl was about to give him a sermon?

'You know, where it says: "A man shall leave his father and mother and be joined to his wife and they shall become one flesh . . ." So you see, I don't think the Church of England thinks there's anything wrong with two young people falling in love, Harry, if that's what this is?'

She looked sideways at him and noticed his eyes were glistening.

'That's my answer then, you're a man and I'm a woman; isn't that where Adam and Eve began?'

'Yes, but . . .'

'No buts.' Taking his hand in both of hers, she raised it to her lips. 'I'm just glad you're not a Catholic priest.'

He started to laugh and then Maggie joined in.

She was correct, he thought, there was no barrier to an Anglican padre falling in love and although he still had to deal with all the dreadful scenes that constantly replayed in his mind over the last four years, here, at last, was someone who might help him to replace the war memories with love.

He remembered the conversation he'd had with his uncle while they'd sat quietly in Emmanuel Church and said, 'But perhaps you're right, maybe I need some help with this,' he finally conceded. 'I could go and see the Deputy Assistant Chaplain General. He's in London this week.' That realisation prompted a huge grin. 'Which would mean I could travel with you back to the boat.'

Harry looked very pleased with himself for finding a reason to hold on to this precious time with Maggie, which seemed just as important as discussing whether a life in the Church was right for him, but, perhaps, he thought, it *was* time he asked for help.

'The bluebells are out,' he said with surprise, noticing they were near to Cringle Brook in Levenshulme.

'Yes, they are, and don't you find that reassuring?' Maggie said. She had no idea what dreadful things Harry had seen but she knew from the lines etched on his face that those recollections would be equally engraved into his consciousness.

'Let me help you, Harry, let me be your hope. When you are holding the hand of a man who is dying, let it be my hand you're holding; when you're looking into the fading eyes of a wounded soldier, remember my eyes looking lovingly at you like they are now. And when you have to throw soil onto a grave, think of the bluebells that will one day grow there.'

Harry bowed his head, but, even so, she spotted the tears falling onto his tunic. Her heart felt it was being compressed in a vice and she clasped his hand tighter.

'I wish we could find somewhere to go,' she said bleakly. 'Somewhere we could blot everything out.'

Harry racked his brains but there was nowhere for two young people to be alone.

'A hotel?' he ventured but then seeing the look of horror that passed over Maggie's face, regretted the suggestion immediately.

'No, no, I didn't mean that.'

They walked in silence towards the shop where they bought enough potatoes for tea and then made their way back to the house.

When they got there, there was a note left for them on the sideboard. It was from Dorothy Harper.

'Sorry you two but the men insisted on going down to the Midway for a pint. We'll pick up some fish and chips so won't be back for tea. Perhaps you could sort yourselves out and we'll hopefully see you before you leave.'

Maggie sent a prayer of thanks in Dorothy Harper's direction and fell into the outstretched arms in front of her.

To be able to hold Maggie without giving in to the terrible longing that was engulfing him took every bit of Harry's self-control.

'I can't wait to marry you, Margaret Carpenter,' he murmured breathlessly in her ear.

She arched her back and said something into his chest.

'Sorry?' he asked, concentrating on touching her hair rather than responding to her warm body that was pressing into his.

'I want you, Harry Moore,' she said out loud, looking up at him with such an open expression, and he groaned.

'I want you too, Maggie, but . . .' His voice faded. He was desperately trying to think of reasons why he shouldn't finally make love to this wonderful woman.

'Is it because you're a bloomin' padre?' she asked, looking deliciously put out.

Harry laughed but then pushed her away from him to hold her at arm's length.

'Partially, yes. But you've been treated so badly in the past, Maggie, and I want our first time to be special with no guilt, you deserve that.'

She started to pout like a thwarted child but once his words sank in, she decided that yes, this had to be different from what had happened with Roger. She lifted her head; this was her chance at a new life – one that was untainted and unashamed.

'But surely that doesn't mean I can't kiss you again though.'

Harry reached out and traced her cheek with his finger before asking, 'How long does it take to eat fish and chips?'

Chapter 37

The pair wondered whether everyone on the train knew how they'd spent the afternoon and each time they caught each other's eye, they had to resist giggling. So much so that eventually, a little girl on the seat opposite said to her mother, 'I think those two know a secret, Mummy. They look like the twins do when they're hiding something from me.'

'Oh, I am sorry,' the woman exclaimed, blushing, 'she really shouldn't talk like that.'

She leaned down to admonish the child but then Maggie bent across the aisle to whisper to the little girl, 'You're right, we're in love but don't tell anybody.'

The little girl clasped her hand over her mouth in delight and gave a knowing grin. She knew all about secrets and this one was just like her storybook of the Sleeping Beauty.

Harry took hold of Maggie's hand to confirm the confession but then the child got to her feet and, delighted with powers of deduction, came across the aisle to whisper in Maggie's ear, 'But isn't he a priest? Is that allowed?'

'Catherine, come here at once,' her mother cried in embarrassment. 'I do apologise, since her older brothers were conscripted, she's been spending too much time with grown-ups and thinks she can say anything.'

'It's OK,' Harry assured her, 'and she's very clever, some priests can't marry but I'm a Church of England padre, so I can.' He looked lovingly at Maggie. 'And I will, just as soon as this war is over.'

* * *

The birds were definitely in fine voice, Maggie thought as the two of them approached the canal.

Harry had telephoned the DCG's office to make an appointment while savouring these last hours with Maggie. When they were off the train, he looked with surprise at how beautiful the trees were at this time of year and how every blade of grass seemed to be growing especially tall and strong even in the blitzed metropolis.

'I think the war's stopped me noticing the daily miracles that are happening all around us,' he said, squeezing Maggie's hand.

'I know,' Maggie said.

As they approached the *Nancy May* at Bull's Bridge, they saw a figure running towards them.

'Maggie, Maggie, thank God you're back!'

Maggie almost didn't recognise the neat figure of Elizabeth; her hair was plastered all down her face, there were tears smeared across her cheeks and her eyes were wide with fear.

'For heaven's sake, what is it?' Maggie said, running to grab hold of her friend. 'What's happened?'

Elizabeth seemed to suddenly register Harry's presence but then shrugged and blurted out, 'They've tracked us down – the gang – and oh Maggie, I haven't dared go in, but the door's all broken and the tiller's been thrown in the cut.' Elizabeth's knees buckled and Harry ran to catch her before she fell.

From behind them, on her own way from the bus stop, they heard Gloria's voice demanding to know what was going on.

She wasn't in the mood for any more dramas after the blazing row she and Will had just had after what should have been an idyllic weekend and her puffy eyes bore witness to the hurt she'd inflicted on herself.

Harry looked towards the boat and gently relinquished Elizabeth's body to the other two. He went purposefully over to the *Nancy May*, his soldier's senses on alert in case anyone was still in the vicinity.

Stepping silently onto the deck, he kept to one side of the hatch and pushed the broken door fully open. As he did so, two figures pushed him out of the way making him fall into the canal with a loud splash. They then fled along the towpath and as soon as they found a break in the hedge, went at full pelt across the nearest field.

Ignoring Gloria's screams, Harry hauled himself onto the bank and dripping with bits of reed, pursued the men as fast as he could. As he ran, Maggie yelled after him, 'Be careful, please, Harry.'

A boat pulled up behind the *Nancy May* and *Florence* and two burly men that Maggie recognised from the bar at Stoke Bruerne jumped straight to shore, taking their check neckerchiefs off and tying them round their fists as they followed Harry. Maggie, desperate to help, grabbed a rope hung up by the hatch and left Elizabeth to Gloria's care to run after them.

'Maggie, you can't do anything,' Elizabeth cried between sobs. 'Oh, this is all my fault, this is all my fault.'

Gloria patted her arm and manoeuvred her towards *Florence*. Her priority was to calm Elizabeth down. She looked really pale.

The pound seemed uncharacteristically quiet apart from a strange chattering that Gloria finally realised was from her own teeth. She pushed Elizabeth down the steps and heard her flop onto the bunk, making little whimpering sounds and then she put her hand over her eyes to peer into the distance at the fleeing figures. Clutching her hands to her mouth, Gloria watched as Harry gained on the two men in mackintoshes and nodded in approval at his fitness. Maggie was setting a surprisingly good pace too but the men from the boat were puffing and panting, more used to pints in the canal-side pubs than running.

Harry suddenly leaped into the air and grabbed one of the men by his coat tail to bring him crashing to the ground and as the other one turned to intervene, Maggie caught up and, with her best skipping rope skills, looped the rope around his ankles to trip him up. The manoeuvres gave the two boatmen enough time to reach the brawling figures and the taller one picked up the first man like a doll and flung him into the air while the second used his knuckles to stop his accomplice in his tracks.

'Stay there, Elizabeth, I'll go and help,' Gloria shouted down to the cabin, and she too sprinted across the field to where Maggie was now sitting astride one of the two men lying face down in the field while the other one was being expertly held from behind by Harry. The two boatmen were standing with their fists raised threateningly.

A furious argument was taking place between the two men on the ground.

'So much for that revenge yer wanted. Boss told yer to leave it be, the heat was already on us – it were too dangerous – but yer wouldna, would yer?'

The second man was being held face down in the grass so could only retort in a muffled voice, 'I thought three bitches'd be easy and they 'ad it comin' to 'em for getting one o' our own put away.'

'Yer can tell that to the boss when 'e's in the cell next door to yer at Scrubs.'

Harry put an end to the conversation by yanking the first one to his feet and, with Maggie's help, frogmarched him towards the boat, his arm twisted firmly up his back. Behind him, the two boatmen kept an equally tight grip on their captive to march behind.

When she reached the little group, Gloria jumped up and down with glee, all thoughts of Will erased from her mind and the only thing that did occur to her was that Joe would have loved this.

*　*　*

The police van had just driven off when Elizabeth finally came out onto *Florence's* stern. She was shaking so Maggie handed her the mug she'd just offered the two policemen in vain. They were in a hurry to get their prisoners locked up and had politely refused, just taking time to praise Harry, the two boatmen and, with disbelief, the slim, young lass who'd prevented the larger villain of the two from moving. One of them gave veiled hints that the force had been after 'this lot' for a long time and that finally, they were going to put them all behind bars where they belonged and that maybe, just maybe, this would lead them to the boss.

Harry looked in dismay at his watch; he'd missed his bus into London and would be late for his appointment with the Deputy Assistant Chaplain. It was all going to take some explaining, he thought, but then catching sight of Maggie's face he saw a mix of triumph and exhilaration and started to laugh. This was a woman who thrived on challenge, and he couldn't wait to spend the rest of his life with her. One by one, the rest of them joined in and then Gloria said, 'I suppose we'd better see what damage they've done; we won't be able to explain all this to the company, will we?'

Standing up, Maggie said quietly, 'I'll go.' She stepped gingerly on the top step, took a deep breath and then disappeared from view.

'Hmm, well, I think Harry disturbed them; it's not as bad as I feared,' she called up.

Gloria and Elizabeth squeezed down the narrow opening and blinked in the gloom.

Gloria gasped. '"Not as bad" . . . ? Oh Maggie, this is going to take pounds to fix. It'll take all our earnings. Look, they've slashed the bedding and broken all the crockery, not to mention the ram's head that I saw floating off down the canal.'

After the day she'd had with Will, it was the last straw and she sank down onto the top step and started to cry. Harry gently placed his hand on her shoulder and gave it a squeeze.

Gloria had never been closer to giving up and going home, like so many of the girls who, she thought bitterly, only had normal hardships to survive on the cut. Those girls had had nothing like this, and her mouth formed a childish scowl.

Three gloomy faces turned towards the boatmen standing respectfully on the grass.

'Now, dunna you worry, you lasses,' one of them said, 'it'll all be all right.'

But after an embarrassingly warm hug from all three girls, they shuffled off back to their own boat and Harry turned to say his own goodbyes to Gloria and Elizabeth. Maggie walked with him back to the bus, hanging on to his arm like it was a lifeline.

'I can't let you go,' she said, plaintively.

'I know, but I have to leave, Maggie. We . . .' He paused, unable to tell her that he was likely to be dropping out of a glider into enemy territory within a few weeks. 'Oh, Maggie, Maggie, Maggie, how do we do this? How can fate . . . or God . . . do this to us?'

'I suppose because we're not the only ones,' she replied with a catch in her voice. 'All over the world, there are young people, just like us, being torn apart by this war. But—' and here, she forced her voice to brighten '—we've got God on our side, so that gives us the edge.'

The two of them mirrored other couples standing at the bus stop, who were also held together by love and hope, defiant against the harm that awaited so many of them. The scene in front of him of smart uniforms and strong arms was replaced in Harry's mind by bodies like these splayed out on a beach in Dunkirk, splattered with blood and surrounded by severed limbs. He shook his head angrily; there wasn't a hug in the world strong enough to combat a howitzer gun, he thought. Maggie saw the despair in his eyes and pulled him closer to her. She had watched him fiddle uncomfortably with his dog collar on so many occasions and knew what agonies of conscience he was going through but now, there was something more. The newspapers were full of speculation about when the Allies would invade France and she had assumed a padre would be safe at the back of the action, but Harry seemed like someone standing on hot stones. A sick feeling arose in her stomach.

Unwilling to let him go, she tried to commit the warmth and passion in her arms as an imprint on his body to get him through whatever else the war had in store for him, but she knew it wasn't going to be enough to protect either of them. Maggie let out a slow sigh.

Harry drew back and looked quizzically at her. 'Are you OK?'

'No, of course not. I need you by my side. I don't want to let you go, not knowing when I'll see you again or what dangers you're about to face. I tell you something, Harry Moore, you're going to need every bit of divine help you can get so you just keep asking for it and don't worry whether you've got through on the right telephone wire, just keep talking. I'm sure someone is listening. And do you know what, even if they're not, it won't do any harm.'

The fierceness of her expression made Harry burst out laughing. 'I don't think God would dare not to exist after that little tirade,' he told her, hugging her to him for one more precious second.

The bus station tannoy announced the next departure so, an inch at a time, they slowly released their hold on each other and Harry stepped backwards onto the bus platform and wrapped his fingers around the cold, silver pole. He took in the way her hair curled around her face, the mistiness of her eyes and the shape of her incredible body and then closed his own eyes to commit it all to memory. He couldn't believe how much it hurt to watch her disappear into the distance as the bus pulled away.

Chapter 38

Back at Ringway camp, the tension had increased. All around Harry, men with taut faces were scurrying in all directions and in the distance, instructions were being shouted on the training ground. No one was in any doubt how much depended on Operation Overlord and their own glider operation, called Operation Coup de Main. If these failed, then the Allies would find it very hard to get a stronghold in Europe again. The discussion with his clerical superior in London had been far more intense than Harry had anticipated, and he'd been subjected to a string of questions about his feelings, his beliefs and his experiences. There were no solutions offered – that wasn't the answer – but when the older man clasped his hand at the end of the interview, Harry felt he was being supported in a way he'd never expected.

Reverend Canon Michael Howe had watched the young man walk away from Erdington army camp and then turned away to make some telephone calls. He'd seen the hunger in this young chaplain's eyes and knew if the Church was going to keep him, it would need to offer more than a cosy peacetime job at the end of the war. In the meantime, he just prayed this man would survive the next few weeks.

* * *

Harry called at the post room to pick up a letter from his parents in which his mother expressed her usual concerns about whether he was getting enough to eat, endorsing Harry's belief that, thankfully, they had no idea what their son was about to undertake. There was also one from his uncle which resonated much more deeply:

Dear Harry,

It's a very strange time and I am sure you are feeling it more keenly than all of us further north. I have to prepare my sermon in a minute but first I wanted to get this off to you as I thought you might be a more suitable recipient of my kindly meant advice than any of my dwindling congregation, most of whom are too deaf to hear me anyway.

Whatever you are about to face, know that you're not alone. I know you've been feeling that none of this makes sense, but this is not the time to try to work it all out. All you have to do is whatever your country expects of you. Know that I will have a word in the right department on your behalf, even if you can't make that call for yourself and, remember, not only your parents and I, your men and that lovely young woman, Maggie, all believe in you and even though you will have no weapon, you have the strongest ammunition of all – love. That is more powerful than any bullet.

Keep safe, my son, and yes, I am going to say it – God be with you,

Your Uncle Peter

It was a thoughtful young man who made his way back through Central Landing School at Ringway to his hut but then he heard a shout from behind him.

'Padre! I've been looking for yous. I knew you couldn't escape me.'

He spun round to see the beaming face of Paul, his batman and friend, and sprang forward to shake his hand enthusiastically.

'Paul, it's so good to see you, but I thought you were still in Italy.'

'Well, them boffins sent word that yous were pinin' for a proper cuppa, so, 'ere I am.'

The grin on the Liverpudlian's face was such a welcome sight that Harry stepped forward to give his friend a hug.

'Eh, none of that. I've got me reputation to think of as a tough soldier. You can't bring them softie Church ways 'ere.' He took a pace backwards to thoroughly assess the man in front of him. 'Hmm, as I thought, not lookin' after yerself. Ah well, good job I'm 'ere now. We'll get yous all fattened up so you bounce when they drop yous on France.'

'You sound like my mother,' Harry laughed. 'For some reason, she's convinced army rations aren't a patch on her Sunday roast; imagine that.'

Paul chuckled. 'Anyways, do you know the trouble I've gone to, to get 'ere. I was 'aving such fun in Italy but I knew you'd never survive without me to look after yous so I had to beg old Forsythe to get me bundled off to Blighty.

'Right, first of all,' the older batman said, addressing the padre like he did his three younger brothers, 'I've 'ad us transferred to the five-star accommodation in hut four. Much more genteel for the likes of us. Then yer 'aving dinner with the lieutenant colonel. No more of this cavorting with the hoi polloi.'

He leaned forward to confide: 'I've 'eard the old man's just 'ad a consignment of whisky that's arrived. If you're very good, I might be able to persuade him to share a dram or two with yous.'

'Oh, I've missed you, Private,' Harry said with a grin and with that, he allowed himself to be marched off towards hut four where a fresh shirt was waiting for him and a kettle was waiting to be boiled for the best cup of tea he'd had since Italy.

* * *

The moment of luxury was thoroughly erased by the training that followed over the next few days as Harry and the rest of the men were drilled and re-drilled in the operation to come. By the time the beginning of June came, Harry was dropping out of aircraft in his sleep. He tried to keep up with letters to Maggie, saying as little as possible about what he was about to face, but he hardly had a moment to himself.

Finally, his division travelled to the south coast and the 5th of June dawned, putting every single man of the 6th Division was on standby. The briefing was short and to the point. The gliders were to attack the Orne bridges to protect the flanks of the seaborne operation by seizing strategic points and communication centres to stop German forces reaching the beachhead. It was imperative that the high ground that overlooked the beaches including the Merville Battery was captured.

As the little group of men on Harry's plane gathered beneath the wing to synchronise their watches, he noticed one young parachutist's knees were shaking so he put his hand gently on the man's shoulder.

'What's your name, soldier?'

'Bill Peters, Padre,' and then in a hushed voice, he added, 'I'm going to die today, I know I am, I've had a premonition.'

Harry took one look at the young, pale face in front of him and made a decision.

'I'm going to hold a short service before we take off if anyone wants to join me.'

Turning towards the wing, Harry put his hands together to recite the Lord's Prayer. Bill Peters was the first to start mouthing the words but then several more men made their way to the wing that was shadowed under the early morning light, their faces blackened for action. Communion was unearthed from the small box that all padres carried at all times and distributed to the men. It only took a few moments, but by the time Harry ended with a heart-felt blessing, Bill's colour had returned to his face. He nodded his thanks to the padre and slowly climbed aboard, turning at the last moment to say, 'That really helped, Padre. Now, I know that if I do die today, He'll be ready for me. Thank you.'

The landing seemed to have gone like clockwork until Harry realised the glider had dropped them at the wrong place. Instead of Orne bridge, they dropped at a place called Benouville where a Panther tank and a self-propelled gun was picking the parachutists off one by one. Harry looked up at the small figures still in the air and was furious at the German practice of shooting parachutists while the Allies simply carted them off to POW camps. He ducked down into a ditch to assess both the situation and the appalling loss of life. The futility of having a cross and a Bible rather than a weapon left him with no choice but to crawl his way back behind the front line to the dressing station where wounded men were being brought in at a terrifyingly regular rate. He immediately started offering compassion to the injured, but the Germans were beginning to overrun the place. The doctors were frantically trying to ignore the fighting that was breaking out at the flap of tent. Forgetting his role as a non-violent participant, Harry darted over and punched one astonished young German directly in the face. As he fell to the ground, the men around Harry cheered. More Allied soldiers moved swiftly in to protect the entrance and Harry simply put himself between the injured men and the Germans, carrying on doing whatever he could to help the beleaguered medics who were trying so hard to save as many lives as possible. Harry paused next to one stretcher to give a blessing to the next dying man. The automatic words he was saying over each one suddenly stuck in his throat and he froze on the spot. The prone figure on the stretcher in front of him with his eyes closed and his chest shattered was Bill Peters.

It broke his heart.

Chapter 38

Instead of moving back up the 'road' as they now called the Grand Union Canal, the girls discovered that their engine was making such a terrible noise they had to turn back towards London to get it fixed. Frustrated that the new load of wood, so nicely sheeted up on the two boats, was going to be late for delivery, they had no choice but to delay their departure north. Gloria had claimed she could fix it but the other two were insisting that, this time, they needed an expert. In an effort to escape Gloria's protestations, Maggie volunteered to go and get some supplies and while there had picked up a newspaper which warned of some secret weapons that Hitler had in store for the capital. Maggie shrugged. She had no more idea than anyone else what the papers were talking about.

It was only a few days after D Day and, without a true picture yet of the losses, the country was feeling more hopeful than it had since the beginning of the war that the tide was finally turning

There was just one thing that cheered Gloria and the other two up. Every time they moored up, they would emerge in the morning to see a pan or a sheet or a bowl left out for them on their stern area. It was Gloria who solved the puzzle for them.

'It's the boat people. They've all heard about our "visitors" and they're sharing what little they can with us.'

Elizabeth was completely stunned. 'But they have so little themselves. I can't believe they're being so generous. Gosh, I'm not sure you'd find the people from the country club sharing their cut glasses or precious china.'

'Believe me,' Gloria said, her eyes misting over, 'these things are more valuable than any country club cut glasses to the people who've left them for us.'

Maggie leaned over the tiller to press Gloria's arm. 'You should be really proud of this community of yours, Gloria. They are very special.'

'Do you know what? I am. I've spent years trying to pretend I don't come from the boats but this job's made me realise, I'm actually honoured to say I'm one of them.' She paused for a moment and then blurted out, 'Will and I are finished. He was just a fantasy. I'd have spent my whole life trying to be something I wasn't.'

There was a chorus of sympathy but the other two both quietly acknowledged it had been inevitable that a relationship of two people such poles apart couldn't be salvaged by love.

'Besides which,' Gloria was saying, 'don't you think there's something a bit off about a fit and healthy man hiding behind a desk doing boring admin when others are out there fighting?'

Elizabeth kept quiet. Her knowledge of the higher echelons of command in the navy had made her aware that no one actually simply sat behind a desk and every time they'd passed the little groups at Bletchley she'd noticed how pulses twitched on their faces and how bloodshot their eyes were. She had much deeper suspicions about what was going on there than she could ever share with Gloria, but something else her young friend had said had resonated with her.

She, too, had been playing a part, trying to be the perfect wife for a naval captain and while she loved Christopher, she'd been suppressing a part of her that had meant she was always hiding behind a mask and she had had enough of it.

Elizabeth gave a small noise: 'I need to tell you both something too. I've applied to be a nurse and I'm going to write to Christopher tonight and tell him I'm joining the Queen Alexandra Nursing Corps,' she announced. 'I'm not going to be something I'm not anymore either.'

There was a moment's pause while the other two absorbed her words and then Gloria said: 'Yes, but it won't happen before the war ends, will it? We can't manage without you.' 'No, I shouldn't think so,' Elizabeth replied with as much confidence as she could muster.

Maggie looked at Elizabeth's face which was glowing with determination.

'OK, well, that goes for me too, I'm going to stop being ashamed of what happened with Roger. That man took advantage of me; I'm not going to spend the rest of my life feeling guilty. If Harry can put it behind us, then so can I.'

It seemed this war had changed them all, Maggie thought.

They took up their mooring ropes and set off to chug haltingly down the canal towards London and, although the early summer of 1944 had been relentlessly wet and they had struggled to keep the timber dry, today was brighter and, despite the worrying noises from the engine, it seemed all the wildlife on the cut was celebrating with the birds, coots and moorhens chirping, flapping their wings and darting in and out of the reeds. Maggie felt a moment of pure joy; she had a man who loved her and had, it seemed, forgiven her for her affair with Roger and she had two friends she would be close to the for the rest of her life. Then her thoughts went to her father and in an instant, the bubble of happiness burst like a child's balloon. That was a happiness she would never deserve.

The boat edged its way down through Haggerston and onto the locks of Mile End that would take them to the repair yard. Keeping their fingers crossed that the engine would get them that far, they worked really efficiently with Gloria running ahead to set up the locks and Maggie and Elizabeth easing the boats into them. There was no longer any need for words; they were a team.

Maggie shivered as she tied the mooring ropes for the night at the stern while Gloria secured the bow; it was colder than she'd thought and she was just wishing she'd brought a coat out from the cabin when there was a definite chill in the air and ripples started to appear on the water. Above her came a strange buzzing noise and she looked up to see the shadow of an ominous shape like a short-winged plane partially on fire and, she couldn't believe it – it was hurtling towards them at enormous speed. The buzzing noise got louder and louder until . . . it suddenly stopped. At that point the pointed nose of the harbinger of doom turned downwards and Maggie screamed.

'Take cover, take cover. It's coming for us!'

'Bloody hell, we're sitting ducks here,' Gloria yelled, running back from the lock with her neck craned upward. 'What the hell is that?' She leaped onto the deck as if the sturdy beams of their little home could save her.

'Hitler's secret vengeance weap—' Elizabeth was in the middle of saying when a huge explosion assaulted their eardrums and the railway bridge in the distance cracked in two, falling to the ground in a hail of dust and rubble. Gloria fell through the companionway and the other two sank to the ground with their hands over their heads while the canal reverberated with the blast making the boats bang heavily against the side of the towpath. It was like a hurricane but, with its targeted impact, even more devastating.

'Cover your heads,' Elizabeth's shaky voice called. 'There'll be glass and rubble.'

Maggie crouched down as low as she could, only able to hear muffled sounds coming from Elizabeth. Trembling and unable to feel any of her limbs, Maggie peered through her fingers to see the pillars on either side of the bomb collapse like jelly. A blast-wave rippled out from the area of the bridge creating a vacuum which caused a second rush of air. The two girls felt pulled towards it like they were being sucked into a tornado and even though they were over 500 yards away from the bridge, they felt its power in every fibre of their beings.

Gloria's loud rendition of the Lord's Prayer from inside the cabin penetrated Maggie's deadened hearing so she too started to mouth them, hoping against hope that Harry's doubts that anyone was listening were without foundation.

Feeling that time had stood still, Maggie glanced down at her feet beneath her bent knees, checked her left then her right before gingerly wriggling her toes and starting to rise to stand. From the inside of the *Nancy May* they heard a scream from Gloria.

'My leg! Oh God, it's agony.'

'Gloria, have you been hit?' Maggie tried to make her way towards the stricken girl but stumbled as her own knees buckled. Her ears were gradually readjusting to let in a cacophony of screams, shouts, the noise of houses collapsing and she bent over coughing as the dust reached the area around the towpath.

Elizabeth caught up with her and saw blood spurting from Maggie's scalp from a shard of the glass that showered down on the boat. 'Get inside and put something clean – and I mean clean, Mags – on that wound. We need help.'

As the only one uninjured, Elizabeth started to run towards the road above but when she reached Grove Road, she came to a sudden halt. She'd never seen anything like it.

On all sides, shops, terraced houses and pavements had been ripped apart as if some monster from another planet had burst his way out from the clouds to destroy the innocent people below.

The initial shock had developed into a frenzy of digging, sirens blaring and people running in all directions, but some were frozen in time as they gazed on the piles of rubble that used to be their homes. It hadn't yet sunk in that those they'd left moments earlier to nip to the shops or walk the dog were never going to emerge from their cosy little homes ever again. One man had his hand uselessly hanging on to a dog's lead next to a prone animal that was hardly recognisable as a dog. As Elizabeth watched, the man dropped like a stone to the ground and with his eyes still open, left this earth forever.

Seeing a woman with a red cross on her arm rushing towards the rubble, Elizabeth grabbed her arm.

'Where's the medical equipment, bandages, sulfur for wounds?'

The girl ignored her, pulling away to start scrabbling over the mountain of bricks and stones that marked where the end of the terraced houses had been.

Elizabeth was overwhelmed for a minute, wondering where she could give the most help. She felt a deep, visceral need to stop all these people's pain but with so many rushing to give assistance she made herself concentrate on the gash on Maggie's head and the agony of Gloria's scream and shouted again to the Red Cross girl, 'Where's your ambulance, I need help. I need bandages.'

The girl, her face as ashen as the dust around them, waved vaguely towards Old Ford Road and Elizabeth sprinted as fast as her shaking legs would allow.

The smell of burning metal combined with dust from the damaged houses choked her, making her cough and splutter, so she pulled her jumper up over her mouth and ran on until she spotted a dark-coloured ambulance merging with the grey of the scene that surrounded it.

'I need a stretcher.'

'You and a few others, I'm afraid, miss,' an ambulance man said and was about to hurry on when he noticed her pale face.

'Please,' she begged. 'My friend has a terrible head wound; she's bleeding so much . . . and I think the other one has broken her leg . . .' At this point she looked so stricken he patted her hand.

'I'm sorry, love but you're going to have to manage for a bit, there's kiddies in that house at the end but you leave that to us professionals and you go and see to your friends,' he said.

Elizabeth stared through the mist of debris to see a crowd of people heading towards the end of the street. There were so many of them, she decided they didn't need another helper but her friends did and she ran back towards the canal, thanking heaven that they hadn't chosen to moor nearer the railway bridge. As she passed along the towpath, she grabbed a large stick and tucked it quickly under her arm.

'Right, I'm going to have to strap this leg up for now,' she told Gloria when she got back. Maggie was cradling Gloria who really had gone very white with one leg bent under her at a very odd angle. Maggie had ignored Elizabeth's instruction and had simply wiped the blood from her face with her sleeve not even noticing that her jumper was actually saturated with red but she was beginning to feel queasy every time she looked at Gloria's leg. She had no idea it was her own wound that was making her feel sick.

'Actually, first, we have to stop that bleeding, Maggie.' Elizabeth delved into the drawer and unearthed a clean shirt. She had no idea who it belonged to and she didn't care.

Giving it to Maggie, she told her to hold it tightly against the wound then immediately stripped off her petticoat, thanking heaven that she rarely wore those trousers she'd bought at the jumble sale all those months ago. Elizabeth used her teeth to tear the worn lace garment into strips while she measured the stick against Gloria's leg.

'This is going to hurt,' she told the wounded girl and then before Gloria could react, she tried to manoeuvre the leg so that the splint of the wood supported above and below the break. It took a moment for the pain to register but then Gloria screamed, her voice resounding in the confined space of the domed ceiling above.

Elizabeth sat back but wondered what the hell she was going to do next.

'Need some help?' a gruff voice shouted.

'Yes, thank God. Oh yes please,' Elizabeth called back and, in the hatch appeared the familiar face of Ernie Spencer with Dolly hovering in the background.

A young woman who had been brought up never to show emotion, Elizabeth burst into tears with relief.

* * *

That night, Maggie curled up in her bunk with a pounding headache. She had a wide bandage across her forehead and the bloodied clothes were in a pile on the floor. With Gloria in hospital, the bunk at her feet was eerily empty and because Elizabeth had gone back to help the rescue attempts on the road above, *Florence* was equally quiet. The cabin had never looked so big – or empty. There was dust everywhere but miraculously, the two boats- and their loads- had survived relatively unscathed which was more than could be said for the area around them. It had taken both Elizabeth and Dolly to help Maggie walk onto Grove Road, while Ernie carried an almost-fainting Gloria. Both invalids silently registered the devastating impact of one of the bombs that were being called 'V1s' and they begged in vain that their helpers should put them down and go and deal with the 'real' wounded. When they reached the hospital, it was mayhem and it took hours for the two girls to be seen by a nurse, let alone a doctor. During their long wait, police officers, worried that such a powerful weapon would cause panic, were using a loud hailer to issue strict instructions that no one should tell anyone outside the area about the hit, but every person in a fit condition to listen knew that was a false hope.

Maggie had wanted to join Elizabeth on Grove Road to give what assistance she could but was told very firmly by the doctor that she needed to rest as the shard of glass had been perilously close to her frontal lobe, which, if not allowed to heal, could cause lasting damage to her brain. Ernie had helped her back to the boat but instead of giving in to the overwhelming need for sleep, Maggie was being plagued by disturbing thoughts. The power of the bomb had been a brutal reminder that the war was not done with them yet and she shivered at the fragility of life. It had been obvious how close the three of them had come to being obliterated and she'd watched in silence as the rescuers scrabbled with their bare hands to try to reach any possible survivors under the piles of bricks. Someone had said several people had been killed but the final toll of all those injured and those who had lost their homes, she knew, was going to be higher. Maggie started to shake, and she clasped her arms around herself, longing for the warmth of Harry. As her fingers grasped her own flesh, a thought ripped through her. Harry could have been involved in the D Day landings. The newspapers had tried to put a positive perspective on the story over the past week, but the extent of the losses was beginning to filter through. She had no idea whether he was still alive.

Maggie Carpenter had never felt more alone.

Chapter 39

Penning a letter in the cramped tent behind the front line of the fierce fighting for Normandy was not an easy task but Harry knew he had to complete it before he chickened out. Reading it back to himself, he felt a huge abyss opening up and wondered for the umpteenth time whether he knew what he was doing.

It was addressed to his superior, the same deputy assistant chaplain general he had met, asking to be relieved of his duties as a padre. His explanation was simple; he had lost his faith, but the words failed to give justice to the depth of agonies Harry had put himself through over the last couple of years.

His decision to write the letter had been consolidated by the un-chaplain-like anger he had felt towards the German he'd knocked to the ground and then the death of Bill Peters. To be unable to protect yet another of the men under his pastoral care had been the last straw and Harry had decided enough was enough.

He was about to put the flimsy sheet of paper into an envelope when Paul came in. His uniform was dishevelled and his blackened face was streaked where he had wiped the back of his hand on it.

'Yous all right, Padre?'

Harry got to his feet wearily and gave a weak smile. 'I think so, I mean I'm alive so that's one up on many poor souls out there isn't it.'

'Yous not wrong there,' the batman replied, 'but I've just talked to some of the men and they're all saying the same thing...'

He paused, waiting for a response but gave up after taking one look at the blank face in front of him.

'All right, well I'll tell yers, seein' as how desperate yer are to know. They're all sayin' that padre's an 'ero. That's you, yer numbskull. The way yer floored that German was just what they all needed. To see God fighting back ... it made it all worthwhile.'

Harry looked stricken. The fact that he'd resorted to violence had been one of the reasons he had finally picked up the pen to the DACG.

'Oh, they mustn't,' he said uncomfortably. 'No, I'm supposed to be a man of peace.'

'Yep, and I do remember hearing about some man of peace throwing the moneylenders out of the temple, so I think yer allowed to give a facer to an odd German, Padre.'

A rueful smile broke out on Harry's face. He loved this Liverpudlian's logic. There was never any answer to it. He said, 'You, of all people, know I can't keep this up, Paul. I'm pretending all the time.'

For once, the batman's voice became serious. 'Yeah, but yer know, you're not on yer own. We're all pretending to be brave, pretending to make jokes, even pretending we're goin' to survive all this. You're part of the charade and personally, I don't think I'm going t'let yous be the first to bail out. You can't let the men down by breaking the illusion. You're in it as much as we are and besides, we need that direct line to heaven that you've got.'

With that, Paul gave a sharp nod of his head demonstrating that he was glad that was all decided and went off to make a cup of tea for them both leaving Harry staring at his letter before he simply ripped it in two.

*　*　*

A few days later after a man in blue overalls had spent the morning clanking and swearing in the engine room Maggie and Elizabeth were on their way again, leaving Gloria to the tender care of the medical staff at St Peter's Hospital in Stepney. Despite a constant nagging headache, Maggie adjusted her head bandage and assured Elizabeth she could certainly manage the butty. It was obvious that Gloria's leg would take at least six more weeks to heal, leaving them with no alternative but to manage on their own. Taking one look at the ashen face and the bandaged head of Maggie the lock keepers realised this was the boat that had narrowly escaped being obliterated near Grove Road and they kept their normal jibes about women and boats to a minimum .

Elizabeth asked twice at the depot when she went to pick up the post but there was only one for her- nothing for Maggie. It was heartbreaking to see her friend's expectant face fall each time when there was still nothing from Harry and her puffy eyes each morning bore witness that she spent her nights crying into her pillow imagining all sorts of terrible scenes. The other letter that Elizabeth quickly tore open, though, was one offering her training as a nurse. She hugged herself with delight but with a sigh, Elizabeth popped that one into her pocket with a quivering hand. It was obvious she couldn't abandon Maggie as each day was going to be a constant challenge just to keep moving- to protect this current load of wood from the rain while avoiding doing physical damage to themselves by attempting to do a job that three of them had found almost impossible at times.

They both threw themselves into their work, which was incredibly hard going but somehow, each time the girls were really at their wits' end, a friendly face from another boat would appear to give assistance. Any attempt to express their appreciation to these proud boat people was rebuffed and all they could do was make sure they always had an extra mug of cocoa or a biscuit ready that they could offer in return.

By the second week, they were really struggling. The job was impossibly physical for three of them, let alone two, and after mooring up at Marsworth in the late afternoon, they had to accept the inevitable – they were going to have to ask for help.

Two dejected figures were making their way along the towpath to telephone the company when they heard the familiar tones of a Limehouse accent.

'You Elizabeth and Maggie?' a girl with auburn hair called out from the other side of the canal and then, not waiting for an answer, walked to cross the stone bridge ahead with her curls flowing in the wind. She looked like an even smaller version of Gloria.

'I'm Lottie,' she told them and then, seeing their blank faces, explained: 'Gloria's younger sister. She said you'd need some help so I put the word out to find where you were and . . . well, here I am.' She flung down a small bag with a satisfied smile and waited.

It took a moment for her words to sink in before Maggie grabbed hold of the girl and swung her round with delight.

'Oh, that's just perfect. We were about to go and ask for some help but if you can fill in, well,' she repeated, 'that's just . . . perfect.'

Elizabeth picked up the small bag, wondering how anyone could have so few belongings and with a beaming smile, led Lottie over to the *Nancy May* where the new girl carried out an expert examination; looking at every bolt, every seam and every fix of the tarpaulin. There were little noises of an equal mix of approval or dismay before Lottie disappeared into the engine room.

A shout emerged from the gloom. 'You say this engine's just been fixed, well to my mind, it still needs a good overhaul. I'll get it cleaned up straightaway and then we can get off. Where are we heading for?'

'We were, umm, giving up for the day,' confessed an exhausted Elizabeth,

'Nonsense,' Lottie replied, emerging to peer over Elizabeth's shoulder at the map

'I think with the three of us, we can get through these next couple of locks,' Elizabeth ventured.

'Nonsense. We can make Great Seabrook,' an indomitable voice replied and Lottie jumped ashore to untie the ropes. Feeling as if a cyclone had swept through the boat, Maggie suddenly started to race around getting everything ready, giving a quick grin back at Elizabeth.

This Smith family from Limehouse were indomitable.

* * *

Lottie proved to be as invaluable as Gloria, but her constant chatter about film stars, hairstyles and fashions soon wore thin for her room-mate and Maggie had to regularly make a point of opening her new Betty Smith novel, *A Tree Grows in Brooklyn*, and turning over with her torch to signal the endless cosy night-time chatter was at an end.

Despite Hitler's last-ditch efforts to quell the British into a constant state of terror with regular bombardments with his new weapon, the rhythm of life on the canal took on its normal contradiction of the two boats gliding to the regular chug, chug of the perfectly restored engine and the hectic schedule that the girls were trying to keep up. With Lottie's help, they were able to keep to time and get their deliveries up and down the Grand Union but each time they approached Limehouse Basin, Maggie and Elizabeth held their breaths.

'I've ne'er seen such a quick turnaround,' one bemused London warehouseman said, watching as one of the girls got one load levelled out while the other sheeted up the the tarpaulin neatly to protect their latest cargo of concrete.

'You'll be putting us out o' a job, you lasses,' he was about to say but Lottie had already fired up the engine and was heading for the winding hole to get them turned round and on their way.

Maggie was becoming an expert at suppressing the surges of panic that threatened to overwhelm her at regular intervals. On top of regularly checking the skies above, she had never prayed so hard or argued with fate as much as she did during those endless weeks without a letter. On their way back through Stoke Bruerne on a chilly September day, three months after the D Day landings, Elizabeth yelped with delight when she spotted a hobbling figure making her way towards the canal.

'It's Gloria!' she shouted to Maggie and the pair of them quickly tied their mooring ropes to race to encompass the young girl in such an enthusiastic hug that she almost fell over.

'Careful. I'm still delicate,' she laughed.

The other two stood back to assess the damage.

'Hmm,' Elizabeth said, 'you look peaky and I'm sorry to say, Gloria, I'm not sure you're going to be up to this.'

'I can stay on for a bit,' Lottie put in, grinning at her sister.

Maggie suppressed a groan thinking of the three of them crowded into that tiny cabin but Elizabeth looked delighted. She'd come to rely on the capable tiny figure of Lottie and to have Gloria as well could be the answer to her dilemma. She still hadn't worked out how she was going to tell them that the offer of nursing training was due to start at the beginning of October . . . in just three weeks' time.

In the meantime, Gloria and Lottie somehow managed to snuggle up in one bunk and it became a regular occurrence that one of them would thud onto the floor during the night. Maggie was amazed that neither of them seemed to wake up as a result, and whichever girl it was who had fallen out would simply climb back on the bunk and start snoring again.

By the time the girls reached the now-familiar Tyseley, Maggie was at screaming pitch. The tension of not having had one letter from Harry for months was putting her on edge and she found herself snapping at Lottie in particular.

'Here, this might help,' Elizabeth told her with a grin when she returned from the office to hand over a grubby letter that had obviously been forwarded several times.

Maggie squealed with excitement and hugged the letter to herself.

'Go on,' Gloria said, 'you go and read it, we'll sort out the paperwork. Lottie, you'd better keep out of sight.'

Elizabeth gave a small cough.

'Umm, you may have to tell them about Lottie and hopefully, they'll let her stay.' She paused, looking at their puzzled faces. 'I start my training at Birmingham next week – as a nurse. I've got a long way to go but hopefully, I'll be all done before this war's over, and I can be of some use.'

Maggie and Gloria looked horror-stricken. They'd been sure Elizabeth's plans wouldn't involve her abandoning them before the war ended.

'But you can't leave us,' Gloria exclaimed, failing to notice Lottie's affronted expression.

'I'm not good enough for you, huh?' Lottie said from behind.

Maggie applied basic reasoning; she'd seen how Elizabeth's eyes had shone when she was tending to Lenny or helping Mrs

Spencer so she capitulated: 'Of course, you are, Lottie. We couldn't have managed without you and I think we all know Elizabeth's calling is elsewhere; I, for one, am sure she'll make a really good nurse. And—' she grinned '—if she *is* going, it would make sense for me to move onto the *Florence*.'

That prospect cheered Maggie up, thinking that she could read in peace, not have to put up with Gloria's snoring and have her own space to think – and, she thought with a delighted shiver, read Harry's letter she'd finally received over and over in peace. She left the others to sort out the paperwork for their auburn-haired new recruit and went to find a bench, where she ripped through the envelope. When she saw his firm handwriting, she exhaled loudly with relief.

It was only as she was scanning his loving words that she glanced at the date and huffed with exasperation; this one had been written not long after the D Day landings. The joy that he had survived that momentous invasion was immediately crushed by the knowledge that fierce fighting was still going on while the Allied troops battled their way across Normandy. Maggie screwed the envelope up in her fist.

Chapter 40

Harry couldn't move his legs. They'd been hiding in a ditch for twenty-two hours, not daring to make a sound. He tried to shuffle his backside, but it was numb with cold. Next to him, Paul was asleep, a handkerchief stuffed in his mouth to stop him snoring.

Tentatively, Harry nudged him. 'Shhh,' he said as Paul jerked awake. 'I think it's OK, but we need to be careful.'

'You stink,' was Paul's whispered reply, noting the damp patches down both their trousers, 'and I'm starving.'

'Yes, well, being unable to move for twenty-two hours does nothing for my ablutions routine,' Harry answered quietly with a grim smile.

The two soldiers were a far cry from the pristine figures they had once been but, as both men conceded, at least they were still alive and somehow, not prisoners of war. They were in their present predicament because, after yet another fierce battle for the fields of Normandy, Harry had followed the stretcher-bearers out to an area at the back of the camp to gradually pass along the long line of bodies, laying his hand on each breast and muttering a prayer when, all of a sudden he heard a German officer's loud proclamation in the tent behind him announcing to the surrounded soldiers and medics that they were now the 'guests' of the Third Reich. Harry had heard the murmur of shock of his own soldiers as they absorbed the information that instead of marching triumphantly through the crowds waving flags in the welcoming villages of northern France, they would be heading to a railway station to be transported to a camp on the Polish border.

It had been Paul's urgent whispering in his ear that if they didn't get a move on, they'd be dead meat that had resulted in the pair of them quietly tiptoeing away from the mayhem in the tent behind them and, under the cover of encroaching darkness, moving slowly along ditches on their elbows until they found one deep channel that was far enough away from gunfire and angry German voices. Aware that if they were discovered they would be shot without ceremony, they'd used their fingers to scrabble down into the bottom of this sodden ditch to hide from view overnight. Paul's pack, which he'd thought to grab, remained tantalisingly close but useless to two men who had been too afraid to move one inch.

Now, as morning light came and the only sound was from the dawn chorus, Paul spoke again.

'Well, I got yous away, now it's your turn. What the bleedin' hell do we do now, Padre?'

Edging his head slowly out above the hollow, Harry looked in all directions. It was flat farmland and about four fields in the distance, he could see a French farmer ploughing his fields as his ancestors had done before him, in denial of the chaos just a few miles away.

'I think if we could get over there,' he said, pointing, 'we might be able to get help. Surely our forces can't be far away?'

They slowly left the sanctuary of their hiding place and crouching down, kept the hedge on their left to make their way towards the farm buildings in the distance.

As they approached, the farmer suddenly spotted them and grabbed a pitchfork, which he brandished above his head, yelling and screaming. A woman in a floral pinny ran from the house behind him and then stopped in her tracks looking carefully at the dishevelled men approaching with their hands in the air.

She spoke in rapid French to her husband, tutted and made her way towards Harry and Paul.

'You are English?' she said in a strong accent.

'Yes,' Harry replied and pointed to his dog collar. '*Je suis prêtre.*'

'Oh Jeez, now this miracle-worker speaks French,' Paul muttered to himself.

The man dropped the pitchfork, crossed himself and ran over to the newcomers. He took Harry's hands and gabbled in French.

Harry tried to keep up but then laughed and the woman took over.

''E is too excited' and turning to her husband, she said, 'Claude, Claude, *calme-toi, enfin, grâce à Dieu, ils sont là pour nous libérer.*'

'Well, there's only two of us so not exactly to liberate you.' Harry smiled, finally extricating his hands from the farmer's strong grasp. 'But we do need your help.'

He explained in rusty French that the Germans had surrounded their camp and had taken a load of captives but that they had manage to escape.

'*Prisonniers?*' the man asked, his delight turning to fury and he spat on the ground.

'Animaux. Ce sont des animaux.'

His wife stepped forward and held out her hand. 'Je m'appelle Colette Dubois et, voici, mon mari, Claude. Soyez les bienvenus.'

As she introduced herself, she was eyeing up the state of the two men and her nose wrinkled at the stench.

'First, I think, you must wash and I will clean these . . . *vêtements. Ils sont vraiment sales.*'

'She wants our uniforms, she can obviously smell them,' Harry told Paul with a grin.

'Yeah, but tell 'em, Padre, we'll be putting 'em at risk if the Germans find us,' Paul said through the side of his mouth.

'Bah,' Claude said, understanding the sentiment if not the words, and picked up the pitchfork again to shake it threateningly towards the camp in the distance.

'How on earth did 'itler get away with invadin' this country,' Paul laughed but the woman was already dragging him towards the scullery of the farmhouse where she unceremoniously ordered him to strip.

By the time the two naked men had been given old sacks to cover themselves, she was already pummelling their uniforms in the cracked old sink with her gnarled fingers while her husband emerged from the kitchen with two small glasses of wine in his huge hands.

'*Buvez,*' he ordered. '*Buvez, il faut célébrer, je pense que la fin viendra rapidement maintenant.*' He disappeared again to bring out two more glasses and gave one to his wife who was grinning just as broadly as her husband.

'We need to celebrate,' she said, 'it is, *certainement*, near the end now, *n'est-ce pas?*'

Sipping slowly, knowing the liquid was reaching empty stomachs and it was still early in the morning, Paul said quietly to Harry, 'They see us as bloody angels heralding victory, Harry. They've no idea what's going on out there.'

Harry put down his glass and told them that they would have to be on their way immediately, the Germans were not far away, and it would be too dangerous for their hosts.

Colette simply raised her eyebrows and glanced down at the sacks that were just about covering the men's modesty.

'She's got a point,' Paul conceded but Colette was moving towards a trapdoor at the back of the scullery that was hidden by shelving. Harry and Paul moved the heavy racks out of the way and raised it to see a cellar full of wine.

'I may never get you out of here, Paul.' Harry grinned and made his way down the stone steps, shivering. Five minutes later two blankets appeared and ten minutes after that, a warm dish with cabbage and one piece of meat each was handed down the hatch. Knowing they were taking the valuable rations of this kind couple, Paul tried to hand up some of the dry biscuits from his pack, but Claude shook his head, looking affronted.

It wasn't long before both men, snuggled in the rough blankets, fell asleep but they were woken by a small cough and looked up to see both Colette and Claude, dressed in their best clothes, now frayed at the seams but gleamingly clean, standing in front of them.

'Mon père,' Colette was saying, 'je vous en prie, bénissez-nous? Ca fait longtemps que nous n'avons pas reçu de bénédiction sans que les Allemands ne nous observent.'

'Mais je ne suis pas catholique,' Harry protested to blank looks. As far as these two good souls were concerned, he was a man of God and to be able to talk to Him without the Germans watching their every move would bring them extra protection.

The ridiculousness of standing there in nothing but a cloth sack and a blanket to give a religious blessing to the trusting couple in front of him should have made Harry laugh but for some reason, it gave his entire vocation meaning. Harry adjusted the sack around his middle to maintain some semblance of modesty, held his hand up in readiness and trusted for the first time in two years that God was listening.

* * *

The two British men were told they had no option but to stay hidden as above them, the Allies were fighting tooth and nail to push the Germans back. Every evening, after dark, Claude and Colette would come down for prayers and a blessing. It made Harry worry to see how their tense features gradually relaxed as if, with a man of God in their house, it gave them protection from the cruel vengeance of the fleeing Germans. From the gloom of the cellar, they'd heard fighting getting nearer and then even distant shouts and both Harry and Paul sat with clenched fists, feeling impotent. Every day though, the trapdoor bolt was firmly fixed and the shelves moved back in place. This couple had no intention of letting their divine protectors go.

'Do you know how hard it is not to drink meself to death with all these bottles?' Paul asked one night. 'If I'm no bloody use out there, I may as well pickle meself in wine 'ere.'

The boredom was relentless and they were both on the point of insisting they should be allowed to take their chances up in the fresh air when Claude came down looking exceedingly pleased with himself.

'*Les prisonniers . . . ils sont libres.*'

Harry looked puzzled.

'*Vos amis,*' his host explained. '*Les soldats.*'

How on earth had those potential POWs escaped their captors? Harry mused. Claude touched the side of his nose and with a wink said: '*J'ai des amis . . .*'

'What's 'e talking about?' Paul asked.

'I think he's saying the newly formed FFI – the French Forces of the Interior – have been busy. They've sort of taken over from the Resistance. Our tip-off must have helped.' Harry's automatic reaction was to bow his head reverently in grateful thanks that so many men he'd worked alongside would soon be free rather than interned in a POW camp. To give thanks to some higher being was a natural act and one, he realised, was engraved into his whole being.

'*Vous êtes tous les deux, des héros!*' Claude pronounced reaching for a dusty bottle of wine above them.

Harry looked extremely embarrassed, but Paul stood up and as soon as the cork had popped, reached out for the bottle to take a swig.

'Always wanted to be a bleedin' hero,' he said. 'Wait till I tell 'em down at The Albion 'bout this!'

Claude had no idea what had just been said but was grinning his head off.

'Eh, *maintenant* ... Paris!' he said and started to hum 'La Marseillaise'.

The trapdoor closed above them and the two men dropped down onto the old mattresses.

Paul spoke first. 'That's amazing, Padre. A real miracle. All those men ... saved from a camp.'

He raised the bottle to his mouth again.

Harry was preoccupied with the emotion that had just gone through his body as he'd automatically offered his thanks to heaven. He heard his uncle's advice: to stop trying to control faith and just let it be there.

Finally, it all made sense. He couldn't be the one to find a rational explanation for something completely irrational; after all, cleverer people than him had tried to find proof for years. It was his choice, and he chose to have faith.

'I'm also going to have faith that I'm going to marry Maggie and spend the rest of my life with her,' he told Paul who was getting too drunk to realise that was a complete non sequitur.

'When we finally get out of here,' Harry was continuing while Paul examined the dregs of the bottle in his hand, 'we're going back to where we landed and I'm going to dig up my parachute so that my lovely bride will have white silk to make a beautiful wedding dress.'

'OK, good idea,' Paul answered, taking a last gulp before falling backwards into a deep sleep.

Chapter 41

It was after another boring month that Harry and Paul heard whoops of joy from upstairs and with a flurry, the trapdoor was flung open. Above them, as they blinked into the light, were about twenty French people, several of whom had their arms outstretched to help the two Englishmen up the steps.

Although they'd performed a regular routine of exercises, both their legs were weak and they stumbled into the scullery.

'*La libération! La liberation!*' the French were all shouting and behind them one bottle after another was hauled into the daylight to be passed around.

On the table to his left, Harry noticed an old newspaper from the summer before. It was faded and torn and had been used to wrap apples, but its bleak headline proclaimed: '*Une nouvelle bombe allemande frappe Londres*'.

He went cold.

* * *

Just after Elizabeth took her tearful leave of the little crew, reports filtered through about the liberation of France but Maggie had no idea of the significance of that news for her and Harry, instead all her concentration was on the increasingly cold temperatures that were starting to blight their progress. By the time the start of 1945 came, the snow covered everything from the tops of hedges to the telephone wires and the canal was frozen too. Maggie, Gloria and Lottie spent so long waiting for the ice cutter or using boiling water to try to break the frozen surface on the canal themselves that they lost valuable time on their journeys, and it was a constant battle to try to find enough coal to fire up their stove, especially as young boaters' offspring seemed to be making a career out of stealing unwitting canal dwellers' stocks. Without being able to keep up any sort of schedule, the girls were all struggling for money and in any case, the shopkeepers they visited on their route all shook their heads waving vaguely at empty shelves as yet another delivery failed to arrive on the snow-covered roads. As the month wore on, they were able to celebrate the success of the Battle of the Bulge on the Belgian and Luxembourg borders, but there seemed little progress elsewhere in the world and every time the British celebrated a step nearer to the war finishing, they were given a stark reminder by the V1 and then V2 rockets that were still hitting England's streets.

'They're not giving up,' Gloria moaned, her thoughts constantly turning to her family near Limehouse, 'these Buzz Bombs are killing thousands still.' She turned away to take her anger out on some congealed oil in the engine.

Over the next few weeks, all thoughts of doing anything except survive the physical hardships were expelled from their minds and it was only at night that an exhausted Maggie would finger Harry's last letter and try to convince herself he was still alive.

The cold, dark nights were giving her too much time to think and her letters to Reverend Phillips at Broughton House revealed nothing. He disguised his concern in good news about Lenny and Alfie who were now making their way up to Berlin, apparently still in good health. He even told her that Alfie, patiently coaxed by Lenny, was starting to talk more and that he believed that by the end of the war, Alfie would be a complete chatterbox! But there was no word of Harry.

Gloria was receiving letters from Joe who was still in the Mediterranean but was shore-based and claimed to be bored.

'Bored, my foot,' Gloria said in between peeling potatoes and trying to stoke up the fire. 'He's been to some variety show in a place called Valetta where they've got dancers and everything.' A flash of jealousy showed in her eyes and Maggie grinned. 'But, he did say, it's all a bit dodgy,' Gloria was continuing, wanting to keep her heroic image of Joe alive. 'Apparently, there are fights and stealing. Even though that terrible siege is over, I think a lot of the Maltese are still trying to survive on the breadline and he keeps having to intervene to keep the peace.'

'I think he deserves a bit of peace,' Maggie said, folding down the tabletop for them to eat off, 'it's not been a barrel of laughs in the Med.'

'Maybe not,' Gloria said, patting the dishcloth in her hand, 'but I do think Elizabeth's Christopher had a word in someone's ear to keep him safe.' To see Joe back safely was her nightly prayer.

'I've heard Churchill and Roosevelt are meeting Stalin on the island to talk about what happens after the war,' Maggie said. 'There'll be no speaking to Joe if he's part of the detail for that little gathering.'

Gloria couldn't help it; her face glowed with pride.

*　*　*

The 'great freeze' as it was called lasted until March and it wasn't until a few weeks later that Maggie was able to get home. She raced down the streets of Didsbury, ridiculously excited to see her grandfather and her old room, where she fully intended to sink into her own pillow and not get up until noon.

'Grandad, I'm home,' she yelled, letting herself in but there was such a cacophony of noise coming from down the hall it seemed no one could hear her. She opened the door into a crowd of people, all with a glass of old sherry in their hands. In front of the window was a beaming Charlie Carpenter and next to him, Mrs Harper, looking resplendent in a maroon hat and tweed suit.

'What's going on?' Maggie asked with suspicion.

Her grandad moved forwards to grasp her in his arms and swing her round.

'I've only gone and got married,' he said with delight.

Maggie looked at the couple in front of her and pouted. 'You could have told me.'

'We did, love,' Mrs Harper tittered, 'didn't you get our letter?'

Maggie thought back. She'd been in such a rush at Tyseley to catch the train she had forgotten to pick up the post. It was a recollection that made her start; had she really given up on ever hearing again from Harry?

'No . . .' she faltered. 'When was all this decided?'

Handing her one of granny's best glasses, Mrs Harper paused to look down at it for a second and caught Maggie doing the same thing. The glance between them was like a film on fast speed with all the hurt her granny had suffered living alongside a silent husband, the hours of shared confidences with her best friend and the protective love for the young girl whose hand was reaching out to take the glass.

Dorothy Harper took hold of her new granddaughter in a matronly hug and whispered, 'We hope it's all right with you, love. He just couldn't manage on his own and I think your granny would know that.'

Maggie took a large gulp of the liquid and spluttered for a second at the unexpected strength of it before saying, 'Do you know, Mrs Harper, I think you're right.' And she raised her glass to her grandfather with a gentle smile on her lips.

'Call me Dorothy, love. I can't replace your granny, but I do think we can be on first name terms.'

The door burst open again and Mr and Mrs Mullins came in.

'The front door was open, so I hope you don't mind,' Mrs Mullins was saying but her husband was hopping from foot to foot with excitement.

'He's dead, Hitler's dead,' he said bluntly, as always, the newspaper man to be the first with news hot off the press.

A huge cheer went up and glasses were recharged.

'We're going to run out of sherry at this rate,' Dorothy was saying, her cheeks now quite pink.

'Never mind, love,' Maggie's grandad chirped in: 'We'll soon be able to buy a new bottle,' and he kissed his new wife firmly on her mouth, making her titter with embarrassment.

Once everyone had gone, Maggie left the happy couple to make a celebratory cup of tea and made her escape to her own bedroom. As soon as she opened the door, the memory of the last time she'd been home with Harry hit her like a mooring mallet. Feeling winded, she sat down heavily on the bed and then flung herself over and sobbed into the yellow counterpane.

* * *

It was a subdued Maggie who made her way back to Birmingham two days later. The vortex churning in her stomach had convinced her that she would never again see Harry's dark brown eyes or feel his warm arms around her. She couldn't even cry but with detachment noticed all the streets looked grey, the people around her looked grey and the skies above her weren't doing any better. She refused to be drawn into enthusiastic conversation by the chatty woman with a shopping basket on her first visit in two years to see her sister in Erdington and simply gave a wan smile as the woman prattled on.

Reaching Tyseley, Maggie wasn't sure she could face another gruelling journey up and down the Grand Union Canal and an overwhelming fatigue swept over her, so much so that she found the nearest bench and sat down with a thud.

'No point sitting there,' Lottie's voice said from along the cut. 'We've got bricks to load and we've been waiting for you. What took you so long?'

It was only as the loading was complete that Maggie remembered the post and saying she'd meet them at the first lock, wearily walked towards the office where one letter and a parcel were waiting for her. She glanced at Elizabeth's writing and then turned to the other one.

She jumped to her feet and exclaimed: 'It's from Harry, it's from Harry!' The man in the faded uniform and peaked cap behind the desk looked singularly unimpressed until the lovely young woman leaned across the counter to plant a huge kiss on his cheek.

'Well, well,' he muttered, rubbing the spot. 'Good job she din't 'ave lipstick on. I'd 'ave had trouble explaining that one to Celia.'

But by now, the girl had clattered down the iron steps outside and was skipping along the canal towpath.

Before she reached the *Nancy May*, Maggie stopped again at a bench and biting her lip, stared at the envelope.

'Please God, let him be all right, please God, let him be all right,' she said, forcing herself to rip open the parcel.

It was a pile of beautiful white silk neatly folded and for a moment, she feared it was a shroud that had been used to wrap

Harry's body in. A chill edged up her body as she grabbed the letter that was on the top.

Dear Maggie, it read, *I just want to let you know I am all right.*

She let out a sob of relief.

It's a long story but first and foremost, I desperately need to hear you're OK too. I heard about those bombs hitting London and every night I've been imagining terrible things. My nights have been plagued by dreadful thoughts and I am desperate to hear from you. I realise you haven't been able to reach me – it's a long story – but if you reply to this army address, it should now reach me.

I'm sending this parachute silk because I picture you one day, walking down the aisle towards me, wearing it. I cling on to that dream.

I can't write any more until I know you're safe but oh, my love, I long to be able to hold you again and then we can have the rest of our lives to exchange our experiences, but I beg you, just reply, PLEASE!

All my love,
Harry

Lottie and Gloria couldn't believe the speed Maggie worked at that morning, loading bricks, sorting out the tarpaulin and whistling all the time.

Gloria glared at the relentless cheerfulness; she'd had a difficult weekend at home in Limehouse where she had been surrounded by the post-bomb misery and destruction that had been wreaked once again on the East End. She had been seventeen when she'd first boarded the *Nancy May*; now she was twenty and still not married. Her relationship with Will had been a disaster and left her scared of falling in love again. In her pragmatic way, she was trying not to dwell on the memory of it and instead, chalk it up to bitter experience, but she still shivered at the thrill and excitement of being in his arms.

Lottie, as usual, was oblivious to the emotions going on around her and was too busy loving every minute of tuning the beautiful Lister engine so that it purred to the envy of many of the boat people around her.

It was only when the girls had moored up for the night that Maggie finally had time to sit down and write back to Harry. She decided not to tell him about the dramas of the Grove Road bomb but delighted in regaling him with details of her grandfather's wedding party. Writing to the man she loved made her realise how much she'd missed being able to share her thoughts with him and she kissed her letter over and over before putting it in the envelope and racing off to the post box.

She was about to put it in when she bristled at footsteps behind her. It was dark and the girls were always alert to the dangers of the towpath at night but then she heard a familiar voice.

'Hello, is that Maggie?'

She peered into the gloom and then yelped with delight. 'Joe? Is that you?' She almost didn't recognise the tall, upright man approaching her. His hair was sleeked back and his naval uniform buttons gleamed in the moonlight.

He stepped forward to hold out his hand formally, but she put her arms around him instead and gave him a hug, much to his surprise and delight.

'Oh, it's wonderful to see you, how long are you home for? We must tell Gloria, she'll be thrilled.'

It was too dark for her to see the blush that crept across his cheeks but on the walk back to the boats, he told her that he was being moved back to Portsmouth where he might sign on for peacetime – when it came. She noticed how his eyes shone when he talked about the navy and suspected he had found a home that he'd never had on *Buffalo*.

His heavy footstep on the counter deck alerted Gloria who came out to see what was happening. When she saw Joe, she put her hand to her mouth to suppress a squeal while Lottie came up behind, watching her sister's reaction with interest.

The two young people hovered at a distance, suddenly shy when Lottie butted in: 'Oh, for crying out loud, I don't know who you are but if you don't kiss her, she's going to fall in the canal.'

Without another word, Joe stepped forward and put his arms around Gloria who melted into his embrace. She gave a deep sigh. *Will who?* she thought.

Chapter 42

8th May, 1945

The bunting was out all over Stoke Bruerne and, without buses, some boaters had hitched a lift or crowded onto a train to go to London, but the girls decided the one place they wanted to be was on the cut. Lottie and Gloria had scrubbed the *Nancy May* and the *Florence*, and Maggie had made some drop scones on the stove to put on the little trestle tables that had been erected all along the edge of the canal.

The sun was shining like a delighted deity after a thunderstorm in the morning that had made many jerk their heads upwards in fear before remembering that the skies would never again rumble with the sound of German aircraft. The bells from St Mary The Virgin in Stoke Bruerne finally rang out again and as they pealed, there were several who took a moment to bow their heads, to try to blot out the sorrow they were going to have to live with for the rest of their lives.

The cabin on the *Nancy May* that morning had resounded with cries of horror as Gloria, Lottie and Maggie examined their wardrobes.

'I can't wear corduroy dungarees,' Gloria moaned and Maggie looked down at her threadbare skirt with desperation.

'I just want to look pretty for once,' Maggie said, pushing her fingers through her hair and she scanned the cabin in vain for anything that might bring a bit of brightness to the occasion later that day. With scant options, they had each donned their best clothes, pulling them out of the back of a cupboard where they had been squashed, only to emerge for an occasional Sunday service and, looking as pathetic as possible, they'd begged Betsy to allow them to waste precious water by washing their hair over the scullery sink with a white enamel jug, which made them all feel more human, at least.

As they emerged from their cabins, smoothing down their skirts with their hands, Dolly Spencer called them over to join her. She was wearing a clean lace blouse with a brooch attached to her breast and the brasses on *Buffalo* gleamed in the sunshine. Gloria hung back, embarrassed that her relationship with this woman might now change but Dolly stretched out her hand to grab Gloria's.

'You're a good lass and if some'at comes of this, I couldn't be more delighted,' she said.

Ernie, from behind her was more direct. 'Oh yeah, you'll make a great daughter-in-law,' he laughed.

Dolly was looking particularly pleased with herself and while the others were laughing and joking, she went below to emerge with some different coloured ribbons and ceremoniously handed them to the three girls.

'Here you are,' she said with a grin. 'They were my mother's but as I've got two boys, I'd really like you girls to 'ave 'em. They're not posh dresses but yer could thread these through your 'air, and they'll look grand.'

And grand they did, she thought with a satisfied smile, once the three girls had pinned up their hair to fall naturally around the strands of fabric: Gloria in red polka dot ribbon, Lottie in a light blue and Maggie in a bright yellow. None of them realised that their eyes were sparkling to reflect the little bit of glamour until they saw Ernie's jaw drop, appreciating for the first time, how lovely these young women were underneath the oil and the muck.

Dolly nudged him with a cheeky smile. 'Enough of that, Ernie Spencer. I'm the only woman for you now, and don't you forget it.'

He swept her up in his strong arms and she giggled like a young girl, throwing her head back in delight. Gloria caught Maggie's eye and winked but her friend was looking pensive.

'I wish Elizabeth had been here with us, today of all days,' she said, 'it doesn't seem right to be here celebrating without her.'

'No,' Gloria replied, 'but she's loving her training, you know she is and I've a feeling that while everyone else is taking time off, she'll be as happy as Larry emptying bedpans and changing dressings.'

'You're right,' Maggie conceded but there was still a gnawing feeling of an empty space around her.

'It's not Elizabeth you're missing,' Gloria said bluntly.

'I know. And you're feeling it too with Joe not being here.'

'Yes, I just hope he doesn't get sent to the Far East,' Gloria said, biting her lip and then, in a brighter tone: 'Come on, let's see if we can get a cider, the queue's going down a bit.'

Maggie looked doubtful but the pair of them linked arms to join the long line along the lock in front of the pub. Betsy glanced up with delight.

'It's over, girls, it's over. Well, at least in Europe it is. Let's pray it won't be long before the east follows.'

She handed over two glasses of cider and raised one of her own to salute them.

'Yer've brought a bit of glamour to the cut, yer 'ave. When I first laid eyes on yer, I thought you'd never 'ack it, but yer 'ave and I'm gonna miss yer.'

'We all are,' the man next to her said and he too raised his glass, shouting above everyone's heads, ''Ere's a toast to these lasses who've brought kindness, 'ard work and . . . nice legs to the cut!'

Then someone started singing, 'For they are jolly good fellows,' and the whole crowd joined in, swerving and swaying with their pints in their hands.

Gloria gripped Maggie's arm making a bruise and then Lottie pushed in, protesting she was not going to be left out.

Maggie wiped away a tear.

Just before three o'clock, everyone crowded into The Boat or tried to listen at the windows to Churchill's statement. His words: 'This is not victory of a party or of any class. It's a victory of the great British nation as a whole' were drowned out by the cheers of the crowds.

Other boats in the vicinity had made an effort to get there for the national holiday to celebrate Victory in Europe so there was a carnival atmosphere when Betsy started serving pints from a table outside the Boat Inn. Someone, Maggie thought it was Ernie, started a conga and the girls were swept up to join in. She tossed back her hair and laughed, no school staffroom could ever feel like this this, she thought.

Maggie took in the scene around her. When she'd first seen these people, they'd seemed gruff, scruffy and, frankly, quite terrifying, now she was one of them and was being greeted with friendly comments, some harmless joshing and an odd shy smile from some of the younger boys. She felt like a completely different person from the one who had been so clumsy in those early days and could now take a boat up and down the cut like a professional; she even had a fair idea how to strip down an engine, thanks to Gloria's tutelage. But it wasn't just her practical skills that had improved, she thought, she was no longer an impressionable girl who would be at the beck and call of a man.

She really believed she'd found someone who would allow her to be an equal.

Pushing her hair out of her eyes, she glanced along the tow-path. It was heaving with people, all with glasses in their hands and laughing and joking but then she saw one figure standing in the distance alone. His gaze was fixed on her.

'Harry,' she breathed.

Epilogue
1947

The boat was packed. Crate after crate of belongings had been lowered onto the deck and were now being stowed for the voyage from Dover across the Channel. It was going to take some time and a succession of trains before the newly married couple arrived at their posting in the south of Austria. Maggie hugged her books to herself; she was going to teach the children of the military families posted in the peace-force occupied countries of Europe and could hardly keep her excitement muffled.

She watched Harry stride across the deck and took a sharp intake of breath. He looked so commanding, and she thought, with a wicked grin, so sexy.

She took out a black and white photograph from her purse and touched it lovingly. They looked so young, she thought, and in her beautiful white, parachute silk dress, there was no sign of the coal dust, cement fragments or the red-brick stains that had defined her life for three years of war on the canals; now she was a wife, and touching her stomach, a mother-to-be, heading off on an adventure that she had always craved. There was one notable absence at her wedding, and that was her father, but Maggie had finally decided she was not going to live her life feeling she had failed because her father didn't love her. She had her own family to think about now.

Their marriage ceremony had been proudly performed by a frail Peter Moore with David Phillips at his side at Emmanuel Church. On the first row had been her grandfather and Dorothy and behind them, her two brothers and their two wives. Further back in the pews, Gloria desperately tried to keep baby Florence quiet, eventually giving in to hand her over to a beaming Joe. Elizabeth was there in her Queen Alexandra nurse's uniform next to a tall, slightly bemused Christopher and at the back of the church, Dolly and Ernie Spencer, at Gloria's insistence, had braved the train to be there. Unfortunately, so had Dolly's rumbustious son, Thomas, who was running up and down the aisle pretending he was still on the railway track that had brought him there.

Maggie felt a burst of pride when she saw Harry. He no longer looked as if he didn't belong in that dog collar but wore it with pride.

'All right, Mrs Moore?' he asked, barely able to conceal his excitement at the challenge ahead.

'*Ja*,' she replied, laughing. 'You see, I'm learning the language already,'

He took her quietly to one side and said with deep conviction, 'I know I'm taking you away from everything you know but I do hope you want this adventure as much as I do.'

She took his face in her hands and kissed him, slowly.

'Well, I think that's my answer then,' he chuckled. 'There's just one more thing before you leave. I need to tell you about your dad.'

The excitement on Maggie's face faded like a child's invisible ink. 'I don't want to hea—'

'Yes, you do, Margaret Carpenter, or you'll be carrying this burden around for the rest of your life.' He took a deep breath and then launched into the speech he'd been practising for months. 'You know that your father was at Gallipoli where he watched his entire platoon being massacred. Well, he couldn't do a thing to help but he's carried this burden around ever since. I think he's not the only one. We're all coming out of this war with burdens, Maggie.'

He watched carefully as Maggie repeated the words over to herself. She turned towards the sea. So many memories came back to her of a father who couldn't hug her, couldn't help or even talk to her but she also knew how she'd felt when the girls had sacrificed Lenny to the Birmingham gang and how the shame had eaten away at her.

Harry knew what she was thinking and said, 'Yes, and I let that poor soldier slip between the waves. We all have our guilt to bear, Maggie but I talked to your father before we left Manchester and he, well, he wanted you to have this.'

He handed over a small package which Maggie tore open.

It was a copy of *Little Women* by Louisa May Alcott and inside the cover was a letter.

Dear Maggie,

I do hope this gets to you before you leave. I wanted you to have this book about a father who, even though he's at war, manages to send guidance, help and love to his daughters. I have been in my own war for far too long and you and the boys have been the victims.

I cannot tell you how sorry I am that I haven't been a better father to you all. It shouldn't have been your grandfather walking you down the aisle, it should have been me, and I will spend the rest of my life regretting that.

Now you are leaving the country, I've realised how many conversations we never had, how many books we never shared and how much love I was never able to give you.

*I hope you'll read this book and imagine that Mr March
could have been me.*
Your loving father x

Harry was there, ready to catch just as she fell onto the iron
railings and held on to her very tightly.

Acknowledgements

A book is always a team effort and my team seems to grow with each book. So, I would like to start with thanking Kate Saffin, poet, writer and performer, who has a vast knowledge of both the women on the canals and the waterway network; she very kindly read *Maggie's War* through for me, and a special thank you to Alastair Clarke for putting me in touch with her. Tim Coughlin at Braunston Marina set me off on my research with his work on the diary of Evelyn Hunt and led me to contact Peter Hoon of Mikron Theatre Company while the books of people like Susan Woolfitt, LJC Rolt, Geoffrey Lewis, Emma Smith, Sheila Stewart and Tim Wilkinson all provided me with the framework and the colour to be able to write the story. For the army padre character, I'm indebted to the Cheshire Military Museum and in particular to Regimental Researcher, Geoff Crump, who could not have been kinder or more helpful. In addition, the British Modern Military History Society's research into Padre George Parry helped me to visualise Harry's work. Jack Stephenson at Broughton House gave me an insight into the incredible work they do with veterans and thanks to residents there, Jean Mack and Peter Belcher, for sharing their stories with me. Thank you to the Ormond family for so generously lending me their book of letters from their father who was at Dunkirk while

The Deserter by Charles Glass gave me a valuable insight into the stories of those who abandoned the army. I found the people at Crick Boat Show incredibly helpful with their advice and snippets of information, as were the people all along the canal when I asked seemingly strange questions, in particular, Benny Chambers who explained how the traditional cabins worked and Michael and Nicola of MJ Pinnock who took time to talk about the working boats on canals. The museum at Stoke Bruerne was invaluable, as was the London Canal Museum. I appreciated Pam and Terry Anderson's forbearance when I trailed them around Limehouse Basin and the people at St Anne's Church, including Charlie Hinds who was visiting the church and could not have been more willing to help.

I'd like to thank Ann McLean, Alexander Anderson Hall and Martin and Theresa Mann for inviting me to 'go international' with an event at an amazing hat factory in France that featured a play about the women on canals by Alexander Anderson Hall. Thank you all for a great evening and a wonderful play and thank you too to Nora Connolly for her interest. Sean Mason was a useful contact for my questions about Lister engines and I would like to thank all those at Emmanuel Church in Didsbury who hardly blinked an eyelid when I asked where the vestry was in 1942, where the altar used to be and all those crucial questions that help my books to be authentic. For my French efforts, I am indebted to Marie Paurin and once again, I could not do these books without my agent, Kate Barker, my publisher, Claire Johnson-Creek and all the team at Bonnier Books – your guidance and encouragement are just so valuable to me. The eagle eye of Sandra Ferguson, who did the copy edits, and Gilly Dean, who did the proofread, saved me embarrassment and Florence Philip is working hard on the publicity to get *Maggie's War* noticed and Enisha Samra is doing the marketing. The audio edition is beautifully read by Rosie Jones.

As always, my family and friends are incredibly supportive and encouraging when I'm struggling. In particular, Kevin,
my husband, my daughters, Sarah and Jayne and my friends,
Carol Taylor, Heather Lounds, Sarah Price and Pippa Mansel.
Your belief in me – and the glasses of wine – have really helped.
In addition, I want to mention my readers in Wirksworth, at
Scarthin Books and my followers on social media; the fact that
so many of you take an interest in my books and even come to
my talks means more than I can say.

Hello Reader,

Welcome if this is your first foray into my books and welcome back if you've travelled this journey alongside me. *Maggie's War* is my fifth book inspired by the amazing women of WWII. With each book, my admiration for the women of the 1940s grows and they never cease to surprise me with the roles they undertook. It was only when I started researching *Maggie's War* that it occurred to me that our family has actually had its own long history with canals. My brother-in-law ran a canal boat company and his daughter ran a trip boat on the Trent and Mersey, my husband worked for British Waterways for some years, and we had our own narrowboat on England's canals. That was a very special time in our lives when I would come nose to nose with a swan out of my little galley window on a beautiful spring day with coots and ducks gliding past. But I also remember being absolutely frozen with icicles on my eyelashes trying to get a rusty lock gate open after months of lack of use. I experienced bruises and sprains and everything ached but when the boat slid with a gentle chug on a summer's evening, I would forgive the canals everything. That's why I couldn't wait to write about the women who travelled up and down the Grand Union Canal carrying essential supplies of goods like steel, bricks, cement, wood and coal. Hundreds applied but only about thirty were still working for the Inland Waterways by the end of the war. The rest had gone home with blisters and bad backs.

For me, part of the joy of these books is the research into what life was really like for my characters and I've had great fun pretending that walking up and down tow paths, talking to boat people and scurrying around in engine rooms is research. The vast difference between a towpath through the centre of a city and a rural setting summed up for me the character of

these incredible waterways but as always, it's people's genuine interest and willingness to help that makes my writing journey so much easier.

When I started to research the book, I was told very firmly, not to call them the Idle Women – a term that was only applied to them after the war because of the small IW badge they wore. So, I very happily complied because idle they certainly were not. They worked long hours in confined spaces, dealt with heavy loads that men struggled with, and they learned how to strip and mend an engine, splice ropes and live without any luxuries.

As time moves on, the women who could tell me their first-hand experiences are obviously dwindling but I've loved scouring the books written by some of these girls and talking to experts whose knowledge of the waterways has helped me formulate the story.

One of the joys of writing these books is to explore areas of the war people might not have considered before and that's why I wanted to include a little-known member of the armed forces – a padre – which was quite a challenge for a partially secular audience. Also, partnering him with Maggie, a woman with a past, offered the chance for a relationship that I thought would be full of potential disasters.

Once I heard that there were a hundred thousand deserters in the Second World War, which is another area that's rarely talked about, I was intrigued, so in my quest to take you, the reader, somewhere you haven't been before and maybe wouldn't be expecting, I decided to include a deserter in this book.

As always, I don't want to sugar-coat what was a terrible experience and I try really hard to give an authentic mix of the trauma with the abiding sense of humour that got the British through those difficult years, while acknowledging the repercussions that ripple through future generations.

I always find it sobering to examine the long-term effects that former servicemen and women have to suffer and again, I hope I depict their struggles realistically.

One thing writing this book has made me do is to fall in love with our waterways once again. Their liquorice strands that weave their way through towns and countryside are now a national asset for tourism but once were an essential supply route that was heaving with a strong community with their own traditions. I hope I've done justice to their way of life and their sense of pride.

I've loved travelling with Maggie and her friends and hope you enjoy the journey too and learn about the vastly different worlds that the canals pass through. I'm aware that I have probably under or over-estimated timescales for their journey to fit in with the story but hope waterways experts will forgive that and any other variations in fact about life on the waterways – after all, the fictional element is as important as the historical facts.

I really hope you enjoy *Maggie's War* and I would love to hear your thoughts about it on my Facebook, Amazon or Instagram pages or in your reviews. And do sign up to the Memory Lane Book Group, where you can hear more about what I, and other saga writers, are up to.

So, thank you for reading this, my fifth novel. I never thought I would feel the evangelical zeal to get these women's stories across to new audiences when I first wrote *Lily's War*, but these girls get under my skin and I feel very strongly that their legacy has to be preserved for future generations. I hope you agree with me.

Best wishes,

Shirley

A Recipe from *Maggie's War*

I looked back through *Maggie's War* and was very tempted to offer you the definitive version of a cabbage and Marmite sandwich but then I relented. My baking is renowned – and not in a good way. However, I did find this lovely oat biscuit recipe on the 1940s' Experiment Website. https://the1940 sexperiment.com/tag/oat-biscuits/ so I hope they'll forgive me for using it. I've tried it and even I couldn't go wrong – and that's saying something.

I could imagine the inimitable Dorothy Harper making these. Apparently, her biscuits were legendary – or so I read somewhere. So here goes – obviously you *could* make them with reconstituted egg if you wanted to, but . . .

Ingredients

4 oz (115 g) margarine or butter or half and half

3 oz (85 g) sugar or unrefined caster sugar

7 oz (200 g) rolled oats

5 oz (150 g) self-raising flour or plain flour sifted with 1 teaspoon of baking powder and a pinch of salt

1 reconstitued dried egg or fresh egg or you can make these without an egg

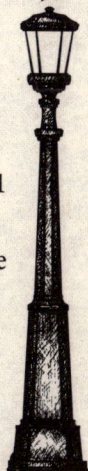

A little milk

Method

- Pre-heat the oven to 180C (350F) or Gas Mark 4
- Grease two baking trays well or use parchment/baking paper instead
- Cream the margarine/butter with the sugar until soft and light
- Add the rolled oats and mix
- Sift the flour, baking powder and salt and add the egg (if used) into the * mixture and mix well again before adding in a little milk to moisten. The dough should be stiff and quite dry but sticks together. Knead together
- Divide out mixture into about 20 lumps the size of a walnut
- Press between palms to flatten to about 1/4 inch thick and place on baking tray and press into shape
- Bake for about 15 minutes until edges are golden
- Leave on baking trays to cool

*You can add sultanas and lemon extract if you want to be really fancy!

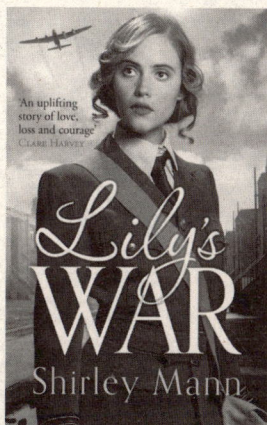

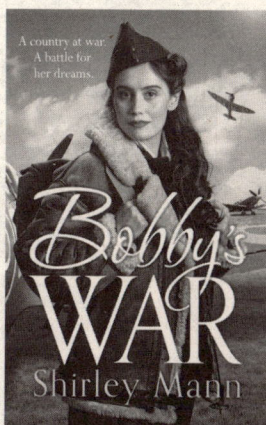

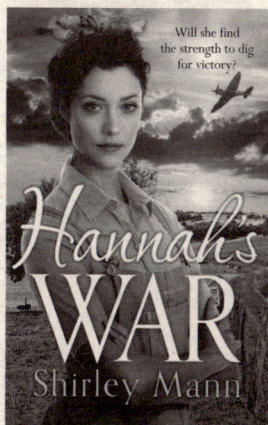

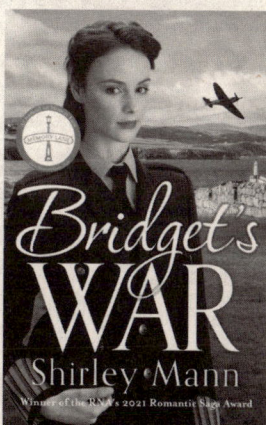

AND LOOK OUT FOR
FAITH'S WAR

COMING 2026. PRE-ORDER NOW.

Introducing the place for story lovers – a welcoming home for all readers who love heartwarming tales of wartime, family and romance. Join us to discuss your favourite stories with other readers, plus get book recommendations, book giveaways and behind-the-scenes writing moments from your favourite authors.

· MEMORY LANE ·

www.MemoryLane.Club